BOOKS BY STUART JACKMAN

NOVELS

A Game of Soldiers
Sandcatcher
Portrait in Two Colours
The Daybreak Boys
Guns Covered with Flowers
Slingshot
The Davidson Affair
Burning Men

PLAYS

Giving and Receiving
Post Mortem

ESSAYS

The Numbered Days

A GAME OF SOLDIERS

A GAME OF SOLDIERS

by

Stuart Jackman

Atheneum   *New York*

1982

The characters in this novel and the events in which they are involved are fictional. The town of Marazag does not exist. If there was (or is) an 87 Maintenance Unit in the RAF it is not the one portrayed in this book.

Library of Congress Cataloging in Publication Data
Jackman, Stuart Brooke, ——
    A game of soldiers.
    1. World War, 1939-1945—Fiction. I. Title.
PR6019.A18G3   1982   823'.914   81-14950
ISBN 0-689-11237-8   AACR2

For Sheena, with love

Between the acting of a dreadful thing
And the first motion, all the interim is
Like a phantasma, or a hideous dream:
The genius and the mortal instruments
Are then in council; and the state of man,
Like to a little kingdom, suffers then
The nature of an insurrection.

Shakespeare, *Julius Caesar*

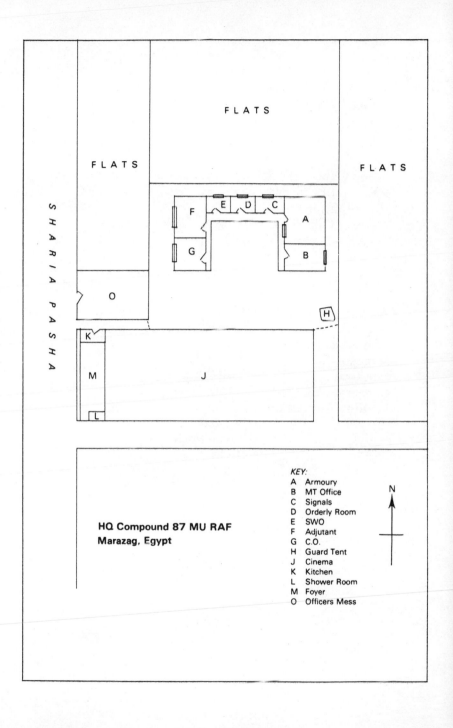

PERSONNEL

HQ 208 GROUP, RAF EGYPT

Group Captain Ludovic Watson, Officer Commanding
Squadron Leader H. 'Hobo' Hobey, SSO
Flight Officer Jane Roper
Warrant Officer M. Wilkinson, GWO (Admin)
WAAF Sergeant Pat Robens

TOP HAT FORCE

Wing Commander Ben Hanwell, RAF Regiment, Officer
Commanding
Flight Lieutenant J. Curtis
Sergeant R.A. Scott
Corporal Miller
Corporal Shepherd
Leading Aircraftmen: Lewis
                           Mason
                           Butterworth
                           Hicks
                           Bell
                           Peters
                           Jackson

87 MAINTENANCE UNIT, RAF MARAZAG

Wing Commander E.F. Gatley, Officer Commanding
Squadron Leader R. March
Flight Lieutenant D. Roper, Adjutant
Flight Lieutenant P. Frant, Medical Officer
Flight Lieutenant J. Prince
Flight Lieutenant H. Bush
Warrant Officer F. Scobart, SWO
Flight Sergeant J. Smart, MT
Sergeants: Lever
           Ryder
           Street
           Collins
           Fenner
Corporals: Vince
           Wooten
Leading Aircraftmen: Mainston
                      Minter
                      Fisher
Aircraftman (1) McCann

A GAME OF SOLDIERS

87 MAINTENANCE UNIT, RAF MARAZAG, EGYPT
15 OCTOBER 1944

He had opened the curtains a little the night before. At 06.40 the sun topped the roof of the block of flats on the east side of the compound, speared in through the gap and touched his face. Had he been asleep it would have wakened him, which was the way he had planned it.

In fact, he was already awake. Had been for the better part of an hour. And before that had dozed only fitfully in the basket chair. He stood by the window drinking a cup of sweet, milky tea, forcing himself to relax, the .303 Lee-Enfield propped against the wall beside him, the five-round clip of ammunition heavy in the breast pocket of his shirt.

He was twenty-two, thin, of medium height, with short brown hair and a tanned, young-old face, the eyes intelligent, the mouth sensitive. Not a professional killer. But a determined one.

Outside the window the killing ground lay silent in the sun; a wired-in square of hard-packed sand in the centre of the town. It was hemmed in on three sides by five-storey blocks of flats and on the fourth by the high, blank wall of the cinema in which the NCOs and Other Ranks were billeted. He was in the kitchen of a first-floor flat in the west side block, looking down against the sun on to the corrugated iron roof of the low brick building which housed the offices of the CO and the Adjutant. The two windows in the living room of the flat provided a good angle of fire. But from the kitchen window it was perfect. From here he could not miss. Must not miss.

Across the compound, on the east side, were the Armoury and the MT office. The Signals office, the Orderly Room and the Station Warrant Officer's office were set along the north side, linking the two wings of the HQ block. On the south side a line of trucks parked at right angles to the cinema wall masked the main gates to the right of the Guard Tent. Tucked away below him out of his line of vision a wicket gate led into a passage which ran up between the cinema and the commandeered hotel which was the Officers Mess and gave on to the main street. Down this passage and through this gate at exactly 07.05 Gatley would come, as he came every morning, to sit in his office before breakfast, read Daily Routine Orders and initial them for publication.

He drank the last of his tea, rinsed the cup under the tap, wiped it dry and set it back on the shelf above the sink; a deft-fingered, methodical man who liked things to be neat. The flat belonged to Rose, a black haired, wide-mouthed cabaret girl with greedy eyes. He had paid her three pounds to move in with a friend for the night and let him use it. She hated Gatley as much as he did, but for different reasons. Three pounds was too much, but it included the price of her silence.

He checked his watch. 06.53. He crossed to the window, picked up the rifle and sat down on the edge of the chair. He snapped the full magazine into place, worked the bolt to inject a round into the breech and thumbed on the safety-catch. His movements were economic, his hands steady. But his face was tight and hard, the muscles round his mouth stiff, the tension in him peaking now.

'Good luck, Babee,' Rose had said last night, putting on her coat in the little hall of the flat, smiling her wide, inviting, garlic scented smile.

10

He had shrugged irritably. 'I'm organised. Done my homework. Luck I don't need.'

But he did. He knew that now, sitting there with the sun warm on his face and the rifle heavy in his hands. Luck or the favour of the gods or whatever it took to bring the guard truck down from the main compound on schedule when the man he was going to kill was at his desk, silhouetted against the sunlight streaming in through the office door.

He got down on one knee behind the curtains, slid the barrel of the Lee-Enfield through the gap and out of the open window and lined it up. He made a tiny adjustment to the sights, re-checked the angle of fire and lowered the rifle, letting the butt rest on his right thigh. He felt his mind empty itself, all the pressure of the last three months, all the disappointments, the growing sense of disillusionment draining out of him. Now there was no confusion, no doubting, not even anger. Only the rifle and the silent, sunlit compound. A kind of brutal, satisfying simplicity.

He heard the rattle of the chain on the wicket gate as the padlock was opened, settled the rifle barrel on the window sill and slipped off the safety-catch. The window of the C.O.'s office was a black oblong in the sights. He concentrated on it, his eyes half-closed, careful not to look up lest the dazzle of the sun blur his vision.

The crunch of desert boots on the sand was startlingly loud in the stillness of the morning. He heard the smack of a hand on a rifle butt. That meant the guard on the main gates had seen Gatley across the compound. The sound of the footsteps changed, hollow on the wooden steps below the veranda, solid on the veranda itself. The footsteps stopped.

There was a moment's pause and then the dark window lit up as the door of the office was unlocked and pegged wide open. He saw his enemy come round the

11

end of the desk and sit down: saw him through the fine mesh of the fly-screened, unglazed window, profiled against the sunlight filling the open door – shoulders and arms, a head wearing a peaked hat. Blurred by the fly-screening, coarse-grained as a press photograph. But a target, back-lit, static. All he had visualised. All he needed.

His finger curled round the trigger of the Lee Enfield. He breathed deeply, slowly, willing his muscles to relax.

The guard truck turned into the alley which ran down behind the cinema to the main gates. He could hear the lumpy tick-over of the big, eight cylinder engine bouncing off the wall as the driver waited for the gates to open. The profile of the man in his sights seemed to expand, filling the sunlit window. He saw the head turn away to look out of the door.

'Come ON, damn you,' he said between clenched teeth, the sweat running down his back under his shirt. 'Get your bloody finger out for God's sweet sake.'

The gears grated as the driver slammed into first. The growl of the truck engine deepened. Its blunt nose butted into view beyond the line of parked vehicles. He took a deep breath, held it and squeezed the trigger. The butt of the rifle kicked back into his shoulder, the sound of the shot lost, as he had known it would be, in the thunder of the engine. He saw the figure in the chair jerk upwards under the vicious impact of the bullet, teeter for a moment and then fall away out of sight.

He snatched the rifle back into the room and cradled it in his arms, kneeling against the wall, shaking, soaked in sweat, his lips drawn back in an unconscious grin of triumph.

In killing, as in loving, there is sometimes ecstasy, a kind of fulfilment.

12

PART ONE

15 OCTOBER 1944

1. 11.00 – 12.05 HOURS

She had come off watch at 02.00 and slept late. The phone wakened her just before 11.00. She groped for the receiver in the darkened bedroom of her flat. 'Jane Roper.'

'Duty Corporal here, ma'am. Squadron Leader Hobey's compliments and can you come in please?'

'Come in? When?' She was not due on watch until 18.00; had planned an afternoon's shopping in Cairo, tea at Groppis.

'Now, ma'am. We've got a car laid on to collect you.'

'For heaven's sake, man,' she said. 'I'm still in bed.'

'Yes, ma'am.' The corporal hesitated. 'Mr Hobey says to tell you it's rather urgent.'

Which meant there was a flap on. 'Hobo' Hobey was the Group Senior Signals Officer; a quiet spoken, self-contained man who had done his time as a W/OP on Coastal Command Sunderlands, sheep-dogging convoys in the Western Approaches. If he said it was rather urgent it had to be bloody desperate. She said, 'Look, let me talk to him, will you?'

'Sorry, ma'am. He's not taking any calls.'

Damn, she thought. She sat up, pushing her fingers through her thick black hair. 'OK, Corporal. Ask them to pick me up here in fifteen minutes.'

At 11.25 the car dropped her outside the block of flats near the Almaza tram terminus which housed the HQ of 208 Group, RAF Egypt. She booked in and walked down the hall to the lift; twenty-three, trim in clean khaki drill, her eyes an astonishing light blue under level black brows, her long legs lovely even in regulation stockings. The Duty Corporal watched her go, admiring the stretch and slide of the tight uniform skirt over her bottom, cursing the narrow blue rings on her epaulettes which put her out of his reach.

She got out of the lift on the fifth floor. Wilkinson was standing outside the Radio Room looking slightly harassed. Wilkinson was the Group Warrant Officer (Admin.); an urbane, balding man, portly, discreet, who wore his uniform apologetically like a bank manager caught in gardening clothes on his day off. He gave her a quick smile. 'A word with you, ma'am.'

'Have to be a quick one, Mr Wilkinson. I'm relieving Sergeant Gray early.'

'That's been taken care of. The SSO took over from her just before 11.00.'

Jane raised her eyebrows. 'Why? Is she sick?' There was a gastric bug going the rounds and they were short staffed in Signals.

Wilkinson pursed his lips. 'Not sick. Upset.' He jerked his head towards the door of the Radio Room. 'The C.O.'s in there and he's a bit twitched, if you know what I mean?'

Jane nodded. The C.O. was Group Captain Ludovic Watson. Twenty-eight, five-eleven, muscular, with a big black moustache and the quick eyes of a fencer; Ludo Watson was a man to be wary of. Ice-cold in action, he flared and sparked like an incendiary bomb

16

when frustrated. A Cranwell pro, he had collected a second bar to his DFC the hard way, flying Beaufighters on low-level shipping strikes in the Mediterranean before a sliver of hot steel from a German flak ship chipped a piece of bone off the top of his spine and grounded him with a permanently stiff neck and a temper as spectacular as it was uncertain. If little Mavis Gray with her wispy hair and glasses and a tendency to come unravelled under pressure had been on the receiving end of that...

Jane said, 'What's the flap?'

'Unacknowledged signal.'

'Oh. What sort of signal?'

'Pack Up.'

'Oh, my God,' she said, shaken. A Pack Up was a meticulously designed logistical air-drop. Weapons, ammunition, rations, medical supplies – a total back-up, life-support system for a task force holding a newly established beach-head, poised to break out and go for the target, unable to move until the Dakotas had made their dropping run. A Pack Up was like a hand-grenade. Once it was primed you didn't hold on to it. You got rid of it. Fast. 'How long ago was this?'

'Just over an hour,' Wilkinson said flatly. 'The executive signal went out at 10.30 hours.' Top priority, most urgent, lives depending on it.

'JACK KNIFE?'

He nodded sombrely. JACK KNIFE was the code name for an assault force briefed to capture an island in the Aegean, neutralise the German garrison and liberate the airfield. That much she knew.

Wilkinson said, 'The SSO thought you should be put in the picture before going...'

'Yes,' Jane said. 'Thank you.' She reached for the door handle. 'Whose Pack Up is it?'

Wilkinson looked at her unhappily. She saw the

17

answer in his face before he spoke. ' 87 MU, ma'am I'm sorry.'

She nodded and pushed the door open. 87 MU was in Marazag. Where David was. There were no windows in the Radio Room; ventilation was by air duct and fan. Because it was manned twenty-four hours a day, the room was always stuffy, always stale.

As soon as Jane walked in she was aware of the acrid smell of cigarette smoke. And of something else. Tension. A mega-volt net of nerves centred in the tall figure of the Group Captain standing behind Hobey who was seated at the console of the big, multi-band radio transceiver. She felt a pricking along her spine but her voice was calm. 'Good morning, gentlemen.'

Watson swung round stiffly, head and shoulders moving together like a gun turret. 'My God, girl,' he said harshly, punching the words at her. 'You took your bloody time.' His voice was deep and gravelly, like stones swirled in an iron bucket. 'Please God you'll be some use to us now you are here.'

Hobey caught her eye and smiled wryly. 'Flight Officer Roper knows her stuff, sir.'

'Yes?' Watson said sceptically. 'Well, she couldn't be more of a disaster than the last girl.'

Hobey stood up quickly; a solid, chunky man in his late twenties, brown hair flecked with grey, his face round and open like a schoolboy's. 'To be fair to Sergeant Gray, sir,' he said evenly, not making a production of it but not letting it slide either, 'if 87 fails to acknowledge our signals that's hardly her fault.'

Watson rounded on him awkwardly. He had almost no lateral movement in his neck and turning made him appear clumsy, which he was not. 'Damn it, Hobo, you know better than to argue the toss about whose fault it is. Those poor bloody pongos are somewhere off the Turkish coast right now, due to hit the beach at first light tomorrow morning. If our Daks aren't over the

18

dropping zone on schedule they'll all be for the chop whosever fault it is.'

Jane walked past him and sat down at the console. He watched her going methodically through the routine on watch check. 'Take your time, won't you?' he said bitterly. 'We're over an hour adrift on a Pack Up signal, but don't hurry yourself on that account.'

She turned deliberately and looked up at him, her eyes steady. 'No, sir, I won't. Time spent checking now is time saved later. So will you please stop bullying me and let me get on with my job?'

Watson's hands balled into fists. His head came forward, brows drawn together. Hobey recognised the signals. The incendiary was fused and fizzing. He blinked, waiting for the explosion.

In the corner by the door the teleprinter stuttered into life.

'Well, God damn it,' Watson rasped. 'It's about bloody time.'

Jane said coolly, 'That's not 87, sir. That's Cyprus.'

'How the hell d'you know that?'

'I recognise his touch.'

Hobey put up his hand to hide a grin. Watson crossed to the teleprinter, ripped out the flimsy and read it. 'You're right, damn it. It is Cyprus.'

Jane gave him a small, tight smile. 'Shall I try 87?'

'God, yes. See if you can work the oracle.'

She eased the headphones over her ears, fine-tuned the frequency and opened the microphone. '208 to 87. Are you receiving me? I say again, are you receiving me? Over.' She switched the set to *receive*. An intermittent crackle of static filled her headset. She cut in the speaker for the men to hear, listened for a moment and then turned the volume down and pushed back the headphones.

Hobey said, 'And that's all we've had out of 'em since 10.30.'

19

'For God's sake,' Watson said. 'Why the hell don't they get a grip? Damn it, you acknowledge a Pack Up if you have to open the window and bloody shout.'

Jane checked the log. It was all there in Mavis Gray's neat writing. The routine Wakey-Wakey check call sent out to all units at 08.00. Acknowledged immediately by 87. The Pack Up red alert received from GHQ at 10.27, transmitted to 87 at 10.30. Unacknowledged. Confirmation sent to GHQ at 10.50. She looked up, surprised. 'You confirmed with GHQ without prior acknowledgement from 87?'

Hobey shrugged awkwardly.

'On my orders,' Watson said, his voice hard.

'I see, sir,' Jane said. So you've taken a gamble, she thought, and backed a loser. No wonder you're twitched.

It was typical of Watson, of course. Part of the press-on, Cranwell image. Jealous of the honour of the Service he would always put his head on a block to cover for his units.

'That wingless wonder, Gatley,' Watson said savagely. 'He's only got three companies of infantry depending on him for every damned thing from mortar bombs to mepacrine.' Gatley was the C.O. of 87 MU, three months in Marazag, new to command status. 'He's probably got the entire unit standing by their beds for a kit inspection or an FFI or some such bull.'

'Since 08.00 hours?' Anxiety flawed Jane's voice like a snagged thread in a silk stocking.

Watson looked at her, puzzled. She's got the shakes, he thought. Why? She's not scared of me like that other clueless little bint. In any case, it's my problem, not hers. He said, 'I wouldn't put it past him. Those Admin bods are all the same. No sense of priorities.'

Jane said, 'I don't think David would agree with that.'

'Who?'

20

'My husband. He's the Adjutant of 87.'

Of course, David Roper, Watson thought. So that's what's bugging her. He searched the filing cabinet of his memory, came up with a mental picture of a wiry man with tow-coloured hair and a narrow, intelligent face. He said, 'He was in heavy bombers, wasn't he?'

She nodded. 'Lancasters.' And halfway through his second tour when he lost most of his left hand over Essen. 'I'm quite sure he's fully aware of the urgency of the situation.'

'So am I,' Watson said gruffly. He saw the tension in the set of her shoulders, her hands clenched white-knuckled on the metal desk. 'Not to worry,' he said awkwardly. He was awkward with women in uniform. Especially pretty women. 'There'll be some perfectly straightforward explanation. There always is.'

'Gremlins in the tubes,' Hobey said, backing him up. 'Or a power cut in Marazag.'

Jane nodded, unconvinced. There was a battery bank for use in a grid failure. And if the radio went on the blink there was always the teleprinter. So why didn't 87 answer?

Watson checked the wall clock. 'Whatever it is, we can't wait any longer,' he said. 'I'm scrubbing round 87 as of now, Hobo. We'll give it to Bisset at 90 MU as an emergency. OK?'

Hobey nodded.

'Right,' Watson said briskly. 'Clear it with him, Hobo. Load at Devasoir. Ask Bisset for his earliest loading time and knock thirty minutes off it. That'll get him moving. Instruct the controller at El Fard to divert the Daks to Devasoir.'

'He won't like that,' Hobey said. El Fard was on the Delta coast, only an hour by truck from Marazag. Devasoir was down on the canal south of Ismalia.

'So he'll have to lump it,' Watson said. 'Earn his pay for once. Alert the Yanks at Devasoir to stand by for the

21

Daks, assist in loading and give 'em priority clearance.
All right?'
    Hobey nodded. 'Sir.'
    'Manage it between you, can you?'
    'No problem,' Hobey said.
    'If that Yank colonel at Devasoir tries to give you a
hard time, put him through to me. I'll be in my office.'
Watson turned and walked to the door.
    Jane said, 'And 87, sir?'
    'What?'
    'Shall I keep trying to . . .'
    Watson saw the plea in her eyes. Not for the first time
he cursed whoever it was in Postings who had wished
WAAFS on the Middle East. Women were all right in
hospitals or munition factories or working on the farm,
but put them in Airforce blue and you introduced a
whole new emotional problem; a dimension of stress
with which he had never been able to come to terms.
'JACK KNIFE's your first priority,' he said sharply, saw
her face tighten and added more gently, 'Oh, God, yes.
Keep plugging away at 87 whenever you've got a spare
minute.'
    She smiled. 'Thank you, sir.'
    Wilkinson was waiting in the corridor.
    Watson glared at him. 'I used to fly Beaus, Mr
Wilkinson.'
    'Sir,' Wilkinson said warily.
    'Know what I'm doing now?'
    'Sir?'
    'Running a bloody lonely hearts club,' Watson said
disgustedly.

2.   14.40 – 15.30 HOURS

'Nothing?' Watson said.

Hobey shook his head. 'No joy at all, I'm afraid, sir.'

'Damn.'

Hobey shifted uncomfortably on his chair, feeling the sweat oozing down his chest. Watson's office was on the top floor. A small, white-walled room, sparsely furnished, functional. And, at this time in the afternoon, hot. In spite of the open window the temperature was up in the eighties. 'It's been seven hours now since we heard from them,' he said.

'Damn it, Hobo, I know that,' Watson said, upright in his special, high-backed chair with its padded headrest, everything on his desk – telephones, pencils, wire baskets, ashtray, lighter, cigarette box – set out neatly like the plumbing in a cockpit.

'Yes, sir,' Hobey said, waited a moment and added, 'I don't think it's an equipment failure.'

'Nor do I. They'd have fixed it by now. Or sent a car to El Fard to talk to us from there.'

'So we keep trying?'

'God, yes. What else?' Watson pressed his head back, easing the ache in his neck. 'Who's on watch now?'

'Section Officer Robens.'

'Robens? Is that the blonde with fat legs and too much lipstick?'

'Yes.' Hobey grinned. Watson described women the

23

way he identified aircraft, picking out the salient features. Accurate but not always flattering.

'Competent, is she?'

'Oh, she's mustard,' Hobey said, loyal as ever. 'And of course Jane's still in there.'

'Jane Roper?' Watson's eyebrows rose. 'Doing what, for God's sake?'

'Waiting.'

Watson scowled. 'We're all doing that, Hobo.'

'Bit different for her, though.'

'Yes.' Watson picked up the table lighter made from an aircraft cannon shellcase. He looked at it fiercely, put it down again. 'How is she?'

'Jane? All right. Too tired to feel tired. She'll be OK as soon as we hear something.'

Depends what we hear, Watson thought. 'What d'you reckon's happening up there? Panic stations in the compound? Local wogs on the rampage?'

'I wondered about that,' Hobey said. 'Had a discreet word on the blower with the Provost Marshal's office, as a matter of fact. They liaise quite a bit with the civvy police, apparently. But so far as they know it's all sweetness and light in Marazag.'

'Um.' Watson stood up and walked to the window. Below him in the MT yard across the street the staff cars parked in the bays looked like scale models, their roofs gleaming in the sunlight. The HQ compound at Marazag was like that. Surrounded by high buildings. Vulnerable to snipers or a man with a grenade. All it needed was some poor bastard who'd got a Dear John letter from his wife and gone round the twist.

Behind him, Hobey said, 'We could contact El Fard again, sir. Ask them to nip down there in a radio truck and give us a sitrep.'

'No.'

Hobey looked at his watch. 14.50. 'We'd know for sure in an hour then, sir.'

24

And so would they, Watson thought. El Fard, GHQ, British Troops Egypt – every damned unit in the Command monitoring the signals. If it wasn't equipment failure or a mob riot it had to be internal, within 87 MU itself. A domestic flap between the MU and Group, Gatley and himself. And that was how it was going to stay. He wasn't having any damned inquisitive outside brass poking their noses into his problem. Not yet, not at this stage. He swung round. 'No, Hobo. I'm keeping this in the family. At least for now.'

Hobey nodded. It was entirely in character, what he had expected.

'Another hour,' Watson said, 'If we haven't heard by 16.00 I'll talk to El Fard.'

'Roger.' Hobey stood up. 'If you'll excuse me, sir, I'd better get back down there.'

When he had gone, Watson walked back to his desk and sat down, drawing the little office round him like a familiar garment. The large scale map on the wall showing all his units marked with coloured pins. The noticeboard above the filing cabinets, papered with the day's DROs, the Group Transport graphs, the status reports. The desk itself, workmanlike, tidy. The visitor's chair angled to catch the light from the window. This was how it had been, where Gatley had sat, that day three months ago when he had come to make his number.

'Squadron Leader Gatley, sir,' Wilkinson said and stepped to one side as Gatley came into the office.

'Take a pew,' Watson said, not rising, not offering his hand. He nodded to the GWO. 'Thank you, Mr Wilkinson.'

'Sir.' Wilkinson withdrew, closing the door firmly behind him.

Gatley sat stiffly upright, his feet together, his hat balanced on his knee. He was in his middle thirties,

25

slightly-built, of medium height. His fair hair was
thinning and brushed back without a parting, his eyes
a faded blue. There were freckles on the backs of his
hands. He looked oddly incongruous in his newly-press-
ed uniform, like a family grocer miscast as an officer in
some amateur production of *Journey's End*. Yet there
was a certain dignity in the set of his head, a kind of
prim integrity. If he was intimidated by the big man
behind the desk he did not show it. Except possibly
about the eyes. His eyes were watchful, wary.

'Good trip?' Watson said. His neck was giving him
hell, the grandmother of all headaches gripping his
skull, squeezing his brain.

'Very pleasant, sir.' Gatley's voice was neutral,
without colour, matching the thin lipped mouth.

'And how are things at home?' Watson said, making
an effort.

'Busy.'

God, Watson thought, it's like interviewing a speak-
your-weight machine. He opened a manilla folder on
the desk in front of him, looked at it for a moment or
two and then said, 'I need a C.O. for 87 MU. Think you
can handle it?'

'Yes, sir.' No surprise. No pleasure. No hesitation,
either.

'It'd be your first command.'

'Yes, sir.'

'Um.' Watson frowned as the ache in his head flared
and subsided. He riffled through the papers in the folder.
'You're not a career officer, of course.'

'No,' Gatley said. But he was a volunteer. That had
meant something back in September 1939 when he had
walked into the Recruiting Centre in Kingsway and
offered his services. RAF VR. And a little badge on his
sleeve to prove it. Looking across the desk at Watson
now he knew it meant nothing to him. Conscript or

26

volunteer, to this man he was just an amateur; a civilian masquerading in uniform.

'What were your qualifications in civilian life?' Watson said.

Gatley looked at him coldly, concealing his anger. He had nothing to set alongside Cranwell. No public school. No university. During the last five years it had not been a noticeable disadvantage. Why was it important now?

Watson noted his hesitation. 'I've no wish to pry, Gatley, but a bit of background is always helpful.' He worked his shoulders, leaning forward, his elbows on the desk. His head felt as though it were balanced very precariously on his neck. 'What was your profession before the war?'

Damn you, Gatley thought, mistaking the pain in Watson's eyes for contempt. You arrogant, bloody fly-boy with your wings and your flashy ribbons. Where the hell would you be without men like me to carry the can for you? He said carefully, 'I've never thought of myself as a professional man, sir.'

'No?' Watson's voice was politely surprised.

'Before the war I was with a firm of timber importers. Assistant General Manager.' And a good one. The facts at his fingertips. All the know-how, the market expertise, the financial acumen. Respected by his colleagues. Not liked, perhaps, but respected. In line for the manager's job. A seat on the Board eventually.

'Useful experience,' Watson said without conviction. Civilian life was alien territory to him; untidy, slightly seedy, boring.

Gatley nodded. 'I've found it to be so.' He was at home with figures, thrived on paperwork. It was people he found difficult.

Watson checked the papers in the folder. 'You've always been on MUs, have you?' The pain in his head

27

shifted its grip, blurring his vision momentarily. He blinked. Saw the typed words slide back into focus.

'Yes,' Gatley said.

'In the UK?'

It was like a cross-examination, the evidence against him building up. Gatley nodded. Why ask? he thought. It's all there in my documents. It's not a brilliant record, but not one to be ashamed of, either.

'Never served on an operational squadron?'

'No.' That had been his ambition in the early days. Equipment Officer on a bomber squadron. Working little daily miracles to get the spares to keep the kites airworthy. But whenever he had put in for a posting they had turned it down. Said he was too valuable where he was.

'So,' Watson said as if to himself, 'no operational experience.'

Gatley's eyes fastened on that striped ribbon with the two glinting bars. 'We can't all be death or glory boys,' he said bitterly.

'What? Oh, quite.'

'Somebody has to stay home and mind the shop.'

'Yes,' Watson said. It doesn't matter, he thought. Leave it, man, for God's sake.

But Gatley could not leave it. 'I've always tried to do my duty.' He ducked his head slightly, his scalp shining through the thin, pale hair. 'I think my record speaks for itself, sir.'

So you're a bang-on, upper-echelon clerk, Watson thought irritably. What d'you want me to do? Pin a bloody medal on you? He said abruptly, 'Married, are you?'

Gatley blinked, unprepared for the question. 'Pardon?'

'Are you married?'

'Separated,' Gatley said. Or a widower, even? He did not know for sure. His five years with Hilda had been

28

a disaster. An invasion of his privacy by a woman whose natural appetites, restrained before the wedding, given a free rein afterwards, had appalled him. On the first night of the honeymoon he had felt like a novice in a brothel. 'My wife left me three years ago.'

When he had gone home on leave that last time and found the house empty he had felt only relief. There had been no note, no explanation. She had taken her clothes and the car and disappeared. Alone? With another man? He neither knew nor cared, had made no inquiries, no effort to trace her. He had moved into a hotel, put the house on the market and discovered a kind of peace.

'I see,' Watson said. 'Children?'

Gatley shook his head. No children, thank God. He did not approve of bringing children into a world at war. It was one of the things Hilda had been unable to understand about him. One of the many things. She had goaded him with it, flaunted herself at him, using her large, plump body shamelessly to provoke him. When he had failed to respond she had called him a queer. But he was not that; simply a solitary man, insecure in the company of both men and women, secure only in his own mind.

'Good,' Watson said and meant it. It would take this man all his time to cope with 87 without having the worry of a wife and family back home to distract him. 'No hostages to fortune, then.' He smiled, the polite, slightly puzzled smile of a judge at a dog show confronted with a breed previously unrecognised by the Kennel Club.

Gatley watched him warily, sensing the lack of warmth in his smile. In his experience most people smiled at him like that, pushing him away rather than drawing him towards them.

Watson sat back, changing his position to ease his neck muscles. 'I see you've come direct from Y Depot. That's Southampton, isn't it?'

'Just outside,' Gatley said. A square mile of stores stacked in the open under tarpaulins, assembled before D Day, continuing now to supply the thrust of the armies eastwards across France towards the Rhine. A week ago he had been there in the thick of it. Working eighteen hours a day, catnapping at night on a stretcher in his office. Already it seemed another world, another life.

'Yes,' Watson said. He had seen the secret file on Y Depot, regarded now as a model MU for handling the immense amount of traffic necessary to support an advancing army. 'Well, you'll find 87 a bit different from that show.' He nodded stiffly towards the map on the wall. 'A small unit in a grotty little wog town miles from anywhere. Your nearest neighbour's El Fard and that's a good hour's drive over bloody awful roads.' If you could call them roads. They were just narrow dirt tracks built along the tops of the dykes in the Delta marshes, the hard-packed soil black and gritty with small stones washed down in the Nile silt. They were designed for ox-carts and donkeys, not trucks.

It was on one of those tracks that Jock Hammond had bought it when the front offside tyre of his Humber shooting-brake blew out. The car had rolled twice, bounced off the dyke and dropped into four feet of muddy water. When they found it, Hammond had still been in the driving seat, pinned there by the boss of the steering column buried in his chest, both knees shattered against the lower edge of the dashboard, his face under water, his lungs full of it. For a man who had survived fifty-two raids over Germany as a Flight Engineer it was, as Scobart had said at the funeral, a helluva way to die.

'Seems an odd place to have an MU, sir,' Gatley said, staring up at the map.

'Bloody stupid,' Watson said. 'We've got those damned strategic boffins in GHQ to thank for that. They

30

moved the unit up there just before Alamein. Part of the dispersal panic when it looked as though Rommel was all set to take Cairo and push on across Sinai.'

'Alamein?' Gatley said. 'But that was . . .'

'1942.' Watson nodded disgustedly. 'Three months, they said. Six at the outside. And we've been waiting two years for them to give us a re-location.' 87 had been a good unit; a small, mobile MU pushing well up into the blue behind the armour, servicing the advanced airstrips of the Desert Airforce. Cooping it up in Marazag was like caging a cheetah.

'I see,' Gatley said.

The hell you do, Watson thought, remembering the rows of beds in the converted cinema, the compound wired in like a POW cage, the boredom, the heat, the flies. You're used to green fields by the Solent and the mutter of guns across the Channel; English beer in an English pub, Vera Lynn on the BBC and the feeling that what you're doing makes sense. No, my friend, you don't see. But you damned soon will.

And he thought: I'm making a botch of this interview, not getting through to him at all. And cursed the ache in his head that blurred his concentration.

He pulled open a drawer in his desk, took out a bulky folder and pushed it across to Gatley. 'Something to read in the train tomorrow. Just the usual bumf, I'm afraid.' But beautifully presented, meticulously typed. That was Vince's work. Corporal Vince who ran the Orderly Room at 87 with the same unobtrusive efficiency with which Scobart, the SWO, handled the discipline; without whom, to quote Jock Hammond: 'The unit'd be an even bigger bloody shambles than it is.'

'Ah, good.' Gatley leaned forward, hovering over the folder, his face animated for the first time, his eyes bright with interest. The contents of the folder were listed neatly on the cover: Nominal Roll, Stores Inward, Stores Outward, Leave Roster, Health, Transport, Defaulters, Native Labour. This was something he knew about; the nuts and bolts of the job. 'Thank you, sir. I'll get right on to it.'

Watson was reminded of a praying mantis presented with a particularly juicy fly. He said, 'That's only the whitewash on the wall, y'know. If you want the real gen you'll need to talk to Bobby March.'

'March?'

'He's the Senior Engineering Officer. Been acting C.O. since Hammond bought it. Good type. Knows his way around.'

Gatley nodded. 'I'm sure he does. But I prefer to find things out for myself, make my own judgements.'

What clot in UK Postings wished this bastard on us? Watson thought. 'Every C.O. needs the support of his officers, Gatley,' he said. 'In a unit like 87, men of the calibre of March and Roper, the Adjutant – they're worth their weight in gold.' God, he thought, I'm beginning to sound like him. 'They've got their fingers on the pulse. They know what makes the place tick. And they hear a lot of things you'll never hear yourself.'

Gatley looked at him sharply, his eyes hard. 'Are you trying to tell me there's something wrong up there, sir?' He sat up straight in his chair, braced his shoulders. It was as though the sight of the folder had given him stature, a presence.

'Not wrong,' Watson said carefully. 'Just a bit – well, tricky.' It was what he had said to Hammond twelve months previously. And Hammond had understood, grinning his shrewd, extrovert grin, sitting where Gatley sat now; a casual, easy man with the Flight Engineer's single wing on his shirt and amusement in his eyes.

But Gatley was not grinning. His face was tight, stubborn.

Rowelled by his headache, clutching at straws now,

Watson saw the stubborness as determination. Maybe you'll do, at that, he thought. Rise to the occasion. Get a grip. Make a go of it. Some men – even the most unpromising – were able under pressure to do that. Was Gatley perhaps one of them? He said, 'The unit ticks over well enough work-wise.' The monthly returns summarised in the folder proved that. 'Trouble is, there's not enough work. This whole Command's been put into mothballs pending the end of hostilities in Europe and the big switch to the Pacific theatre when we start ferrying troops and equipment out there to clobber the Japs. When that happens we'll be needed again, run off our feet probably.' And he couldn't wait for it to begin. The old, pre-Alamein razzmatazz. The sweat, the panic stations, the marvellous, hit-'em-for-six-damn-their-eyes spirit. 'Meanwhile, apart from the odd Pack Up, we're more or less marking time. You see the problem?'

'Morale?'

Watson nodded. 'We've got two hundred men up in Marazag trying to spin out a work-load fifty could do. Most of 'em have been over three or four years, done their time up the blue, seen their share of action. But for the last two years they've been marooned in the middle of nowhere. Give 'em a real job to do and they're magnificent. But with time on their hands, damn-all in the way of off-duty facilities and the nagging suspicion that the little woman back home's shacked up with a Yank. . .' He spread his hands.

'I understand,' Gatley said smugly.

Watson looked at him doubtfully. Even in a man with a much more exciting personality such confidence would be disquieting. Somewhere in his head, deep down under the throbbing, griping ache rooted in the steel plate that topped his spine, a warning voice was clamouring to be heard. But he was too tired to listen to it, his energy sapped by the struggle to keep his brain

33

clear. His bad days were fewer now than they had been in the early months following his discharge from hospital. But when they came they were savage. 'Hammond did a wizard job up there,' he said. 'Ran that unit like a family.' He saw Gatley's lip curl. 'I'm not saying that's the only way to do it, of course. But...'

'I understand,' Gatley said again. 'Concern for the men's welfare will be a high priority second only to efficiency.' He smiled, a curious, almost patronising smile, as if he had somehow changed roles with Watson, become not the interviewee but the interviewer. 'An efficient ship is a happy ship.'

Pompous little squit, Watson thought. You'd make a proposal of marriage sound like a share prospectus.

'It's a question of organisation, isn't it?' Gatley said. 'Filling the unforgiving minute.'

Is it hell, Watson thought. We're talking about people, damn it. Not spare parts on a hangar floor. He tugged at his moustache as the pain thrust upwards from his neck, branching out into his head, tenacious as ivy, spiked like blackthorn. He's not unintelligent, he thought. He has a sense of responsibility and he's obviously honest. So why don't I trust him? And knew the answer as he asked himself the question. Gatley was a man who would do the right thing at the wrong time and for the wrong reasons. Given a choice, Watson would have rejected him. But there was nobody else to send.

Watson stood up. 'Well, good luck to you, Wing Commander,' he said. You'll need it, he thought. 87'll break you before you break them. And was in some small measure comforted by the thought.

Gatley got to his feet, surprised. 'Wing Commander?'

'Didn't they tell you? It goes with the job. Temporary, of course. But paid.' He held out his hand.

'Thank you, sir.' Gatley shook hands briefly. He

34

disliked touching people. He put on his hat, picked up the folder and tucked it under his arm, doing it deliberately, with care; assuming the accoutrements of command.

Watching him through a haze of pain, Watson thought: For God's sake, man, just go. Take your facts and figures and bloody well get out of my sight.

Gatley said, 'You can rely on me, sir. I'll certainly do my best to justify your...'

'Don't give me any promises, Gatley,' Watson said curtly. 'Just give me results.'

Which, he thought now, Gatley had done. The monthly returns from 87 for August and September had made that clear. Watson had read them with a kind of awe. Discipline had been tightened, the main stores compound at the railhead completely reorganised, the serviceability of the MT section dramatically improved, a comprehensive training programme put into operation.

'Made an impressive start, hasn't he?' Leach had said. Leach was the Senior Group Equipment Officer, a thin, bespectacled man with a mind as balanced and complex as a rotary engine. 'Really got them going up there.'

But going where? Watson wondered uneasily. This training programme he's set up. When he's got 'em trained, what's he going to do with 'em then?

The Pack Up for JACK KNIFE came at exactly the right moment, seemed the logical, custom-built answer. Something for 87 to get their teeth into; a test of Gatley's influence and methods. And, after the sort of bulk supply programmes he had been involved in at Y Depot, a piece of cake.

'So what the hell's gone wrong?' he said aloud, staring at the map on the wall opposite his desk as if it were a window through which he could see into Gatley's mind.

35

'Five Dak-loads of stores, for God's sake. It's not exactly bloody D Day.'

He got up and was halfway to the window when the phone rang. He swung round and pounced on it. 'Watson.'

'Hobey here, sir.'

'Yes?'

'They've made contact.'

'87?'

'Yes. I'm sorry, sir. It's not too good, I'm afraid.'

'Hold on to 'em, Hobo,' Watson said. 'I'll be right down.'

3.   15.30 – 17.00 HOURS

Hobey was waiting at the foot of the stairs. He had a signal pad in his hand and his face was grave.

'OK, Hobo,' Watson said. 'Let's get on with it.' He made to push his way past but the SSO stood firm.

'Just a minute, sir.'

'Bugger that,' Watson said. 'We don't want to lose 'em again.' In his mind he was already rehearsing what he would say to Gatley.

'I'm sorry, sir. I'm afraid we've already lost them.'

'Lost 'em?' Watson's face went red. 'For God's sweet sake. Three of you in there and you can't even hold on to a . . .'

Hobey pushed the signal pad at him. 'You'd better read this. It's a transcript of their signal.'

Watson snatched the pad, scowling. The top third of the page was in shorthand, the longhand version, in a neat, feminine hand, below it. 208 FROM 87. UNABLE TO HANDLE YOUR PACK UP. WE HAVE AN EMERGENCY SITUATION HERE AS OF 09.00 THIS MORNING. ADJUTANT HAS BEEN SHOT AND IS SERIOUSLY WOUNDED. MEN ARE BARRICADED IN CINEMA. GATLEY HAS ORDERED SIGNALS BAN AS PART OF SECURITY BLACKOUT. THIS IS A MAYDAY. I SAY AGAIN, THIS IS A MAY—

Watson looked up. 'Is that it?'

'Yes.'

'Cut off at the end like that?'

Hobey nodded. 'We heard shooting. Then the set went dead.'

'Good God,' Watson said. 'You had it on the speaker, did you?'

'Yes.'

'Who actually sent the signal?'

'He didn't identify himself. Not by name.' The voice had been hurried, sharp-edged. 'Jane says it wasn't one of their regular W/OPs. My guess is somebody sneaked into the Signals office and...'

'Jane?' Watson looked at the signal pad. The words ADJUTANT SHOT SERIOUSLY WOUNDED hit him like a fist. 'Was she on the set when...?'

'Yes.'

'Damn. How is she, Hobo?'

Hobey shrugged. 'All right. Shaken rigid, of course, poor kid. But – all right.'

'The other girl – whosit ...?'

'Pat Robens. She's in there with her now. I thought it best to leave the two of them together for a minute or two,' Hobey said. And stop you blundering in like an eager war-horse, he thought.

Watson nodded. 'You've tried to get through again?'

Hobey nodded. 'No joy, I'm afraid. I think they've shot up the set.'

Or the chap working it, Watson thought grimly. Security blackout be damned. What the hell was Gatley trying to hide? 'OK, Hobo. We've got things to do.' He hesitated, his hand on the door. 'She's – not weeping or anything, is she?'

'Not yet,' Hobey said.

Jane was sitting at the console talking into the microphone, Pat Robens beside her. '... read me? I say again, do you read me? Acknowledge. Over.' She flicked the switch. Watson saw the rigidity in her shoulders, saw her shake her head miserably as the static hissed and stuttered through the speaker. She moved to open

38

the microphone again and he said quickly, 'No. Leave it, Jane.'

She turned her head and looked up at him. Her face shocked him; a white, frozen mask, the eyes huge and empty.

'It's probably just a flesh wound,' he said. 'They always look worse than they are.'

As if he had not spoken, she said dully, 'We've got to keep trying, sir.' Her voice was dry and brittle.

'We've got to do a hell of a lot more than that,' Watson said. When you got a Mayday you didn't hang about. Especially when it was from one of your own. He looked up at the clock, his mind racing. 15.42. Two hours to get a relief column together. Four hours to drive up to Marazag. If they made it by 22.00 they'd be damned lucky. 'How d'you feel about staying on watch? With Section Officer Robens, of course.'

Hobey said quickly, 'Pat can cope on her own, sir. I think we should let Jane get some ...'

'I'll stay,' Jane said.

'No,' Hobey said. 'The best thing you can do is ...'

'Stay here and work,' Jane said. 'I'm not going back to sit in that flat and wait for the phone to ...'

'Good girl,' Watson said, his voice gruff. He saw Hobey's mouth open to protest and hissed at him, 'Shut up, Hobo. Use your bloody imagination for once.' He touched Jane's shoulder briefly. 'I want you to handle Bisset and Devasoir. See that Pack Up safely on its way.' Whatever was happening at 87, whatever the outcome, when the official questions were asked, JACK KNIFE would be at the top of the list. If the troops on the beachhead got their air-drop on schedule he might, just might, be able to keep the crisis at 87 private to Group. 'All right?' he said.

Jane nodded.

'You'll be hearing from Bisset pretty soon now.

39

Meanwhile, keep a channel open for 87. Listening watch, eh?'

She said, 'You don't want me to keep calling them?' And her eyes pleaded: I want to know what's happening. David's hurt and I want to know. I want to know.

'Waste of time,' Watson said shortly but not unkindly. 'There's obviously nobody manning the set up there.'

'I realise that,' she said, 'but – well, it's just that . . .'

'Look,' Watson said, impatient to get on, knowing he had to settle her mind first. 'There's just a chance whoever sent that Mayday might come through again. If he does he'll only have seconds to get the word to us. I don't want the channel blocked if that happens.'

'We'll put them on the monitor, sir,' Pat Robens said.

Watson looked at her gratefully, with approval. Her blonde hair was rolled neatly above her collar. Her voice, like her eyes, was warm, composed. Nice girl, he thought, in spite of all that lipstick. Pity about her legs. He turned to Hobey. 'Conference in my office in ten minutes. Bring Jack Curtis with you.' He glanced down at Jane, wanting to say something, finding no words. It would have been easier with a man. 'It's a bastard,' you could say to a man. Or, 'Dee-dah dee-bloody-dah.' And he would grin and understand. But a girl was different. He nodded to her. 'Don't let Bisset flannel you. I want those Daks loaded and airborne by 18.30.'

Back upstairs in his office he sat down at his desk, lit a cigarette and dialled a number on the internal phone. 'Hanwell.' The voice in his ear matched the man. Ben Hanwell, ex-infantry Major, now a Wing Commander in the RAF Regiment, was an even tempered, deceptively casual man who masked a kind of exuberant

40

ruthlessness behind a slightly bored manner and a Sandhurst accent.

Watson said, 'Can you come up here, Ben?'

'Now?'

'Yes.'

'Fun and games, is it?'

'Something like that.'

As Watson hung up, Hobey knocked on the door and came in.

'Take a pew, Hobo. Curtis coming?'

Hobey nodded. 'He was down in the yard.' Curtis was the Group MT Officer.

'I've asked Hanwell to join us,' Watson said.

'You're sending the Regiment up there?'

'Yes.'

'Going to be tricky,' Hobey said. In his vocabulary tricky was an urgent word; the word he had used on Ops over the North Atlantic when the Sunderland was two hundred miles out, rounding up a crippled tanker in a Force eight gale.

'That's why we need Ben Hanwell,' Watson said. Hanwell and his hard men and a spectacular helping of good old-fashioned luck.

Curtis and Hanwell came in together. They sat down beside Hobey opposite Watson. The Group Captain passed round his cigarette box, picked up the signal pad and read out the Mayday from 87, using the clipped, flat voice once familiar to Ops Room Controllers right down the North African seaboard from Alexandria to Tripoli.

Hanwell smiled his lazy, unruffled smile. He sat with his arms folded, the cigarette in the corner of his mouth; a tough, ginger-haired man in khaki drill, the bottoms of his trousers tucked neatly into gaitered boots, the brass buckle of his webbing belt unpolished, the belt itself a faded, sand-stained blue. His shirt sleeves were rolled up. The hairs on his arms glinted redly among the freckles. 'Dear, oh dear,' he said.

Watson gave him a hard, tight grin. 'Very probably,' he said. 'So I want you to go up there and have a shufti.'

'My pleasure,' Hanwell said.

'How many men will you need?'

'Have you got a street plan of Marazag showing the compound?'

Watson opened the deep filing drawer in his desk, thumbed through the maps in it and pulled out a large scale plan of the town. He unfolded it and spread it out on his desk. The 87 HQ compound was outlined in heavy black ink; a small square set in the heart of the town. Hanwell leaned forward, noting the maze of narrow streets.

'Hell of a place to get at, Ben,' Watson said.

'Bit dicey,' Hanwell said. 'Especially in the dark.' He pointed to the compound itself. 'Brick buildings?'

Watson nodded. 'Corrugated iron roofs. Wire-mesh fly screens on the windows.'

'No glass?'

'No.'

'That helps.'

'All the doors are wooden with an inner fly-screened frame. The Armoury window has wooden shutters.'

'Check,' Hanwell said, taking out a pencil. 'I can have this, can I?'

'Yes, of course.'

Hanwell began to make notes on the plan. 'Guard Room?'

'Here, just inside the main gate.' Watson tapped the plan. 'It's an EPI tent. Dug in. Sandbagged.'

'Um. And these flats overlook three sides?'

'Yes.'

'Oh dear. Wired-in, I take it?'

42

'Yes. Lights at each corner. Mounted above the wire. Controlled from the EPI.'

'And the cinema's where the men are bottled up?'

'Roger. It's their billet. Airmen on the ground floor and stage. Senior NCOs in the balcony. It's been boarded off to make it private. They mess in what used to be the projection room and the manager's office, knocked into one now. The airmen mess in the foyer. The cookhouse is beside it.'

'Um. It's not exactly the Ritz, is it?'

'No,' Watson said. The cinema was dark and infested with bugs. The cookhouse swarmed with cockroaches.

'The Roxy, actually,' Hobey said.

Hanwell grinned. 'The Officers Mess is – where?'

'Here in Sharia Pasha. It was a small hotel.'

'Right.' Hanwell made a note. 'OK. I'll take fifty of my chaps.'

'Fifty?' Watson frowned. 'There's a couple of hundred bods in that cinema, Ben.'

'Fifty's enough. Any more and we'll be treading on each other's arses.' Hanwell shook his head. 'Not pleasant.'

Watson looked at him with affection. They both spoke the same language, these two. 'How soon can you be ready?'

Hanwell looked at his watch. 'Mind if I use the phone?' He dialled and waited, staring down at the plan, his face composed, his eyes intent. 'Sar'nt Scott? Hanwell here.'

'Sir.' A mile away in the camp beside the Almaza airfield, Scott sat in the Regiment's Orderly Tent.

'I want fifty men in full combat order paraded and ready to go by 17.00.'

'Sir.' Pronounced: 'Surrr.' The r sounds like tearing silk.

'Haversack rations. Tea in the thermoses.'

'Sir.'

'Hand pick 'em, Sar'nt. It's going to be a long night.'

'Are we going far, sir?' Scott said politely. He was a lowlander, deep-chested, big-thighed, rope-muscled in the back and shoulders. A long-distance man, all stamina and guts, built to stay, like his forebears who had run all night across the border hills rustling English cattle. English women, too.

'Just up the road,' Hanwell said. 'I'll come up with the transport directly.'

'It's not an exercise, sir?'

'No, Sar'nt. Not this time. This one's for real,' Hanwell said happily and put the phone down.

Watson looked at Curtis. Flight Lieutenant John Curtis. He was a large, loose-limbed man of twenty-two who had sailed through the Aircrew Selection Board, been classified as Fighter Pilot material and come totally unstuck over the colour-vision test. 'Over to you then, Jack.'

Curtis nodded eagerly. He had already done his homework. 'Four troop carriers. Three-tonners. And a fifteen-hundredweight as the command vehicle.'

'And a radio jeep, please,' Hobey said. 'If, as I suspect, their set's u/s up there, I'll need that.' He caught Watson's eye and grinned. 'I'd like to go in the jeep, sir.'

'I rather thought you would, Hobo,' Watson said. He was the obvious choice; the diplomat behind the Regiment's muscle. If anyone could make Gatley see reason it was Hobey.

Curtis was on the phone talking to the Duty MT Corporal. ' . . . and five drivers. Including at least two who know their way around in the Delta. And I want the gharries double-checked and topped-up, ready to move by 16.50. Oh, and get the drivers to draw side-arms and ammo.'

44

As Curtis put the phone down, Watson said, 'Five drivers?'

'I'll be driving the command vehicle, sir,' Curtis said, phrasing it like a request. But his eyes were adamant.

'Yes,' Watson said with a kind of envy. A fifteen-hundredweight was a poor substitute for a Spitfire. But something. Better than sitting in an office. He swivelled in his chair to face Hanwell. 'You'll have to play this one by ear, Ben. God knows what you'll find up there. But I'll spell out what I want. OK?'

Hanwell nodded. 'Of course.'

'I want that unit put back together again bloody quick. And without casualties as far as possible. When you brief your chaps – when will you do that, by the way?'

Hanwell looked at the street plan of Marazag. 'Somewhere here.' He jabbed his finger at a point about two miles outside the town.

'You'll go in from the north?' Watson said.

Hanwell nodded. 'Up through Talkha. We'll stop there to eat and get organised. That way I'll have time to think about it on the trip up.'

'Yes,' Watson said. 'Well, when you brief 'em, you make damned sure they understand. Minimal casualties. I don't want to get clobbered by GHQ for starting a civil war.'

'Check.' Hanwell hesitated, pulling at the lobe of his left ear. 'We are, of course, talking about a night action to quell a mutiny.'

'No, we're damned well not,' Watson said. 'Night action, yes. Mutiny – no way.'

Hanwell said silkily, 'They have barricaded themselves in that cinema.'

'Self-defence,' Watson said. 'Gatley's probably got the SPs dodging round that compound taking pot shots at anything that moves.'

45

Hanwell raised an eyebrow. 'He's that twitched, is he?'

'Round the bend,' Watson said. 'Has to be.'

Hobey said quickly, 'We don't know that, sir. It could be . . .'

'We know damn-all,' Watson said harshly. 'Except that Roper's been shot and Gatley's lost control of the situation.' He swung back to Hanwell. 'I want him relieved of command and brought back here for me to deal with. Put March in the chair. He knows how to cope.'

He's still trying for a cover-up, Hobey thought. Everything screwed down tight and no outside interference.

'How you do it's your affair, Ben,' Watson said. 'You're in command and you have my full support. But I want that unit back on its feet by 09.00 tomorrow morning.'

Hanwell nodded. 'I hear you, sir.'

'Good.' Watson sat back. 'Hobo, I'm relying on you to keep me in the picture as things develop. But discreetly. Gatley's clamped a security blackout on 87 – about the only sensible thing he has done. Let's keep it like that. I don't want some damned inquisitive W/OP monitor at GHQ picking up your signals and spreading alarm and despondency.' He scowled, black eyebrows drawn down. 'If those politicians in uniform get wind of this God knows where it'll end.'

'We'd better code it,' Hobey said. He tore a sheet off the signal pad and began to write.

Watching him, Watson said, 'Keep it simple.'

'This do?' Hobey passed the slip of paper over.

The code was based on the game of Monopoly. Watson read it aloud. 'Arrival at Marazag: ADVANCE TO GO. Objective achieved: COLLECT £200. Departure for 208 with Gatley: GET OUT OF JAIL FREE.' He looked up. 'Yes. You do that, Hobo, and I'll give you Park Lane and Mayfair with a hotel on each. Right. Any questions?'

'Call sign?' Hanwell said.

Watson grinned, remembering Monopoly sessions in the Mess. 'You always win with the top hat, don't you, Hobo?'

'TOP HAT, then,' Hanwell said. 'And if we snafu it, which God forbid?'

Hobey said sombrely, 'Bankrupt.'

The phone rang, ominous as a fire-bell. Hobey snatched it up, listened and held out the receiver to Watson. 'Jane Roper. Another signal from 87.'

'Put it on the squawker,' Watson said tightly.

Hobey cradled the receiver on the speaker box.

'Yes, Jane?' Watson said.

'Signal from 87 reads: MEN HOLDING GATLEY HOSTAGE IN CINEMA. MAIN COMPOUND GUARD REPORTS BEGINNINGS OF A MOB COLLECTING OUTSIDE GATES. SITUATION DETERIORATING. WE NEED . . .'

'Yes?'

'That's all, sir. We called right back but they don't answer.' Jane's voice was rock-steady. Fine-drawn but cool.

'Thank you, Jane. Well done. Keep listening.' He broke the connection. 'Well, Ben?'

'Shaky,' Hanwell said.

Watson nodded grimly. Shaky, like Hobey's tricky, was a disaster word. The crisis in 87's HQ compound was beginning to overspill into the town. Inevitably, of course. Alerted by the firing the native population of Marazag was turning instinctively, with the peasant's built-in greed, towards the main compound out by the railhead where hundreds of thousands of poundsworth of equipment waited in the open behind the wire, vulnerable, tempting. It was like displaying the Crown Jewels on the grass at Tower Green and then calling the

47

Beefeaters out on strike. The wire would hold the mob back for a while. Until darkness, perhaps. But once they cut through that...

Hanwell stood up, smiling, calm. 'Well, gentlemen,' he said. 'I think perhaps it's time we went.'

4. 17.00 – 22.00 HOURS

The TOP HAT column turned in through the camp gates off the Almaza track, the fifteen-hundredweight leading with Hanwell in the cab beside Curtis. Hobey brought up the rear, tailing the three-tonners in the jeep.

Scott had fallen-in the men in three ranks outside the Orderly Tent. They wore boots and gaiters, khaki denim overalls, webbing harness, big packs with tin hats strapped to them, water bottles and the blue berets of the RAF Regiment, the brass badges left green and tarnished so as not to reflect the light. Each man carried a sten gun slung from his right shoulder, spare magazines in the thigh pockets of his overalls and a sheathed commando knife in his bayonet frog. The knives were not standard issue. Only Hanwell's company wore them, had been specially trained in knife fighting by Scott. Stacked on the sand were fifteen rope-handled wooden boxes of ammunition, two cartons of flares and five two-gallon thermos containers filled with hot tea sweetened with condensed milk.

The trucks came round in a circle over the sand, driven with precision as if tied together, their white canvas tilts rippling in the late afternoon breeze.

Scott brought the men to attention as the trucks stopped in line astern. Hanwell got out of the command vehicle and walked towards them. He returned the sergeant's salute, casually touching the peak of the khaki hat, army pattern, he had worn as a Major during Wavell's big push up the desert in the early days. 'Get the stuff loaded on, Sar'nt,' he said. 'Quick as you can. Then I'll have a word.'

Hobey sat in the jeep with his driver and watched the men toss their packs into the three-tonners and swing up the ammunition boxes over the open tailgates. The tea containers went into the back of the fifteen-hundredweight and were secured with webbing straps. The men moved easily, economically. They were fit and tanned and incredibly young.

Just boys, Hobey thought, listening to their laughter, the excitement in their voices. Trained and smart and unblooded. And he wondered what the night held for them.

When they had finished loading he got out of the jeep and walked down the line towards Hanwell who was leaning against the side of the fifteen-hundredweight, his hands thrust comfortably into his trouser pockets. As he joined him, Hobey saw a staff car swing into the camp and accelerate away up the far side of the column towards the tented area.

The men came running to gather round Hanwell, jostling and pushing good-humouredly.

'Right,' Scott said. 'Settle down and pay attention.'

Hanwell smiled. 'Thank you, Sar'nt.' He straightened up and folded his arms, suddenly tall in the waning sunlight, his badgeless cap tilted slightly over his right eye, the heavy service revolver big on his hip. '87 MU. At Marazag in the Delta. They're having a spot of bother. Our job's to go and sort it out. Should be a piece of cake. Probably all over by the time we get there. There'll be a meal stop when we're within striking distance of the town. I'll give you a full briefing then. Meanwhile, don't start dreaming of deeds of derring-do. This is just a police action, not an assault. Those boys up there are on our side. Remember that. I'm not having

50

you barging in like a load of trigger-happy cowboys. Clear?'

Heads nodded. There was a murmur of assent. Hobey heard the sound of an engine, turned his head and saw the staff car driving out through the gates again.

Hanwell grinned. 'On the other hand, there's absolutely no reason why we shouldn't enjoy ourselves. Show the flag a bit. Let those store-bashers see we're not just toy soldiers.'

The men grinned back at him eagerly. The Regiment were the odd men out in the RAF. Originally formed to take over airfield defence from the army, they were regarded with amused cynicism by the operational squadrons they guarded. Rather as the Marines had once been regarded by the Navy. And, like the Marines, their reaction had been to build up a tough, disciplined image. They drilled hard, trained hard and, given the chance, fought hard. By late 1944 the squadrons' cynicism had changed to grudging respect. But the old Toy Soldiers jibe still rankled.

Hanwell said, 'OK, Sar'nt. Let's get weaving.'

'Sir.' Scott turned smartly on his heel. 'Right. You heard the Wing-co. On the trucks a bit sharpish. Come on, come on, let's be having you, then.'

Hanwell opened the door of the cab. Curtis already had the engine ticking over. 'See you at dinner then, Hobo.'

Hobey nodded and walked back down the line to the jeep. The driver had put up the canvas tilt. Somebody was sitting in the back seat. He put his head in to see who it was. 'Jane,' he said, startled. 'What are you. . .?' and remembered the staff car.

'Hullo, Hobo.' She smiled at him, her eyes defiant. She was wearing overalls and a blue battledress blouse, her hair tucked up under a woollen cap comforter, a scarf wound round her neck. The effect was to emphasise the good, strong bone structure of her face.

51

'Start up, sir!' the driver said, looking to his front, disassociating himself from her. He was thin and young with a sharp, Cockney face and a Ronald Colman moustache. He wore a sleeveless leather jerkin over his shirt.

'What?' Hobey said. All down the line the trucks were vibrating now as the drivers gunned their engines. 'Oh, yes.' He looked at the girl. 'What the hell is this, Jane?'

She said quickly, 'We were thinking – Pat and I – if 87 comes through again . . .'

'They won't. You know that.'

'No, but if they do – you'll want to know, won't you? So we've fixed for her to call you every hour on the hour if there's any . . .'

'And you've come to tell me to listen out?'

'Yes.'

Hobey nodded. 'OK. Thanks. You've told me.'

Curtis sounded two short blasts on the fifteen-hundredweight's horn. The column began to roll. Hobey swung himself up into the passenger seat. 'We'll drop you off near Group.'

'No,' Jane said firmly. 'I'm coming with you.'

Hobey twisted round. 'Does Watson know you're here?'

'Oh, be your age,' she said. 'You know damned well he doesn't.'

Hobey nodded and turned to the driver. 'Stop at the tram terminus, Lewis. Flight Officer Roper's getting out there.'

They drove left through the gates on to the strip of tarmac laid like a black ribbon across the sand, linking the camp with the open square on the edge of Heliopolis where the Cairo tramway terminated.

Jane leaned forward and put her hand on his shoulder. 'Ah, Hobo,' she said softly. 'Come on.'

'No,' Hobey said, not turning his head, watching the

52

back of the three-tonner they were following, grateful that the jeep's tilt hid the girl from the men in the truck. 'Watson wouldn't wear it. Nor would Hanwell. Nor will I.'

The fifteen-hundredweight entered the square and swung right round the steel and glass tram shelter on the island in the middle. The three-tonners wheeled after it, keeping station at ten yard intervals. Hobey pointed to the Greek café on the corner of the El Khanka road. 'Pull in over there, Lewis.'

Jane said warningly, 'I'm not getting out, Hobo.'

'Then I'll have to put you out, won't I?'

'Try,' she said. 'You just try and I'll scream blue murder.'

Lewis began to brake, easing the jeep in towards the kerb. On the pavement outside the café two MPs were standing watching the column go by; large, impassive men in starched shirts and shorts, white webbing belts, red-banded peaked caps tilted low over their eyes. Hobey looked at them unhappily.

In his ear, Jane said, 'I mean it, Hobo. I'll scream the roof off this damned jeep.'

The MPs turned their heads as Lewis stopped just short of the café. 'By the time those two beauties have finished asking questions,' Jane said quietly, 'TOP HAT'll be way past Khanka. But you won't, Hobo. You'll still be here struggling in a tangle of red tape with a hysterical woman on your hands. It won't be funny.'

Hobey bit his lip, his round, honest face troubled.

Jane's hand tightened on his shoulder. 'Please, Hobo. I've got to come with you. You know why.'

He turned his head and saw the urgency in her eyes. 'There's nothing you can do if you . . .'

'I can be with him,' she said. And the wanting was in her voice, a kind of hunger. For better, for worse, in sickness and. . . 'He needs me, Hobo.'

53

'Everything all right, sir?' One of the MPs had come to stand beside the jeep.

Hobey looked up at him from under the tilt. 'What?'

'Only you're parked a bit awkwardly here, sir,' the MP said politely. But his eyes were unfriendly.

Jane's fingers dug hard into Hobey's shoulder. He heard her draw in her breath to scream. 'Just checking,' he said.

'Checking, sir?'

'That's what I said.' Hobey nodded to Lewis. 'OK. Drive on.'

Lewis let in the clutch and accelerated away after the column.

Jane said, 'Thanks, Hobo. You're a good, kind man.'

'I know,' Hobey said. But Hanwell wouldn't think so when they stopped to eat beyond Talkha.

Coming up fast behind the last three-tonner, Lewis felt his head swim, saw the truck shimmer, slip out of focus, float above the road like a mirage. He blinked and braked fiercely. The jeep's tyres squealed, its blunt nose dipped sharply.

Hobey grabbed the handle on the dashboard. 'For God's sake, man.'

Lewis shook his head. The three-tonner came back into focus. He eased the jeep into gear and took proper station.

'What was all that about?' Hobey said.

'Sorry, sir. Had the sun in my eyes.'

Hobey looked at him quickly. Lewis's face was shining with sweat. 'Are you all right?'

'Yes, sir,' Lewis said. He had a slight headache and his mouth was dry. He sat braced in the driving seat, watching the tailgate of the three-tonner, waiting for that curious, disconnected feeling to come back. It didn't. After a couple of miles he began to relax.

'By the way,' Jane said. 'Devasoir came through before I left. The Pack Up's on schedule so far.'

'What?'

'The Pack Up. It's all under control.'

'Oh,' Hobey said. 'Good.' He was ashamed to discover he had forgotten about the Pack Up, his mind wholly concentrated on 87 MU and the new problem of Jane. That morning JACK KNIFE had been top priority. Now it was somebody else's problem. He wondered what had happened at 87 to make Gatley shift priorities. The attack on Roper, perhaps? It was not more important than the many lives involved in JACK KNIFE, but in a small, isolated unit it might well appear to be. Especially to Gatley. For the first time he felt a certain sympathy for the little Wing Commander.

They drove up through the date plantations into El Khanka, a tumble-down, one-street village that stank of goat and human excrement, and pushed on towards Bilbeis. In the fading light the irrigation ditches gleamed like silver veins feeding the lifeblood of the dying Nile into the black soil of the Delta. This was the womb of Egypt; a great, water-logged triangle of immense fertility with its base in the sea and its apex in Cairo. All the rest was desert; arid, barren sand. But here, where the mighty river died, there was life; rooted in the oozing silt, nourished by the mineral-rich water. Everything grew here – grapes and corn, figs, dates, melons, pomegranates, chick-peas, beans – everything. They said if you ground a cigarette-end into the mud with your heel a tobacco plant would sprout.

The legendary garden of the gods, Hobey thought. Older than time and unchanging. The gods wore different faces but the legend was always the same. River-god, corn-god, the great bull-god of Mithras – they all had to die that their subjects might live. Die and rot in blood and corruption. And rise to die again.

And it seemed to Hobey, brooding on the presence of the girl in the jeep and on what waited for them in Marazag, that the air washing in through the open sides

55

was clammy with the smell of death. But whether an ancient, remembered death or a death still to come, he could not decide.

It was dark when they got to Zagazig. Approaching the little town, Jane clipped on the headset over her cap comforter and switched to Group's frequency. She listened for a moment or two, switched off and shook her head.

Twisted round in his seat, Hobey said, 'Anything?'

'No.' She pulled off the headset, disappointed.

He grinned. 'No news is good news.'

She nodded resignedly. She didn't believe it any more than he did.

Three miles beyond Zagazig they came to El Qanayat and turned off on to the dyke track for Simbillawein. They were deep into the Delta now, the track narrow, the surface friable and treacherous under the heavy-duty tyres. Curtis was pushing the fifteen-hundred-weight hard, hunched over the wheel with Hanwell beside him, his face intent in the reflected glow of the instrument panel. The track was no more than twelve feet wide, its edges crumbling. On either side there was an eight foot drop to the soggy fields. There was no moon. The sky was as black as the earth lying wet and invisible beneath the long, probing spread of the headlights. It was like flying through heavy turbulence. The trucks bounced and shuddered on the uneven surface, suspended between earth and sky, rushing through the vacuum of the night. Curtis's hands were locked white-knuckled on the wheel, his left foot braced against the steel bulkhead, his right sensitive on the throttle pedal. The windscreen was thickly spattered with dead insects and they had rolled up the windows to keep the cab clear. Back in the jeep they had no protection. The air swirled in under the tilt, gritty with flies. Jane wound her scarf round her head, covering her nose and mouth, holding on to the back of Hobey's seat as the little vehicle bucked and slithered in a cloud of fine black dust sprayed up by the three-tonners.

In the fifteen-hundredweight, Hanwell was navigating, reading the map by the light of a torch. Every few miles they had to slow down, dropping quickly through the gears to crawl, transmissions howling, brake lights glowing, across a rickety plank bridge without side rails where the dyke switched abruptly from one side of the irrigation canal to the other. There were no road signs, no warning lights. The track in front of them simply disappeared in the headlights as the bridge showed up on left or right of them. Driving at fifty plus, even with Hanwell reading the map, it was an unnerving experience.

It was at one of these cross-overs that Lewis suddenly doubled-up behind the wheel with a gasp of pain as the stomach cramps hit him without warning. He braked instinctively and whipped the gear shift into neutral. The jeep slewed wildly across the track, recovered and swung the other way, slid on locked wheels and came to rest on the lip of the dyke. He sat for a moment, unable to move, his head pressed against the rim of the wheel, his arms folded tightly over his stomach.

Hobey had been thrown forward against the dashboard. He pushed himself back into his seat, bruised and shaken. 'What the hell're you trying to...?'

Lewis straightened a little, his face crumpled with pain. 'Sorry, sir. I don't feel ...' He gulped, swung his legs out of the jeep, stood unsteadily for a moment and then jack-knifed and vomited on to the track. He wiped his hand across his mouth, turned dizzily back to the jeep, gasped, 'I'll be OK in a ...' and vomited again.

Hobey got out and went round to him. 'Easy, boy,' he said. 'Just relax and let it come.'

Lewis raised his head. In the glare of the headlights

57

his face was chalky, his mouth slack. The sour stench of vomit clogged his nostrils. Already insects were starting to cluster on his chin. He brushed them away with a shudder of disgust and hung on to the bonnet of the jeep, swaying on his feet. He opened his mouth to another gush of vomit, retching and sobbing, his eyes streaming with tears. He shook his head, gasping for breath like a swimmer. 'Oh, God,' he said weakly. 'I feel so . . .' and his voice choked on vomit and his knees buckled and he went down in a heap.

Hobey pulled him upright and together they got him into the back of the jeep. Jane took out her handkerchief and wiped his mouth and chin. He was shivering now, his skin dry and hot, his breath very foul. The transceiver and batteries took up a lot of room. He lay huddled on his side on the seat, his knees drawn up to his chest, his arms crossed, hands tucked under his armpits. He was still getting cramps but there was nothing left in his stomach to vomit except a thin, watery bile. He was breathing noisily through his mouth, his eyes beginning to roll as the fever took hold of him. There was an old groundsheet folded down behind the rear seat. They wrapped that round him and made him as comfortable as they could.

Jane got into the passenger seat and Hobey took the wheel. He reversed the jeep, edging it carefully away from the lip of the track, drove over the bridge and set off to catch the column.

'Something he ate?' Jane said, sitting sideways to keep an eye on Lewis.

'Probably,' Hobey said. But he knew it was more than that. The sudden, compulsive vomiting, the fever, the shivering – these added up to only one thing: gastro-enteritis. 'I thought there was something wrong,' he said. 'That business on the Khanka road when he damned near pranged into the back of the three-tonner.' He peered through the fly-smeared windscreen and saw the white glow and red tail-lights of the column up ahead, rolling slowly over a bad stretch of track. He gunned the engine and brought the jeep into line behind them.

'Will he be all right?' Jane said.

Lewis groaned, semi-conscious, in the beginnings of delirium.

Hobey nodded. 'We'll try to get some water into him presently when his stomach muscles have relaxed a bit.' Dehydration was the real danger in that climate, wasting away the flesh at an astonishing rate, drying out the body fluids, building the fever.

Lewis stirred uneasily. An indescribably foul smell filled the jeep. Jane wrinkled her nose.

'Diarrhoea,' Hobey said apologetically. 'Poor devil, he's running at both ends.' It was an aspect of war not featured in the recruiting posters, the lords-of-the-sky image of the RAF. Lacking even the gory honour of battle wounds.

Jane swallowed. 'Shouldn't we..?'

'Waste of time,' Hobey said. 'We'll get him cleaned up when we make Marazag. He'll be about empty by then.' And hated himself for the callous, sensible words.

The column picked up speed beyond the bad patch. The night air flooded into the jeep, cleansing and freshening. Lewis was making a curious spluttering noise with his lips. Jane leaned back and wiped his mouth again. The groundsheet, tucked under his chin, crawled with a mat of insects feeding on his vomit. She brushed them away in disgust. 'God,' she said. 'This bloody country.' There was revulsion in her voice. And something else. A kind of practical, the-hell-with-it determination.

Hearing it, Hobey grinned to himself approvingly. She worked in a clean office, lived in a comfortable flat, showered twice a day, was fastidious about her clothes and person. She had not been trained to ride the Delta after dark with a sick man lying helpless in his own

59

filth. But she was coping, discovering within herself a hitherto unsuspected ability to accept. He said, 'It is a bit basic, isn't it?'

Three hours out of Almaza they bypassed Simbilla-wein, turning north-west over little-used tracks, making for the jump-off point at Talkha. Jane checked her watch, turned in her seat and switched on the radio for the third time. Nothing came through the headset from Group. She switched off. Lewis was unconscious now, muttering and jerking under the groundsheet. She wiped his face gently, shocked by the burning skin, the hollows in his cheeks under her fingers. 'Have you got a spare hanky, Hobo? This one's about had it.'

Hobey dug into his pocket and gave her his handker-chief. She threw hers out of the jeep, settled in her seat and said, 'David was on Lancs, y'know.'

'Yes.' Hobey kept his voice neutral, masking his surprise at the sudden statement. Masking it well, too. But not quite well enough.

She smiled, looking at him sitting square and compe-tent behind the wheel. 'It's all right, Hobo,' she said. 'I'm prepared for the worst. I'm not expecting it, but I'm prepared for it.'

'Yes,' Hobey said to keep her talking, knowing it was what she needed to do. Fears put into words lose a little of their power.

'Where did you meet him?' Hobey said.

'In a taxi,' she said, remembering.

She was standing on the pavement outside Heliopolis House Hotel and she saw the old black Plymouth taxi coming up the main street and flagged it down. She had been playing tennis that morning and was wearing white shorts and a shirt, a cardigan draped round her shoulders, her racquet tucked under her arm. The taxi stopped and she gave the driver the address of her flat, opened the rear door and stepped in.

60

The man in the back seat said, 'Hullo. I'm David Roper.'

'Oh.' She hesitated, bent forward, one foot still on the pavement. 'I'm sorry. I didn't realise there was...'

'Be my guest.'

'Are you sure?'

He grinned. 'That address you gave. Is it anywhere near 208 Group?'

'Well, yes,' she said. 'But...'

'Then I'm sure.' He took her elbow and helped her into the seat, reached across and pulled the door shut. 'OK, driver.' He sat back and held out his hand. 'I'm David Roper.'

'Yes. You said.' He had tow-coloured hair and his eyes were grey, older than his face except when he smiled. She shook hands, feeling the strength in his fingers. 'I'm Jane Smith.'

'Smith?'

'Yes.'

'Ridiculous name. Had it long, have you?'

'All my life.'

He shook his head. 'Time you changed it. Doesn't suit you.' He smiled. 'Jane, yes. Jane I like. But Smith, God love us.' His uniform was creased and obviously new, the khaki colour deep, unbleached by the sun.

Straight off the boat, she thought. But the wings on his shirt were faded. 'Are you posted to 208?' There was a large khaki valise on the floor between his feet, more luggage on the seat beside the driver.

'Under their umbrella,' he said. 'Place called Mairsey Doates or Marzipan or something equally unlikely.'

'Marazag?'

'That's it.' He raised an eyebrow. 'I say, you're not a spy, are you? I mean, careless talk costs wives and all that bull.'

'Lives,' she said.

'Those too.'

61

She smiled back. 'No. I'm not a spy.'

He nodded. 'You could be with those looks.'

'Oh?' She was oddly disconcerted by the directness behind his banter, the way his eyes held hers.

'Definitely.' He looked at the shape of her breasts under her shirt. 'All female spies are ravishing.'

'And usually ravished, I believe.'

He shrugged. 'Occupational hazard.'

This isn't real, she thought. And felt like a character in a wartime film. Clipped understatement and brittle laughter. Pints and popsies and bandits at twelve o'clock high. The taxi overtook a tram. It sounded like an engine being run-up on dispersal. 'So,' she said. 'Fighters or bombers?'

'What?' Oh, bombers. Lancs.' And his eyes were suddenly old, dark with memories like a slate roof in the rain. Like the eyes of the boys she had resisted in Lincolnshire. 'And you?'

'WAAF,' she said. 'Signals.' And just managed to stop herself adding, 'Actually.' Which would have been in the script but out of character.

He grinned. 'Commissioned, of course?' She had the poise of rank even in those brief white shorts which left her long thighs bare. And the accent to match: pleasant, Home-Counties-girls-grammar-school.

'Yes.'

'Good show,' he said. It made life easier if they were both in the Officers Mess. 'Based at Group?'

'Yes.'

'Been there long?'

'Six months.' There was a confidence about him which should have been brash but somehow was not. 'What is this? A pre-flight check?'

He grinned. 'Yes, please. You're sure you've always been Jane Smith?'

'Positive,' she said, sticking to the script. Not sure where it was leading but staying with it.

62

'So,' he said. 'You're not married?'

'Oh, I see. No, I'm not married.'

He nodded, pleased. 'Cleared for take-off, then.'

She turned her head and looked out of the window, hiding her smile. The taxi swung into a side street and stopped outside her flat.

He said, 'This it?'

'Yes.'

'Home sweet home.'

'Be it never so humble. Thanks for the lift.'

'My pleasure, ma'am.' He opened the door and got out, putting on his hat. When she joined him on the pavement he was taller than she had expected, possessed of an authority beyond his years. She had seen that before. Boys grew up quickly in the driving seat of a Lancaster. Or failed to grow up at all.

'Group's just around the corner from here,' she said for something to say.

'Wizard.'

They stood in silence for a moment, actors without a script. Aware of each other, absurdly tongue-tied by their awareness.

'One small request,' he said then.

'Yes?' she said warily, willing him not to say the wrong thing, not to spoil it. And thinking: Spoil what?

'Have you any social engagements this week?'

'I might have. Why?'

'Cancel them.'

Her eyes widened, amused, relieved. 'Just like that?'

'Roger. I've got seven days before they banish me to – where did you say it was?'

'Marazag.' Lovely, squalid, safe Marazag with no runways, no Ops Room, no women waiting in the dawn.

'Yes. Well, that ought to give us a chance.' He was

smiling but his eyes were serious, almost anxious. 'OK?'

He's shy, she thought happily. Under the Rattigan dialogue, the obligatory aircrew image, he's really quite a shy person. Easily hurt. She said demurely, 'That can be arranged. I lead a very quiet life.' There had been men, of course. But not many and none serious. They were either old – in their thirties – or married. Or both.

He said, 'Well Miss Quiet-Life-Smith, will you be lunching in the Mess today?'

She nodded. She had been going to make herself a sandwich in the flat, relax for an hour before going on afternoon watch. But she nodded.

'See you there, then,' he said. 'We can work on it together while we're eating.'

'Work on what?' she said innocently.

He looked surprised. 'Changing your name to Roper. What else?' He touched his cap and got back into the taxi. The window was open and as he shut the door she saw there were three fingers missing on his left hand. She looked up quickly, startled. His eyes held hers, grey and steady, with just the hint of a question. He kept his hand there in full view, making no attempt to hide it. The truncated palm, the index finger unnaturally long in isolation. It was, she realised, deliberate. A declaration inviting a response.

'One o'clock in the bar,' she said.

'Iced lager?'

'Lovely,' she said. And saw him grin delightedly as the taxi drew away.

'He'll be all right, won't he, Hobo?' she said.

'Sure he will.'

'I mean, they'd have said if he ...'

'He'll be fine.' Hobey gripped the wheel, remembering too many conversations like this. Foolish, defiant

64

words flung in the teeth of the evidence, standing in the rain on the jetty waiting for a Sunderland two hours overdue.

She said, 'He's a very honest person, y'know. Straight. No tricks.' If David Roper said he loved you, you knew he meant it.

'Damned good at his job, too,' Hobey said.

'I know,' she said. 'So who'd want to shoot...?' Hammond and Watson, March, Scobart. Even that nice little Orderly Room clerk – what was his name – Vince. They all liked David. March had been his best man. Hammond had given her away.

Married in Cairo, they had gone up to Palestine for the honeymoon. A night in Jerusalem, five more in Tiberias at a little guest house by the lake. Picnicking in the grass-grown ruins of Capernaum, swimming naked together in the cool, clear water, waking every morning to the view of Hermon and the scent of oranges. That they had had, and a seventy-two in Luxor and a weekend together in the flat every six weeks. Until Gatley took over from Hammond. Gatley did not approve of weekends.

'This bloody war,' she said. You thought you were safe, in a back-water, a long, long way from the fighting. And you tasted happiness and looked forward and dared to hope. And the damned thing sneaked up on you out of nowhere and chopped you down.

'I'll second that,' Hobey said.

She stared through the windscreen at the tailgate of the three-tonner pounding along in front. The back flap of the tilt was rolled up and the faces of the men inside loomed and faded in the jeep's headlights like ghosts in a dark cave. Is this how it ends? she thought. It began in a taxi in the morning, blossomed marvellously through a golden afternoon we thought would last forever. Does it end like this in the haunted darkness and the stink of vomit?

65

Behind her, Lewis cried out in delirium. She turned quickly. 'It's all right,' she said. 'Just hold on, boy.' His chin was bearded with insects and she wiped them away gently and touched his hollowed cheeks and stroked his hair. 'Just hold on,' she said. 'Please.'

And Hobey knew she was not talking to Lewis. She was talking to David.

5. 22.00 – 23.00 HOURS

Hanwell took a final mouthful of tea, swirled the dregs round in his mug and tipped them out. 'OK, Sar'nt. Story time I think.'

'Right,' Scott called. 'Gather round.'

The trucks were parked nose-to-tail along a line of date palms beside the track a couple of miles beyond Talkha. One of the drivers had rigged an inspection lamp in the back of the fifteen-hundredweight, looping the lead from the battery over the tilt support above the tailgate. In the yellow light from the low-wattage bulb Hanwell's face was calm, the professional mask in place. But his eyes were bleak. He was still twitched about the girl.

'You mean she's here now?' he had said incredulously when Hobey told him. 'You let her come with us?'

'I'm sorry, Ben.'

'So am I.'

'I tried to persuade her to...'

'Persuade her? Damn it, Hobo, you've got the rank. You should've just dumped her back there in Al-maza.'

Hobey had looked at him unhappily, knowing he was right.

'Who else knows she's here?'

'Nobody. Except Lewis, of course. And he's...'

'You told me.' Hanwell had bitten into a sandwich,

67

checking over the operational plan in his mind, looking for a place to fit the girl into, not finding one.

'She's OK, Ben. Very capable.'

'Capable of jinxing the whole show,' Hanwell had said bitterly. He had had it all worked out, aims and methods carefully balanced, risks calculated and accepted. And now, this. 'If I'd any sense at all I'd leave her here. Pick her up on the way back.'

'You can't do that.'

'No.' A man, yes. You could leave a man. Give him a sten and a couple of spare magazines and tell him to keep his head down. But not a girl. 'OK. When we hit the town I want you in the jeep tucked in right behind me. We'll stop outside the Officers Mess and I want her in there under cover bloody fast. Got it?'

'Roger,' Hobey had said. And after a moment, 'You can't really blame her, Ben. Roper's her husband after all.'

'What's that got to do with it?' Hanwell had said. 'This is supposed to be a task force not a bloody lonely hearts club.'

'She could be useful once we're there.'

Hanwell had shrugged and said no more. But he was still twitched, the presence of the girl one risk too many.

As the men clustered round the back of the fifteen-hundredweight he opened his map case and spread the street plan of Marazag on the tailboard. 'Well, here we are, friends.' He put a finger on the edge of the plan. 'Two miles north of Marazag, the town God forgot. With anything like luck, nobody'll be expecting us to come in this way. So we don't knock on the door and wait politely. We bash straight in through this rabbit warren of streets and come out into Sharia Pasha – here. I'll lead. Then the jeep. Then the three-tonners. Mason, you'll drive number one. Flight Lieutenant Curtis'll be riding with you. Butterworth, you're on number two.

68

Hicks number three with Corporal Miller. Bell, you're back-stop on number four with Sar'nt Scott. Right.' he gave them his lazy, this'll-be-a-doddle-chaps, smile. 'This is how we do it ...'

Hobey listened to that easy, drawling voice detailing the plan with a cool logic which broke down the danger endemic in it and fed it to the men in manageable portions. Not minimising it, not trying to flannel them. Simply cutting it down to size. And he thought: This is what it's all about. The x factor in the equation. Expertise plus training plus x equals success. And x was courage, the ability to inspire trust, a kind of love. Leadership.

'... all nice and tidy,' Hanwell said. 'The street staked-out, the HQ compound occupied and secured, everything under control.' He folded his arms, leaning comfortably against the tailgate. 'Any questions?'

One or two, Hobey thought. Like, for example, when we've occupied the compound how do we get the men to come out of the cinema? And what about Gatley, held hostage in there? And what happens if the mob's got into the main stores compound and armed themselves with mortars?

'Play it by ear,' Watson had said. And it had sounded feasible up there in his office at Group. But standing out here in the dark under the trees with the graveyard smell of wet mud in your nostrils it was a different story.

'One more thing,' Hanwell said. 'There'll be no firing until you get the word. Those boys've been cooped up in that God-awful cinema for the best part of twelve hours. My guess is they'll be bloody glad to see us.'

I hope you're right, Hobey thought. I hope to God you're right.

Hanwell folded the street plan. 'That's it then, friends.' He smiled at Hobey, no longer twitched, his

69

mind cleared for action 'I think you should get that signal off now, Hobo.'

Hobey walked down the line to the jeep. Jane was sitting in the passenger seat. 'Finished your supper?' he said.

She nodded. 'Very nice. Except the tea. That was stewed.' She looked at his face as he got in behind the wheel. 'Hanwell give you a bad time?'

'God, no. He's dead chuffed you're here. Thinks you'll be a great help.'

She put her hand on his arm. 'Thanks, Hobo. You're a very bad liar. But thanks for trying.'

Hobey pressed the starter. 'Call Group and tell 'em we're off.'

She turned in her seat and put on the headset. 'This is TOP HAT. Do you read? Over.'

'We read you TOP HAT. Go ahead, Over.' Pat Robens' voice. Calm, professional, with just a touch of tension. Which meant Watson was beside her.

'ADVANCE TO GO. I say again, ADVANCE TO GO. Out.' Jane switched off, unplugged the headset and left it round her neck in the readiness position.

Hobey let in the clutch and pulled the jeep out on to the track, driving up past the three-tonners to take station behind Hanwell. 'How's Lewis?'

'Not good. I got some tea into him but it all came back.' He was frighteningly weak and she had supported his head in the crook of her arm, holding her breath against the smell, fighting down her disgust. 'He needs a bath and a bed.'

'We're going straight through to the Mess,' Hobey said. 'Hanwell wants you both in there on the double. OK?'

Out of the way, she thought, off his hands. She stared at the back of the fifteen-hundredweight as the column picked up speed. 'He did give you a bad time, didn't he?' she said. 'About me.'

'Forget it,' Hobey said. If there was a bad time it was in the future not the past; waiting for them in Marazag.

'Oh no,' she said warmly. 'No, Hobo. I won't forget it.'

They came out of the trees on to a broad, level stretch of open ground. On the far side, the town was a dense black mass under the stars. Hanwell checked in the mirror and saw the three-tonners crowding in behind him, lights blazing. He grunted in satisfaction. This was how he had briefed them. 'Close-up tight and keep moving. Tilt flaps down, loosely secured. Lights on full beam. If there's anybody watching – and there will be – they've got to think we're just another freight convoy bringing in stores.'

The mouth of the street was a black hole in the headlights' glare. He drove into it, the walls rising up round the truck, the snarl of the engine suddenly loud. He held his speed, thrusting up into the heart of the town, smelling the familiar, cloying stink of camel and goat and ancient human dirt. The street was empty, the crumbling houses blank-faced, shuttered against the night air. This was the poor part of Marazag, a verminous huddle of rotting mudbrick hovels tucked away behind the main street. He glanced upwards, checking the parapets of the flat roofs where men had been known to wait with baulks of timber and heavy stones to block the street. And with rope nets to drop on the crews when they got down to clear the way. But there was nobody.

The street forked and he swung left, the plan clear in his mind. Behind him, the column divided. The jeep and number four three-tonner followed him; the other three bore right. He saw them go in the mirror, glanced ahead and braked hard as a corner loomed up. He dropped into third, revving the engine, hauling on the wheel. The

71

truck drifted, tilting on its suspension, the big tyres fighting for a grip on the dirt surface. He controlled it with the throttle, grateful for the stability of the wide, short wheel-base, and came out of the corner exactly on line and accelerating.

Thirty feet in front of him an enormous carpet blocked the street like a painted wall, hanging vertically from a wire slung across from roof to roof, twenty feet high, twelve wide. The braking distance was impossible. He double-declutched, ramming the gear shift into second. The engine howled as he stamped on the throttle pedal. The broad, blunt nose of the truck smacked into the carpet, thrusting it forward and up. He saw it curl away above the cab, heard it slap on the tilt as he went through.

The street beyond was laid out for a wedding feast. A long strip of straw matting ran down the centre covered with white cloths on which were set large dishes of mutton stew, platters of bread and cakes, flat baskets piled with grapes and oranges and figs, earthen-ware jugs of water and fruit juices. In the light of dozens of oil lamps ranged along the window sills the guests were sitting cross-legged opposite each other with the women standing discreetly behind them. Somewhere in the middle of the line, in the place of honour, the bridegroom faced his bride; he splendidly dressed in a long, striped galabeyah and a white burnous, she magnificent in bridal gown, gold and silver filigree bracelets on wrists and ankles, silver coins glittering on her ceremonial veil. Perhaps a hundred and fifty people eating and drinking and laughing together to the music of a flute and a one-stringed fiddle. And the bride's eyes dark and shining above her veil in the gentle lamplight and her husband watching her and smiling, his beard trimmed to a point and freshly oiled.

The fifteen-hundredweight smashed in under the hanging carpet in a bomb-burst of light and sound. High

72

in the cab, Hanwell had a blurred confused impression of instant panic – startled faces, gesticulating arms, figures scrambling back against the walls of the houses, oil lamps flaring as they toppled. The truck ploughed brutally through the feast, spattering the guests with a glutinous spray of food and fruit. A child began to run in terror, tripped and went down, sprawling only inches from the off-side front wheel. There were screams and shouts, the splintering of breaking glass, an acrid, burning smell as the hot oil from the shattered lamps set fire to the matting. Ahead of him a second carpet hung across the street. He held the truck steady and watched it rush towards him. Fender and radiator grille butted into the carpet, lifted it, tossed it up high above the cab. The fifteen-hundredweight shuddered and broke through into the empty street on the far side.

The jeep was not so lucky. It came in under the first carpet in the slipstream of the fifteen-hundredweight and was immediately showered with a thick, greasy mash of food and crushed fruit thrown up by the truck's rear wheels. The windscreen was plastered over in an instant. Hobey felt the wheel go slack in his hands as the tyres skated over the semi-liquid debris slathered across the matting. Instinctively he eased his foot off the throttle, tried to change down and missed the gear. The jeep slewed out of control, pulling to the right as Hobey wrestled with the gear shift and clutch. He found second gear and dabbed at the throttle. The jeep jinked out into the centre of the street, the tyres thrashing for a grip on the loose white cloths now crumpled and coated with a gluey mess of stew and cake and fruit juice. He felt a thud and saw the windscreen wiped partially clear by the body of a man sliding over the bonnet against the glass. He glimpsed a dark face contorted with shock and pain. And then the man was thrown clear to smash against the wall. The second carpet came swinging down behind the fifteen-hundredweight, hit the front of the jeep squarely, heavily, and stopped it dead.

Watching in the mirror, Hanwell drove thirty yards, hit the brakes, flung open the door, grabbed the sten clipped to the back of the cab behind his seat and dropped down. He began to run back towards the carpet, cocking the sten as he ran.

Bell brought the number four three-tonner in through the first carpet, lights blazing, the heel of his hand screwed down on the horn button. The impact of the big truck snapped the supporting wire and the carpet dropped away against the wall on his left, smothering a group of women in its heavy folds. Bell braked fiercely.

Beside him, Scott had his sten gun in his hands. 'Bloody hell,' he said, his voice awed. 'Will ye look at that?'

The street was a shambles. In total disarray the wedding guests milled and struggled in the slippery morass on the torn and burning matting, the women shrieking hysterically, the men bellowing with rage as they converged on the stalled jeep, pulling at the tilt, hammering in the bonnet, thrusting each other aside in their passion to get at the occupants.

Inside, Jane and Hobey crouched together in a nightmare of fists and grasping hands which beat at their faces and clawed their clothes to drag them out. Hobey locked his right arm round her shoulders, braced his feet on the steel floor and lashed out with his left fist. Lit by the flickering flames from the burning matting, the faces of their attackers were dark, savage masks streaked with red, the mouths stretched wide in grimaces of hatred to show rotting teeth, the eyes bright and hot with fury. The jeep shook and swayed under the press of bodies, threatening at any moment to overturn. A hand snatched the cap comforter off Jane's head. Her thick, black hair tumbled round her face. The men

74

shouted, 'Bint. Bint,' excited to find she was a woman. She shrank down, pressing against Hobey. He saw the gleam of steel as a knife was drawn. A thin, curved knife, held low, point upward, poised for the classic, upthrusting stroke of the Arab knife-fighter – in through the soft stomach wall, up under the rib cage into the heart. He jerked his knee up, twisting away in his seat, awkward behind the wheel. The knife penetrated his trouser leg just above the knee-joint, sliced deeply into his thigh and up his side. He felt it scrape over his ribs, curving away from him now behind his shoulder. He felt a sharp, burning sensation, as if he had been stroked with a hot wire, but no real pain. The knife dropped down for a second thrust. A stone shattered the windscreen in front of Jane, showering her with needle-sharp shards of glass. The mob howled; a deep, angry, blood-hungry howl that changed to one of terror as Hanwell pushed round the edge of the hanging carpet, pointed his sten at the sky and squeezed the trigger.

Up the street, Scott had the cab door open and was standing on the step of the three-tonner. He lifted his sten and fired an answering burst, aiming high over the roofs. The mob round the jeep fell back, hesitated and then panicked, throwing themselves down against the walls, piling on top of each other, jamming frantically into the doorways of the houses. The screams of the women rose in a high, shrill wail as Hanwell fired again, spraying the bullets along the wall above their heads. He ran across the street in front of the jeep, dragging the edge of the carpet with him, opening the way.

'Go,' he shouted to Hobey. 'Go, go, go.' He heard the whirr of the jeep's starter motor. The engine coughed, ran unevenly for a moment and died. 'For God's sake, man,' he shouted, hampered by the weight of the carpet, unable to fire the sten one-handed.

Hobey crouched over the wheel of the jeep, blinking
the sweat out of his eyes. He was dizzy with shock and
the first cruel stab of pain as the numbed nerves in his
leg and side began to re-awaken. Through the crack-
crazed glass on his side of the windscreen he could see
the fifteen-hundredweight down the street. It seemed
impossibly distant, haloed in the glow of its headlights
like a ghost truck. Under the screaming of the women
he could hear Hanwell shouting. The words were
meaningless but their urgency was unmistakable, lacer-
ating his fuddled mind like a spur. Light-headed, close
to blacking-out, the blood running warm down his leg,
his breathing quick and hoarse and shallow, he fumbled
for the starter button. The engine fired. He let in the
clutch clumsily, his wounded leg heavy. The jeep
leap-frogged and stalled. His head snapped forward and
hit the rim of the steering wheel.

'Hell's teeth.' Scott thumped the tilt of the three-tonner with the flat of his hand. 'You men in there. Give
us some back cover.' He ducked back into the cab and
snarled at Bell. 'Don't just bloody sit there, man. Get up
behind that jeep and give its arse a shove.'

Bell put the truck into first gear and fed in the revs.
The three-tonner rolled forward ponderously, the thunder of its engine breaking over the heads of the mob like
a wave. Bell edged it up to the jeep and stopped with the
front fender just touching the spare wheel strapped on
the back.

'Right. Now shove the bastard through,' Scott said,
watching Hanwell through the open window of the cab.
He saw the Wing Commander's head come up suddenly,
staring down the street past the three-tonner. In the
back of the truck a sten rattled briefly. Scott leaned out
and looked behind. A man with a rifle toppled forward
over the parapet above one of the houses and dropped
heavily into the street. His fall acted like a catalyst,
injecting fresh anger into the mob. They began to gather

76

themselves again, sensing the crisis in the jeep, aware of the vulnerability of Hanwell as he clung to the curtain unable to defend himself. A low, muttering growl rolled down the street like the rattle of pebbles in an undertow.

'Come on, come ON,' Scott shouted to Bell. 'We haven't got all bloody night.'

Bell eased in the clutch and shunted the jeep forward. Behind him the sten was firing again; brief, sharp bursts over the heads of the men grouped menacingly round the dead Arab, pinning them down, holding them, buying time. Inside the jeep, Jane pushed Hobey back in the driving seat and leaned across him, gripping the steering wheel, aiming for the tailgate of the fifteen-hundredweight. Her teeth were clenched, her lips drawn back in a grimace of concentration. She was slathered in sweat, her clothes clinging wetly to her body.

Hanwell let the three-tonner go past him and then released his grip on the carpet. It swung down behind the truck, hiding it from the mob. The growl was louder now, a deep, bass drum-roll under the keening of the women. The growl of a lynch mob. Hanwell had heard it before, knew they had only seconds left before the anger overcame the fear and the mob exploded into action. He ran down alongside the three-tonner to the jeep.

Jane had scrambled out and was struggling to drag Hobey from behind the wheel. He was semi-conscious now, shaking his head to clear it. There was a large, dark swelling coming up on his forehead where it had smashed against the rim of the wheel and his trousers were slicked with blood. Hanwell dodged round the bonnet, reached in and freed Hobey's boots which were jammed under the pedals. Together he and the girl manhandled him across into the passenger seat, pushing him well down, his knees doubled under the dashboard, his head supported on the back of the seat.

'Can you cope with the driving?' Hanwell said.

Jane nodded. In the glare of the three-tonner's lights her face was white and sweaty, streaked with dirt and blood. There was more blood – Hobey's blood – smeared down the front of her blouse and overalls and little slivers of glass in her hair. But her eyes were steady. Bright with fear but steady.

Hanwell helped her into the driving-seat. The sten in the back of the three-tonner was firing intermittently through the carpet. The growl of the mob swelled and deepened. Every second was vital now.

'Hobo's in trouble,' Jane said. 'He's losing too much blood. We've got to get a bandage on that . . .'

'Not now,' Hanwell rapped, fighting the impulse to yell at her. It was important to keep her calm. He whipped out his revolver. 'Your scarf. Tie it round his thigh. High up. Quickly.'

She slipped the scarf between Hobey's legs, pulled it up into his groin and knotted it. Hanwell pushed the barrel of his pistol under it and gave it two turns, jamming the butt beneath Hobey's belt. 'Five minutes,' he said. 'We'll be there in five minutes.' If the bloody jeep starts, he thought. If the mob doesn't burst through that carpet and swamp us. If you really can drive. He masked the thoughts with a smile.

Jane started the engine and pushed the gear shift forward into first.

'Good show,' Hanwell said. 'Piece of cake now.'

She smiled back; a wobbly, ashen ghost of a smile. But a smile. He was relieved to see it. 'Stay close,' he said. 'Right in under my . . .' and ducked as a bullet smacked into the tilt and ricocheted off the transceiver.

Bell cut the lights on the three-tonner. Behind the carpet the matting was burning fiercely now. In the narrow gap between the wall and the edge of the carpet,

78

Hanwell saw the figure of a man with a rifle silhouetted against the flames. He brought the muzzle of the sten up in a smooth, quick arc, firing from the hip. At so short a range the impact of the bullets was horrifying. They hosed into the man's stomach, threw him back against the wall, chopped up through his chest and pulped his head.

Hanwell turned, ran crouching to the fifteen-hundredweight, vaulted into the cab and whipped into gear. In the mirror he saw the jeep tailing him and the three-tonner behind it; saw the carpet suddenly torn down, the mob scrambling over its folds. And then there was a corner and they were round it and away, out across a small marketplace and into another narrow street and up to the end and round into Sharia Pasha.

The other three-tonners were waiting there, parked at the foot of the street, lights blazing, engines ticking over. Hanwell touched the horn button briefly and swung away left up the street, the jeep and number four three-tonner following him round as if roped to his tailgate. Ahead the street was empty; wide and silent and empty. The hard white lights of the trucks washed the colours out of it and it looked like an old photograph; a faded still from an early Western film – the main street at high noon, cleared and deserted, waiting for the showdown.

Hanwell checked his watch and was astonished to see they were only six minutes behind schedule. The cinema was a couple of hundred yards in front of him now, the name ROXY picked out in empty light sockets on an iron frame bracketed above the main doors. He pulled over to the left, braking gently. The jeep and Bell stayed in behind him. The other three trucks shot past. He glanced in the mirror and saw Bell drop back, swing the three-tonner hard right and stop broadside-on across the street, blocking it neatly.

Beyond the cinema, Hicks turned left, making for the

alley that led down to the main gate of the HQ compound. Mason and Butterworth drove on up the street, braked short of the corner and parked side by side.

Hanwell ran the fifteen-hundredweight up on to the narrow pavement outside the cinema and stopped. Jane brought the jeep in behind him. He switched off the engine and cut the lights. They were in position, the street staked-out and blocked, their field of action secured. He opened the cab door, picked up his sten and climbed out.

6.   23.00 – 01.00 HOURS

'Seems quiet enough, sir,' Scott said. He had left six men with the three-tonner down the street, brought the other six up and deployed them outside the cinema and the hotel, using the jeep and the fifteen-hundredweight as cover.

Hanwell nodded. 'Yes.' It was quiet. Too damned quiet. A tense, brooding silence, chill as the night air.

They were standing in deep shadow in the doorway of a shop opposite the cinema with Jane behind them. Lewis and Hobey were still in the jeep parked across the street under the first floor balcony of the hotel.

'I'm worried about Hobo, sir,' Jane said. 'He needs . . .'

'I know what he needs,' Hanwell said.

She bit her lip, pressing her shoulders against the shop door behind her, fighting the reaction to the horror of those desperate minutes in the jeep which was beginning to catch up with her.

Hanwell stared across the street. The cinema was in total darkness, the main doors shut behind a steel trellis, the windows above blank and blind. He had expected that. They probably had a couple of men up there, standing well back out of sight, watching the street. Beside the cinema the mouth of the passage that led down to the compound was a black oblong, dense as a wall. But there were lights in the hotel, shining through the curtains drawn across the windows. So why

81

the hell didn't they open the door? They must know we're here, he thought. You don't come belting up the street with six trucks in the middle of the night undetected. He watched the windows, looking for a twitch of curtains, seeing nothing.

Jane said quietly, 'Something's wrong, isn't it?'

'They're just being over-cautious,' Hanwell said. But he knew it was more than that.

If it was Germans holed-up in that hotel, he thought, there'd be no problem. Kick down the door, lob in a couple of grenades, wait for the dust to settle and go in hard with the stens. As it is . . . He said, 'I'm going in, Sarn't. If there's any trouble, one of your chaps takes Flight Officer Roper up to Mr Curtis in the fifteen-hun-dredweight. The rest of you come in and join the party. In that order. Clear?'

'Sir.'

Hanwell cocked his sten, ran across the street and ducked down beside the jeep. 'How's it going, Hobo?' he said softly.

'Not too bad,' Hobey said, his voice thready.

'I'm just going to pop in and book you a room for the night.'

'With bath.'

'Naturally.' Hanwell looked at the men crouching behind the two vehicles. 'Nobody moves till Sar'nt Scott gives the word.' He stood up, walked round the bonnet of the jeep and up the steps to the hotel door. There was a big brass knob on the door and he turned it, easing the door open a fraction. He took a deep breath, settled his sten on his hip, put his boot against the door and kicked it wide open.

The little entrance hall was brightly lit. And empty. No duty corporal. No mess orderlies. He waited a moment and then walked in. The staircase was on his left. He walked past it, his footsteps muffled by the carpet, turned right and saw the lounge door standing open at the end of a short passage. He got up against the wall outside the door and stood poised, listening.

'Anyone there?' he called.

'In here.' The voice was hoarse, ragged. 'Quickly, man. We need help.'

Hanwell stepped through the doorway in one long stride. Scobart was sitting in an armchair with his back to the bar counter, his right leg extended in front of him. His foot, heavily-bandaged, rested on a low coffee table. The muzzle of the Lee Enfield rifle in his hands was levelled on Hanwell's stomach. 'Good evening, sir,' he said. 'Come in. We've been expecting you.'

Hanwell stood just inside the door and stared at him, seeing the lines of fatigue in his face, the dull shine of pain in his eyes. Something small and hard jabbed into his back just above his kidneys. He froze. A voice in his ear said, 'You heard the SWO. Go and say hullo to him.' A hand came round his right shoulder and took hold of the sten. 'You won't be needing this.'

Hanwell said, 'My name's Hanwell.'

'From where?' Scobart said.

'Group.'

'US cavalry?'

'Something like that,' Hanwell said. 'Where's Squadron Leader March?'

'I'm asking the questions,' Scobart said. 'Sir.'

Hanwell's eyes flicked left and right, measuring distances, calculating odds. He pressed his feet firmly into the carpet, bent his knees slightly. The voice in his ear said gently, 'I wouldn't if I were you.'

Scobart said, 'You're not alone, of course?'

'No.'

'How many?'

'Enough,' Hanwell said. The pistol in his back pressed harder. The signal had said nothing about the NCOs. Were they also involved in the mutiny?

Scobart said, 'You're Regiment, aren't you?'

'Yes.'

Scobart nodded. He lowered the rifle and pushed the safety-catch on with his thumb. His movements were slow, deliberate; the movements of a very tired man trying to do the right thing, going through the motions, stretched beyond his limits. 'OK, Harry,' he said. 'He's on our side.' He put the rifle on the carpet beside his chair and held out his hand. 'I'm Scobart, sir. Glad to see you.' He managed a wry, apologetic grin. 'Sorry about the reception but it's been a long day and we're all a bit twitched.'

Hanwell felt the pressure of the pistol ease, stepped forward and shook hands. 'As well to be careful, Mr Scobart.' He turned and saw a short, plump man in white drill, button-up tunic and trousers. He had pale blue, slightly protuberant eyes and held the pistol and sten gun in his hands.

Scobart said, 'Harry Ryder, sir. Sergeant cook.'

Ryder put the guns on a table and smiled warily. 'Sorry, sir.'

Hanwell grinned and nodded.

'You got my signal then, sir?' Scobart said.

'That was you, was it?' Hanwell looked at the bandaged foot. 'Was that when you . . .?'

'Bullet through the instep.'

'Bad?'

'Only when I get angry and stamp.'

Hanwell smiled, liking the man. He was long-backed and solid, built for the parade ground. All the swank and swagger, all the presence. Built for a bar-room brawl, too. A broken-bottle, knee-in-the-testicles man. A few pounds overweight perhaps, but there was a lot of good hard muscle under the fat. 'So, where is everybody?'

'Main stores compound. All the officers and SNCOs. Except Harry, here. And the M.O. He's upstairs with the Adjutant.'

84

'Natives a bit restless, are they?'

'Greedy, anyway,' Scobart said. 'There's a helluva lot of loot up there.' Which had to be protected. Stores were the top priority, what an MU was all about. Material first, people second.

'How is the Adjutant?' Hanwell said.

'Rough. Chest wound. He needs a hospital.'

He's not the only one, Hanwell thought seeing the shine of sweat on the SWO's face, remembering Hobey and Lewis outside in the jeep. 'And the C.O.? Still held hostage?'

'Yes.' Scobart's lip curled. 'And bloody lucky to be alive.'

Hanwell said evenly, 'You're all bloody lucky he's alive, Mr Scobart.' He turned on his heel and went out into the hall, calling for Scott.

'Sir?' The sergeant came running across the street and up the steps.

'Two men to guard the trucks,' Hanwell said. 'The rest of you in here on the double.' He walked back into the lounge. 'Sar'nt Ryder, d'you think you can rustle up some hot water? Disinfectant. Bandages. I've a wounded officer coming in.'

'No problem, sir. What about the M.O.? Shall I ask him to . . .?'

'Just get the necessary,' Hanwell said. 'I'll get word to the M.O.'

'Coming right up, sir.' Ryder went out towards the kitchen.

Scott came in with Hobey slung over his shoulder. Behind him, two of the men carried Lewis in the groundsheet. Jane was with them. Scobart stared at her incredulously; at her tangled hair, the blood dried on her face, streaked down her battledress blouse and overalls.

Scott settled Hobey in one of the big armchairs, easing him down gently. The Squadron Leader looked as

85

though he had fallen into a combine harvester. His shirt was ripped from waist to armpit, his left trouser leg gaping and drenched in blood. His face was a dirty grey colour below the purple ridge of the bruise across his forehead. His eyes were slitted in swollen lids, his lips stretched thin and tight in a grimace of pain. He lay huddled in the chair like a broken puppet, Hanwell's revolver still thrust through Jane's scarf on his thigh as a tourniquet.

Scobart said, 'Hell's teeth. What happened to him?'

'We gatecrashed a wedding,' Hanwell said in his best Sandhurst drawl. 'The guests were – upset.'

Scobart looked at Lewis lying limp and still on the groundsheet. 'And him?'

'Gyppo guts. He'll be OK.'

'He won't,' Jane said quietly. 'He's dead.'

'What?' Hanwell knelt on one knee beside Lewis, saw the small, dark hole in his right temple where the ricocheting bullet, glancing off the radio in the jeep, had entered his brain. Lewis's eyes stared up at him. He closed them with his thumb and forefinger and stood up. 'Wrap him up and put him out in the hall for now,' he said to the men.

As they carried him out, Jane said, 'Where is . . .?'

'Upstairs in his room,' Hanwell said.

'He – he's not . . .?' Her eyes followed the still form in the groundsheet.

Hanwell smiled. 'Good Lord, no. He's all right.'

She nodded, her face very pale. 'Can I see him?'

Hanwell turned to Scobart. 'Which is the Adjutant's room?'

'Number seven. First floor. End of the corridor.'

'The M.O.'s up there with him,' Hanwell said. 'Give him my compliments and ask him please to come and have a look at Hobo, will you?'

'Yes,' she said. 'Thank you,' and turned and ran out into the hall.

Scobart said, 'Is she a nurse, sir?'

'No.'

'Only he – the Adjutant – he's a bit roughed-up.'

'She's Mrs Roper,' Hanwell said flatly.

'Oh, my God.' Scobart looked shocked. 'She's not going to like ...'

'She's his wife, Mr Scobart,' Hanwell said. 'She'll cope.'

Scott was kneeling in front of Hobey's chair with his clasp knife open. He slit the trouser leg from ankle to hip and peeled it back, exposing the thigh wound – a long, deep gash curving away from the groin towards the hip-bone. He straightened the leg slowly, carefully, and released the tourniquet. A thick ooze of blood welled in the open wound.

Hanwell said, 'That's veinous not arterial.'

Scott nodded. He reached up and pulled Hobey's shirt out of the waistband of his trousers. Deflected by the bulge of the hip-bone, the curved knife had jinked over his webbing belt and cut down again into his side; a shallower cut this time, glancing over the rib cage and up round the back of his armpit. His shirt was split from waist to sleeve. Scott ripped it away.

Ryder came in with a bowl, a steaming kettle, a bottle of disinfectant and a couple of clean bed sheets. He put them down beside Scott, looked at Hobey's leg and sucked in his breath. 'Nasty.'

Scott said, 'How's your M.O. on embroidery?'

'Not bad,' Ryder said. He turned to Hanwell. 'I've got the coffee on, sir. Hot, black and sweet. That suit?'

'With a little rum to give it body?' Hanwell said.

Ryder grinned. 'Five minutes.' He went back to the kitchen. Hanwell followed him out into the hall. The men from Scott's truck were waiting there. 'You two,' Hanwell said. 'Upstairs. Top floor window. Anything happens in the street, I want to know. Anything at all. Clear?' He watched them run up the stairs, turned to the other two. 'Check out the radio in the jeep. Might be damaged. If it is, fix it. If you can't, come and tell me.' He lit a cigarette and stood for a moment looking down at Lewis's body wrapped and tied in the groundsheet like a mummy. He would have to write a letter. 'Dear Mr and Mrs Lewis, I regret to have to inform you that your son . . .' A bug in the intestines and a stray bullet in the head. Hardly a hero's death but he would have to make it sound like one. For Lewis and for how many more before the night was out?

'Wing Commander Hanwell?' The voice was pleasant, educated.

Hanwell looked up and saw a slight, grey-haired man, very clean, with dark eyes in a smooth, sensitive face. 'I'm Hanwell.'

'Peter Frant. I hear you've got a customer for me?'

Up in the northern sector of the town Hassan Shawish Meguid sat on his donkey amid the ruins of the wedding feast and watched his four bodyguards slide their ancient rifles butt-first down through long slits cut into the sides of their galabeyahs so that only the tips of the foresights showed under their armpits. Meguid was an ex-omdeh (mayor) of Marazag; a merchant in his fifties, grizzled and paunchy. Rich, too, as the silver dowry coins stitched to his daughter's wedding veil proved; his only daughter, married that afternoon, who should now have been safely in bed with her husband but who was standing among the mourners in the doorway of his house in her torn, filth-spattered wedding gown, her cheeks under the veil streaked with kohl-stained tears.

Meguid settled his long, curved knife in its sheath under his belt and held out his hands for the lamp. Housed in a metal box which contained the batteries, the lamp had a powerful wide-angle lens. It was designed for use as an emergency landing-light on

88

forward airstrips and had been stolen from the main stores compound by one of the native labourers some weeks before. Meguid balanced it on the pommel of his saddle, clutching it against his stomach. 'Death to el asakar Ingleez,' he shouted, kicked his heels into the flanks of the donkey and rode up the street with his bodyguards trotting on bare feet beside him.

'Death to el asakar Ingleez.' About thirty men armed with knives, shotguns and iron bars took up the cry and bunched in behind him, spurred on by the keening of the women who lined the street to watch them go.

Hicks coasted the three-tonner down the alley behind the cinema, lights and engine switched off, and ran it gently up against the main gate of the compound. In the starlit darkness beyond the gate the Guard Tent and the HQ buildings were vague shadows, silent, still. Two of the men ran back up to guard the mouth of the alley. The rest followed Miller over the padlocked gate, climbing on to the bonnet of the truck and dropping down on to the hard-packed sand.

The Guard Tent was deserted, blankets and biscuits (mattresses) folded neatly on the iron beds, the rifle rack empty. From there they spread out across the compound, moving quickly, quietly to take cover behind the end walls of the HQ block and in the black shadow behind the Ford pick-up parked near the wicket gate in the south-west corner. Hicks waited in the tent, watching through the open flap, his hand on the main switch mounted on the centre pole.

Miller went up the steps on to the veranda outside the C.O.'s office and padded down to stand in the angle of the wall between the offices of the Adjutant and the SWO. A slab-shouldered, heavy-thighed East End docker with a wide, flat face, broad-tipped nose and small, shrewd eyes, Miller was basic Regiment material; tough, cheerful, disciplined. And, when the chips were down, totally ruthless. He went down on one knee, tilted his steel helmet forward over his eyes, gripped his sten firmly and whistled – a brief, low whistle. Instantly the compound was flooded with hard, white light as Hicks tripped the switch and the big arc lamps at each corner blinked on. Miller froze in the shadow cast by the sloping iron roof of the veranda. He stared down its length past the Orderly Room and the Signals office to the Armoury window. He studied it uneasily, the hairs rising along his spine. He had a bad feeling about the Armoury, sensed eyes watching him through the close mesh of the fly-screened window. It was the obvious place to occupy. You could attack any of the other offices; poke the barrel of the sten through the windows and hose them down. But not the Armoury. God only knew what they had stashed away in there; ammo, grenades, mortar bombs. Firing into that lot would blow the whole damned block sky-high. And you with it.

He straightened cautiously and began to crab down the veranda, moving silently in the shadow, his back pressed against the wall, his eyes fixed on that black window at the end. He felt the handle of the Orderly Room door in his back, reached behind him and turned it slowly. He tensed, bracing his feet on the concrete, threw his weight against the door, turning on the ball of his foot as it flew open, the sten swinging in a short, level arc.

There was nobody in the Orderly Room.

Miller stood just inside the door and took stock. A trestle-table with a typewriter, telephone and wire baskets neatly arranged. Filing cabinets against the far wall, a truckle bed beside them made up but not slept in. He crossed to the table and picked up the phone. It was dead.

He went back to stand in the shelter of the doorway out of sight of the Armoury. The men from the truck were well hidden. He could see only the pick-up, the blank brick wall of the cinema and the bonnet of the three-tonner nudging the gate, blocking the alley. In the brilliant light of the arc lamps the compound was like a stage, empty in front of the backdrop of the cinema wall, waiting for the players to make their entrances.

Miller was not an imaginative man. Brave and shrewd but not imaginative. And he had been schooled in the hazardous techniques of house-to-house combat, accepting the appalling risks involved with phlegmatic calm. But the emptiness of the compound and the silence that brooded over it disturbed him. He hesitated a moment longer, summoning up his nerve. And then sidled out on to the veranda.

The bullet glanced off one of the upright supporting pillars six inches above his head, sparked along the wall and thudded into the door-frame of the Adjutant's office. Miller jerked back inside the Orderly Room. He had been right to be wary of the Armoury.

He sat down by the trestle-table to consider his next move. The bullet fired above his head had been a warning. He knew that. Whoever was in the Armoury could have taken him then; would certainly take him with the next shot. But why? What was so special about the Armoury? Who was in there? And why wasn't he holed-up with the others in the cinema?

He put his left hand on his thigh and felt the hard, round bulge of the grenade in his pocket. That was the answer, of course; laid down in the training manual. Pull the pin, count three, stick your hand out through the doorway low down and roll the grenade along the veranda. Throw yourself flat with your arms locked over your head and wait for the Armoury to disintegrate. He shook his head, remembering Hanwell's briefing. They were here to rescue and relieve, not destroy.

There was a wastepaper basket on the floor under the table. He prodded it with his boot and grinned. He stood up quickly, wriggled his shoulders out of his overalls, unbuttoned his shirt and pulled it over his head. He fastened his overalls again, tipped the wastepaper basket upside down to empty it and worked his shirt down over it. The bottom of the basket came up through the collar opening and he put his steel helmet on top, jamming the buckle of the chin-strap through the basket weave to hold it firm. He stooped and picked up a piece of crumpled paper, smoothed it out and tucked it over the basket below the helmet. The effect was crude and unconvincing, a paper-faced, helmeted scarecrow that wouldn't fool the dimmest of birds. But on the shadowed veranda, seen through the wire mesh of a fly-screened window, it might just work. He found a broom in the corner behind the door, reversed it and crammed the basket down over the bristles, wedging it tightly. He picked up his sten and walked to the door. 'OK, mate,' he said quietly. 'Try this one for size.'

Half crouching, he pushed the grotesque basket head out through the door, turning the paper face towards the Armoury. The impact of the bullet wrenched the broom handle out of his hand. The steel helmet fell off and rolled drunkenly down the veranda on its rim. But Miller did not stay to watch it. He was through the door and down to the corner and crawling on hands and knees under the Armoury window to safety before the helmet stopped rolling and fell over with a metallic clatter.

Three hundred yards beyond the cinema up Sharia Pasha where the flats gave way to smaller, mud-brick houses, Curtis got up on the step on number one three-tonner and nodded to the driver. 'Right, Mason. Nice and easy, now.'

They had off-loaded the boxed ammunition and

stacked it against the walls of the houses behind the two trucks. Right down to the corner, Curtis had men stationed in every doorway. Others lay prone in the litter of decaying rubbish on the flat roofs, cursing the insects which swarmed over them, scratching bitten hands and faces.

Mason edged the truck forward ahead of number two parked alongside to seal off the street.

'No lights,' Curtis said, 'until I give the word.'

The truck ground along in low gear, came to the corner and nosed slowly round it.

'That's far enough,' Curtis said. He got down and stood by the cab listening. Then he said, 'OK. Lights.'

The headlights' full beam sliced through the darkness. The street seemed to leap into focus, rising up in front of him like a pop-up picture in a child's book. It sloped away between the houses to the waste ground beyond the southern limits of the town, silent and empty. Except for something propped against the wall of a house about fifty yards up on his left. Curtis stared at it suspiciously. It was humped and shapeless, like a sack. He checked the roofs on both sides of the street, looking for an incautious movement, a glimpse of a face, the glint of light on a rifle barrel. He saw nothing.

Up in the cab, Mason leaned across and said, 'Could be a trap, sir. Bait, like.'

Curtis nodded. He had seen it all before. Earlier that year a man who had gone to investigate a similar sack-like object in the main street of El Khanka had been shot in the back from the roof of the house opposite. Killed for the clothes he was wearing, the loose change in his pocket and – most valuable of all – his pay book for which German agents in Cairo would give fifty pounds.

'Put the lights out, Mason,' Curtis said. He shut his eyes, squeezing the lids tight to blot out the after-image, and opened them again to darkness. He waited three minutes, eyes wide open. He had the exceptional night vision of the colour-blind and watched the street come into focus, a perspective of dark and lighter shadows tunnelling away from him under the black, star-sequinned velvet of the sky. He looked for the sack and saw it take shape as a black splotch in the darkness.

'No lights, Mason,' he said quietly, 'unless there's trouble. Then give 'em me damned quick.' He slid off the safety-catch of the sten and began to move up the street, dodging from doorway to doorway, his rubber-soled boots making no sound on the dirt surface. Three yards from the sack he stopped and crouched low against the wall, seeing its top half now profiled clearly against the strip of sky above the street. He waited, poised to spring, his night vision improving with every half minute.

The sack stirred, changed shape, seeming to grow a little taller. He realised it was a man squatting on his haunches, swaddled against the night air. He saw the head lift and turn towards him. The wrappings fell away to reveal the barrel of a gun. Curtis lurched sideways, tucked his shoulder in, rolled once and came up with the sten bucking and blazing in his hands. The squatting man screamed and rose up, twisting and writhing as the bullets slammed into him, shredded him and nailed him to the wall. And Curtis was across the street and crouched in a doorway when Mason switched on the lights of the three-tonner, released the clutch and came barrelling down the street towards him. The empty street, the silent, deserted, innocent street.

There were no answering shots from the roof-tops, no concerted rush of men from the doorways. Just the shuttered houses and the crumbling, mud-brick walls. And lying against the wall, the bullet-riddled corpse.

Curtis ran round the back of the truck and stood looking down at the man he had killed. The man lay on

94

his back, his stick-like right arm which Curtis had mistaken in the darkness for a gun barrel still stretched out stiffly. His face was wizened, covered in sores, without a nose. Blind white eyes stared fixedly at the stars. His toothless mouth gaped open, a grey-white, ulcerated tongue, slimy as a slug, protruded between withered lips. The torn rags of his clothing were soaked in blood over his pulped chest and stomach. At close range a sten kills, but not tidily.

'All right, sir?' Mason said.

'Yes.' Curtis tasted bile hot and sour in his throat, hawked and spat disgustedly. 'Just a beggar, damn it.' Dumped on the street by relatives too poor to feed him. Left to rot through the days and nights in misery and darkness. Unwanted, an embarrassment, loved only by lice and flies. A helpless blind beggar and he had killed him. 'I thought he...'

'You've done him a kindness, sir,' Mason said. 'Put him out of his misery.'

'Yeah,' Curtis said, knowing it was true; knowing also that it didn't help. He had joined the RAF to fight the enemy not to kill blind syphilitics.

He opened the cab door and was about to climb in when he heard it; a low, angry mutter like the sound of distant surf. He turned his head sharply, looking up the white tunnel of the street. The mutter swelled ominously, spiked now with the percussion of rifle fire. He saw the sky over the waste ground flicker; a bright, orange light which flared and subsided and flared again. The mutter was much louder now, deep and growling and savage; the voice of a mob on the rampage. He shouted, 'Back up, man. Quickly.'

Mason began to reverse. Round the corner in number two truck, Butterworth heard the snarl of the engine, saw the tail-lights come into view and switched on dipped headlights to guide Mason back into position.

95

When the trucks were side-by-side again, Curtis ran back between them calling for his corporal.

'Sir?' Corporal Shepherd was a slight, perky sparrow of a man. Quick on his feet. Good with a knife. Bright.

'Get this ammo back on the trucks. Pull in the men off the roofs and stand by to move out.' Curtis looked round for Peters, his runner. Peters was the youngest man there; nineteen, fit, on his first Op with the Regiment, full of it.

'Double back to the hotel,' Curtis said. 'My compliments to the Wing Commander and there's a bloody big fire up at the main compound and what sounds like amateurs' day at Bisley. Request instructions. Got it?'

'Got it, sir.'

Curtis grinned at the healthy, sunburned English face. 'Off you go then. You should be there now.'

'They're good lads, sir,' Scobart said. 'It's just that they've been buggered about too long.' By the planners in GHQ. By the climate and the flies and the boredom and the loneliness. By the lack of facilities and the lack of women, the anxieties about their families back home, the want of something positive to do. And by Gatley, the little disciplinarian who went by the book, had set out to re-build the unit and had, instead, destroyed it.

Hanwell nodded. It was always the same. Good lads. Honourable men. But attempted murder was attempted murder, mutiny was mutiny. 'And they're not armed?'

Scobart shifted in his chair. The stiffness in his foot was creeping up his leg, the muscles in calf and thigh cramping painfully. 'There were some rifles in the Guard Tent. They've got those.' Including the missing one? he thought.

'Ammunition?'

96

'Not much.' Scobart winced, massaging his thigh. 'Not now.'

'And the Armoury's secure?'

The SWO nodded. It was the first thing Lever had done when the parade had broken up. Bolted the shutters, double-locked the door. 'I don't think they're looking for a fight.'

'No?' Hanwell said sceptically. 'So we try talking them out. Is the phone working?'

'They've taken it off the hook.'

'I've got a PA system in the jeep. We'll use that.' Hanwell grinned. 'The right word at the right moment in the right tone of voice.'

Scobart nodded doubtfully. It was what he had suggested to Gatley.

But Gatley had rejected it, as he had rejected every suggestion, all advice. 'And if they sit tight?'

'We'll have to force 'em out,' Hanwell said. He saw the anxiety in Scobart's eyes and grinned. 'Not to worry, Mr Scobart. It won't come to that.'

Behind him, Frant finished bandaging Hobey's leg and straightened, easing his shoulders. 'How's that?'

Hobey nodded. 'Fine.'

'I think we can get you up to bed now.'

Hobey lay on a blanket on the bar counter, the stitches in his thigh and side nagging through the shot of morphine Frant had given him. 'No way, Doc,' he said. 'I'm good as new now.'

But he didn't look it. His eyes were fever-bright slits in his bruised, grey cheeked face, his hair matted with sweat. He propped himself up on one elbow and gave Hanwell a sketchy grin. 'That PA system...'

'Forget it, Hobo. We can cope,' Hanwell said. Whoever set up the PA it wouldn't be Hobey.

'I've not come up here to lie in a bloody bed drinking bloody barley water,' Hobey said.

'Don't be a damned fool,' Hanwell said. 'Bed's the best place for you.'

Hobey shook his head. 'Get me off here into a chair and I'll be OK.'

Hanwell looked at Frant. The M.O. shrugged. 'If that's what he wants.'

They picked him up and carried him to a chair and settled him in it with a blanket tucked round him. Scott brought one of the coffee tables and slipped it under his left leg.

Scobart grinned at him. 'Join the club.'

Hobey nodded, breathing hard.

'Couple of Chelsea pensioners,' Hanwell said. He turned to Scott. 'Go and see if they've got that radio serviceable will you, Sar'nt?'

As Scott went to the door, Miller knocked and came in.

'Ah, Corporal Miller,' Hanwell said. 'All quiet in the compound?'

'Sir,' Miller said stiffly, ill-at-ease in officer territory.

'Good show.' The familiar drawl settled the corporal as it was meant to do. 'Lights working all right, are they?'

'Sir. Only...'

Hanwell looked at him, his eyes questioning. 'Only?'

'There's somebody in the Armoury, sir. And I don't reckon he likes us much.'

At the north end of Sharia Pasha, thirty yards beyond number four three-tonner, LAC Jackson lay prone on the first-floor balcony of a block of flats. His thighs were spread, his feet turned outwards, a .303 rifle snuggled into his shoulder.

Jackson was a rifle man. Always had been right from the day on his square-bashing course when they had marched him down to the range for the first time and put a Lee Enfield in his hands. He had been just eighteen then, awkward, half-fledged, with acne and crooked teeth and a king-size inferiority complex. He had left school at fourteen to work in a grocer's shop, unpacking crates in the backyard, stocking the shelves with bottles and tins and paper bags of flour, riding an old bicycle through the streets delivering the orders on Fridays. He had been out of his depth in the RAF. No trade, no special skills, scruffy in his ill-fitting uniform. An erk with blistered boots and frayed collar-tabs, the lowest form of airforce life, doomed to serve as an ACH/GD for the duration.

Until they had given him a rifle.

The old drill-sergeant's line about your rifle being your wife was true for Jackson. Between him and the Lee Enfield it had been love at first sight. He had cherished it, serviced it, oiled and cleaned it; polished the brass butt plate, blancoed the webbing sling, built his life round it. Without it he was a nobody; a rear-rank, for-Gawd's-sake-lad-keep-out-of-my-sight no-hoper. But married to his rifle he was alive, complete.

He had fired ten rounds that first day on the range – an outer, two inners and seven, smack-in-the-middle bulls.

'Beginner's luck,' the sergeant had said sourly. But the next time Jackson had made it eight bulls and the time after that, ten. The perfect score. 'He's still wet behind the ears, sir,' the sergeant had said to the flight commander, 'and he looks like an orphan in a Bombay brothel. But he's a natural-born shot.'

Which was why Scott had posted him on that balcony.

He lay comfortably relaxed, both eyes wide open, the right one gazing calmly down the sights of the rifle lined up on the mouth of the alley across the street, the left

99

one feeding peripheral information into his brain. Only amateurs closed one eye to shoot. Real pros thanked God for binocular vision and used it.

Thirty yards to his right the three-tonner stood broadside-on, blocking the street, its canvas tilt a pale glimmer in the darkness. He raised his head slightly and looked beyond the truck, changing his focal range to rest his eyes. He could see the outlines of the jeep and the fifteen-hundredweight in the patch of light from the hotel doorway and a faint glow in the sky behind the cinema from the compound arc lights. The quietness of the town gathered round him; an uneasy, electric silence which he tested warily, as a cat tests the air before a storm. He looked back into the mouth of the alley, pressing his cheek against the stock of the rifle, and saw the shadows move, heard the muted pad of bare feet, the sudden nervous snort of a donkey. He eased off the safety-catch gently. The rifle was fully loaded with one up the spout. The donkey snorted again. Jackson curled his finger round the trigger, stroking it, his touch as light as a lover's.

Meguid halted a couple of yards inside the alley. His bodyguards closed in round him. The men behind stood still. He gave them whispered instructions, took a fresh grip on the heavy lamp and urged the donkey forward.

Jackson watched them emerge into Sharia Pasha, the donkey's head a grey shadow in his sights. They turned left towards the three-tonner, Meguid and his four bodyguards, walking slowly, openly, in the middle of the street. Behind them the shadows in the alley converged into a solid mass as the men grouped together and waited, hidden from the truck. Only when Meguid had opened the door with the key of the lamp would they come out in support.

Jackson tracked the donkey with his rifle, letting it pass.

100

'Let 'em go by, Jacko,' Scott had said when he had posted Jackson on the balcony. 'That way, if they get stroppy, you can take 'em from behind.'

Meguid reined in the donkey. The four men stood round him, clutching their rifle barrels under their galabeyahs.

'Eh, Ingleez,' Meguid shouted. 'Sayeeda effendim.'

Jackson lifted the foresight of the rifle, aiming it at the nape of Meguid's neck. He opened his eyes wider, building the pattern of shadows – the grey of the donkey, the white of the galabeyahs, the blackness under the walls – fitting these together to make a picture, a target of which the man on the donkey was the bullseye.

Meguid waited for a reply, but the men round the three-tonner crouched in silence. He shouted in English, 'No trouble, effendim. We come in peace and as friends.'

In a pig's eye, Jackson thought, listening to the rustling of the packed shadows in the alley. He began to breathe slowly, carefully. In shooting as in singing it was important to get your breathing right. He saw the pattern in the street below him break up and change as the four bodyguards spread out on either side and took station against the walls. At the same instant Meguid switched on the lamp.

The intense white beam, widened by the lens, transformed the street. It was as if a slide had been slipped into position under a microscope. The three-tonner towered in huge perpective, its tilt gleaming like an iceberg, every detail of wheels and cab and metal body brilliantly delineated. The men lying beneath it and crouched at either end covered their faces with their hands, helpless and blind as rabbits pinned in the glare of a car's headlights. It was as though a star had fallen in the street, impossible to look at with the naked eye, impossible to see through. Behind it in the

101

darkness, Meguid and his men were as invisible and as safe as if they had been behind a wall.

But not from where Jackson lay. To him they were clear-cut, sharply-defined silhouettes. Black shapes pasted on to a white background like target figures in a fairground shooting gallery. He saw the bodyguards pull their rifles up through the slits in the galabeyahs and go down on one knee. Saw them tuck the butts into their shoulders. Saw their hands close over the bolts, slide them back and forwards and down in the locking position. It all seemed to be happening in slow motion, every movement deliberate and separate, giving him plenty of time.

He swung the barrel of the Lee Enfield up and left, settled the foresight on the front bodyguard on the left of the street, took first pressure and squeezed the trigger. The man fell forward, his head split open. Before he hit the ground Jackson had shot the one behind him, swung the rifle across right and lined up on the third man. The Lee Enfield was a part of him, an extra arm growing out of his shoulder, its small, round muzzle an extra eye. The movement of his hand from trigger to bolt and back again was a smooth, continuous blur, impossibly fast. He shot the third man and the fourth – this one in the chest as he turned towards the balcony. Then he sighted on Meguid.

Meguid gripped the donkey with his knees, sitting in a haze of bewildered terror; a small, fat man caught in a trap of his own devising. His hands held the lamp that was to have been his guarantee of safety and had become, without warning, a weapon turned against him. He twisted in the saddle, his mouth open in a scream of panic, his fingers fumbling sweatily for the switch. Jackson's fifth bullet took him in the throat just above the rib cage, angled down to break his spine and burst out of his back in a mushroom of blood and flesh and splintered bone. The donkey put his head down,

102

wheeled and bolted. Meguid was thrown off, the lamp still clutched to his stomach. He fell heavily on top of it, rolled off and lay still.

The men in the alley broke and ran.

'To recap, then,' Hanwell said, 'You've got the compound staked out and fully lit. Main gate blocked. A man on the wicket gate at this end. The rest positioned under cover.'

Miller nodded. 'The bod in the Armoury doesn't seem to mind us being there, sir. So long as we keep well away from that corner of the veranda.'

'Hmm.' Hanwell got up and began to pace between the bar and the door. He had taken off his cap and his ginger hair, cut short and crinkled, glinted in the lights. Miller watched him approvingly. This was the Hanwell he knew from half-a-dozen ops; the incisive, determined man behind the casual, drawling mask. 'And all the other offices are empty?'

'Sir.'

'Any noise coming from the cinema?'

'No, sir. All quiet.' Miller stood by Hobey's chair, properly at ease, big and solid in his sand-stained overalls.

'Probably all got their heads down,' Scobart said.

'Yes.' Hanwell looked down at him. 'What about this chap in the Armoury? Any clues about who he is?'

Scobart shook his head. 'I don't understand it, sir. Lever had that place sewn up tight.'

'Lever?'

'Sergeant Lever. Armourer. He opened it up to issue arms and ammunition to the party going up to the main compound. And double-checked it was secure again before he left with them.'

Hanwell said to Miller, 'Is the door damaged at all?'

'No, sir.'

'Not been forced?'

103

Miller shook his head.

'Got in with a key, then,' Hanwell said. 'Who has the keys to the Armoury, Mr Scobart?'

'Only Lever and the Adjutant.'

'Yes,' Hanwell said. 'Well, whoever's in there it's not either of them.' He looked across at Scott. 'Right, Sar'nt. Let's go and have a little chat with our trigger-happy friend.' He picked up his hat and put it on, went to the table by the door for his sten.

Miller said, 'With respect, sir, he's not in a chatty sort of mood.'

Hanwell nodded. 'I hear you, Corporal. We'll just have to . . .' He broke off as the door opened and Peters came in, excited, eager. It was all still a game to Peters. Urgent messages and the sound of distant firing and his mates laughing and singing in the trucks. Then he saw Scobart and Hobey and his face went tight. He licked his lips and looked at Hanwell.

'Well, Peters?' Hanwell said. 'What can we do for you?'

'Mr Curtis's compliments, sir,' Peters said and recited the message exactly as Curtis had told him, word perfect right down to 'Request instructions.'

Hanwell smiled. 'Thank you, Peters,' he said calmly.

But Scobart was not so calm. 'Bloody hell,' he said, all the frustration of his immobility in his voice. 'They're all up there. Every officer. Every SNCO. If that mob's . . .'

'Yes, Mr Scobart,' Hanwell cut in evenly. 'You said.'

Scobart flushed. 'Sorry, sir. It's this damned foot. I ought to be up there with them.'

'I understand,' Hanwell said. And to Peters, 'Is Mr Curtis ready to move out?'

'Yes, sir. They were reloading the trucks when I left.'

104

'Right,' Hanwell said. 'Let's re-jig the programme a little, shall we?'

'Hush,' Jane said. 'Please, darling. I can't stay if you talk.' Frant had been adamant about that. 'The Doc says you must rest, conserve your strength.'

'Frant's an old woman,' Roper said huskily. 'A couple of days and I'll be ...' His voice choked on a cough and he struggled for breath, his face pale and sweating.

'That's enough,' she said. 'One more word and I'm off downstairs.' She leaned forward in her chair and wiped his face with a small towel. 'I mean it, David.'

'Yes, ma'am.' He gave her the ghost of a smile and closed his eyes for a moment, lying propped up high on the pillows in the narrow bed in the little, white walled room.

The bullet had gone in under his right clavicle, passed through the top of his lung and out under his left arm. Frant had done a first class emergency job on him, cleansing and packing the wounds with sulphonamide, strapping the broken ribs, giving him morphine and plasma. But it was only an emergency job. He needed the full facilities of a hospital Intensive Care Unit.

'How is he?' Jane had said, standing in the corridor with Frant before she had gone in.

'Fair.'

She had looked at him, her eyes questioning. Was that part of his professional vocabulary? A categorical word like the ward sister's 'comfortable', cautious, noncommittal? 'What does that mean? I want to know exactly what his chances are.'

'He's young and strong,' Frant had said. 'That helps, of course.'

'Please,' she had said.

He had shaken his head. 'I don't know. I honestly don't know. He's got a collapsed lung and a couple of broken ribs and he's lost a lot of blood. The way he is

105

now I think he's got a chance. A good chance. But to be absolutely honest with you ...'

'Please.'

'It could go either way. If he gets through the night. If my patching stays together. If there's no infection ...' Frant had smiled and spread his hands, 'I'm sorry I can't be more positive.'

She had nodded. 'Thank you. You've told me what I want to know.'

She sat now holding his hand in hers. In the gentle light from the bedside lamp his face was waxy, lined with fatigue and pain. But it was still the face she knew and loved. She was grateful for that. Grateful the bullet had not disfigured him, smashed his face as the German shell splinter had smashed his left hand.

He opened his eyes, focused on her face and smiled. She had tidied herself before coming in. Washed her face and hands, combed the glass out of her hair, stripped off the stained battledress blouse and overalls. He saw her through the haze of morphine, fresh and smiling in slacks and shirt. 'How's Ludo Watson?'

'Oh, he's in tearing spirits, as usual,' she said. 'He sends his love.'

'Decent of him to let you come.'

She nodded.

Frant had said, 'He doesn't know, of course – about the trouble with the men.'

'Who brought you?' he said.

'Hobo. He had to come up anyway. Routine inspection. So I thumbed a ride.' She saw him open his mouth and put her hand on it lightly. 'No more talk or I'll ...'

He nodded. After a moment his eyes closed. She bit her lip and blinked back the tears, ready to smile if he should open them again.

Hanwell slung his sten gun over his shoulder. 'OK. Let's go.'

Scott said quickly, 'You won't change your mind, sir? About me?'

Hanwell shook his head. 'I'm sorry, Sar'nt. I need you here.' He was leaving him with Hicks and six men. Miller and the rest were going with him in the fifteen-hundredweight. 'If anything breaks you can't handle, send Hicks up in the jeep.' It was not the way he wanted it. In the sort of chaos he suspected was waiting for him in the main compound, the big lowland sergeant would have been worth ten men. But with Hobey and Scobart out of action and the girl to think of, it was the way it had to be.

'The lads'd be with you if they knew, sir,' Scobart said.

'I don't doubt it,' Hanwell said, recognising the SWO's loyalty to his men. But, holed-up in the cinema, they didn't know; would suspect a trick if they did. By the time they had been persuaded it was true it would be too late.

He went out into the hall. Miller was standing with the men by the front door. 'All right, Corporal,' Hanwell said. 'Everybody into the fifteen-hundred-weight.'

Miller grinned. 'We going up there to sort 'em out, sir?'

Hanwell nodded. This bit at least was straightforward, right out of the training manual. No pussyfooting about. No punches pulled. And he had Miller.

He followed the men down the steps into the street and stood for a moment looking north towards number four three-tonner.

Beside him, Miller said casually, 'Bit of a flurry down there just now, sir. No panic. Everything's under control.'

'Sure?' Hanwell said. He needed that street block. It

107

was a vital element in the security of the HQ compound and the hotel. Especially now.

'Jackson's there,' Miller said, his wide, flat face impassive.

'Ah,' Hanwell said. 'That's all right, then.' Only a tank could get past Jackson. 'Right. In the truck then.' He climbed up into the cab behind the wheel. Miller opened the other door and got in beside him. 'This is more like it, sir.'

Hanwell nodded and pressed the starter button, aware of the corporal's enthusiasm; sharing it. This was what they were trained for. Not to negotiate, to attack.

7.   01.00 – 02.45 HOURS

They came out of the mouth of the street in a smother
of dust, Curtis leading in the fifteen-hundredweight,
the two three-tonners tucked in behind. They were
running fast without lights, relying on Curtis's superb
night vision to get them through. Beside him, Hanwell
stared across the waste ground beyond the southern
limits of the town and saw the mosque standing by itself
a quarter of a mile away, halfway between the last of
the houses and the main stores compound. A big, black
shape against the stars, topped by its minaret. A bonus.
Custombuilt for their purpose. Perfect cover.
  'In behind there, Jack,' he said crisply.
  Curtis hauled on the wheel. The three trucks raced
across the sand and swung in behind the mosque. They
stopped in the black shadow below its wall, the nose of
the fifteen-hundredweight projecting slightly beyond
the corner. Curtis switched off the engine and sniffed,
smelling smoke in the cold night air.
  Hanwell took a pair of night-glasses out of the canvas
pocket on the door, unclipped the hatch above his head
and pushed it open. He stood on the seat, resting his
elbows on the cab roof, settled the glasses comfortably
against his eyes and turned the knurled focusing screw.
Curtis spread out the plan of the compound and flicked
on a small torch.
  The compound was long and narrow, lying in a
north/south axis with a single-track railway spur

coming in through the wire on the south side and running like a backbone down the centre to within fifty yards of the main gates in the north side wire. Wooden sheds with corrugated iron roofs stood inside the wire on either side of the gates. Behind them, stacked in rows at right angles to the railway and on both sides of it, crates of stores set on heavy baulks of timber and covered with tarpaulins rose twenty feet into the air. The passageways between the rows were just wide enough to take a flat-bed loading truck.

Hanwell swung the glasses left. The north-east corner of the high wire fence filled the lenses, outlined faintly against the dull glow from a dying fire. He called down to Curtis, 'Nine o'clock from the main gates.'

Curtis checked the plan. 'Main clothing stores.'

'That's where the fire was. Just about burned out now.' Hanwell panned the glasses slowly right along the line of sheds to the gates. One of the twin arc lamps mounted on wooden gantries above the gates had been shot out. The other was still working. In its glare he could see the gates sagging open on broken hinges. Between them on the trampled sand a number of bodies sprawled lifeless in bloodied galabeyahs. He lifted the glasses, adjusting the focus. Flashes of rifle fire starred the darkness beyond the pool of light. The sound of the shots rattled distantly like pebbles thrown on an iron roof. Shadows moved against the blackness. A sten chattered briefly, irregularly,like bad morse. He said, 'Left of the gates, about thirty yards in.'

'Guard Room,' Curtis said.

'And on the right?'

'MT workshops.'

'They've smashed through the gates – a bit expensively by the looks of it – and they're attacking the Guard Room from the cover of the workshops.' Hanwell ducked down into the cab and leaned towards Curtis, looking at the plan.

110

Curtis rubbed his hand over his face. His skin was itchy under the stubble on his cheeks; itchy and tight, the way it always was before action. 'So let's go and clobber 'em.' Which was the frustrated fighter pilot talking; throttle through the gate, wing over and dive on target.

'Easy now, Jack,' Hanwell said. 'There are a couple of questions need answering first. Like how many of the bastards are there? And how far in have they penetrated?'

'Hundred? Hundred and fifty?' Curtis said, remembering that moment in the street when the fire had mushroomed against the sky and the roar of the mob had come sweeping back like a wave.

Hanwell nodded. 'My guess is our chaps are holding the Guard Room.' He jabbed the plan with his finger. 'Probably pulled back in there when the gates went.' He looked at Curtis. 'So how many wogs does it take to keep 'em bottled-up in there? Twenty?'

Curtis nodded. 'No more.'

'OK. So where are the others? Don't forget most of 'em work in there on the Native Labour force. They know their way around. They could be all over the place. Right through to the south wire by now. And they're in there to loot. Knocking off March and his team's a side-show. What they're really after is the stores.' He pointed to the south-west corner of the plan. 'And this.'

'The petrol dump?'

'Roger. They'll go out through the wire that way. And fire the dump as they leave. Twelve thousand gallons of high octane.' Hanwell shook his head. 'Make quite a blaze, won't it?'

Curtis clenched his fists on the rim of the wheel. 'Three bloody trucks and a handful of men in that rabbit warren. We haven't got a prayer. We can bust March

111

and the others out of the Guard Room, fair enough. But how the hell are we going to secure the compound?'

Hanwell smiled grimly. 'There's always a way, Jack. The trick is to recognise it when you see it.' He looked down at the plan, tracing his finger along the railway spur towards the south wire. 'I want you to go up round that side and take a quick look. Without lights. Can do?'

Curtis nodded. 'I'll need somebody with me,' he said, looking at the drawing of the railhead and its siding just outside the wire. On the plan the lines were neat, uncomplicated. But the reality in the dark would be different.

'Shepherd,' Hanwell said. He opened the cab door. 'I'll have a word with him and Miller.'

He walked back to the three-tonners. Miller was in number one, Shepherd in two. He called them down from the cabs and briefed them. His voice was clipped now, almost curt. No trace of the lazy drawl. Shepherd ran forward and got up into the fifteen-hundredweight. Miller went back to talk to the men in the three-tonners.

'One circuit, Jack,' Hanwell said, standing beside the open window of the cab. 'Go out wide at this end, as close as you can get on the far side. Shepherd knows what to look for.'

Curtis nodded and started the engine.

'Just a recce,' Hanwell said. 'No heroics.'

'Understood,' Curtis let in the clutch and pulled away. Hanwell watched him take the truck out wide round the north-west corner of the compound and then got up on to the step of the first three-tonner. 'Edge her up a bit, Mason.'

Mason ran the truck forward six yards.

'Right.' Hanwell climbed on to the bonnet with his night glasses. He checked his watch and began to search systematically along the north wire from west to east.

112

Behind him, the men in the second three-tonner, briefed by Miller, were stripping off the canvas tilt and stowing it in the back.

Curtis eased his foot on the throttle pedal. The truck jounced over the railway line and he turned left, driving up towards the big steel buffers in their hydraulic mounting at the railhead. A string of goods waggons stood on the siding between the compound wire and the main track. He looked at Shepherd. 'Better check.'

Shepherd nodded, unslung his sten gun and laid it on the floor of the cab as Curtis rounded the buffers and stopped. Shepherd was a Birmingham barrow-boy, nurtured in the roaring street-markets, hard headed, impudent, fly. A bantamweight with small hands and feet and a narrow, wiry frame, he had bought himself a flick-knife for his seventeenth birthday after being brutally worked over by a couple of muscle men intent on moving on to his pitch. He had the knife-fighter's long reach and cool, unblinking stare and he moved like a dancer. Twenty-three now, with four years of desert service behind him, he was a tough, resourceful loner, cheerful, sharp-tongued, dangerous. He opened the cab door and dropped down on to the ground.

'Make it quick,' Curtis said.

Shepherd grinned and ran back along the main line, the faint gleam of the rails guiding him. Beyond the last waggon he crossed the tracks to the siding and began to work his way back towards the fifteen-hundredweight. There were six waggons in the string, open-topped, wooden-sided; secondhand English rolling stock with the old LNER markings still discernable under the paint. At each one he pulled himself up to peer inside, the knife in his bayonet frog tapping his thigh.

The native guard was waiting for him, crouched beside the coupling between the first and second waggon, an old shotgun in his hands. He heard

Shepherd's footsteps stop, heard the creak of the second waggon as the corporal hauled himself up to look inside, and hooked the hammer of the shotgun back with his thumb. Shepherd went pounding past him, a dark shadow against the stars, put his foot on the wheel of the first waggon and reached up to grip the top edge of the side.

The guard straightened, bringing up the gun. His galabeyah brushed against the light chain on the locking-pin of the coupling. Shepherd heard the warning rattle, lowered himself quietly and drew his knife. He pivoted on his left foot, knees slightly bent, shoulders hunched, stomach sucked in. He saw the barrel of the shotgun appear round the corner of the waggon, put the knife between his teeth, seized the gun barrel with both hands, forced it up and twisted his shoulders, using the barrel as a lever. The guard came out from between the waggons, off-balance, stumbling. Shepherd turned him with the gun and rammed it back hard. The heavy brass plate on the heel of the butt dug into the guard's stomach and he jack-knifed. Shepherd transferred the gun barrel to his left hand, pinned the guard against the side of the waggon, took his knife in his right hand and stepped forward. He let go of the gun, put the heel of his left hand under the guard's chin, straightened him and thrust the knife into his stomach and gutted him like a fish. The guard sagged, blood spraying out of him. Shepherd jerked the knife out and let him crumple down against the wheel. He wiped the knife on his overalls, picked up the shotgun, smashed it over the coupling and threw it away. He dragged the dead guard clear of the track and turned and ran back to the fifteen-hundredweight.

Three minutes later Hanwell picked up the fifteen-hundredweight in the night-glasses two hundred yards east of the compound wire, travelling fast. Curtis brought it

114

in round the back of the mosque and braked to a halt alongside the three-tonners.

Shepherd got down, smiling. 'There's a string of goods waggons on the siding, sir. All ready to roll on to the spur.'

'Empty?' Hanwell said.

'And unguarded,' Shepherd said. 'Now.'

'Good show.' Hanwell saw the dark stain down the front of Shepherd's overalls where the guard's blood had spurted. He jumped down off the bonnet of the three-tonner. 'Get the men out, will you?'

He briefed them quickly, tersely, the way he had briefed so many men in the last five years, communicating not only the detailed orders, the precise sequence of events, but also confidence, a kind of rapport. They bunched round him against the black wall of the mosque and listened to his voice, the telegraphic words punctuated by the sound of rifle fire from the compound, their faces intent, absorbed, their eyes shining. When he had finished they broke away and began to climb back into the trucks. He watched them, masking his own inner feelings behind a grin of encouragement.

All this, he thought, for a few crates of machinery that'll probably sit out the war here unused, unwanted. We must be mad to do it.

The fifteen-hundredweight moved out first, Curtis driving, Hanwell in the cab with him, six men in the back. Behind it, Mason drove number one three-tonner carrying twelve men. Shepherd rode with him. Number two three-tonner waited in the shadow of the mosque, Butterworth at the wheel, six men crouched on the folded tilt under the naked steel arches of the supports. Corporal Miller, designated NCO i/c Diversion, stood with his back to the radiator grille, a cigarette cupped in the palm of his hand, and watched the two trucks

115

swing out wide west of the compound following the route Curtis had taken on the recce with Shepherd.

Curtis drove without lights, reading the surface of the waste ground easily, every patch of shadow, every ridge, every hollow. But to Hanwell, peering blindly through the dark windscreen, it was like being hurtled down a black tunnel. The truck bounced and swayed, the wind whistled eerily over the open hatch above his head and drummed on the tilt. He fought down a sense of panic, forcing himself to relax. Coming up to the railway, Curtis dabbed the brake pedal twice. In the three-tonner Mason saw the brake lights wink their warning and swung left, changing down through the gears as the big truck bucked over the sleepers on the siding and came to rest with its front bumper inches from the buffers of the last waggon in the string.

Curtis took the fifteen-hundredweight down between the siding and the main line, braked to a halt beside the first waggon and cut the engine. In the silence that followed Hanwell heard the snarling of dogs fighting over the corpse of the guard Shepherd had knifed. He put his head and shoulders up through the hatch and lifted the nightglasses to his eyes. In the lenses the compound showed in sharp focus. He traced the line of the spur in under the wire and down between the rows of crates towards the arc lamp hanging like a low star in the sky beyond the Guard Room nearly a mile away. There was still some firing going on down there, but the south end of the compound was silent and dark.

The men were tumbling out of the trucks now, running along the siding and climbing into the empty waggons. Curtis opened the cab door and got out. He reached in behind the seat for the box of flares and the Very pistol, slung his sten over his shoulder, tucked the pistol into his belt, patted the grenades in his thigh pockets and grinned up at Hanwell. 'I'll be off, then.'

Hanwell nodded.

116

Curtis walked down to the junction where the siding fed into the spur. Shepherd was there and together they threw the heavy lever, opening the points for the waggons. As the curved metal plates clicked into position the first bullet kicked into the sand a yard from their feet. They ducked and ran under cover behind the leading waggon in the string. A ragged fusillade stitched an uneven seam along the wooden sides of the waggons. Shepherd hoisted himself up into the first waggon, took the box of flares from Curtis and crouched with the three men already in there. The firing continued sporadically. One of the dogs was hit and the rest ran yelping under the waggons and away across the main line.

Curtis ran down towards the three-tonner. Mason saw him coming and started the engine. Curtis got up on the step and locked his hands on the cab door. 'OK,' he said. 'Let's go.'

Mason reversed slowly, braked, engaged first gear and four-wheel drive and fed in the revs. The big truck lunged forward. The steel bumper smashed into the buffers of the rear waggon in the string. The buffers recoiled, absorbing the shock. All down the line the couplings clanked. The waggons shivered and groaned. Inside them, pinned down by the bullets whining over their heads, the men braced themselves on the steel-ribbed floors.

Mason backed off and came in again. This time the waggons eased forward a little and rocked back. Mason reversed again, taking a longer run. The engine howled as he stamped on the throttle. The three-tonner bucked over the sleepers, its heavy tyres spraying stones. The bumper thudded into the buffers, striking sparks. The waggons lurched forward. The wheels of the truck lost their grip and spun and the waggons groaned to a halt.

Watching from the fifteen-hundredweight, Hanwell

muttered, 'Come on, come ON. Get your bloody foot down, man.'

Curtis shouted, 'On my signal,' and jumped down and ran forward calling the men out of the waggons. The bullets were coming more thickly now and the men wriggled over the sides of the waggons and stood ready to shove. Mason had his head out of the cab window, peering down the line in the darkness. He heard Curtis shout, released the clutch and accelerated. As the truck slammed into the buffers the men humped their shoulders and braced their feet and heaved. The hammering of the engine drowned the sound of shots from the compound and the waggons began to roll, slowly at first and then picking up speed.

'Everybody on,' Curtis yelled and pulled himself up into the first waggon.

Hanwell slid down into the driving seat of the fifteen-hundredweight and started the engine, watching the waggons rolling past him over the points on to the spur, curving round now towards the wire. As the three-tonner came alongside, he slipped into gear and drove forward.

The leading waggon butted into the wooden-framed, wire-mesh gate and burst it open. As it entered the compound Curtis fired a flare.

Standing by the corner of the mosque, Miller saw the flare streak up into the sky, explode and hang above the compound. He hauled himself up into the cab of the three-tonner as Butterworth let in the clutch. The truck came out of the shadows in a blaze of headlights and raced across the sand towards the main gates, its horn blaring, the men in the back shouting and banging the butts of their stens on the metal sides. Ten yards short of the gates Butterworth put the wheel over hard. The truck swung right, heeling sharply on its suspension. Miller pulled the pin of a grenade with his teeth and

118

hurled it out through the cab window. The truck was broadside on to the compound now, the men in the back spraying bullets in a long, sustained burst. The grenade burst behind the Egyptians crouched against the wall of the MT workshops. They turned in a panic and the bullets scythed into them.

'Once more and then in,' Miller said.

Butterworth brought the truck round and drove back across the gates, the men in the back slotting fresh clips into their stens and pouring a stream of bullets into the Egyptians. Beyond the pool of light cast by the arc lamp Miller could see a broken, moving pattern of shadows – a black and white jigsaw of flapping galabeyahs and dark faces – as more men came running back down the spur, firing wildly as they ran. The truck came round in a tight circle, shuddering on full lock, straightened with a lurch and headed directly for the open gates. Butterworth felt the wheel jerk in his hands as they went bucketing in over the bodies lying on the sand. The headlights ripped open the darkness exposing a yelling mob of men desperately diving for cover behind the bodies of their fellows slumped against the workshop wall.

'We've got 'em,' Butterworth shouted. 'We've got the. . .' and his voice stopped abruptly as the windscreen shattered and a bullet smashed into his jaw and took away the lower half of his face.

The flare drifted slowly over the south end of the compound. In its hard, white light the rows of crates under their black tarpaulins stood out clearly, the narrow passages between them flecked with shadows. The waggons rolled in along the spur, moving easily now, nudged forward at a brisk walking pace by the three-tonner. The men knelt behind the wooden sides and hosed each passageway with bullets from their stens as it came into view.

119

'A sort of mobile slit-trench,' Hanwell had said at the briefing. And it was exactly that, giving them cover, keeping them together as a unit, bringing passageway after passageway into their line of fire. Trapped between the walls of crates, out in the open, off-balance, the Egyptians fired back with courage but without discipline. Their old rifles and shotguns were no match for the stens and as Hanwell had said they were looters not soldiers. By the time the last waggon was fifty yards into the compound they were beginning to break and run for the main gates.

Two of the men in the last waggon dropped off and made for the petrol dump in the south-west corner, running down between the crates, stumbling over the bodies as the flare withered and died. The dump was a big shallow pit dug out of the sand, surrounded by a four-foot wall of sandbags. The petrol was stored in unpainted metal tins which dimly reflected the starlight, shimmering like a small, pewter lake. The two men vaulted over the sandbag wall and dived into the shadows. Their job was to protect the dump without drawing fire on themselves.

'Knives, boots and fists,' Hanwell had said at the briefing. 'No guns. It only needs one bullet to blow that lot to hell and back.'

In the leading waggon Curtis fired another flare. By its light Hanwell manoeuvred the fifteen-hundred-weight into the gap in the wire where the waggons had broken through, switched off, got up on the seat and put his head up out of the hatch. He needed no night-glasses now. The whole of the southern half of the compound was flooded with light from the hanging flare.

Miller grabbed the wheel of the three-tonner, shouldered Butterworth to one side, kicked his feet clear of the pedals and tramped down hard on the brakes. The glare of the headlights was a white, opaque mist beyond

120

the starred and splintered windscreen. Unable to see, he held the wheel steady, felt the truck slide on locked wheels and braced his left foot against the bulkhead, waiting for the crash. Wedged behind his right shoulder, Butterworth was screaming in a froth of blood and shattered bone, a stolid, unremarkable man, good at his job, faceless, for whom death could only be a friend. The truck ploughed heavily into the men bunched in front of the workshop wall, slewed sharply left, rammed into the corner of the building and stalled. Miller went out through the windscreen head first, slid across the bonnet and somersaulted off on to the sand. He fell on his right shoulder and felt the collar-bone snap. He rolled on to his back, dazed and bleeding, his face lacerated by the splintered windscreen. The sten gun was still clenched in his left hand and he shook the blood out of his eyes and turned on to his stomach in an automatic reflex action, grunting with pain as the edges of the broken bone grated and pierced the skin.

The men in the back of the truck lay in a tangled heap up against the cab wall, bruised and shaken. In the cab Butterworth was dead, sprawled over the steering wheel, his head with its ruined face thrust through the wreckage of the windscreen, the top of his skull split open. All around the truck and pulped under the front wheels the Egyptian dead lay on the bloodied sand. In the silence that followed the impact water gurgled out of the riven radiator, petrol dripped on to the hot engine from the ruptured fuel line.

In the cab of number one three-tonner Mason concentrated on keeping the truck jammed firmly against the buffers of the rear waggon. In spite of the cold he was sweating profusely, the wheel slippery under his hands, his shirt clammy against his skin. He struggled to control clutch and throttle, jouncing in the seat as the truck jolted and rocked over the sleepers. In front of him

121

the waggons rolled ponderously up the slight incline towards the main gates. The temperature gauge was nudging the red danger line and he kept the revs up, knowing that if the hot engine stalled it would be a pig to re-start. Knowing, too, that the brakes would probably fail to hold the waggons if they started to run back. Through the top of the windscreen he could see into the rear waggon where the sten guns spewed out fiery streams of bullets, flushing the alleys between the rows of crates as efficiently as hoses flushing a drain. The noise was indescribable – the howl of the labouring engine, the stammering of the stens, the screeching of iron wheels on the track, the whine and thud of occasional bullets striking the metal sides of the cab. Mason was no stranger to gun fire. He had run ammunition up the desert with 52 MT Company and been harried and strafed by Stukas and German 88s. But that had been out in the blue, pounding down the long sand tracks with plenty of room to manoeuvre. This was different; shunting railway waggons through a forest of crates with the engine tearing its guts out and the clutch pedal juddering under his boot. Caught in a cross-fire and nowhere to go but forward.

In the leading waggon Curtis fitted another flare into the pistol and fired it as the previous one died. They were two-thirds of the way through the compound now, the surviving looters running down the spur in front of the waggons intent only to escape from the murderous fire of the stens. He peered over the rim of the waggon and saw the Guard Room clearly now, the white light of the flare dimming the arc lamp above the shattered gates. The firing seemed to have stopped up there and he saw the jumble of bodies on the sand and the blunt, battered nose of the three-tonner rammed into the corner of the workshops. He turned and shouted, 'Hold your fire. Cease firing.'

The men in the waggons put up their guns. The sound

122

of the truck engine behind them was suddenly do-
minant. Above them the flare was dying quickly,
dropping and drifting and fading. As it went out Curtis
shouted, 'Mason. Stop the truck.'

The men repeated the order, shouting back to Mason.
The waggon string ran free for a moment and creaked
to a halt as the darkness closed in again.

Shepherd went over the side of the leading waggon,
grabbed the brake lever and hauled it on, tugging with
both hands. All down the line the couplings clanked,
taking the strain. The brake held. He looked up and saw
Curtis's head and shoulders dark against the sky. 'Get
the men out,' Curtis said and vaulted down beside him.
A hundred and fifty yards up the track the Egyptians
were grouping, silhouetted now against the arc lamp.
About fifty men, Curtis judged. 'They're to stay by the
waggons until the truck passes them and then follow it
up.'

Shepherd nodded. 'Sir.'

'And tell Peters I want him on the double.'

Shepherd ran back, banging the butt of his sten on the
waggon sides. 'Out. Everybody out.'

The men scrambled out and stood crouched by the
wheels. Peters came running up, breathing hard, excited.

Curtis said, 'Nip back down to Mason. Tell him to get
the truck up here fast.'

'Sir.' The boyish voice a little hoarse.

God, he's keen, Curtis thought. 'And then report back
to Wing Commander Hanwell. Tell him we're just going
to mop up now. Right?'

'Right, sir,' Peters said and was gone.

A long minute later the truck came grinding up
alongside the waggons, the men running in behind it.
Curtis got up on the step. 'All right, Mason?'

'Sir.'

'OK. Full lights, bottom gear, dead slow. Got it?'

'Sir.'

Curtis nodded. 'Be all over in five minutes.' He dropped down and hit the cab door with the heel of his hand. 'Go, go, go.'

Mason let in the clutch gently. The men fanned out, shoulder to shoulder in line abreast on either side of the truck and began to walk forward with it. Mason flicked on the headlights, his foot light on the throttle pedal. Caught in the glare, clustered between the Guard Room and the MT workshops like trapped moths in their dirt streaked galabeyahs, the Egyptians jostled and murmured, staring at the truck, on the edge of panic.

'Hold your fire,' Curtis shouted.

Shielded by the lights, his men advanced steadily, fresh clips in their sten guns, fingers curled round the triggers.

Butterworth's three-tonner went up with a roar and a whoosh of flame as the petrol ignited under the bonnet and the fire blew back along the fuel line and ripped the tank apart. The explosion and the great billow of fire broke the Egyptians' nerve. They dropped their weapons and ran towards the advancing men, their hands held high above their heads. Behind them the door of the Guard Room opened cautiously.

Peters was just over halfway back to the fifteen-hundredweight, running through the darkness, following the line of the spur, when the truck blew up. He sidestepped instinctively and turned, close in against the end of a row of crates. He saw the flames from the burning three-tonner leaping high above the roof of the workshops, heard the triumphant yell from the men with Curtis and stood eyes wide, lips drawn back in a grin of shock and excitement, his hands clenched round his sten gun. 'Bloody hell,' he said softly. It was a precise expletive. The scene outside the Guard Room was like a medieval tapestry brought dramatically to life. The

124

terrified Egyptians scattering panic-stricken now, caught between the fire and the menace of the guns flanking the advancing truck. The guns themselves like pitchforks jabbing and herding the fear-crazed figures in the shroud-like galabeyahs. The shouts and screams, the hungry, tearing crackle of the fire, the lurid, orange-yellow flames, the choking smoke. 'Bloody hell,' Peters said again and turned to continue his run to the fifteen-hundredweight. Turned to the vicious swing of a rifle butt which smashed solidly into his face and cracked his skull like an egg and killed him.

Driving down beside the spur in the fifteen-hundredweight Hanwell saw it all like a shadow puppet play against the flickering screen of the burning truck. He snapped on the headlights as Peters' head split open and saw the Egyptian leap down from the top of the end crate in the row and stoop over Peters' body, dropping his rifle to snatch up the sten. Hanwell put his foot down flat on the floor over the throttle pedal and drove the truck into and over him. He braked and opened the cab door and ran back. The sprung steel bumper of the fifteen-hundredweight had caught the Egyptian in the moment of straightening and broken his back. He lay face-down on the sand, squirming in agony, blood spreading and seeping up through the back of his galabeyah. Hanwell turned him over with his foot and shot him through the head. Then he holstered his pistol and bent and picked up Peters in his arms. He looked with grim compassion at what was left of the runner's face and remembered the eagerness with which he had come bursting into the hotel lounge bright-eyed and excited, a small but vital link in the chain of command. He carried him to the truck, gently, tenderly, as if he were still alive to feel pain, and lifted him in over the tailgate and laid him down.

It's always the young ones, he thought. The kids with everything to live for. And he shook his head angrily over the waste of it all and got back in behind the wheel. There would be another letter to write, another tissue of comforting lies to be woven. 'Your son died bravely for his country.' But the truth was otherwise. Peters had died for nothing more than the failure of Commanding Officer to match up to his job. Peters and Lewis and how many more?

'Three, I'm afraid,' Curtis said. 'Butterworth and two others.' Regiment men whose names he did not know. Fried in the back of the truck when the petrol tank blew. 'The other four made it OK.'

'Miller?' Hanwell said.

'Busted shoulder. Cuts and bruises. Nothing that won't mend.' Curtis jerked his head towards a chair in the corner of the Guard Room where Miller was sitting with a cigarette between his teeth and the sweat dripping off his face while they put a first field dressing on the ragged tear in his shoulder and strapped his right arm across his chest to immobilise it. 'He did a good job for us.'

'They all did.' Hanwell pushed back his hat and rubbed his hand over his face. This was always his bad time, the action over, the reckoning to be made.

The Guard Room was packed with officers and senior NCOs, noisy with talk and sharp, abrupt laughter as taut nerves relaxed. There was an aftermath smell of sweat and cordite and too many cigarettes. They had opened the door wide and unshuttered the windows and the cold night air drifted in and pushed a layer of stale smoke up into the roof. He shouldered his way through the crowd and went to stand beside March in the doorway.

March said, 'Thanks.' A big-boned man with a heavy-jawed face and a Lancashire accent, he was wearing a sleeveless leather jerkin open over his shirt. He stood with his feet planted firmly apart, hands in his

126

trouser pockets, a pipe in his mouth. He looked solid and easy, like an off-duty police sergeant about to go into the garden and spray the greenfly off his roses. 'I'm damned glad you came.'

Hanwell shrugged. 'You'd have been all right in here till morning.'

'By which time,' March said, 'those bastards would 've picked the compound clean.' He pointed the stem of his pipe at the surviving Egyptians squatting dejectedly in a huddle under the arc lamp.

'Yes,' Hanwell said. 'There is that, of course.' The stores, he thought bitterly. Always the bloody stores. He looked at the Egyptians, seeing them now for what they were, what they had always been; frightened peasants doomed to a life of squalor and poverty, tempted into an action for which they had neither the stomach nor the equipment. And for what? Several hundred thousand poundsworth of sophisticated engineering they could not use and would have smashed in their frantic search for the one thing they coveted – guns. 'What do we do about them?'

'Boot their arses and let 'em go,' March said flatly. 'File a report with the local police, of course, just for the look of the thing. But nothing'll come of it. This is Marazag not England's green and pleasant.' He nodded towards some of Hanwell's men collecting the bodies and laying them out in rows on the sand. 'That's what counts up here. They'll think twice before they try this again.'

Shepherd came down past the waggons and into the pool of light with his easy, barrow-boy's walk. He saluted Hanwell, jaunty as ever and as cold-eyed. There was blood on his overalls. Not his blood. 'We've patched-up the wire over by the siding, sir.'

'Any stragglers?' Hanwell said.

'Not now, sir, no.' Shepherd touched the hilt of his knife, a casual gesture more meaningful than words. He

127

was not a man to take prisoners, 'We've checked out all the stores huts.'

'Petrol dump?'

'Intact. I've left Harris and Potter up there just in case.'

'Right,' Hanwell said. 'Post sentries on the gates. And I want a six-man patrol inside the wire till first light. Everybody else back in the trucks.'

'Sir.' Shepherd hesitated. 'You want me to stay up here, sir?'

Hanwell grinned. 'No, Corporal.'

Shepherd nodded, relieved. He turned and walked away, calling to the men. In the light of the arc lamp the scene had a strange, Daliesque quality – the burned-out truck, grotesquely twisted, smothered in grey foam from the extinguishers; the Egyptian dead laid out in orderly rows, the survivors blank-faced, blank-eyed on the sand, their resignation in sharp contrast to the workmanlike activity of Hanwell's men. He said, 'I'd like to leave one of your people in charge up here, if that's all right with you?'

March nodded. 'No problem.'

'You're OK for transport?'

'Yes.' The 87 MU trucks were parked in the wired-in yard behind the MT workshops.

Hanwell adjusted his hat to its customary angle above his eyes. One crisis resolved, another waiting. 'Best get back down the town then.'

March knocked out his pipe on the heel of his boot. 'They're still tucked up in the cinema, are they?'

'Yes.'

'Daft buggers. Gatley still in there with 'em?'

'So far as I know,' Hanwell said.

'How're you going to winkle him out?'

'Gatley?' Hanwell's face was hard. 'To hell with him. It's the men I'm concerned about.' But he knew it was not as simple as that. So long as Gatley was alive

128

something could be arranged, the whole affair smoothed over. Watson would see to that. But if anything happened to him . . .

'Amen to that,' March said. 'But he's still the C.O. and . . .'

'I understand,' Hanwell said shortly. 'You don't have to spell it out.' Rank was everything; to be saluted, respected, preserved at all costs. The bony skeleton which held the Service together. The fact that the man who wore it was an incompetent, paranoic, twenty-two carat bastard was irrelevant.

'Like the Yanks are always telling us,' March said equably, 'war is hell.'

Hanwell grinned. 'It's not the war, it's the bloody awful people you meet in it.'

PART TWO

16 OCTOBER 1944

1. 01.15 – 03.00 HOURS

'What are his chances, Doc?' Hobey said. He felt himself floating in the chair as the pain-killers did their work. A not unpleasant sensation which left his mind surprisingly clear.

'Roper?' Frant shrugged. 'He's got a lung wound. And lung wounds arc fickle. One minute you've got a patient, reasonably comfortable, weak but alive. The next, you've got a corpse.'

'That dicey, is it?'

'He's lasted this long and his wife's here now. Do him more good than I can. If she can hold on to him till morning I'll start hoping.'

Hobey nodded. 'She's a good kid.'

'Two nice people,' Frant said.

'Damned nice,' Scobart said. 'They deserve better than this.'

'We all do,' Hobey said. 'Or think we do.' After five years of war the old feelings were beginning to reassert themselves, questioning the slogans and the propaganda, the patriotic jingoism of the newsreels. Feelings of hope and compassion. A reaching out for tenderness and Integrity, the elusive will-o'-the-wisp idea that men should somehow be brothers, that human life was the basis of all true values. 'So why was he shot, Mr Scobart?'

'It was a mistake,' Scobart said.

'An accident, you mean?'

'Not an accident. A mistake.' The last of many mistakes. And the worst. How long did it take to line a man up in the sights of a rifle and squeeze the trigger? A couple of seconds? Less, probably. But that was only the punch line. The tragic joke which led up to it had been three months in the telling.

'What are you trying to tell us, Scobart?' Hobey said quietly.

'The bullet was meant for Gatley, not the Adjutant.'

'Ah,' Hobey said. 'I see. You're quite sure of that, are you?'

'I am, sir.'

'Mmm.' Hobey looked up at Frant. But it was no use asking him. The M.O. was stationed at El Fard, visited the MU only for a morning surgery once every ten days. Fortunately for Roper, today had been one of them. 'And the man who made this mistake – d'you know who he is?'

'No, sir, I don't,' Scobart said, his voice flat, his eyes hostile.

You're lying, Hobey thought. You know damned well who it is. 'I think you'd better tell us something about what's been going on up here,' he said. 'There'll obviously have to be an inquiry – statements taken, records examined, all that official bull.' And a verdict reached and the necessary action taken. 'But we might as well start fitting the pieces together while they're still clear in your mind.'

Scobart shook his head. 'I'm not really the man to ask. Squadron Leader March . . .'

134

'Will make his own contribution in due course,' Hobey said. And thought: Assuming he survives that bit of nastiness up the road. 'Meanwhile I'd like to hear what you have to say.' It was standard operational procedure in this sort of situation. Only one man had a foot either side of the barrier between officers and ORs. The SWO. 'Off the record, naturally.'

'Yes.' Scobart lit a cigarette, sucked the smoke down into his lungs, held it for a moment and then exhaled. 'Off the record, then. Wing Commander Gatley is a walking disaster.' Had been from the minute he stepped out of the pick-up, done up like a dog's dinner, back there on the first Tuesday in August.

Roper met him at the station and brought him back to HQ in the old Ford pick-up Hammond had salvaged from the desert for his own personal use. Fifteen hundred hours on an August afternoon and the sun like a polished brass lid clamped down over the compound. Scobart saw him get out of the little truck and mount the steps of the veranda outside Roper's office. In spite of the heat, Gatley was in full parade dress: khaki drill tunic, shirt and slacks, black tie, black shoes, belt and holstered pistol. Through the close-mesh fly-screening on the Orderly Room door he looked a little like Wavell; the same quick, short-legged walk, the same jerky movements of the head. But without Wavell's presence, without his panache.

Scobart nipped out his cigarette, stood up and put on his forage cap. 'Harps at the high port, Corporal Vince,' he said. 'God has arrived.'

Alec Vince twisted round in his chair; a fresh-faced man, two months past his twenty-second birthday, neat, pleasant, intelligent. Too intelligent for his rank. But there was no establishment at 87 for an Orderly Room Sergeant. 'Already?' he said, surprised. 'So what happened to the tea-party in the Mess?'

135

'Looks like he stood 'em up,' Scobart said.

'Umm. Bit on the small side, isn't he?'

Scobart smiled his hard, Brasso-and-blanco smile. 'It's the small ones you want to watch out for, son. If there's one thing worse than a big bastard it's a little bastard.'

Vince grinned. Scobart was six feet one, bullet-headed, iron-hard, with a voice like a slide trombone. He had come up through the ranks and done his time up the blue. And it showed.

Scobart watched as Gatley stood talking to Roper, hearing the murmur of their voices without being able to distinguish the words. Then Roper saluted and went into his office. Gatley stood a moment or two longer, his right thumb hooked into his belt over his stomach as he surveyed the compound. It was an oddly Napoleonic stance, rather mannered in so small a man. Then he turned and walked down the veranda towards the Orderly Room.

Scobart stepped forward and whipped open the door a split-second before Gatley's hand touched it. 'Good afternoon, SIR,' he said, the slide of the trombone fully extended. He produced his famous C.O.-on-parade salute, heels snapped together, stomach pulled in.

Gatley acknowledged it, squinting up under the peak of his hat, his mind checking quickly down the nominal roll he had memorised in the train. 'Mr Scobart, isn't it?' he said approvingly. He liked big smart men whom he out-ranked.

'Sir. And this is Corporal Vince, Orderly Room Clerk.'

Gatley nodded to Vince who was now standing by his chair. Behind him on the table sheets of paper were laid out neatly. 'I'm glad to see not everybody's lounging about over tea and cakes,' Gatley said. 'Daily Routine Orders?'

136

'Yes, sir. I'm just getting ready to type the stencils,' Vince said.

A pleasant voice, Gatley noted. Unmilitary, educated. Probably called up between Grammar School and University. A useful man who would need to be kept in his place. 'Good,' he said. 'Before you finalise them check with the Adjutant. He has something to go in.'

'I already have his notes, sir.'

'I think you'll find there's more,' Gatley said smoothly. 'Now.'

'Sir.'

Gatley smiled, a thin, humourless smile, sharp as an opened tin. 'I'm a creature of habit, Vince, as you'll discover. I like to go into my office before breakfast, read through the DROs and initial them for publication. You will oblige me by ensuring they are ready on my desk at 07.00 hours every morning. EVERY morning. Understood?'

'Sir.'

'Good.' Gatley looked round the office approving its neatness, feeling suddenly at home for the first time since leaving the UK. 'Well, carry on Vince. Mr Scobart, perhaps you will accompany me?'

'Sir.' Scobart opened the door and followed Gatley out on to the veranda. He fell into step beside him, shortening his stride. 'Vince is a first class man, sir. Very genned-up. Conscientious, too.'

Gatley nodded. 'I had already formed that impression, Mr Scobart. I trust closer acquaintance will confirm it.'

Scobart's mouth tightened. Why make a production of it? Hammond would just have said, 'Wizard type', and left it at that.

'You what?' The telephone emphasised March's flat, Bradford vowels, underlined the indignation in his voice.

'I'm sorry, Bob,' Roper said. 'The little man wants to play soldiers apparently.'

'Does he, by God? What's he like, Dave?'

'Keen,' Roper said, making it an insult. 'He's come to win the bloody war. If necessary single-handed.'

'Damn. Like that, is he?'

'Probably brushes his teeth to numbers.' Roper could hear a gramophone playing in the background. The Andrews sisters belting out 'Jack of all Trades.' He visualised the Mess with its comfortable chairs and the table laid for the special welcome tea they had planned. Sandwiches, some of Ryder's cordon bleu scones, jam, a cake.

March said, 'Damn it, Dave. We're all standing round here like mourners at a wake with no bloody corpse. Can't you sort of steer him in this direction?'

'No, I can't,' Roper said irritably. His office was like an oven under its corrugated iron roof. 'He wants the mountain to come to Mahomet.'

'But what the hell for?'

'I don't honestly know. But I suspect a pep-talk.'

'Bloody hell. Didn't you tell him about the party?'

'Oh, yes,' Roper said bitterly. 'I told him.'

'And?'

'He doesn't think we'll beat Hitler by holding tea-parties in the middle of the afternoon.'

'Hitler?' March said. 'What the hell's he got to do with it? This is Marazag not the bloody Falaise Gap.'

Somebody turned the record over. The sisters oozed into 'The Shrine of St Cecilia'.

'Look,' Roper said. 'I know it's a bind, but just get over here, will you? Please. After less than half an hour of his company I've had friend Gatley in small and grisly lumps.'

'That sounds like a Mayday. Is it?'

'You're damned right it is.'

March chuckled. 'Don't panic. Help is at hand.'

138

'Thanks, Bob. He wants everybody, remember.'

'Roger,' March said. 'If that's what he wants, that's what he'll bloody get. God help him.'

Gatley walked past the Signals Office towards the Armoury with its heavy wooden door and the shutters folded back beside the window. Scobart knew Lever was in there watching. Hank Lever, Sergeant Armourer; twenty-nine and already grey, thin as a pull-through, smelling of gun oil. Hank who was a loner; who lived and worked in conditions of almost clinical hygiene, every weapon racked in its place, every gleaming round accounted for; who sat at his bench in a pair of bleached overalls, endlessly stripping and cleaning and re-assembling his guns on a piece of oiled silk. Now if Gatley went in there . .

But Gatley turned right and walked on towards the MT office. He glanced up at Scobart and smiled slyly as if guessing the SWO's thoughts. 'Not the Armoury,' he said in his prim, precise voice. 'I'll look in there later. Tomorrow, perhaps. I'm sure it'll be in apple-pie order.'

'Always is, sir. Sergeant Lever runs his section like an operating theatre.'

'Precisely.' Gatley stopped just short of the MT office. 'It's my experience that if you want an accurate indication of a unit's status you skip the Signals and the Armoury and go for the MT. If that's satisfactory everything else is likely to be on the top line. Am I right?'

'Fair comment, sir,' Scobart said. So, he thought, not just a little bastard. A clever little bastard.

On any RAF station the Motor Transport section tended to be scruffy. Efficient but scruffy. It was regretted but accepted; a fact of Service life. Drivers and fitters were a separate breed, independent, exercising considerable power. They brought in the rations and the mail, which meant they controlled morale. Without them everything would be paralysed; stores would not move, men would not eat, aircraft would be grounded. They knew this. They were poorly paid, lived in oil-stained overalls and did a dirty, often monotonous job with irregular hours. But they were indispensable. Excused all parades and guard duties, they were there to keep the trucks rolling, the unit operational. So long as they did that most people were not too worried about appearances. Hammond certainly had not been. But Gatley was not Hammond.

Scobart pushed open the door of the MT office and stood aside. Gatley went in.

The office was long and narrow and smelled of stale tobacco smoke. There were a few old bucket seats salvaged from scrapped vehicles, a small table and a metal filing cabinet. Cigarette-ends littered the floor and clustered in the sand of the fire buckets. A clutch of battered enamel mugs stood on a wooden bench beside the filing cabinet with a primus, a packet of tea, a bag of sugar and an open tin of condensed milk on which flies were feeding. The whitewashed walls were grubby, papered with servicing charts, standing orders, duty rosters and an eye-catching display of pin-ups and nudes cut out of magazines bought under the counter on leave trips to Cairo. Other sections had their pin-up galleries but none of them featured girls with breasts so large and bottoms so rounded as those on the walls of the MT office. Scobart saw Gatley stiffen and grinned to himself. A clever little puritanical bastard, then.

Jack Smart, Flight Sergeant MT, was perched on the edge of the table with his back to the door, talking over the phone to one of his fitters in the workshops up in the main compound by the railhead. ' ... don't give a monkey's how you do it, mate,' he was saying. 'Just bloody do it and get a bloody iggeri on. I need that gharry first thing in the morning and...' He listened for

140

a moment or two. 'Well, that's your bad luck, mate. You've been arsing around up there like a gelded camel for the last two days. Sort it out and sort it out a bit sharpish or I'll have you on a fizzer and up in front of the new C.O. so fast your feet won't touch.' He slammed the phone down, picked up a mug of tea and drank noisily.

Scobart cleared his throat. Smart looked round unhurriedly, grinned and eased himself off the table. He was small and wiry in khaki overalls open to the waist, scuffed desert boots and an elaborately-tooled leather belt with a massive silver buckle. The belt was a gift from the pilot of an American Liberator who had been stranded in a jeep with a blocked fuel pipe in the middle of the night on the Cairo/Alex road until Smart had come barrelling out of the darkness in a five-ton Crossley and fixed it for him.

Smart wore no shirt under his overalls and his chest was bony, the sternum prominent. His face was sharp beneath a widow's peak of lank, black hair, thick eyebrows meeting over a broken nose, the mouth wide and not unfriendly, the eyes dark and small and quick. Before the war he had been in the secondhand car trade, operating on a patch of waste ground in south London, fixing not selling, working on whatever came in, asking no questions about swapped number plates and suspiciously new log books. Cars were his passion. Engines, gearboxes, prop-shafts, differentials – he knew them as a surgeon knows the human body, talked to them the way some men talk to horses, cursing them as he cherished them.

'Afternoon, gents,' he said cheerfully. 'Just in time for a cuppa.'

Behind Gatley, Scobart frowned warningly. He liked Smart. Foul-mouthed, damn-your-eyes, let's-get-stuck-into-the-bastard Smart whose approach to life was like that of a hopeful mongrel living a day at a time in a hostile world where kicks and juicy bones arrived unpredictably and without logic. Liked him, admired his skill, relished his cheerful profanity – and despaired of his total disregard of protocol, his cavalier attitude to rank.

'Jack knows his job,' Hammond had said once when Smart had slouched past with a casual nod, hands deep in the pockets of his overalls. 'That's all that matters.' But Scobart doubted Gatley would agree. He said carefully, 'This is our new C.O., Flight. Wing Commander Gatley.' And to Gatley, 'Flight Sergeant Smart, sir.'

'Smart?' Gatley said coldly. He pursed his lips. 'His appearance belies his name. But it certainly matches this – this pig-sty.' He picked up one of the mugs off the bench. The inside was stained dark brown. He looked at Smart, speaking directly to him for the first time. 'You expect me to drink out of this?' He dropped the mug on the floor.

Smart scowled. 'Not now I don't.'

'Sir,' Gatley said.

'Sir.'

'And these cigarette-ends.' Gatley tapped one of the buckets with the toe of his shoe. 'Fire buckets, Flight Sar'nt. Fire buckets. Not ashtrays.' He looked slowly round the office. 'Filthy. The place is filthy. A shambles.' His eyes flickered over the pin-ups. 'Disgusting.'

Smart shrugged. 'End of the day, see?'

'That's no excuse.'

Smart's eyes narrowed, the line of his jaw hardened. 'I'm not making excuses. I'm telling you why. First thing in the morning when the chico's done his stuff you could eat your breakfast off this floor. But by the end of the day it's ...'

'Not good enough,' Gatley said curtly. 'Clean up as you go along. That's my way.'

142

'Yeah? Well, it won't work here. We're not on some bullshitting Blighty training base. We've got more to do here than ponce about with floor bumpers and feather dusters every five minutes. The chico looks after that side of things. His job, not ours.'

'The what?' Gatley said.

Scobart said quickly, 'Native boy, sir. All the sections have them. They do odd jobs. Make the tea. Sweep up.'

'Do they?' Gatley said. 'Do they indeed?' He turned back to Smart. 'How many men in your section, Flight Sar'nt?'

'Twenty drivers. Four fitters and a couple of u/t mechanics,' Smart said, paused and added, 'Sir.'

Gatley nodded. 'Very well. In future they will be responsible for keeping this office tidy. You can do without native labour. Understood?'

'No, sir,' Smart said levelly, his eyes angry.

Hell's bells, Jack, Scobart thought. Take it easy. You'll give the little squit a heart attack in a minute. Can't you see he's round the twist? Has to be. No senior officer in his right mind would get himself into this position, arguing the toss with an NCO about something as trivial as a dirty floor. Would he?

Gatley drew himself up. 'Now you listen to me, Smart. And listen good. If you think I'm making a suggestion you're very much mistaken. I'm giving you a direct order.'

'I understand that,' Smart said. 'What I don't understand is how you expect me to obey it. I'm five drivers under strength for a start. And with the sort of clapped-out heaps I'm supposed to keep on the road I could use another three fitters at least. If I've got to detail men every day to tart this place up for ...'

'If they have time to sit around smoking and drinking tea,' Gatley said, 'they've got time to clean up. Right?'

Smart shook his head wearily. 'You still haven't got

143

the message, have you? Nobody's sitting around are they? Why? Because they're too bloody busy, that's why. They dodge in here between trips, grab a mug of chai and a fag and belt out again. You can't expect 'em to ...'

'I can,' Gatley said. 'And I do.'

Smart shrugged. 'OK. If you want the whole bloody shooting-match to grind to a halt while we blanco the cobwebs and hang net curtains over the windows ...'

'I'll tell you what I want, Smart. I want an immediate apology from you. Your appearance is disgraceful, your language appalling and your manner little short of insolent.' He stared fixedly at Smart, his eyes very bright, his mouth quivering. 'Well? I'm waiting.'

Smart hesitated, shrugged and said, 'OK. I apologise.'

'Sir.' Gatley's voice was almost shrill. 'You will address me as Sir.'

'Sir,' Smart said grudgingly.

Gatley nodded, tight-lipped. 'Thank you. Your apology is accepted. This time. Meanwhile I'm putting this office out-of-bounds to all MT personnel as of now and until further notice. Is that clear? They can use it to book their vehicles in and out and collect their orders. And that's all.'

'You can't do that,' Smart said angrily. 'My lads work their guts out to keep this unit operational and they need a place to ...'

'When I'm satisfied they're able and willing to make this office presentable I'll review the situation. Until then it's out-of-bounds.' Gatley looked up at Scobart. 'See that goes in DROs, Mr Scobart.'

'Don't bother,' Smart said scornfully. 'I'll tell 'em myself. I don't hide behind bits of bloody paper.'

'In DROs, Mr Scobart,' Gatley said. He turned back to Smart. 'And get these obscene pictures off the walls. And for God's sake, man, put a shirt on. Naked women

144

and half-naked men – you're supposed to be running an MT section not a brothel.'

Smart stood rigid with anger, his fists bunched at his sides, his face thunderous under those heavy black brows. 'Is that all?' he said thickly.

Scobart felt the tension rise like the mercury in a thermometer. He knew he had to get Gatley outside quickly before there was real trouble. Court martial trouble. Smart was strung up tight as a piano wire, needed only one more injudicious word to snap his control and explode him into action.

'I believe so,' Gatley said calmly. 'For the moment, at least.' He turned towards the door. Scobart pulled it open, relieved.

Smart said wickedly, 'I see. Sir.' The sibilants splintered like a bottle broken for a fight.

Gatley's shoulders stiffened. He swung round, red spots of anger burning in his cheeks. 'Something on your mind, Flight Sar'nt?' He smiled unpleasantly. 'Something you want to tell me?'

And that's the red alert, Jack, Scobart thought. So watch it, mate. Back off, for God's sake.

'Isn't that what you came in for?' Smart said. 'For me to tell you something about how the section's coping, what the problems are?'

'I've seen all I need to see,' Gatley said.

Smart's lip curled. 'You've seen nothing. Sweet F.A. When Wings Hammond came in here he got down to basics. Vehicle status. Spares availability. How the men were bearing up. Morale, not morals, that was his line.' He shook his head disgustedly. 'All you seem to be interested in is a bit of dust and a few fag-ends.'

'All right, Smart,' Gatley said. 'I'll spell it out for you. This once. Never again. I'm interested in seeing this section run in an airmanlike manner. And that includes keeping this office fit for inspection at all times. A clean office is an efficient office. An efficient office means an efficient NCO. And an efficient NCO means an efficient section. Now, have I made myself absolutely clear?'

Smart looked past him at Scobart, saw the plea in the SWO's eyes, the quick, urgent shake of his head. His eyes met Gatley's mockingly. 'I hear you. Sir.'

Gatley nodded. 'Very well. See to it, then.'

'Where are we supposed to meet him?' March said. He sat in Roper's office with his hat pushed back on his head and his shirt sleeves rolled up, the hairs on his arms damp with sweat. He had a green and white polka-dot bandana knotted loosely round his neck and his eyes were sharp with annoyance.

Roper shrugged. 'I dunno, Bob. In his office, I suppose.'

'Oh, come on, Dave, get a grip. There's fifteen of us, damn it. How are we all going to pack in there, for God's sake?'

'Unless he plans to see us one at a time.'

'While the rest of us kick our heels on the veranda?' March's eyebrows rose. 'It's not on, old son. It's just not on.' He looked at his watch. 'In about five minutes from now the trucks'll start rolling in from the stores compound. There'll be a couple of hundred bods milling about out there gawping at us. How's that going to look, eh? Every bloody officer in the unit lined-up outside that office like a bunch of naughty boys waiting to see the headmaster. Good God, man, it's tough enough trying to keep this dump running smoothly without that sort of carry-on.'

Roper said, 'I've already organised that. I've rung main stores and told 'em to hold the trucks for half an hour.'

'Oh, great,' March said. 'That'll really cheer the troops up, won't it?'

'OK,' Roper said irritably. 'You're acting C.O. – or have been. See what you can do with him. I've done my

146

best to make him see sense. But it's like talking to a damned teleprinter.'

March shook his head. 'Talking's a waste of time with a type like that. Five minutes behind the Armoury with no badges of rank and no witnesses and I'd sort the bastard out, no problem.'

Roper grinned wry-faced. 'I know, Bob. But it's not that simple, is it? We've got to live with the bloody man.'

'Something wrong, Mr Scobart?' Gatley said.

The SWO was staring across the compound at the officers grouped outside Roper's office. 'I don't know, sir. The officers ...'

'My orders,' Gatley said smugly.

'Sir?'

'And I was right, wasn't I? About the MT office?'

'I know how it must look,' Scobart said carefully. 'But Smart knows his job. He tends to do things his own way, of course. And he doesn't mince his words. But ...'

'No. He doesn't, does he?'

'He gets results,' Scobart said.

'Does he?' Gatley said. 'Well, from now on things on this unit will be done only one way, Mr Scobart. My way.'

'Sir.'

'And that goes for everbody – officers, NCOs and ORs. Understood?'

'Understood, sir.'

Gatley nodded, standing on the edge of the veranda, thumb hooked in his belt in that curiously mannered stance. 'Right,' he said briskly. 'I'll have the officers fallen-in please.'

Scobart looked shocked. 'You want me to parade them, sir?'

'I do.'

'Here?'

147

'Here.'

Scobart swallowed. 'With respect, sir, is that wise?'

'I propose to address them. Introduce myself.'

'On parade? Now?' Scobart said.

Gatley looked at him sharply. 'What's the matter, Mr Scobart. D'you want me to put it in writing?'

'No, sir.' Scobart hesitated. 'It's not for me to say, of course, but wouldn't it be more – er – appropriate to do that informally in the Mess before dinner?'

'No,' Gatley said. 'It's not for you to say. And no, it would not be more appropriate in the Mess. I'm taking command of this unit, not indulging in a fireside chat over a glass of sherry.'

'Sir.'

'Fall them in below the veranda outside my office. My compliments to the Adjutant and ask him to join me here.'

'Sir,' Scobart said, his face a mask of disbelief. He saluted and marched himself off down the veranda, the tap of his heels on the concrete as ominous as a drum-beat at an execution by firing squad.

148

2

'He did that?' Hobey said incredulously. 'Paraded the officers?'

Scobart nodded. 'And inspected them.' They had come as they were, casually dressed for the welcome tea party in the Mess: slacks tucked into suede ankle-boots, off-white safari jackets, bleached shirts, bright bandanas. Only Gatley had been properly dressed for a parade. He had walked grimly along the ranks with an embarrassed Roper beside him, glared at each affronted face, mounted the veranda, tucked his thumb into his belt in that curious gesture they were to see so often and told them they were a disgrace to the Service.

'What else did he say?' Hobey's voice was hard.

Scobart hesitated. 'D'you know Wing Commander Gatley, sir? I mean, have you met him personally?'

Hobey shook his head.

Scobart looked at Frant. 'You have, sir, of course.'

'A couple of times only,' Frant said and smiled apologetically. 'I've usually managed to keep out of his way.' Like most M.O.s he was more doctor than RAF officer, concerned with the patient's health, not his rank.

Scobart nodded. 'Well, it's not so much what he says. It's the way he says it.' The earnest, defensive face, the wintry smile, the prim, self-righteous voice, the total lack of humour ...

* * *

Scobart stood the parade at ease, took up his position outside the right marker and listened with mounting dismay as Gatley began to speak.

'Isolation demands extra effort ... Example is the first duty of an officer ... Difficult circumstances exist to strengthen, not weaken, morale ... Slackness is an infection, discipline the only known cure ...' The worn clichés were trotted out with absolute conviction as though they were freshly-minted coins of wisdom. 'Noblesse oblige ... Privilege of rank means responsibility ... Firm leadership is the secret of efficiency; efficiency the secret of success ...' It was like watching a man digging his own grave with the spade of rhetoric.

Scobart bit his lip. You could talk like this to young cadets fresh from their school ATCs. But not to men like March and Roper, officers with a lot of service under their belts. You couldn't flannel them with high-sounding phrases out of the training manual. He heard the snarl of a truck engine, turned his head slightly and saw the first of the troop carriers roll in through the main gate. It swung round in a haze of dust to park with its front bumper a foot from the cinema wall. The men began to climb down over the tailgate as the second truck lumbered in.

Five minutes later, Gatley was still speaking, struggling to be heard above the growl of the trucks grinding through the gate in low gear. By now the compound was full of men in dirty, sweat-stained overalls staring at the officers in astonished amusement. Scobart heard their laughter and felt his face go hot. He looked quickly along the line of officers, snapped to attention and took a pace forward. 'Sir. Permission to dismiss the parade, sir.'

Gatley glared down at him. 'Permission refused, Mr Scobart. I haven't finished yet.'

'But sir, the men are ...'

'Be quiet,' Gatley snapped, his face as white as the knuckles of his hand gripping his belt.

Scobart stood like a stone, mouth clamped shut, his eyes bleak. Behind him, March broke ranks and walked forward, head up, heavy shoulders set. He stopped beside Scobart and looked up at Gatley. 'The SWO is only trying to do his job,' he said. 'Since you won't let him, I'll do it for him.'

'You will return to your place,' Gatley said shrilly. 'I have not yet finished what I . . .'

'You've finished,' March said and turned his back on the C.O. 'Parade.' The deep, broad-vowelled voice boomed across the compound. In an instant the watching men stood still and silent. 'Parade, atten-shun. Dee-is-miss.'

The officers turned smartly to the right, fell out and began to walk across to the wicket gate. March nodded to Scobart. 'Thank you, Mr Scobart. Get the men into their billet, will you?' He returned the SWO's salute, swung round to face Gatley on the veranda, saluted him and said with a kind of polite contempt, 'We look forward to your company at dinner, sir.' And he turned on his heel and walked away and left him standing there.

'An unfortunate beginning,' Hobey said, secretly appalled, careful not to show it.

Scobart looked at him bitterly. Unfortunate my arse, he thought. It was a bloody catastrophe.

'Not the first man to get off on the wrong foot, of course,' Hobey said tentatively, feeling his way.

'Sir,' Scobart said, not helping him.

'Everybody makes mistakes, Mr Scobart. We're none of us perfect.'

'No, sir,' Scobart said. So that's the way we're going to play it, is it? he thought. Forgive and forget. Seven days jankers all round to put the record straight. And

151

a cushy Cairo posting for Gatley with a bit of promotion thrown in. The classic closing of the ranks. He had seen it happen before. 'But some of us learn from our mistakes.'

'What are you trying to tell me, Mr Scobart?' Hobey's eyes were cold slits in the swollen mask of his face, his voice sharp with warning.

Scobart lit another cigarette, blew out the match and shook his head. 'We tried, sir,' he said. 'The Adjutant, Mr March, all of us. We really tried to back him up.'

Hobey nodded. 'Yes, I'm sure you did.'

'We realised he was – well, a bit out of his depth. Straight off the boat and into the chair. And everything new and different. Like the Adjutant said, it was down to us to help him all we could.' Scobart sucked at his cigarette, coughed out smoke. 'Trouble was, he wouldn't let us. Help him, I mean. We could see what was happening. See the unit starting to fall apart. The men brassed-off with all the bull and the jankers and the never-ending pep talks and that damned stupid training course he dreamed up. But every time we tried to sort of steer him round the dodgy bits he just shot us down in flames.' He shook his head moodily. 'I dunno, sir. It seemed like he thought listening to a bit of advice – a suggestion or two – would somehow undermine his authority.'

'Yes,' Hobey said. 'I see.'

'With respect, sir, any fool could have seen,' Scobart said. But Gatley was not a fool. Foolish, but not a fool. A fool you could ignore. Walk over. You couldn't do that with Gatley. 'But he didn't. Didn't see a damned thing.' It had been like talking to a blind man. And not just talking. Actions were supposed to speak louder than words. But even when it was put on a plate and shoved in front of his nose, Gatley hadn't seen it.

Scobart stubbed out his cigarette. 'You'll not have heard about the pick-up, sir?'

152

Hobey shook his head.

'A Saturday, it was,' Scobart said. 'Three weeks after he came.'

That Saturday began rather well. The weekly C.O.'s parade Gatley had instituted had showed a marked improvement, the bearing of the men brisker, their general turn-out smarter. Walking down between the ranks in open order he had instructed Scobart to take the names of only four men. Two weeks before it had been twenty-two.

He stood on the veranda outside his office, an oddly insignificant figure in spite of his immaculate uniform, and watched the men pack into the trucks for the morning's work in the main compound. Watched with approval and the beginnings of pride. They still had a long way to go to meet his standards but the signs were there now. They were quieter, more disciplined, cleaner. Another month, he thought, and they'll be a credit to me. It never occurred to him that their quietness was sullen, their briskness striated with resentment.

As the last three-tonner swung out through the gate he noticed Lever lounging in the doorway of the Armoury, arms folded, shoulders wedged comfortably against the doorpost. Gatley bit his lip. He was getting nowhere with Lever. There was a sardonic self-sufficiency about the man he found disconcerting; a laconic expertise he detested. Lever and Smart were two of a pair, the one clean the other dirty, the one taciturn to the point of insolence the other too free with his tongue. But both of them loners, both of them somehow beyond his reach. And that worried him. They were key men in the unit and they despised him. He knew that without being able to understand it. And found it disturbing.

He glared across at the sergeant, willing him to look at him. Lever unfolded his arms and stood up straight.

153

He pulled out a packet of cigarettes, selected one unhurriedly, put it between his lips and lit it. Gatley turned abruptly and went into his office.

Scobart always had a mug of tea laced with a little rum after morning parade. He was sipping it gratefully in his office when the phone rang. He lifted the receiver. 'SWO.'

'Gatley here.' The C.O.'s voice buzzed like a wasp in Scobart's ear. 'I'm right, am I not, in thinking you are responsible for discipline on this unit?'

Hell's teeth, Scobart thought. Here we go again. 'Sir.'

'Then perhaps you can explain to me why Sar'nt Lever is loafing about on the veranda, smoking?'

Because he can't bloody smoke in the Armoury, Scobart thought. He said, 'I didn't know he was, sir.'

'It's your job to know these things.'

'Sir.'

'I can't carry the whole damned unit on my shoulders, Mr Scobart. I do have other things to do besides
. . .'

'I'm sorry, sir,' Scobart said, but his voice was irritated not apologetic. He recognised the speech, had heard it before too many times in the last three weeks. 'I'll have a word with him.'

'You do that,' Gatley said thinly. 'If he's got time on his hands I can very quickly find something to occupy him. Not necessarily to his liking.'

Like Orderly Sergeant for a week, Scobart thought. OK, I've got the message. 'I'll go and see him now, sir.'

'No, Mr Scobart, you will not. You will send Corporal Vince to instruct Lever to report to you immediately.'

'As you wish, sir,' Scobart said, controlling his anger. 'Though knowing Sergeant Lever, he's probably got everything organised and on the top line.'

154

'That's no excuse. A good NCO can always find something to keep him busy.'

Here endeth the first bloody lesson, Scobart thought.

'See to it, will you?' Gatley said.

'Sir.'

'Thank you. We'll inspect the airmen's billets in ten minutes. If that won't incovenience you?'

Scobart scowled at the sarcasm. 'I'll be there, sir.' He put the phone down abruptly. Saturday morning, for God's sake, he thought. Doesn't the little bastard ever let up? This is supposed to be an MU not the bloody Glasshouse.

Sitting at his table, Gatley took the top folder out of his IN tray, opened it and began to read. The neatly-typed page soothed him. The formal report was satisfyingly impersonal, slotting tidily into his mind, drawing him into a world he knew and understood. When the phone rang he reached for it impatiently. 'Gatley.'

The LAC switchboard operator heard the sharpness in his voice and grinned. 'Wing Commander Bisset's on the line from 90 MU, sir.'

'Put him through.'

'Morning, old boy. Just about on your way, are you?' Bisset said.

'I'm sorry?' Gatley said coolly. He disliked hearty men who called him old boy.

'I take it you'll be flying down from El Fard. If you give me your ETA Devasoir I'll lay on transport.'

Gatley said, 'What's all this about, Bisset? I've got a rather full morning in front of me and ...'

'On Saturday?' Bisset laughed. 'Now pull the other one, old boy. I say, you did get my note, didn't you?'

'Note?'

'Inviting you down for the weekend. Spot of sailing. Bit of swimming. And a good old-fashioned thrash in

155

the Mess tonight. I mean, you are coming, aren't you, old boy?'

'No,' Gatley said. 'I'm afraid not. Thank you.'

'Oh,' Bisset said. 'That's a damned shame. Tarrant's on his way. And Blake from Kasfareet. I thought we could've ...'

'Sorry,' Gatley said. 'Count me out.'

'I see.' Bisset's voice was suddenly hard. 'You got yourself a Pack Up or something equally bloody?'

'No.'

'You did get my note?'

'Yes.'

'But you've been too damned busy to answer?'

'I'm sorry. I didn't think you'd expect an answer.' The note had been a casual, come-if-you-can-old-boy invitation he had thrown straight into his wastepaper basket and forgotten.

'And you're not coming?' Bisset said.

'I've only been here five minutes, damn it,' Gatley said.

'I know, old boy. That was rather the idea. A bit of a get-together with some of your fellow C.Os. Welcome to the club and all that bull.'

'I'm sorry. I've got too much to do to take time off for non-essential junketings.'

'I see,' Bisset said quietly.

Gatley flushed. 'There is a war on, Bisset.'

'Yes? Sorry to hear that, old boy. Damned inconvenient. If it's still raging Monday morning and you need any help to repel the enemy hordes be sure to let me know, eh?' Bisset said and rang off.

Gatley put the phone down. His hands were trembling and he clasped them on his desk, locking his fingers tensely. These damned aircrew bods. Who the hell did they think they were with their old boy superiority and their damned country-house weekends in the middle of a war?

156

Scobart knocked on the door and came in, tall, blank faced. 'Ready when you are, sir.'

'What?' Gatley looked up. 'Oh, it's you, Mr Scobart. You've spoken to Lever?'

'Sir.'

Gatley nodded. He stood up and put on his hat. 'Right. Let's go and see if the men are taking my words to heart, shall we?'

The Saturday morning inspection was the highlight of Gatley's week, filed in his mind under the twin headings of DISCIPLINE and WELFARE. He saw it as being an expression of his concern for the men in his charge; a practical concern made doubly necessary by the cramped nature of their living quarters which he privately considered appalling. It never crossed his mind that his manner, his obsession with detail and his refusal to make allowances made them resent it. And if it had he would have dismissed it out of hand.

Scobart held the door open for him and he walked down the veranda steps on to the sand. The pick-up he had inherited from Hammond was parked in the shade behind his office. He paused for a moment to look at it with pride. The once-battered and shabby little truck had been completely transformed. The engine and gearbox had been stripped and rebuilt, the dented panels in the bodywork expertly beaten out, the whole vehicle re-sprayed in airforce blue. A large roundel had been stencilled on the bonnet; another, smaller, one on the tailgate. The floor of the cab had been fitted with black rubber matting and the seats given new covers of white canvas. A white canvas tilt was stretched tautly over the open rear end, roped through gleaming brass eyelets with white sashcord. The tyres glistened under two coats of black tyre paint.

To Gatley it was more than a vehicle; it was a prototype. A model of the MU itself. If the pick-up could be restored, so could the entire unit. It would take a little longer, but it could be done. Would be done. He gave a little nod of satisfaction and walked briskly towards the cinema.

It took him thirty minutes to work his way through the billet. At the end of it he managed a small smile. 'Marginally better this week, I think, Mr Scobart.'

'They've made a real effort, sir. You can see that.' The SWO closed his notebook and slipped it into his hip pocket. The six names Gatley had instructed him to take were, in his view, six too many. The fold in a blanket not quite square, a frayed shoelace, a couple of stray hairs in a hairbrush. This was nit-picking, expected in a training unit for recruits, totally unnecessary here.

'So they should.' Gatley tapped his leg with the fly-swish he had taken to carrying. 'Have Vince prepare the charge sheets. I'll deal with them first thing on Monday morning.'

Just to start the week off right, Scobart thought. He said, 'Is that really necessary, sir?'

'Necessary?' Gatley's smile faded.

'These are very minor faults. I suggest, with respect, you might overlook them, sir.'

'Indeed?'

'There's more than one way to bake a cake, sir. They're good lads and...'

'But only one right way, I think,' Gatley said primly. 'Minor faults, perhaps. But minor faults, unchecked, grow into major ones.'

'Sir.' I tried, Scobart thought. I bloody well tried.

'It's the horseshoe nail syndrome, isn't it?' Gatley said.

'Is it, sir?'

'One small, insignificant nail. But for the want of it everything was lost. Shoe, horse, rider, battle – everything.'

158

Spare me the sermon, Preacher, Scobart thought, his face set and blank.

They were standing on the cinema stage. The curtains and screen had long since been removed and the space occupied by thirty beds, each made up correctly, biscuits neatly stacked, blankets and sheets folded in the regulation sandwich, shaving and cleaning kit laid out on a towel, socks, shirts and spare underwear placed symmetrically, shoes lined up at the foot of each bed.

Below them in the stalls the seats had been ripped out to make room for more beds. A hundred and seventy of them arranged in close-packed rows with narrow aisles between them. Even without the men there it looked impossibly crowded, like a troop-deck. The confusion before breakfast, with two hundred men struggling to dress and make up their beds, would be indescribable.

The balcony had been boarded up to give some privacy to the senior NCOs and a false floor installed, built in broad terraces to take beds and lockers. Behind it, the projection room and the manager's office had been gutted and knocked into one to make the Sergeants Mess. The airmen messed downstairs in what had been the foyer, which they also used as a NAAFI. Washing and toilet facilities were stark, dank, cockroach-infested and minimal.

'It's not the easiest of places to live in, sir,' Scobart said.

'All the more reason to keep it clean and tidy,' Gatley said. He lifted the foot of the nearest bed and let it drop sharply. A small cluster of bugs fell out of the joints in the iron frame. The bugs were everywhere. In the bed frames, the blankets, the woodwork, the cracks in the plastered walls. It was impossible to get rid of them, difficult to keep them in check.

'Time these beds had a blow-lamp on them,' Gatley said.

'Hardly feasible in here, sir. The fire risk's too great.'

Gatley nodded. 'I agree.' He squashed the bugs under his shoe and wrinkled his nose at the smell. 'We'll get the men to take them outside and give 'em a good going over.' He looked with disgust at the smear of blood on the wooden floor of the stage. 'Do it tomorrow morning. 10.00 hours.'

'Tomorrow?' Scobart said, surprised. 'Tomorrow's Sunday.'

Gatley smiled. 'Better the day, better the deed.'

Scobart's mouth tightened. 'Sunday's the men's day off, sir.'

'Thank you. I am aware of that, as it happens.' Gatley looked up at the SWO. 'Damn it, man, do you have to question all my orders?'

'Sir.'

'It's in their own interests, isn't it? And if they do it tomorrow it won't interfere with the work schedules, will it?'

'No,' Scobart said, stony-eyed. Work schedules my arse, he thought. Where the hell d'you think we are? In some bloody Russian factory?

'See Vince puts it in DROs.' Gatley said.

Scobart followed him down off the stage, up between the rows of beds in the stalls and out into the foyer. Gatley turned left and opened the door of the shower room; a small, cramped cell little bigger than a large wardrobe. A concrete floor with a large iron grating set in it. Grey concrete walls. A small, opaque window just below ceiling height in the outer one. Two shower roses protruding from the wooden ceiling. Two taps, waist-high, on opposite walls. It smelled dank and musty, like a disused well. As Gatley opened the door a small tribe of cockroaches scuttled away down the grating.

Gatley frowned. 'We'll have a blitz on this place, too, while we're at it. Plenty of hot water and caustic soda

160

to keep the drain open properly. And a good sluice round with Jeyes fluid. That'll get rid of the cockroaches.'

You must be joking, Scobart thought. The little buggers thrive on the stuff. He said, 'I'm afraid there's no hot water, sir.'

'Then boil some up,' Gatley said. 'There's plenty of dixies in the kitchen.'

'Sir,' Scobart said doubtfully, imagining Street's reaction to half a dozen dixies occupying his calor gas rings. 'What we really need is a new shower block.' It had been Hammond's dream, promised by the planners in Cairo, never materialising.

'Until we get one,' Gatley said, 'we'll make the best of what we have.'

'Sir, there's nearly 250 men in this . . .'

'Thank you, Mr Scobart. I am acquainted with my unit's strength.' He smiled thinly. 'And its weaknesses.' He closed the door and led the way across the foyer into the kitchen.

The kitchen was a narrow room no bigger than a corvette's galley. In it, three cooks were sweating to prepare a meal for NCOs and ORs, working in artificial light with only the pegged-back, fly-screened door for ventilation.

Sergeant Street was in charge; a melancholy man with a pale moon face and myopic, disillusioned eyes. His hair was cropped short, the stubble beaded with sweat. He was bending over a large dixie of potatoes on the calor gas stove, muttering to himself.

'Morning, Sar'nt Street,' Gatley said. 'Everything all right?' His eyes flicked round the hot, steamy room. All the working surfaces were scrubbed clean, the hot-cupboards shining, the pans burnished. He nodded, pleased. The defaulters had been busy. He knew Scobart disapproved of the number of men put on a charge every day. But cookhouses depended on defaulters to keep them up to scratch. The cooks had enough to do preparing the meals.

'Sir,' Street said morosely, mopping his face with a towel. Intruders in his kitchen depressed him, made him nervous.

'What's on the menu today?' Gatley said.

'Soya links, beans, sweet potatoes, rice pudding and jam.' To be eaten in two sittings and washed down with tea in a temperature of a hundred and five.

One of the cooks opened the door of a hot-cupboard to display rows of grilled soya sausages. Gatley peered in. 'Thank you.' He looked round pointedly. 'And where is the menu, Sar'nt?'

'Sir?' Street straightened defensively, blinking sweat out of his eyes.

'The menu,' Gatley said. 'I don't see it displayed anywhere – as it should be.'

No, Street thought. Well, you wouldn't, would you? Seeing as how we haven't put the bloody thing up. He said, 'Sorry about that. We've been a bit pushed this morning. Had a bit of strife with the grill. It's put us behind, like.' Not to mention the flap to get this place bulled-up for you to inspect, he thought. Menu, for Christ's sake. Who needs a bloody menu? They've got eyes in their heads, haven't they? Noses on their faces? They can smell the bloody grub and see what's on their plates without having to read about it. It's not à la carte at the bloody Ritz, damn you.

'We can all make excuses, Sar'nt,' Gatley said in his preacher's voice.

Bloody right, mate, Street thought. But can you make a dinner for a couple of hundred bods in a kitchen the size of a bloody biscuit tin?

'Well?' Gatley said.

'I'll get it done right away, sir.'

'See that you do. I realise you're working under some

162

difficulties in here. But that's no excuse for sloppiness, is it?'

Street glowered at him.

'Is it, Sar'nt?'

'No.'

Hell's teeth, Scobart thought. The man's apologised. What more d'you want? Blood?

'Very well,' Gatley said. He put his hand on the door screen.

Street dipped a ladle into a pan of rice pudding. 'If you'd like to taste it, sir?' Hammond had always done that. Dropped in casually for a mug of special cooks' tea and what he called 'a lick of the pudding spoon'.

Gatley shook his head. 'That's the Orderly Officer's job. Not mine.'

Street and the two cooks exchanged bitter glances. Scobart said quickly, 'Looks smashing, Len. Nice and creamy. I hope you've made enough for seconds?'

Street nodded, recognising the gesture, appreciating it. But why couldn't Gatley have said something like that?

Gatley looked impatiently at his watch. 'If you're quite ready, Mr Scobart? I do have one or two other matters to attend to this morning.'

'Sir.' The SWO followed him out into the alley which ran down between the cinema and the Officers Mess and walked with him through the wicket gate into the compound.

'See that Vince gets on with those charge sheets,' Gatley said. 'If I'm needed I'll be up in the main compound for the rest of the ...' He stopped short, staring at the pick-up, his mouth fallen open. 'What in God's name ...?'

The little truck looked as though it had been parked under a gusher. A thick, black slick of used engine oil obliterated the windscreen, oozed across the sloping bonnet with its red-white-and-blue roundel and dripped

163

slowly down the radiator grille. The off-side cab door hung open, the window black with oil, the door itself streaked and dripping.

Gatley half-ran to the cab and looked inside. There was more oil inside. A lot more. It had been sluiced over the new seat covers and across the instruments on the dashboard. Under the pedals the rubber matting floated half-submerged in a black, viscous pool.

'Bloody hell,' Scobart said softly. Behind the cab the white canvas tilt had been systematically slashed to ribbons and then deluged with oil. The interior was awash with it. Black streaks ran down the metal sides and tailgate, glistened on the tyres, formed little puddles in the sand.

Gatley walked slowly round the truck, white-faced, trembling. He looked across the ruined tilt at Scobart, his eyes wounded.

Scobart shook his head. 'I'm sorry, sir. Damned sorry,' he said gruffly, embarrassed for this insecure, narrow-visioned little man standing forlornly beside his oil-slathered status symbol. Sorry for him and for the sickness of the unit now made brutally plain.

Gatley nodded mutely. He stood bent forward a little, shoulders hunched, fists tightly clenched. Like a man who has just received a stomach wound and is holding himself together waiting for the shock to wear off and the agony to begin. 'Thank you, Mr Scobart.' He licked his lips. 'I was – rather proud of my pick-up.' He took a long breath, closed his eyes for a moment, opened them and straightened his shoulders. 'Right,' he said tautly. 'Get Flight Sar'nt Smart over here, will you.'

Scobart's eyebrows rose. 'Smart? You surely don't think he's responsible for . . .?'

'No,' Gatley said. 'Smart hates my guts. I know that. But he wouldn't get back at me like this.' He shook his head. 'I know who's to blame, Mr Scobart. The native labourers.'

164

'The wogs?' Scobart said. 'You think it was the . . .?'

'Of course. Has to be. It's the only logical explanation.' Gatley's eyes were bleak. 'Mindless vandalism, that's what this is. The work of ignorant hooligans.'

Scobart stared at him in amazed relief. By God, he thought, he really means it. He really is that bloody blind.

'Well?' Gatley said. 'I'm waiting, Mr Scobart.'

'Sir.' Scobart walked across the compound, up the steps of the veranda and into Smart's office. The Flight Sergeant was sitting at his table with the Duty Book opened in front of him. His overalls were reasonably clean and he was wearing a shirt. The floor of the office was still damp from scrubbing. There were no pin-ups on the walls. Smart stood up. 'Morning, SWO. MT office fully operational and ready for inspection. Sir.' He stamped his foot down hard and came elaborately to attention.

'OK, Jack,' Scobart said. 'Never mind the bull. Gatley wants to see you.'

'Bloody hell.' Smart scowled. 'Now what's eating the bastard?'

'You don't know?' Scobart said, watching his face closely.

'Not a clue,' Smart said.

Scobart told him.

'Bugger,' Smart said angrily. 'We sweated blood over that gharry.'

'I know.'

'What a bloody stupid thing to do.'

'Or a shrewd one,' Scobart said. 'It's really hit Gatley where it hurts.'

'Yeh?' Smart grinned. 'Well, that's something, I suppose.' His eyes narrowed. 'Why does he want to see me?'

'Why d'you think?'

165

'Stanna shweir, mate,' Smart said. 'You're not trying to tell me he thinks I did it, are you?'

Scobart shook his head. 'He thinks it was the chicos.'

'Like hell,' Smart said. 'The chicos don't come in on Saturdays. Doesn't he know that yet?'

'If he does, he's forgotten,' Scobart said. 'And God help any bobbing little bastard who reminds him. I'll have his guts for garters.'

'Damn right,' Smart said. 'Least said soonest bloody mended. Sack the chicos and call it quits.'

'And be grateful for small mercies,' Scobart said.

Smart nodded. 'Gatley must be round the twist to put it down to the wogs, though.'

'You don't think it was them?'

'You know damned well it wasn't.'

Scobart nodded. 'So does Gatley, I think. But he can't face the alternative.'

'That one of his own men did it?'

'Yes. I don't think he can live with that – or the implications behind it.'

'Bad luck, mate,' Smart said. 'We've got to.'

'Yes,' Scobart said bleakly. 'I have worked that out for myself.'

'Yeh, SWO. You end up carrying the bloody can. As usual.'

Scobart shrugged. 'That's my job, Jack.' Hammond had put it neatly once over a mug of tea in his office. 'The SWO's a sort of priest,' he had said. 'From the Latin pontifex – a bridge-builder. He builds bridges between officers and men, Mr Scobart. Holds the unit together.' Builds bridges and keeps secrets, Scobart thought now. It had been easy with Hammond. But with Gatley . . .

'So who d'you reckon it was?' Smart said.

'Out of two hundred and fifty? God knows.'

'Not that many,' Smart said. 'It has to be somebody

166

here in the compound. Let's see. The Adjutant, Signals, Vince ...'

'No,' Scobart said.

Smart nodded. 'So that leaves Hank Lever.'

'We don't know that.'

'Has to be Hank. Everybody else is up in the main compound winning the bloody war, damn it.'

'Unless some bod on his day off nipped in through the wicket gate and...'

'No,' Smart said. 'He'd've been spotted.'

'Not necessarily.'

Smart shook his head. 'It's Hank all right. You know how Gatley gets up his nose.'

'His and everyone else's.'

'Yeh, that's true.' Smart thought for a moment. 'Except Vince. Vince likes him.'

'Vince is loyal to his C.O.,' Scobart said in a hard voice. 'Liking doesn't come into it.'

'There you are, then,' Smart said. 'It could be Vince. Gatley gives him a hell of a lot of stick from what I've seen.'

'It wasn't Vince,' Scobart said flatly. 'And Gatley's waiting to see you.'

Smart put on his hat, tilting it over one eye as usual.

'Straighten it, for God's sake,' Scobart said irritably.

Smart grinned and adjusted his hat fractionally. 'I still think it's old Hank, y'know.'

'Think what you like,' Scobart said opening the door. 'But for all our sakes, Jack, keep it to yourself. That's an order.'

They walked back together to the pick-up. Smart looked at it and swore spectacularly.

Gatley nodded grimly. 'For once, Smart, I agree. Not with your disgusting choice of words but with the sentiment behind them.' He looked at his watch. 'We

167

have just over an hour and a half before the men come back for lunch. I want it cleaned up by then.'

Smart shook his head. 'Not a hope of that, sir.' He rubbed his finger in the oil on the bonnet, felt the new paint sludgy underneath. 'We'll have to use heavy detergents to shift this lot. And that'll take most of the paint off too. Which means a complete re-spray, new tilt, new seat covers.' He sucked in his breath noisily. 'There's a week's work here. At least.'

'You're quite sure of that, Flight Sar'nt?'

'Sir.' Smart kicked the tyres angrily. 'These are a write-off, too. Soaked in the bloody stuff. What a bloody, stinking mess.'

'All right,' Gatley said. 'Get a tarpaulin and cover it. All over. Completely, right down to the ground. Nobody else on the unit is to see it like this. Clear?'

'Sir,' Smart said.

'Can it be driven?'

Smart shrugged. 'I'd rather tow it up to the work-shops.'

'But it can be driven?'

'Yeh. I could scrape the worst off the windscreen, drape a groundsheet over the seat and... Yeh, it could be driven.'

'Very well,' Gatley said. 'I want you to drive it out of here tonight. After dark. Say around 20.00.'

Smart looked puzzled. 'You want me to drive it?'

'Yes. You yourself. Nobody else.'

'To the workshops, you mean?'

'No,' Gatley said. 'I'm not prepared to have it standing up there for a week for everybody to see. You will drive it out of town. Take it up the Tira track a couple of miles tonight and burn it.'

Smart and Scobart exchanged startled glances. 'Burn it, sir?' Smart said.

'Yes.' Gatley's face was calm; a sort of white, frozen

calm, the skin tight along the jawline and over the cheekbones. 'It will burn, I take it?'

'Like a bloody bomb,' Smart said.

Gatley nodded. 'That's what I thought.'

Smart said, 'We can fix it, y'know, sir. I mean, it looks a mess now, but it can be fixed. There's no need to...'

'I don't want it fixed, Smart,' Gatley said. 'I want it destroyed. Totally, finally destroyed. Is that clear?'

'Good God,' Hobey said incredulously. 'And is that what you did?'

Scobart nodded. 'I followed Smart with a fifteen-hundredweight. He ran the pick-up off the track into a ditch and we burned it.' It had gone up like a torch, billowing thick black smoke into the night air. They waited until there was nothing left but a tangle of hot, twisted metal and then drove back together in the fifteen-hundredweight. It had been rather like returning from a murder.

'And that was that?' Hobey said.

'Yes,' Scobart said. Vince had typed out the official report to Group HQ stating that the pick-up had been stolen by native labourers and subsequently found as a burned out wreck. Gatley had signed it. And that had been that. But Gatley had learned one lesson. When the C.O. of El Fard presented him with another pick-up a week later (with an apology for its battered, high-mileage condition) he told Smart to put it through the workshops for a mechanical check only. Thereafter he drove it as it was, in shabby brown and yellow camouflage paint with a cracked black tarpaulin tilt and the dents and scrapes in the wings and bonnet untreated.

'But somebody in the unit was laughing?' Hobey said.

Scobart nodded.

169

'Was it Sar'nt Lever?'

'I don't know who it was,' Scobart said.

'You didn't try to find out?'

'No.'

And wouldn't tell me if you had, Hobey thought. He eased his weight in the chair, favouring his heavily-bandaged leg. 'Sensible,' he said. One thing 87 hadn't needed at that stage of the game was an official inquiry with a man – possibly a senior NCO – on a serious charge. 'Water under the bridge, eh?'

Scobart nodded.

Hobey said, 'And after that, did things get a bit easier?'

'They did for a time, yes,' Scobart said. 'He was still riding us on a tight rein, of course, and if anything cropped up he didn't like he was on to it boots and all. But for a week or two – well, he didn't go looking for trouble the way he had before. The lads sensed it, too. They still moaned like hell about the bull, of course. But you expect that. It's like a sort of safety valve.'

'Yes,' Hobey said. 'But it didn't last?'

Scobart shook his head. 'I think he tried, y'know. Really made an effort. But it was always a bit dodgy. A knife-edge. He was playing a part he had no talent for and I knew it wouldn't work. He's too damned honest, y'see. He can't – you know . . .'

'Dissemble?'

'Sir?'

'Hide his feelings.'

'Right. He finds it hard to make allowances. He's got this insecurity thing. That's why he has to go by the book. People think he's just naturally bloody-minded. But it's not that. He goes by the book because it's the only way he knows. And if he tries to ease up – bend the rules a bit – he comes unstuck in a big way.'

He's done that, all right, Hobey thought. Attempted murder and a mutiny. He can't pin that on the wogs and hope to make it stick. He said, 'I see you're a bit of a psychologist, Mr Scobart.'

'No, sir,' Scobart said. 'But I know about men.'

'And Gatley doesn't?'

Scobart shrugged. 'If you'd been in his place, what would you have done?'

'After the pick-up thing?' Hobey grinned, his swollen face creasing painfully. 'I'd have laid on a party for the troops. Got in some decent beer from Cairo. Dug out all available talent and made a night of it. Nothing like a bit of a thrash with people making fools of themselves to get things in perspective.'

Scobart nodded. 'That's what we thought. But it didn't work out like that.'

3

It was the sort of audience comics dream about. Two
hundred and fifty men tanked-up with beer, excited,
uncritical. They crowded together on the rows of beds
in the cinema with the officers in chairs at the front and
Len Street behind the temporary bar under the balcony
at the back. An all-drinking, all-smoking, all-male,
all-ranks get-together with its own special ethos, its
own mystique.

Until Smart walked on to the stage to close the first
half of the programme it had all been innocent and
amateurish. A tenor from the Parachute Store ('Ah,
Sweet Mystery of Life', 'We'll Gather Lilacs', 'Bless this
House'). An overweight, lugubrious Signals corporal
reciting 'Albert and the Lion' in a Birmingham accent.
A wavy-haired LAC from Pay Accounts playing the
'Warsaw Concerto' on the battered old upright with
immense bravura and a rather uncertain left hand. A
conjuror from Works and Bricks who was good with
cards, less successful with a bunch of paper flowers. And
a tall, thin, apologetic Clothing Store sergeant who had
once been told he looked like Jack Buchanan and did a
bit of tap dancing in between the verses of 'Good Night
Vienna'.

But when Smart came on the atmosphere changed to
one of delighted expectancy. He was wearing his Max
Miller outfit – floral-patterned white plus-fours, two-
tone shoes, wide-brimmed white trilby – and he stood

172

centre stage under the spotlight, easy, relaxed, professional, leering at them through the drifting curtains of cigarette smoke.

'Evenin' gents all.' The exaggerated Cockney whine cut through their welcoming applause, gripped them by the throat, held them. 'Lucky to 'ave me at all, you are. Yers. Been 'ere sooner, see? Only – ' he paused, timing it neatly, opening his eyes wide, staring with wicked innocence at Gatley in the middle of the front row – 'only some thievin' wog bastard nicked me motor, didn't he? An' I 'ad to bloody walk it.'

The audience erupted in a roar of laughter. 'Yers,' Smart said bitterly. 'You can laugh. It's all right for you sprogs with white knees and numbers as long as a randy camel's – tail.' And his eyebrows shot up as the laughter crackled round him. 'Nah what 'ave I said, then? Dirty-minded lot. No, but it's all right for you. You 'aven't worked your way through the local talent yet. No you 'aven't, mate. Stop flamin' boastin'. Get yer finger out and yer. . . No, listen now. Listen. I 'ave, see? When I came over they were still diggin' the Suez Canal, weren't they? All the bints in Marazag, I've 'ad 'em. Now I gotter walk all the way to flamin' El Fard to get a new pick-up. No. Wait a bit. Listen to what I'm tellin'. . .' His voice was lost in an explosion of laughter. Only Gatley sat tight-lipped, staring up at him, his eyes frosty.

Smart waved his hand at the bare stage behind him. 'We was goin' to 'ave some proper scenery up 'ere tonight. Ordered it special, we did, from the Old Vic. Only there wasn't no room for it on the boat, see? What with all them kites and tanks bein' shipped out.' He altered his voice, assuming Gatley's prim tone with astonishing accuracy. 'You may not be aware of it, gentlemen, but there is a war on.'

Roper felt Gatley stiffen beside him as the laughter rolled down like a wave. Watch it, Jack, he thought.

173

Enough's enough. Don't push him too far, for God's sake.

'Listen, now. Listen,' Smart said. 'Did you 'ear what Farouk said to Farida when 'er knicker elastic snapped? Out shoppin', they was. Down Sister Street in Alex. An' we all know what sort of shops they 'ave down there. Anyway...'

Roper grinned, relieved. Smart was on safer ground now, picking his way with winks and grimaces through a series of stories, each one outrageously vulgar, some blatantly obscene. But safe.

Sweating under the spotlight, his hat tilted back, his quick, dark eyes flicking shrewdly over the audience, Smart rode their laughter like a surfer, confident, masterly, unstoppable. '... an' the WAAF said, 'Oops, KIT inspection. Sorry.' An' popped 'em back in a bit sharpish.'

He finished with a monologue which started innocuously enough:

> 'There's a little naafi canteen
> on the road to Marazag.
> There's a big one for the Yankees
> further down...'

and worked its way through twenty suggestive verses about the love affair of an airman and a NAAFI girl to the pay-off:

> 'And she murmured, "It's a bastard."
> But it never need have been...'

And he whipped off his hat and pointed it straight at Gatley:

> 'if they'd known there was
> a Preacher in the town.'

The men gave him a standing ovation, whistling and stamping as he stood grinning and bowing, his hat in his hand, his lank black hair plastered to his head, the sweat running down his face.

'Sorry about that, sir,' Roper said as the lights came on for the interval and a queue formed at the bar. 'I'm afraid his humour's a bit on the ripe side.'

'Disgusting,' Gatley said, arms folded, rigid in his chair.

'Oh, quite. Still, you've got to admit he is damned clever the way he puts it over.' Roper looked at March sitting beyond Gatley. 'What d'you think, Bob?'

'Bloody sauce,' March said, grinning. 'But he's good. Bloody good.'

'Filth,' Gatley said. 'Sheer, unadulterated filth. Anywhere else he'd be . . .'

'Yes,' March said quickly. 'But we aren't anywhere else, are we? It's a troop concert, and that's the point. OK, he's a bit smutty. No harm in that once in a while. Helps the men get it out of their systems.'

'I don't agree,' Gatley said. 'The morale of this unit is already . . .'

'Yes, but he's good for morale,' March said. 'Bad for their morals, maybe. But he's a real morale booster is Smart. Like a – whatsaname – catharsis.' He turned in his chair and looked back towards the bar queue. 'Look at 'em. Happy as bloody sandboys. Dirty jokes are a damned good safety-valve. Better than dirty women any day. Ask the M.O. next time he . . .'

'Mens sana in corpore sano, surely?' Gatley said primly.

'I dunno about that,' March said. 'I'd rather have a few dirty minds in healthy bodies than half the unit down with clap. And that's the real alternative, y'know. A couple of hundred chaps in their prime in this

175

dump, living like monks.' He shook his head. 'Something's got to give.'

'I'm sorry. I don't like dirty talk,' Gatley said.

Or people enjoying themselves at your expense, Roper thought. It's not the smut you can't take. It's being on the receiving end of Smart's snide remarks.

Scobart walked in behind the bar, collected a couple of bottles from one of the crates of beer and went into the foyer and out down the alley. The night air was cool on his face, great clouds of insects hazing the lamps above the deserted compound. The sand crunched under his boots. The guard on the main gate stiffened, watching him warily. Scobart went up on to the veranda and into the Orderly Room. Vince was sitting at the table, working.

'Still at it?' Scobart said.

Vince looked up. He looked tired. Neat, as always, but tired. 'Somebody's got to mind the shop.'

'Your idea? Or Gatley's?' Scobart said. And added quickly, 'OK, Don't answer that.' He knocked the caps off the bottles on the edge of the table and passed one to Vince. 'Get this down you, lad.'

'Thanks. Cheers.'

'Cheers.' Scobart took a big swallow of beer, wiped his hand across his mouth and sat down. 'Anything doing?'

Vince shook his head.

'Won't be, either. Saturday night. You might as well jack it in. Come on over and catch the second half.'

'Better not. The minute I leave the office – that's when Group gets on the blower.'

Scobart watched him covertly. Vince's face was tight, his voice brittle. 'I could send someone to spell you.'

'No, I'll stay. Thanks, anyway.'

'Up to you.'

Vince drank from the bottle. 'How's it going?'

'Kweis kateer. Smart's just been on.'

176

'On form, was he?' Vince said bitterly. He didn't like Smart.

'Bang on. Gatley was spitting blood.'

'Did it show?'

'It showed.'

They drank in silence for a moment or two. Scobart got out his cigarettes and they lit up. 'Beer all right?'

'Smashing,' Vince said. and then, 'He's doing his best, y'know.'

'Gatley?' Scobart said. 'Is he?'

'You don't go much on him, do you?'

'Not a lot, no.'

'He's a lonely man,' Vince said quietly, as if to himself. 'All locked up inside that uniform. He pushes himself too hard.'

'You too,' Scobart said, seeing the dark shadows under Vince's eyes. In the last few weeks the paperwork had trebled.

Vince shrugged. 'I can cope. Somebody's got to back him up.'

'Yeh.' Scobart tilted the bottle to his lips.

'He means well,' Vince said.

'Oh, sure. He loves us like a father.'

'Yes,' Vince said slowly. 'In his own way I think he does. Or would do if we'd let him.'

Scobart looked at him, surprised. Saw the tension in his face, his hands clasped too tightly round the bottle. 'OK,' he said. 'Let's have it, Alec. What're you trying to tell me?'

'You're all against him, aren't you?' Vince said. 'Officers, NCOs, the men – you all gang up on him.'

'Oh ah?' Scobart said.

'You don't give him a chance. Everything he does – all his ideas, all his plans for the unit – you do your damnedest to wreck 'em. Sneer at him behind his back. Ridicule him.'

'Is that what you think?' Scobart said, his voice hard.

'Think?' Vince said. 'It's what I know. He knows it, too. He's not a fool, y'know. He's got eyes in his head. Ears. You're all moaning about the training programme and the bull and ...'

'The charge sheets,' Scobart said icily.

'OK. I know about the charge sheets. I type the bloody things, don't I?'

'And enjoy it?' Scobart said. 'Enjoy seeing half the unit shoved on a fizzer every bloody day?'

'No, I don't. And neither does he.'

Scobart shrugged. 'Then why does he do it?'

'You don't leave him any choice, do you, damn it,' Vince said. He was worked up now, his face pale, his eyes glistening.

Close to tears, Scobart thought. Why, for God's sake?

'No enthusiasm,' Vince said. 'No co-operation. I said he was lonely and I damned well meant it. You've isolated him. Frozen him out. You couldn't have cut him off more completely if you'd walled him up in his office and piled sandbags on top.'

'Bull,' Scobart said. 'If there's any walling-up been done, it's him who's done it. Damn it, you know what he's like. Pompous, arrogant, holier-than-thou ...'

'Yes, I know what he's like,' Vince said. 'But do you? What he's really like – the man, not the C.O.' He set the bottle down on the table. Scobart saw his hands were shaking. 'His wife left him,' Vince said. 'Did you know that? Just walked out and left him. On his own. No kids. No relatives. Nobody.' He blinked angrily. 'Getting this command was his big break. A unit of his own. People depending on him, needing him.'

'Like hell,' Scobart said roughly. 'We need him like we need a boil on the arse.'

'We need him,' Vince said vehemently. 'He's exactly

what we need. Somebody to put us back on our feet. Give us a bit of self-respect. A bit of pride again.'

'Esprit de corps,' Scobart said sardonically.

'Why not? OK, he's strict. Regimental. Is that so bad? At least he lays it on the line straight. You know where you are with him.'

'Yeh,' Scobart said. 'Up the creek without a bloody paddle.'

Vince spread his hands in disgust. 'Aw, what's the use? You hate his guts and that's all there is to it.'

Scobart stubbed out his cigarette carefully, watching Vince – the trembling hands, the pale, tense face. He had never seen the corporal like this. Edgy, jumpy, nerves stretched tight. 'How d'you know,' he said then, 'About his wife?'

'He told me,' Vince said.

'Did he now?'

'He talks to me. Comes in here sometimes when I'm working late and talks to me. Is that a crime?'

'What does he talk about?'

Vince shrugged. 'I dunno. Lots of things. Himself. Me. Places back home we both know. After the war.' He looked up at Scobart with a kind of defiance. 'Just normal conversation between ...'

'Friends?' Scobart said with an edge on his voice.

'If you like.'

Scobart nodded slowly. 'Yeh.' But he didn't like it. He didn't like it at all. If it leaked out that Gatley was getting chummy with his Orderly Room clerk ... 'You want to watch it, son,' he said. He tipped the last of his beer into his mouth and stood up. 'Time I was getting back. Sure you don't want to come?'

'No,' Vince said. 'What d'you mean, I want to watch it?'

'With Gatley,' Scobart said. 'Don't encourage him, Alec. People might start jumping to conclusions. Know what I mean?'

179

'Look,' Vince said. 'I told you. He's lonely. He needs someone to ...'

'We're all lonely, lad,' Scobart said heavily. 'Two hundred and fifty of us cooped up here and the nearest white woman eighty miles away in Alex.'

Vince's face reddened. 'What's that got to do with it?'

Scobart met his eyes steadily. 'I don't have to spell it out for you, do I?' He nodded at the bed neatly made-up against the wall. 'Sleeping here again tonight, are you?'

'Yes, I am,' Vince said defiantly. 'Alone.'

'OK, OK.' Scobart grinned at him. 'I'm on your side, son. It's those dirty-minded bastards over there who ...'

'To hell with them,' Vince said. 'It's not like that and you know it. He's just a ...'

'Lonely man?' Scobart nodded. 'Yeh. You said.'

'And you believed him?' Hobey said. He was fitting the pieces together now. Detached from the pain by the analgesics Frant had pumped into him, his mind was building the picture. Seeing it the way Scobart saw it. Knowing a Court of Inquiry with Watson in the chair might see it quite differently.

'Hell, yes,' Scobart said. 'I believed him. Vince is as straight as they come.' Reserved, educated, obsessively neat, not a good mixer. The only son of a Grammar School deputy head. Middle-class, respectable, with all the social inhibitions of a Home Counties dormitory suburb upbringing. Inexperienced with girls, probably a virgin. But straight.

'And Gatley?' Hobey said.

'Gatley takes him for granted. Works him damned hard. Keeps him in his place.'

'And confides in him, apparently,' Hobey said. 'How does he get on with women?'

180

'Gatley?' Scobart shrugged. 'I wouldn't know, sir,' he said, making it formal.

He's warning me off, Hobey thought. Why? Was Gatley a queer? Was that the key to the whole sorry mess? Rebuffed by his Orderly Room clerk, denied his safety-valve. He said, 'His wife left him. D'you know why?'

'No, sir.' Scobart hesitated. 'He's a bit of a puritan. I think he finds sex disgusting.' Which, although he couldn't know it, was what Hilda Gatley had said, but more coarsely.

'Normal sex, you mean?' Hobey said.

'Sex, full stop,' Scobart said. 'That's what smashed up the concert that night. Not Smart's act. Jo-Jo Prince.'

When Scobart got back to his seat in the second row McCann was on stage in the middle of his 'Little Sir Echo' number.

ACI McCann was a Liverpool-Irish Jew; a squat, ugly, short-legged man with a head slightly too big for his body and an impudent grin which masked the temper of a wild cat. Because of that temper he had been stripped from sergeant to ACI, worked his way back up to corporal and been stripped again. Watching him now, strutting like a bantam cock, pumping out the words of the song in a gravel-and-honey voice, Scobart grinned and shook his head, remembering that morning six months previously in Hammond's office.

'All right, McCann,' Hammond had said. 'The corporal was giving you a bad time. I accept that. But did you have to go for him with a broken bottle, damn it?'

'Nothing else handy was there, sir?' McCann had said, rigidly at attention, cap off, eyes staring straight ahead.

'You might easily have killed him. You do realise that, I suppose?'

'Sir.' Impassive. Like a robot.

'Thirty-two stitches. And he damned near lost an eye.' Hammond had searched that blank face for a hint of remorse, found none.

Apologise, man, Scobart had thought, standing beside the CO's chair. Can't you see he's bending over backwards to get you off the hook? Say you're sorry, for Christ's sake. Help him a bit.

'I reckon the bastard asked for it, sir,' McCann had said. And had returned from the Glasshouse fifty-six days later an unrepentant ACI.

'Hello,' he bellowed now, sweating and grinning on stage.

And they howled back, 'Hello,' belting it out, loving him. Loving him even more when he went down on one knee, hands clasped dramatically over his heart, looked straight down into Gatley's face and sang:

'Yer a nice little feller,
I know by yer voice,
but yer always so-oo far a-way-ay ...'

He skipped off on a shock wave of applause. The stage lights dimmed. As the men fell silent, the band slid into 'Moonlight Becomes You', slow and sweet and easy. A single, blue-white spotlight flicked on and moved smoothly across to settle far left. Into it stepped a girl.

She was tall and svelte in high-heeled silver shoes and a full-length white ball-gown, a white turban moulded neatly to her head. The gown was classically simple, beautifully cut, shaped to her breasts and waist, full in the skirt. Her shoulders were bare, her arms slender in elbow-length white gloves. An enormous paste diamond in the front of her turban glittered and flashed in the light as she moved centre stage. And she moved like a dream, graceful, gliding from the hips, the skirt swirling gently against her thighs; a demure, feminine walk with just a hint of sophistication in it, timed,

182

poised, captivating. The men in the audience were silent, watching her hungrily, drinking in every movement, every gesture of her hands, every inviting glance of her eyes – big, dark eyes, the lashes long against her cheeks. And her chin small and rounded, and her mouth smiling to show perfect teeth.

The band eased into 'Yours' and she began to sing in a velvet contralto:

> 'Yours till the stars lose their glory,
> yours till the birds fail to sing;
> yours till the end of life's story . . .'

It was exactly the right song at exactly the right time. Simple, sentimental, but not without a certain integrity. And she sang it as though she meant every word, with a kind of artless intimacy. To every man there she was a different woman; wife, sweetheart, the girl in the faded snapshot in his paybook, the girl who had promised to wait, the girl he hoped one day to meet. The flesh and blood of a dream in a white dress singing to him alone.

'Room Five Hundred And Four,' she sang and 'Lovely Weekend.' And, as the spotlight changed colour 'Alice Blue Gown.' The men swayed to the music, cocooned in the warmth of her voice, knowing who she was, not caring; seeing only what they wanted to see, hearing only what they wanted to hear, needed to hear.

When it was over she stood smiling in the spotlight, blowing kisses as the men stamped and cheered. It was the end of the concert. Nobody could follow her act.

Back in the Mess, Gatley said, 'That girl. D'you know her?'

Roper looked at him quickly. 'Don't you?'

Gatley shook his head. 'She was superb. Presence, voice, everything. Lifted the tone of the whole show. I'd

183

like to meet her. Thank her for what she did. She's local, is she?'

'Yes,' Roper said uncertainly. 'She's local.' He looked at March for help.

March grinned. 'There's a bit of a party in the Sergeants Mess. They'd appreciate it if some of us looked in.'

'Will she be there?' Gatley said.

'Oh yes,' March said. 'She'll be there.'

Gatley smiled and rubbed his hands together. 'So, what are we waiting for, gentlemen?'

Roper said, 'There's just one thing, sir. I think you ought to know it's . . .'

But Gatley was already making for the door. 'Not now, David,' he said in rare good humour. 'You know better than to open the hangar doors in the Mess, eh?'

Roper looked at March. March shrugged, picked up his hat and followed Gatley out.

The Sergeants Mess was jammed solid – all the senior NCOs, all the officers. A gramophone was playing, scarcely audible in the roar of conversation and laughter. Smart looked up as Gatley came in with March and Roper. He was still in his Max Miller suit, sweating and grinning and three-parts drunk. He stamped his heel hard on the hollow wooden floor and shouted, 'Stand by your beds. Order, now. Order if you please.' He pushed his way through the suddenly quiet crowd and thrust a glass into Gatley's hand. 'Glad you could make it, Wing Commander, sir,' he said.

Gatley took the glass and nodded. 'Thank you, Smart.' His eyes looked past the Flight Sergeant. The girl was standing by the bar on the far side of the room.

Smart turned his head, following Gatley's gaze. 'Smashin', isn't she?' he said.

Gatley turned to Roper. 'Perhaps you would introduce . . .?'

'Allow me, sir. Allow me,' Smart said, took Gatley's

184

arm and steered him through the crowd. He stopped in front of the girl, grinning. 'With your permission, ma'am,' he said, slurring the words slightly, 'I'd like to present our Commanding Officer. Wing Commander Gatley.'

The girl smiled enchantingly and held out a gloved hand. All over the room the men stood with glasses in their hands, watching, waiting. There was a kind of electric expectancy.

'Wing Commander,' the girl said. 'This is an unexpected pleasure.'

Gatley took her hand in his, smiled and raised it to his lips.

'The pleasure is all mine,' he said. 'I'd like to thank you for . . .' His voice was drowned in a great shout of laughter. He whipped round, his face thunderous, glaring at the flushed, laughing faces.

Smart clapped him on the back and shouted, 'Bloody good show, sir. You're a toff, that's what you are. A real sport.' He put his arm round the C.O.'s shoulders. 'He's all right, isn't he, lads?'

They began to applaud, grinning at each other in happy surprise. This really was a turn-up for the book. It looked like the Preacher was human after all. Kissing that gloved hand had been a masterpiece. They began, for the first time, to feel close to him.

Gatley stared at them slowly, his face pale.

God help us, Roper thought watching him. He doesn't know. He still hasn't twigged it.

The applause faltered into a puzzled silence as they saw the anger on Gatley's face. He pulled away from Smart and turned back to the girl. 'I must apologise,' he said in a choked voice, 'For this – this vulgar exhibition. I hope you will . . . .'

'Apology accepted, Wing Commander.' Her voice was cool, amused. 'And thank you for your old-world courtesy.' And then she grinned, her face changing

185

subtly. 'You'll do, mate,' she said in a much deeper voice. And she put up a hand and pulled off the turban. Under it the hair was dark brown, cut short back and sides; the face below it, in spite of the skilfully applied makeup, the face of a man. A good-looking, almost pretty man. A man Gatley suddenly, sickeningly recognised. His jaw dropped. 'Prince,' he said in a shocked whisper. 'You're Flight Lieutenant Prince.'

Prince struck a pose, hand on hip, eyes roguish. 'When I'm in my party frock, ducks,' he said, 'just call me Jo-Jo. Everybody does.'

'Prince?' Hobey said. 'He was on night fighters, wasn't he?'

Scobart nodded. 'Radar Op/Navigator in Beaus.'

'Flying coffins,' Hobey said, 'especially after dark.'

'So I've heard. You know him then?'

'I know of him,' Hobey said. Everybody in Group knew about Prince, the gutsy, electronic wizard with the girlish good looks who had left the West End stage to sit back-to-back with his pilot in a blacked-out Beaufighter, homing in through the dark on a blip on the radar screen. Of all the colourful eccentrics among the redundant aircrews now waiting out the war in the Middle East, he was perhaps the most remarkable. 'He's that good, is he? In drag?'

'He's unbelievable,' Scobart said. 'Even when you're in the know you still think he's for real.' He shook his head, grinning. 'He's magic.'

'But Gatley didn't think so?'

'Gatley blew his top. Right there in the Mess with everybody watching.' The choked voice thick with disgust, the fever-bright eyes, the pompous, outraged self-righteousness. 'Christ, it was a shambles,' Scobart said. 'I mean, it was his big chance. All he had to do was grin and take it and he'd have been home and dry. One of us.' He shook his head. 'As it was . . .'

186

Prince had stood straight and still, a small contemptuous smile curling his lip. He should have looked ridiculous in the white dress with lipstick on his mouth and his face painted and powdered below the close-cut hair. But there was dignity in his stillness, a kind of poise. The ridiculous figure had been Gatley, ranting and shrilling at them, spittle flecking his lips, his whole body shaking. 'A disgrace to the commission you hold ..... pandering to the lowest, vulgar tastes .... a shameful exhibition .... obscene, disgusting ... undermining the respect of the men for their officers ...' The words spluttered out against a background of embarrassed silence which hardened into anger; a cold animosity walling him in, isolating him.

'We'd made him look a clot, y'see,' Scobart said. 'He couldn't forgive that.'

'Can any of us?' Hobey said. 'Could you?' Gatley's reaction had been understandable. But also inexcusable. He knew that. Noblesse oblige was not only seeing your men fed before you fed yourself. It was also knowing how to cope with a joke that misfired.

Scobart looked at him bleakly. 'You think it was our fault, then? You think we all ganged up on him? Is that it?'

'What I think's not important,' Hobey said. 'It's what the Court of Inquiry will think that matters now.' Down there in Watson's office at Group HQ, a phalanx of top brass behind the table, the empty chair waiting in front; the formal questions asked, the answers carefully noted; the squalor and stress of Marazag light years away. It would all look quite different then. The bull, the pep-talks on the veranda, the refusal to make allowances for the appalling living conditions, the failure to get alongside the key men in the unit and win their respect and co-operation – all this would be smoothly presented as being no more than the perfectly legitimate actions of a conscientious C.O. intent to put

187

87 back on its feet. Gatley had gone by the book. He would not be faulted for that. 'A deliberate, cold-blooded attempt has been made on the life of an officer. And ...'

Scobart said quickly, 'I told you. That was a mistake.'

'I know what you told me,' Hobey said.

'But you don't believe me?' Scobart's voice was flat, resigned.

'What will the Court believe?' Hobey said. 'That's the point. Nothing I have heard so far is going to impress them unless it can be shown to have a direct bearing on the events of yesterday morning.'

'Damn it, sir, that's obvious, isn't it?'

'It's obvious to you, perhaps.'

'But not to you?'

'I don't know, do I?' Hobey said. 'Until you tell me.'

'Tell you what,' Scobart said angrily. 'What more d'you need to know to convince you Gatley's a walking bloody disaster?'

'What the Court of Inquiry will need to know,' Hobey said evenly. 'Just exactly what happened when Roper was shot. And afterwards.' He managed a small, apologetic smile. 'I'm sorry, Mr Scobart. It's not that I'm unsympathetic. I appreciate the unit's been through a bad patch. But what you must realise is that at the official level this whole stupid balls-up only begins with the shooting of the Adjutant and the damning failure to acknowledge that Pack Up signal. That's what they'll be interested in. Not excuses or mitigating circumstances or even reasons why. Just the facts, as they happened, when they happened. OK?'

'But that's not fair,' Scobart said. 'You can't just ignore ...'

'Oh, for God's sake,' Hobey said. 'Of course it's not bloody fair. Why the hell should it be? This is real life, Scobart, not the Boys Own Paper.'

188

'Yeh,' Scobart said wearily, accepting it. Angered by it, but accepting it. 'Yeh, OK.'

Hobey smiled. 'Good show. Now, take your time. This bit we have to get right.'

4

'One rifle short?' Collins, the Orderly Sergeant, stared incredulously at the Corporal of the Guard. 'Bloody hell. That's all we bloody need.'

Outside the Guard Tent the last of the three-tonners ferrying the men up to the main compound ground out through the gate. Dust and acrid exhaust fumes drifted in through the open flap. It was 08.10 on the morning of October 15 and already hot, the air in the tent moist and heavy. Collins pulled out his handkerchief and wiped the sweat off his face and neck. In accordance with Gatley's Standing Orders he was in full dress khaki drill, shirt, tie and tunic, cap badge, buttons and belt buckle gleaming, boots like black mirrors. Twenty-five, not tall, fidgety.

'Sorry, Sarge,' Corporal Wooten said. He was from Dorset; a big, slow man, mild-eyed like the cows he had used to milk.

'Well, where the hell is it?' Collins said, glowering round the tent.

'I dunno, do I? It was here last night. I checked when I took over.'

'So?'

Wooten shrugged unhappily. 'So some bugger's whipped it.'

'I know that, damn it,' Collins snapped. 'I didn't think it had grown legs and bloody walked.'

'Sorry, Sarge.'

190

'Yeh, mate,' Collins said. 'You bloody will be.' He scowled up at Wooten. 'Well, don't just stand there like a spare man at a wedding. Go and look for the bloody thing.'

'I 'ave,' Wooten said, aggrieved.

'Well, go and look again. And this time try opening your bloody eyes.'

'Sarge.'

'Get on with it, then,' Collins said and pushed past him out of the tent and across the compound to Scobart's office.

Scobart was sitting at his desk reading DROs, a mug of tea at his elbow. He looked up as Collins came in.

'That clot Wooten,' Collins said dropping into a chair.

'What about him?'

'He's only lost a bloody rifle, hasn't he?'

'Bull,' Scobart said. 'Wooten's dim. But he's not that bloody dim.'

'I'm telling you,' Collins said fretfully. 'He's one short in the Guard Tent. All there last night – which is more than he was. One adrift this morning.'

'Damn,' Scobart said. 'Hank'll go spare.'

Collins nodded gloomily. 'He's not the only one. What about Gatley?'

'You haven't told him, for God's sake?'

'Hell, no. But it'll have to go in the report tonight. Unless that swede-bashing clot comes up with it.'

'He won't,' Scobart said. 'Whoever took it's probably flogged it to a wog by now.'

'So we're up the creek, aren't we?' Collins said. 'Once Gatley gets his teeth into this it's going to sound like we've auctioned off the whole damned armoury in job lots.' He altered his voice to a passable impersonation of Gatley. '"Valuable government property. Criminal negligence. Dereliction of duty."'

191

'"You're not fit to wear the King's uniform,"' Scobart said. 'You forgot that one.' He grinned.

'It's not funny, damn it,' Collins said. 'As Orderly Sergeant it's me who'll be carrying the can.'

Scobart gulped down some tea, stood up and put on his hat. 'Don't panic. I'll go and have a quiet word with Roper first.'

He went out on to the veranda and put his head in the Orderly Room. Vince was working at the table. 'If I'm wanted, I'll be in with the Adjutant,' Scobart said.

Vince turned in his chair. 'He's not in his office yet.'

'Know where he is?'

Vince shook his head. 'Haven't seen him at all this morning.'

'He's not been in here?'

'No.'

Scobart went back into his office, shook his head at the question in Collins' eyes and picked up the phone. He dialled the Officers Mess.

'Officers Mess. Duty Corporal.'

'Scobart. Is the Adjutant there?'

'No, sir. He went over to the compound before breakfast. Hasn't been back since.'

'HQ compound?'

'Sir.'

'With the C.O.?'

'Instead of the C.O., sir. Wing Commander Gatley's still in the Mess.'

Scobart looked at his watch. 'Bit late, isn't he?'

'Got a touch of the trots, I think,' the corporal said. 'Didn't the Adjutant tell you, sir?'

'No.' Scobart put the phone down. 'That's damned odd.'

'What is?' Collins said, his voice agitated.

'Have you seen Roper this morning?'

'No.'

192

'He didn't go up with the trucks after parade?'

'No.'

'Right,' Scobart said. 'Come on.'

'What about this bloody rifle?' Collins said.

'Damn the rifle,' Scobart said. 'We've lost more than that, mate. We've lost the Adjutant.'

They went along the veranda together. Roper's door was locked. But Gatley's wasn't. Scobart pushed it open and stepped inside.

The first thing they saw was the pool of blood oozing out from behind the desk. Scobart stepped over it and looked down. Roper was lying on his left side, the chair on top of his legs. His shirt was soaked in blood, his face waxy, covered in flies.

Scobart knelt on one knee, brushed away the flies and felt for the pulse in Roper's neck. It was there, flickering under his fingers, thready, irregular, but there. Just.

'Dead?' Collins said.

'Not yet.' Scobart looked up. 'The stretcher in the Orderly Room. Get it. And bring Vince with you. Go on, man, move yourself.'

When Collins had gone, Scobart knocked away the chair and turned Roper carefully on to his back. He saw the ragged hole below the left armpit, the white gleam of bone in the red, torn flesh. He unbuttoned his shirt and whipped it off and wadded it over the wound, clamping his hand down on it. The flies hovered and buzzed round his head and he waved them away and saw the tear in the window screen where the bullet had smashed its way through. Roper was breathing noisily now through his mouth. His eyes were closed, his lips pale. Scobart touched the ashen face and felt the skin damp and cold.

Collins came in with the stretcher, Vince behind him carrying a blanket. The two senior NCOs lifted Roper gently on to the stretcher. Vince handed them the blanket, his face turned away.

193

'Look at him, laddie,' Scobart said, his voice hard.

Vince's eyes switched down and flicked away again. He gulped, clapped his hand over his mouth and blundered out of the door.

'Not on the bloody veranda, damn you,' Collins shouted.

'Leave him,' Scobart said, tucking the blanket round Roper, pulling it tight over the wadded shirt. 'He'll be all right.'

'More than this poor devil will,' Collins said. 'God what a mess.'

He looked disgustedly at the blood smears on his sharply-creased trousers. 'Where d'you want him taken?'

'Up to his room.' Scobart checked his watch. 'Thank Christ it's one of Frant's days. He'll be here in an hour.'

Vince came back in, wiping his mouth.

'All right?' Scobart said.

Vince nodded, his face very pale, a curious hurt look in his eyes.

You liked him, Scobart thought. We all did. Do, damn it. He's not dead yet. 'OK. Give Sergeant Collins a hand with him.' He stood up, sweat slicking the black hair on his chest and arms. 'And send over one of the orderlies with a bucket of water and a mop. Gatley'll have a heart attack if he sees the place like this.' Probably will, anyway, he thought. He felt his stomach knot. This was going to be one hell of a day.

He held open the screen door for them. 'Go easy with him. And, Alec . . .'

'Sir?'

'On your way back, bring me a clean shirt will you?'

He watched them go down the steps and across the sand towards the wicket gate, then went back inside

194

and picked up the phone. When the Duty Corporal answered, he said, 'Is the CO. still there?'

'Just left, sir.'

'Coming here?'

'Sir.'

Scobart put the phone down and went out on to the veranda. As he did so, Gatley came in through the main gate, acknowledging the guard's butt salute with his fly swish.

Pompous little squit, Scobart thought. Comes the long way round just to get saluted.

Gatley crossed the compound and mounted the veranda steps. His face froze when he saw Scobart standing there naked to the waist.

'In my office, sir, please,' Scobart said and half-turned to lead the way.

'One moment,' Gatley said tartly. 'What the hell d'you think you're doing walking about without a . . .?'

'My office,' Scobart said, took him firmly by the elbow and steered him quickly along the veranda and into his office.

Inside, Gatley said, 'Now, look here, Scobart, I don't know what this is all about but . . .'

'Sit down and I'll tell you.' Scobart walked round behind his desk and sat down.

Gatley hesitated, his face flushed. He saw the hardness in Scobart's face and sat down stiffly. 'Well?'

Scobart told him curtly, almost brutally.

Gatley's face paled, his hands gripping the fly swish across his thighs. 'Is he – bad?'

'About as bad as he can be.'

'But he'll be all right, won't he?' Gatley said, his voice thin and pleading.

'That's for the MO to say, sir.'

'Yes.' Gatley shook his head, his eyes bewildered. 'I don't understand. Who would want to . . .?'

195

'I don't know, sir.'

'Nor do I,' Gatley said. He licked his lips. 'In my office, you say?'

'Sir.' Scobart watched him steadily. OK, Buster, he thought. So what does your little book recommend now?

Gatley took a deep breath and pulled his shoulders back. 'All right, Mr Scobart. I'm declaring an emergency as of now.'

'Sir?'

'Ring through to the main compound. I want all personnel back here immediately. Not the guard detail. They've been up there all night and can't be responsible. But everybody else – officers, NCOs, ORs – I want them recalled. Is that clear?'

'Sir,' Scobart said, appalled.

'Meanwhile, as of now, I want this unit closed up tight. Maximum security. A total clamp down. No outgoing Signals. No phone calls. Understood? Once the men are back we'll lock the gates and mount a double guard.'

'With respect, sir, is all this really necessary?'

Gatley looked at him, surprised. 'One of my officers has been shot.'

'I know that, sir.'

'But you don't consider it very serious?'

'It's not that, sir. Only . . .'

'Are you questioning my orders, Mr Scobart?' Gatley said coldly.

'No, sir. But if we shut down Signals and the switchboard, Group's going to get twitchy.'

'I'll inform Group when I'm ready,' Gatley said. 'The first thing to do is to identify the man responsible for this cowardly attack. Once we've done that we can make a full report to Group.'

'How?' Scobart said flatly. 'How are you going to do that?'

196

Gatley stiffened in his chair. 'I gave you an order, Mr Scobart. The sooner you implement it, the sooner your question will be answered.' He pointed to the phone. 'Now get on to the main compound and recall the men. And when you've done that you will oblige me by putting on a shirt.'

'Sir,' Scobart said and reached for the phone.

Ten minutes later the first three-tonner rolled into the compound packed with men. Standing at the end of the veranda with Scobart at his side, Gatley watched them dropping down over the tailgate. Behind him the orderly came out of the office with mop and bucket. 'All cleaned up, sir.'

Gatley nodded. 'Thank you.'

A second truck came in, the third close behind. The men were in noisy high spirits, welcoming the break in routine.

'You can start forming them up, Mr Scobart,' Gatley said. 'Three ranks facing me.'

'Sir.' Scobart eased his neck in the starched collar of the clean shirt Vince had brought him. 'And the officers?'

'And the officers too.'

Scobart stepped down on to the sand, called out a right marker and began to build the parade. The men fell in as they came off the trucks, dressing tightly in a smother of dust, quieter now, watchful, aware of the double guard on the main gate, the man with a rifle posted at the wicket gate.

March climbed out of a truck and walked across to Scobart. 'What the hell's going on, for God's sake?'

'Bit of a panic, sir. The Adjutant's been . . .'

'Squadron Leader March –' Gatley's voice carried thin and sharp across the sand – 'let me remind you that this is a formal parade. You will oblige me by taking station with the other officers.'

March scowled, thrust his hands deliberately into his trouser pockets and strolled away.

As the last truck ground in through the gates the guards swung them shut and locked them. Scobart called the parade to attention and checked the numbers. Apart from the guards in the main compound, the Duty Corporal in the Officers Mess and one man monitoring incoming signals, they were all there – cooks, armourers, MT personnel, parachute packers, store-keepers – the entire strength of the unit. He turned and marched back to stand looking up at Gatley on the veranda. He saluted, grim-faced, regimental. 'Parade ready, sir.'

'Thank you, Mr Scobart.' In the sudden silence Gatley's voice was tense, unnaturally loud. He stood with his hands clasped behind him, the fly swish hanging down like a tail.

'Permission to stand them at ease, sir?' Scobart said.

'Permission denied.' Gatley stepped forward to the edge of the veranda. 'Now listen to me and listen carefully. Early this morning the Adjutant was the victim of a cowardly attack. He has been shot in the chest and his condition is critical.'

A shock wave rippled across the compound, heads turning as the men stared at each other, stunned.

'Stand still in the ranks,' Scobart barked.

'The Medical Officer will be here from El Fard shortly,' Gatley said. 'We shall know more when he has made his examination. But in my view the Adjutant's chances are very slim. Very slim indeed.'

Standing rigidly at attention below him, Scobart searched the faces of the men. They stared back at him blankly, like men on a police identity parade. Street in his white cook's overalls, Smart, Lever, Jo-Jo Prince, McCann. It could have been any one of them. They all hated Gatley. But so did many others. The parade was full of men who had been marched into Gatley's office

198

on a charge. His eyes flicked up to the flats behind the C.O.'s office. From up there, seen against the sun through a fly-screened window, the figure at the desk would have looked like Gatley; the right sort of shape in the right place at the right time.

'I've had you brought back here for one reason only,' Gatley said then, 'to give the man who is responsible for this outrage the opportunity to do the honourable thing. Make himself known voluntarily.'

Scobart blinked. For God's sake, man, he thought, we're dealing with attempted murder, not a bit of smut scrawled on the latrine wall.

'I want the man who shot the Adjutant to take one pace forward,' Gatley said.

And then what? Scobart thought incredulously. Double round to main stores and fetch a rope to hang himself?

The parade stood rock still.

'I'm waiting,' Gatley said sharply.

Nobody moved.

'I can't make any promises, of course,' Gatley said. 'But a voluntary confession at this stage would not go unremarked by the Court of Inquiry.'

The men stood fast, not looking at him, staring at the HQ block.

'I see,' Gatley said. 'Very well. If you want to do it the hard way that also can be arranged.'

There's the threat, Scobart thought. Now the appeal.

'One last chance,' Gatley said. 'For the sake of the unit.'

Bloody hell, Scobart thought between disgust and despair. They're grown men, damn it, not prep school kids.

'You disappoint me,' Gatley said peevishly. 'Mr Scobart.'

Scobart turned smartly. 'Sir?'

199

'I'll have the officers fallen-out. They will go to the Mess and be confined there until further notice. The remainder will stand fast.'

Scobart looked up at the taut, pale face, thin-lipped below the peaked hat. He saw the anger in Gatley's eyes and knew there was no point in arguing. 'Sir,' he said. He faced the parade. 'Fall out the officers. Parade stand fast.'

March led the officers out through the wicket gate, the guard locking it again behind them. The men waited.

Gatley looked at his watch. 'It is now 09.40. I intend to keep you standing here on parade until the man who shot the Adjutant declares himself.' He raised his voice sharply. 'NO MATTER HOW LONG IT TAKES.'

The men stood wooden-faced, silent on the sand. In the full glare of the morning sun, hemmed in by the high wall of the cinema and the blocks of flats, the compound was heating up rapidly. In another half hour it would be like an oven.

Oh my God, Scobart thought. You've done it now, you stupid bastard. You've really done it now.

'Mr Scobart,' Gatley said.

'Sir?'

'You will hand over the parade to Sar'nt Collins and join me in my office.'

'To Collins?' One of the least experienced senior NCOs, out-ranked by Smart and half-a-dozen others.

'He is the Orderly Sergeant today, I believe?'

'Sir,' Scobart said. By the book, he thought. Always by the bloody book. The bastard probably checks AMOs before he beds his wife. And remembered Gatley's wife had left him.

Taking over, Collins said, 'Christ on a crutch, Jim. I can't cope with this.' His voice was agitated, a hoarse whisper.

'Don't panic,' Scobart said quietly. 'I'll sort him out.

200

Wait till I'm in his office and then stand 'em at ease.' He grinned tightly. 'And don't make a production of it.'

He went up the steps, knocked on Gatley's door and stepped inside. The office smelled of disinfectant. There was a large damp patch on the floor. Gatley was sitting behind his desk. He had taken off his hat and his thin hair was sweat-plastered flat to his head. 'Sit down, Mr Scobart,' he said.

Scobart pulled up a chair and sat opposite him. 'It's not going to work, sir.'

'I think it will,' Gatley said. 'Given time.'

Scobart shook his head. 'Nobody's going to put his head on the block just like that.'

'Not of his own accord, perhaps. But the others will force his hand. And sooner rather than later. You'll see, Mr Scobart. We'll have our man by lunchtime at the latest.'

'You think they know who he is?'

'Of course they know. This is a small unit. Everybody living in each other's pockets. You can't keep secrets here.' Gatley sat back and smiled thinly; not a pleasant smile. 'I'm not saying it's common knowledge. But somebody knows. And that's all we need. A couple of hours out there in the sun and they'll trade him for a mug of tea and a chance to sit in the shade.'

You bastard, Scobart thought. All you need is a pair of jackboots, rimless spectacles and a black hat and you could stand in for Himmler any bloody day. 'And if they don't?' he said.

'We'll cross that bridge when we come to it. If we come to it.'

What bridge? Scobart thought. You've just burned the bloody thing. How long d'you think they'll stand out there before they break ranks and walk away from you? And what are you going to do then, for Christ's sake?

Turn the guards on 'em? He said, 'I still think we should inform Group, sir.'

'No.' Gatley's voice was flat and hard. 'I'll handle this my way.' He clenched his fists on the table, the knuckles white.

He's got the twitch, Scobart thought watching him. He's scared of losing his command. That's why he won't go to Group till he's got it all wrapped-up. All the loose ends tied and some poor devil's head in a basket. 'What about Mr Roper, sir?'

'Roper?' Gatley looked surprised. As if he had forgotten all about the Adjutant.

'He needs hospital treatment. I think we owe it to him to contact Group. They could organise a chopper. Get him flown up to Alex.'

'I'll take advice from Frant on that.' Gatley looked at his watch. 'He should have arrived by now.' He picked up the phone and got through to the Mess. 'Has the MO arrived yet? . . . Ah, good. With him now, is he? . . . Very well. Ask him to report to me as soon as he's finished.' He rang off and smiled smugly at Scobart. 'Frant's having a look at him now.'

You don't care, do you? Scobart thought bitterly. Just so long as you come out of this in one piece, everything under control and the would-be murderer on the hook, you don't give a damn about Roper or any other bugger. 'I can look after things here, sir,' he said. 'If you'd like to go over and see him.'

Gatley shook his head. 'Better let Frant get on with it, I think.' He got up and went to stand just inside the screen door. After a moment he opened it and shouted, 'Sar'nt Collins.'

'Sir?'

'I don't recall asking you to stand the men at ease.'

'No, sir.' Collins licked his lips. 'Parade. Parade atten-SHUN.'

'Thank you, Sar'nt.' Gatley returned to his desk.

202

Scobart said, 'About the officers, sir.'

'Well?'

'With respect, sir, I think they should be put fully in the picture.'

'You want me to discuss it with them?'

'Sir.' Scobart hesitated, feeling as always with Gatley that the conversation was being conducted in some sort of code to which he did not have the key. 'There are some very experienced men among them. I think you might find their opinions helpful.'

Gatley's lips thinned in a cold smile. 'You know better than that, Mr Scobart. Or should do by now. I don't run this unit by committee. When there are decisions to be made, I make them myself.'

'Sir,' Scobart said resignedly.

'Patience, that's all we need.' Gatley sat back and folded his arms comfortably. 'A little patience.'

He means it, too, by God, Scobart thought. He really is that out of touch.

At 10.25 Gatley put on his hat, picked up his fly swish and nodded to the SWO. 'I think perhaps an encouraging word is in order, Mr Scobart.' He stood up and walked round the desk. Scobart followed him out on to the veranda.

It was like walking into a hot oven. Down on the sand the men stood silent and still, sweat dripping off their faces, dark wet patches staining their overalls. On the balconies of the flats a number of women sat watching, sensing a crisis. Scobart glanced up at them uneasily, knowing that by now the whole town would be buzzing with rumours. Gatley might think he could keep it from Group. But he couldn't keep it from Marazag.

The C.O. tucked his fly swish under his left arm, hooked his right thumb into his belt and stared down at the men.

OK, Napoleon, Scobart thought, this is your Waterloo.

'You disappoint me,' Gatley said. 'Not, I may say, for the first time. I had hoped that by now you would have come to your senses. Decided to co-operate. Do the only decent, the only honourable . . . '

Scobart turned his head sharply, blanking out Gatley's voice, the pompous, moralising clichés making no impression on his brain as he listened tensely to the chatter of the teleprinter in the Signals office along the veranda.

'. . . the good name of this unit,' Gatley was saying. 'That surely is something you will want to protect. I understand about personal loyalty. I admire it. But there are occasions when loyalty to . . . '

Scobart saw the door of the Signals office open. The Duty W/OP came out with a flimsy in his hand; a young, fresh-faced man called Minter who had failed his aircrew medical because of his eyesight. He hurried along the veranda now, his glasses glinting in the sunlight, the flimsy held out urgently in front of him.

Scobart took it from him and read it quickly. Minter stood waiting, his face anxious.

'. . . bring this foolishness to an end and enable us all to get back to work without further delay,' Gatley said. 'Is that too much to ask of you? I'm sure, now you've had time to consider . . . '

'Excuse me, sir,' Scobart said quietly.

Gatley shook his head irritably. 'Not now, Mr Scobart. I'm . . . '

'Signal from Group, sir,' Scobart said. 'Top priority. Most urgent.'

'Not now,' Gatley said, his voice harsh.

'But it's that Pack Up, sir,' Scobart said. 'The JACK KNIFE executive.'

Gatley turned on him, his face red with anger. 'I said,

204

not now. Damn it, man, can't you understand plain English?'

'Sir,' Scobart said stiffly, aware of the men's eyes watching.

'Very well.' Gatley turned back to face the parade.

'Will Minter acknowledge it, sir?' Scobart said doggedly.

'No he will not,' Gatley snapped.

'But, sir . . .'

Gatley ignored him. 'Let me make this absolutely clear to you all,' he said, a hard, shrill note in his voice. 'I want the name of the man who shot the Adjutant and you will stand there until I get it. I don't care how long it takes. You can stand there all day if you want to. But I want that man's name. And when I get it, God help him.' He turned and glared up at Scobart. 'Now, Mr Scobart. In my office, if you please. Minter.'

'Sir?'

'Go and lock the Signals and bring me the key.'

Minter gaped at him. 'But, sir, I'm on watch and there's this . . .'

'The C.O. gave you an order, lad,' Scobart said.

'Sir.'

Inside the office Gatley snatched the flimsy out of Scobart's hand and sat down at his desk to read it.

'We've got to acknowledge it, sir,' Scobart said.

Gatley shook his head. His face was pale now, shining with sweat. The flimsy trembled in his hands. 'No,' he said. 'We're in no position to do that.'

'We're in no position not to,' Scobart said. 'That's a Pack Up executive. Men's lives depend on . . .' He broke off as Minter knocked and came in with the key.

'Thank you, Minter.' Gatley took it and put it on the desk.

'I've shut everything down, sir,' Minter said. 'WT, printer, external switchboard.'

'Very well. Ask Sar'nt Collins to send Vince to me.

You can take his place in the ranks.' Gatley smiled his thin-lipped smile. 'I'm sure you wouldn't want any favours.'

'No, sir.'

'Off you go, then.'

When he had gone, Scobart said, 'It wasn't Minter, sir. Not with his eyesight.'

'Of course it wasn't,' Gatley said. 'But he might know something. He's not used to standing in the sun. Half an hour out there may well loosen his tongue.'

Scobart looked at him in disbelief. What was that word the trick cyclists were so fond of? Para-something. Paranoia. 'We haven't got half an hour, sir, have we?' he said. 'Not now that Pack Up's come through.'

Outside in the compound the men were chanting: 'Preacher's pet. Preacher's pet,' the rhythmic words keeping time with Vince's feet as he marched across the sand and up on to the veranda and knocked on Gatley's door. He came in, his face flushed. Scobart stepped past him and shouted, 'Silence in the ranks.' His voice slammed through the chanting and stopped it abruptly. More quietly he said, 'Take the name of the next man who speaks, Sergeant Collins.' And came back in and closed the door.

'Now, Alec,' Gatley said. 'I'm putting you in charge of the HQ block. Everything's locked up now – MT, Armoury, Signals, the Adjutant's office. I want you to stay in the Orderly Room and keep an eye on things for me until I get this business sorted out. Understood?'

'Sir.' Vince hesitated. 'I'd rather stay on parade, sir. With the others.'

'I know you would,' Gatley said. 'And it does you credit. But I need someone to man the Orderly Room and keep a check on things. Somebody I can trust.'

'Sir.' Vince saluted, turned towards the door and paused. 'Excuse me, sir. Is there any news of Mr Roper?'

206

'The MO's with him now,' Gatley said. 'So he's in good hands.'

'Sir.' Vince went out.

Scobart said, 'JACK KNIFE, sir. We've got to do something.'

'We can do nothing, Mr Scobart. Our hands are tied until we've got this sorted out.'

'With respect, sir, I suggest we acknowledge the signal and get the men back to work at once.'

'No. I've stated my terms and I intend to stand by them.'

'In that case, sir, signal Group we can't handle JACK KNIFE.'

'And when they ask why?'

Scobart shrugged. 'Lay it on the line, sir. They'll have to know sooner or later.'

'They'll know when I'm ready to tell them,' Gatley said. 'Not before.' He looked at his watch. 'There's no need to worry, Mr Scobart. They'll realise by now their signal never reached us and they'll already have switched the Pack Up to another MU.'

'I hope to God you're right, sir,' Scobart said.

'I told you. I make the decisions – and take full responsibility.'

'We're responsible for JACK KNIFE, sir. We've done all the preliminary work on it. Everything's on the top line ready to ship out to El Fard.'

Gatley shook his head. 'That's no longer our problem. Nor our concern. I'm responsible for the good order of this unit. That's my first priority and I intend to honour it. Clear?'

'Sir.'

'Very well. Then let's hear no more about it.'

At least until the JACK KNIFE casualty lists are published, Scobart thought. We'll hear plenty then.

'And in future,' Gatley said primly, 'when I am addressing a parade you will not interrupt me.'

'Sir,' Scobart said, his face wooden. 'In the circumstances I thought it right to ...'

'Whatever the circumstances, there is a protocol in these matters,' Gatley said. 'I expect it to be observed to the letter.' He took off his hat and was wiping his forehead with his handkerchief when the phone rang.

'March here.' The Squadron Leader's heavy voice was studiously polite. 'I take it, sir, you'll be coming over to talk to us?'

'When I'm ready, yes,' Gatley said.

'Ah,' March said. 'Only Frant is anxious to have a word with you.'

'And I with him,' Gatley said. 'I expected him here before this.'

'Can't leave the patient, sir.'

'Not for five minutes?'

'Not even to come to the phone.'

'I see,' Gatley said. 'It's not very good, then?'

'It?' March said coldly.

'Roper's condition.'

'Could hardly be worse, I'm afraid.'

'All right. I'll come now.'

'Thank you very much,' March said and put the phone down.

Gatley flushed angrily, stung by the contempt in March's voice. He cradled the receiver and put on his hat. 'I'm going to the Mess.'

'The Adjutant?' Scobart said. 'How is he, sir?'

'That's what I'm going to find out.' Gatley stood up, tugging down his tunic. He picked up his fly swish. 'Keep an eye on Collins. Don't let them take any liberties with him. If anything breaks I want to know. Immediately. Clear?'

'Sir.' Scobart held open the door for him and watched him go down the steps and across the sand towards the wicket gate, flicking his fly swish against his thigh,

208

walking with that curious, short-stepped jerky walk; a kind of jauntiness.

God, he thought disgustedly, he's beginning to enjoy it. He's burned his boats with Group and he's out on his own and it makes him feel important.

'How is he?' Gatley said, standing at the foot of the bed in Roper's room. The Adjutant was still unconscious, his face drawn and white, eyes sunken, cheeks hollow with shock and pain. But he was breathing more easily.

Frant shook his head. 'Not good. I've done what I can but it's only first aid, really. A holding operation. He should be in Intensive Care, round-the-clock nursing, all the facilities. Even then . . .' He shrugged, his finger on Roper's pulse.

'Are you saying we should move him?' Gatley said sharply.

'God, no. We daren't do that. Not now. If we could've flown him out immediately, fine. But not now. The way he is now we'd kill him if we tried to move him.'

Gatley nodded, relieved. 'That's what I thought.'

Frant had strapped Roper's left arm across his chest to support the broken ribs. His mutilated left hand emerged from the white bandages like a claw. Gatley looked at it with distaste, the way he had looked at it across the breakfast table that first morning in the Mess.

He had been first down to breakfast, showered, shaved, fully dressed, brisk and impatient to be at work. The way he always was in the morning. It was one of the facets of his character Hilda had found irritating. As he had been irritated by her sloth.

He was buttering toast when Roper came in, collected a plate of bacon and eggs from the hot-server and sat down opposite him. 'Good morning, David.'

'Morning,' Roper said, guardedly. He looked at Gatley's tie and tunic and wondered if he went to bed in them. He himself was comfortable in khaki drill slacks and an open-necked shirt. Most of the others in the Mess wore their working overalls. Except Prince. He was immaculate in tailored shirt and cord trousers, a blue and white silk square tied round his neck, identity bracelet on a heavy silver chain on his right wrist.

'Lovely morning,' Gatley said, spooning marmalade on to his plate.

'Always is,' Roper said. As you'd know, he thought, if you hadn't just got off the boat. He picked up his knife and fork and began to eat.

Gatley found himself staring at that left hand holding the fork between thumb and forefinger, at the callused pads of skin over the severed knuckles. He swallowed, his appetite gone. 'I've been over to my office and initialled the DROs. Vince has made a neat job of them.'

'Always does,' Roper said. He didn't like people who talked at breakfast.

Gatley pushed his plate away, his toast unfinished. 'Mainston,' he said.

'Sorry?'

'LAC Mainston. He's on guard duty at the main gate.'

Shop talk in the Mess, Roper thought. At breakfast, yet. 'Yes?' he said.

'I've told the Guard Commander to put him on a charge.'

Roper looked at him. 'What for?'

'He let me into the compound without a challenge.'

Roper forked bacon into his mouth, chewed for a moment or two. 'Did he salute you?'

'After a fashion, yes. But . . .'

'That's it, then. He recognised you.' Roper reached for the big white teapot and poured himself a cup.

210

'That's no excuse,' Gatley said, tight-lipped.

Roper added milk and sugar, stirred his tea, drank a little. 'OK, so he boobed. No need to charge him. I'll have a word with the Guard Commander and . . .'

'I'm sorry, no. I happen to think security is important.'

Roper nodded. 'So do I.'

'Well, then?'

Roper put down his knife and fork and sat with his hands flat on the tablecloth. Mainston was paying you a compliment, damn it, he thought. Can't you see that? He said, 'I also think that it's important for this unit that you make a good beginning. Putting a man on a charge for a trivial mistake your first day here is not, perhaps, the best way to do it.'

Gatley flushed. 'You must allow me to be the judge of that. In my book, sloppy security is by no means a trivial matter.'

'I agree,' Roper said. 'But surely in this case . . .?'

'I'll deal with Mainston after parade,' Gatley said. 'Tell Vince to prepare the necessary paperwork.'

'Yes, of course.' Roper rubbed his cheek with the palm of his left hand.

Gatley's eyes narrowed. He stood up abruptly. 'A word with you in private. Say in five minutes?'

He was waiting beside the noticeboard in the entrance hall when Roper came out of the Mess, paused to light a cigarette and joined him.

'Sir?'

'Your hand,' Gatley said abruptly, making it sound like an accusation. 'What happened to it?'

Roper held his left hand out, palm upward. 'A Nazi flak-gunner borrowed three fingers and forgot to give them back,' he said casually. Only a very sensitive ear would have detected the practised effort behind the mocking words.

Gatley's ear was not sensitive. 'Why don't you wear

211

a glove?' he said. 'Keep it covered up. Especially at table in the Mess.'

Roper's eyes hardened. He tucked his thumb under the index finger and thrust his hand quickly into his trouser pocket.

'Never try to hide it,' the physio-therapist had said. 'That only draws attention to it.' She had been about his own age, clinically pretty in her white coat, with a good skin and smooth brown hair. 'OK, so you'll get a few embarrassed stares to begin with. But if you act naturally, nobody'll notice after a couple of hours. You've got to accept it. Then everybody else will.' He had taken her advice and found it valid. But it had not been easy.

He said now, 'I'm sorry if it offends you.'

'Offend is perhaps too strong a word.' Gatley smiled stiffly. 'You're used to it, of course. But for others . . .' He shook his head. 'It's a question of morale, isn't it?'

'You're not doing a hell of a lot for my morale,' Roper said icily. He stubbed out his cigarette. 'I'm not a cripple, y'know.'

'Of course not. You manage very well. Surprisingly well.'

'Thank you,' Roper said. And thought: You patronising bastard.

'Look,' Gatley said. 'If you'd lost an eye you'd wear a patch, wouldn't you?'

'That's a bit different.'

'Is it? I don't think so.' Gatley shook his head. 'A glove, suitably modified, would . . .'

'Are you giving me an order, sir?' Roper said.

'More a suggestion. I'm sure the others would agree with me that . . .'

'Why not take a vote on it, then?' Roper said bitterly. 'A show of hands, if you'll pardon the expression.'

'No need to adopt that attitude. I'm only trying to . . .'

212

'Yes? Trying to – what?'

Gatley shrugged. 'Of course, if you're going to deliberately misunderstand my motives in raising the . . .'

'I understand them very well,' Roper said. 'And you can tie 'em together in a neat little bundle and shove 'em. Sir.'

'We keep him here, then?' Gatley said.

Frant nodded. 'I could use some supplies.' He fished a piece of paper out of his pocket. 'I've made a list. If you could get a signal off to El Fard.'

'Yes, of course.'

'Ask them to treat it as an emergency.' Frant said. 'I need that stuff urgently.'

'I understand.' Gatley put the list in his pocket and stood for a moment looking down at Roper. The Adjutant's eyelids fluttered, the index finger of his mutilated hand curled in a curious beckoning gesture. 'Is he coming round?'

Frant shook his head. 'Not yet. When he does he's going to need the pain-killers on that list.'

'Yes. Well, I'll leave you to it, then,' Gatley said.

March was waiting for him in the hall at the foot of the stairs. 'Any change?' he said.

'They're still on parade,' Gatley said. 'And will remain there until . . .'

'I meant Roper,' March said tightly.

'Oh.' Gatley picked up his hat and fly swish off the side table. 'No. Not yet. Frant seems reasonably happy about him though.'

There was a murmur of voices from the Mess. Cigarette smoke drifted through the open door into the hall. Gatley put on his hat carefully.

March said, 'We're all ready and waiting.'

'For what?'

'I take it you are going to discuss the situation with us? Decide what's the best thing to . . .'

'Nothing to discuss,' Gatley said stiffly. 'All the relevant decisions have already been made and implemented.'

God, March thought, he really means it. He's persuaded himself he's got it all buttoned-up. 'Yes?' he said. 'Including JACK KNIFE?'

Gatley's eyes narrowed. 'You've heard? How?'

'These things get around.' March checked his watch. 'Look, I've had a word with the heads of departments and we're all agreed we can still make it. Everything's packed and ready to load. All it needs is . . .'

'Oh,' Gatley said coldly. 'You're all agreed, are you? Interesting.'

'We can have the men up there in ten minutes. Signal Group to rejig the schedules slightly. Though with anything like luck we'll be able to cut a few corners and . . .'

'May I remind you, March, you are no longer in command of this unit? I am. I make the decisions here and I make them my way. Which does not include private meetings held by my officers behind my back.' He glared up at March from under the peak of his hat. 'In the time I have been here I have learned not to expect very much in the way of co-operation. But I had hoped at least for common loyalty.'

'It's not a question of being disloyal,' March said angrily.

'No? I'm relieved to hear it. You'll forgive me if I find it hard to believe.'

'We're wasting time, sir,' March said. 'I urge you to take the necessary action without further delay. Signal Group and get the men back to . . .'

'Out of the question,' Gatley said harshly. 'It's already too late for that. Group will by now have

214

assigned the Pack Up to another MU. Quite properly, in my opinion.'

'But they won't have been alerted, as we were,' March said. 'They'll have to start from scratch. We could still deliver quicker than they can.'

'I don't agree,' Gatley said. 'In any case, it's no longer our problem.'

'But surely we . . .?'

'The matter is closed, March.' Gatley tugged down his tunic. 'Now, if you've quite finished arguing . . .'

'For God's sake, man,' March said. 'What the hell are you trying to prove?'

Gatley stiffened, his eyes frosty. 'In the circumstances I'll forget you just said that. This time. But in future I advise you to . . .' He broke off as the phone rang, walked down the hall and picked up the receiver. 'Gatley.'

'Vince, sir.'

'Yes, Vince?' Gatley put his hand over the mouthpiece and smiled triumphantly at March. 'I think my tactics have paid off.'

'Mr Scobart's compliments, sir,' Vince said. 'And can you please come over straightaway.'

'Thank you, Vince. I take it we've got our man?'

'No, sir. The parade's broken up, sir. They're leaving the compound and . . .'

'I'm coming now,' Gatley said. 'Tell Mr Scobart I want them fallen-in again. Immediately.'

5

McCann started it.

The tough little Liverpool-Irish Jew was left-hand man in the front rank, facing the blank end wall of the C.O.'s office. That put him out of sight of the window. Out of sight of the Orderly Room, too.

At 11.08, slathered in sweat, tormented by the flies which hovered in a thirsty black cloud over the parade, his eyes smarting, his feet cooking in his boots, McCann decided enough was enough. He stood himself at ease, wiped the sweat off his face with a grimy handkerchief and said loudly, 'Bugger this for a game of soldiers.'

'Stand still, that man,' Collins snapped.

McCann grinned. 'You talking to me, Wack?'

'Yes, McCann. I'm talking to you.'

'Get stuffed,' McCann said pleasantly. He stepped out of line, stamped his feet to ease the cramped muscles in his thighs and patted the pockets of his overalls. 'Damn. I've come without me fags.'

A ripple of nervous laughter ran through the ranks.

'Silence,' Collins yelped. 'Get back in line, McCann and stand to attention.'

McCann put his hands in his pockets, smiling, hard-eyed. 'You shut your face, you bullshitting bastard,' he said.

Collins' face went red. He took a pace forward, the holstered pistol he carried as Orderly Sergeant bumping on his hip. McCann's hands came out of his pockets. He hunched his shoulders, half-crouching, arms reaching, fingers hooked. 'Come on, then, Wack,' he said, his scouse accent gritty. 'Up the Pool we eat fairy cakes like you for breakfast.'

The men tensed, watching Collins, knowing this was the breaking point. Wanting it. Welcoming it. Not sure how to handle it.

Collins licked his lips, sweating hard. He was out of his depth and knew it, with neither the experience nor the stomach to cope with a man like McCann. 'I'm telling you for the last time, McCann,' he said hoarsely. 'Get back in line.'

'Up yours,' McCann said. He began to crab towards the sergeant, moving flat-footed, knees bent, his boots slurring over the sand. His big head was thrust forward, his lips drawn back in a hard, fighting grin.

Collins watched him, on the edge of panic; a rabbit to McCann's stoat. The fingers of his right hand reached down blindly, found the holster flap, tugged it open and closed over the butt of the pistol. McCann's eyes narrowed. 'You haven't got the guts,' he said contemptuously.

They were close to each other now. Collins could see the beads of sweat glistening in McCann's eyebrows, the long, black rimmed nails on those hooked fingers. The pistol was heavy in its holster. His brain screamed at the muscles in his arm to pull it free and level it at that sweating, grinning mask of a face. But his muscles froze, unable to obey.

'All right, Sergeant Collins.' The voice was deep and solid, heavy as a sabre and as sharp edged. Scobart's voice. 'I'll take over.'

Collins gulped in relief and turned and saw the SWO standing tall at the end of the veranda. 'Sir,' he said. 'I ...' He choked as McCann's left arm slid over his shoulder and round his neck. The elbow crooked savagely under his chin, jerking his head up and back, squeezing his windpipe. His eyes bulged, his teeth bit into his tongue, his knees buckled. As he sagged down, McCann whipped the pistol out of the holster, put his knee in the small of Collins' back and sent him sprawling on the sand.

Scobart stood unmoving, his face expressionless, his eyes fixed calmly on the pistol levelled at his chest. 'Don't be a bloody fool, McCann,' he said evenly.

To Vince, watching from the Orderly Room, everything seemed to stop. Like a film jammed in a faulty projector. He stared dry mouthed at the scene framed in the window, sharply focused in the hot, white light of the sun. The motionless ranks of men drawn up in front of the trucks. Collins down on his hands and knees, his forage cap knocked off, his hair falling over his eyes. McCann crouched behind him, both hands locked on the pistol held steadily at arms' length; a lonely, defiant figure in the centre of the frame. And Scobart, massive, commanding; dominating the compound simply by being there, rearranging the almost visible lines of tension with himself at the focal point.

There was a long moment of absolute stillness; a taut, drawn-glass thread of time linking McCann with Scobart, stretched to its limits, vulnerable to the smallest sound, the slightest of movements. It needed only an incautious cough, the blink of an eyelid to snap it.

Vince held his breath, his hands balled into fists. The menace of that cocked and levelled pistol was now a tangible thing, reaching out to him like a cold hand, raising the hairs along his spine. In his shocked imagination McCann had already squeezed the trigger, Scobart had already crumpled on the veranda, slammed back against the office wall by the kick of the heavy calibre bullet.

And then the film started to roll again.

McCann straightened slowly, lowered the pistol and

218

shrugged. 'Sod you, Scobart,' he said without heat, tossed the pistol down beside Collins, turned his back on the SWO and began to walk away.

'Stand still,' Scobart rasped. 'Where the hell d'you think you're going?'

'Got to take a leak,' McCann said over his shoulder. He walked on down past the parade towards the main gate, hands in pockets, jaunty.

The men watched him, grinning, their mood changing quickly from fear-spiced anger to derision as the tension in the compound sagged. Somebody in the rear rank shouted, 'Have one for me, mate, while you're at it.'

'You lazy bastard,' McCann called back. 'Come and do your own dirty work.'

The men laughed. A great shout of laughter bringing release from the long hours of standing rigid in the hot sun. It swung at Scobart like a fist, jolting his concentration, breaking his control of the parade.

'Stand fast in the ranks. Parade – shun.' Every ounce of authority was in his voice, the final word resonant as the slam of a closing door.

But it was too late. Already the parade was a shambles, the men breaking ranks and streaming after McCann. Scobart stood, a helpless spectator now, and watched them drain away from him.

At the main gate, Wooten saw them coming; saw McCann's hard grin, the sweating, excited faces of the men crowding in behind, powdered with dust as their boots churned up the sand. He had six armed men; one beside him at the gate, five more standing in a bunch outside the Guard Tent. Six men with Lee Enfields; five rounds in each magazine, a spare clip in each man's pocket. And more than two hundred men coming at them.

'Open up, mate,' McCann shouted. 'Iggeri, now. Let's be having you.'

219

Wooten stood, legs apart, arms folded, his back pressed against the heavy padlock. Not a quick-witted man, but brave enough in his stolid, unimaginative way.

McCann faced him, hands on hips. Wooten said, 'My orders are . . .'

'Sod your orders, Wooten,' McCann said. 'Who's side're you on, for Christ's sake?' The men packed in solidly behind him. Wooten stared at them, flummoxed, smelling the sweet-sour stench of their sweat.

Those at the back began to sing. 'Why are we waiting? Why-aye are we wait . . .'

'Here, gimme that.' McCann wrenched the rifle out of the guard's hands, shouldered Wooten to one side, brought the butt down hard on the lock and smashed it. The gates swung open.

The men jostled through into the alley with a howl of triumph. Wooten shouted to his guards to stand fast. But if they heard him they took no notice. Shouldering their rifles they joined the mob swirling through the gates and were swept out into the alley with them. Wooten hesitated a moment, shook his head and followed them.

Now only the senior NCOs were left, isolated figures spaced out across the suddenly empty compound. Collins picked up his pistol and turned, white-faced, to Scobart. 'The stupid bastards,' he said in a shocked voice. 'You know what they've done, don't you? You know what this is?'

'I know,' Scobart said heavily.

'A mutiny,' Collins said. 'A bloody mutiny.'

'Can you blame 'em?' Scobart said, as if to himself. He felt exhausted, empty. As though all his resources of energy, summoned up to out-face McCann, had been drained out of him in the flood of men sweeping away up the alley.

220

'Gatley,' Collins said. 'Oh, my God. What're we going to tell Gatley?'

'The truth, it's about time he faced up to it.'

'Yeh, maybe. But . . .' Collins' voice trailed away.

Scobart looked at him bleakly, irritated by the man's weakness. 'You can fall out the NCOs now, Collins.' He walked down the veranda to the Orderly Room with the slow, deliberate steps of a tired man at the end of a long journey.

Vince saw the weariness in his face. And something else – around the eyes and mouth – a kind of hurt. 'Are you all right, sir?'

Scobart nodded. 'Ring the Mess, Alec, will you? Ask the C.O. to come over,' he said bitterly, knowing that the journey was not over. The journey was only just beginning.

'And you let them go?' Gatley's voice was peevish. 'You just stood there and let them go?'

Scobart shrugged. 'We had no choice, sir.' Never mix it with the men. It was the first rule in the book. Disobeying an order was serious enough. But striking a superior was catastrophic; a one-way ticket to the Glasshouse. No NCO worth his salt ever put his men at that kind of risk. You used your voice, kept your distance and pulled rank. If that failed you backed off and let them go. Gave them a chance to cool down and come to their senses. Then you threw the book at them.

'That's no excuse,' Gatley said.

Scobart compressed his lips, not trusting himself to speak.

They were in Gatley's office: the SWO standing stiffly in front of the desk like a man on a charge, Gatley pacing up and down behind it.

'Where are they now?' Gatley said. It was meant to

221

sound crisp, on the ball, but his voice was brittle, his eyes panicky.

'In the cinema, sir. Got their heads down, most likely.'

'Indeed? Well, that's marvellous, isn't it? I turn my back for five minutes and the entire unit goes to bed. Brilliant.'

At least they're not swanning round the town sparking off the wogs, Scobart thought. Be grateful for that, damn you.

Outside, the senior NCOs were grouped below the veranda, waiting for orders, the subdued murmur of their voices filtering in through the fly-screens. Gatley pulled out his chair and sat down. 'Right,' he said. 'If it's a hard time they want, I'm the man to give it them. I want them out and back on parade in exactly five minutes. Clear?'

Scobart winced. 'With respect, sir, you can't do that.'

Gatley's mouth tightened. 'It's not for you to tell me what I can or cannot do, Scobart. I'm the C.O. of this unit and I'm ordering you to get those men back on parade. Now.'

'And if they refuse?'

'I'm relying on you to see they don't.'

Oh, for God's sake, Scobart thought. Stop trying to pass the buck. 'Sir,' he said, 'we've had one disaster already this morning. We can't afford another. We're not going to get anywhere with a direct confrontation. Not at this stage. We're dealing with men who've...'

'Mutinied.' Gatley thumped his fist on the desk. 'They're mutineers, all of them.'

'If you think that,' Scobart said flatly, 'you'd better call the Provost Marshal's office in Alex and...'

'No. No outside interference. We'll handle this ourselves. My way.'

'I'm sorry, sir. It won't work.'

222

Gatley's face went white. 'Are you refusing my order?'

'I'm asking you to reconsider it, sir,' Scobart said carefully. 'Take a little time. Let them settle a bit. Bring the officers into it. And the sergeants. Work out a way to get through to the men and win back their confidence.'

'So,' Gatley said bitterly. 'That's it, is it? I might have known.'

'Sir?'

'The trouble with you, Scobart, is that you're just not up to your job. I've suspected it for long enough. All I ever get from you are excuses, arguments. Every order questioned, every action criticised, every idea...'

'That's not true, sir. I...'

'Will you be quiet when I'm speaking?' Gatley shouted, half-rising in his chair, hands flat on the desk, head thrust forward. He licked the spittle off his lips, his face working. 'I've met your sort before, Scobart. Soft-centred. All mouth and no guts. Hiding behind your rank. Bluffing your way through. And when it comes to the bit, about as much use as a cheque book without a bank account. Well, you listen to me, and listen good: if you're too weak-kneed to do your duty I'll damned soon find somebody who isn't. And I'll break you, Scobart. I'll break you right down to...'

The door swung back with a crash, kicked open by McCann. He nodded to Scobart. 'Giving you a rollicking, is he, Wack?' He pointed at Gatley. 'You. Outside.'

Gatley froze, his jaw dropping. 'What...?'

'You heard. Outside. A bit smartish.'

'Mr Scobart.' Gatley's voice was high-pitched. 'Arrest this man.'

McCann grinned. 'I wouldn't do that, Wack.' He jerked his head towards the window. The muzzle of a Lee Enfield was poked in through the hole in the fly screening, levelled on Gatley's right ear. Gatley turned his head and saw the rifle and the dark shape of the man outside.

'Freddie Mainston,' McCann said. 'He doesn't like you much. Sir.'

Gatley stared at him, dry-mouthed, sitting very still, his fingers pressed down hard on the desk. 'He wouldn't dare to . . .'

'No?' McCann smiled. 'Try him.'

Scobart said, 'OK, McCann. You've had your moment of glory. Don't push your luck too . . .'

McCann ignored him. 'I said, outside,' he said to Gatley. 'You've got thirty seconds. After that . . .' He nodded towards the window and drew a finger across his throat.

Scobart heard the hard reckless note in his voice, knew McCann was close to the edge of violence, dangerously balanced as he had been earlier in the compound, needing only a tiny push to send him over the top. 'It's not too late, McCann,' he said, knowing it was.

'It was too late three months ago,' McCann said, his eyes fixed on Gatley's face. 'An hour after this little bastard took over this dump.' He glanced at his watch. 'Twenty seconds.'

'You're bluffing,' Gatley said, but without conviction.

'You reckon?' McCann grinned.

'Go with him, sir,' Scobart said quietly. 'We'll get it organised.'

'Ten seconds,' McCann said.

Gatley stood up slowly, acutely aware of the rifle tracking his movements. 'You'll pay for this, McCann. And pay dearly.'

'And worth every bloody penny,' McCann said. 'Now, move.'

Gatley walked to the door, stiffly, head up, not

224

without a certain dignity. Outside, Vince was waiting, a man with a rifle behind him. Two more armed men were covering the sergeants. A fourth stood guarding the Signals office.

'Vince,' Gatley said. 'What are you . . .?'

'Miss Vince is coming with us,' McCann said. 'To keep you company.' He put his hand in the small of Gatley's back and pushed him towards the end of the veranda. Vince and the three armed men followed, the men walking backwards, rifles trained down on the NCOs. Mainston was waiting at the foot of the steps. As they went down on to the sand McCann looked back and saw Scobart standing in the office doorway. 'We'll be in touch, Mr Scobart, sir,' he said mockingly. 'Don't ring us, we'll ring you. Oh, and don't get any ideas about bleating to Group.' He pointed to the man outside the Signals office. 'Fisher won't like it.'

Keeping the NCOs covered, they hustled Gatley and Vince through the wicket gate and into the cinema by the kitchen door.

When they had gone, Lever looked up at Scobart, jerked his head towards Fisher and said quietly, 'We can take him. Piece of cake.'

'Not yet, Hank,' Scobart said. So far only Roper had been shot. He was determined to keep it that way. 'Let him stew a bit. Start to feel his mates have forgotten about him.'

'He's not a hard man, y'know.'

Scobart nodded. 'That's what I mean.'

'You did right, Mr Scobart,' March said, standing at the Mess bar, a pint tankard in his hand.

Scobart shrugged. 'Anybody but McCann and I'd have taken a chance. But you know his temper, sir. About as stable as a trembler switch. If he'd cut loose in there . . .'

'Quite. You've nothing to blame yourself for. I think

225

we're all in your debt for keeping things damped down.'

There was a murmur of assent. The senior NCOs had been invited into the Mess and the room was crowded, every chair occupied, men sitting on the window ledges, on the floor. The orderly behind the bar was kept busy opening bottles of beer. The atmosphere was relaxed, almost festive.

The way it always is when Gatley's not here, March thought. And felt a prickle of guilt, remembering where Gatley was. He raised his voice. 'All right, gentlemen. We all know the situation. It isn't good. But it isn't desperate either.' And he added, under his breath, 'Yet.'

They were quiet now, every head turned towards him. He looked at their faces and saw what Gatley had never seen. Trust.

'In the absence of the C.O,' he said, 'I'm taking temporary command. Agreed?'

They nodded, smiling, relieved. You knew where you were with Bobby March.

'As I see it, we play a waiting game,' March said. 'The ball's in their court at the moment. Mr Scobart tells me McCann's going to ring through when he's ready to talk. My guess is that'll be quite soon.'

'Why wait, Bobby?' Prince said, perched on a window-ledge, elegant in cord slacks, cream shirt, fawn chukka boots. 'Why not ring him instead?'

'And let him know we're worried?' March shook his head.

'Who's worried?' Prince said. 'Except possibly Gatley.'

'They are, Jo-Jo. The two hundred men in that cinema.'

'Including McCann?'

'Especially McCann. He's taken the initiative. Snatched Gatley and barricaded them all into the

226

cinema. A gesture of defiance which I'm sure he enjoyed making. But what happens next?' March shook his head. 'That's the question they'll be asking him now. And the longer they stay cooped-up in there, the bigger that question's going to get.'

'And what's the answer?' Prince said.

March smiled. 'That's what he's going to ring up to find out.' He took out his pipe and began to fill it. 'He needs help and we've got to give it to him.'

'The hell we have,' Henry Bush said. Flight Lieutenant Bush, i/c Aircraft Engine Spares; fortyish, solid, methodical. A straightforward, uncompromising man. 'He's made his bed, let him lie on it.'

'It's not that easy, Henry,' March said. 'The longer they stay in there the more desperate they're going to get. And they've got Gatley, remember.'

'You think he's really in danger?' Bush said.

'Not yet,' March said. 'But it could come to that. And quickly. We all know the bullet David got wasn't meant for him. And we all know who it was meant for.' He lit his pipe, got it drawing properly, and said, 'McCann's taken 'em up a blind alley and they're trapped. Our job now is to talk 'em back out.' He looked at them through a haze of smoke, his eyes serious. 'They're our men, gentlemen. And our responsibility. They've done one stupid thing today. It's up to us to make damned sure they don't do any more.'

Prince nodded. 'Fair enough, Bobby. We're all with you.'

'Good,' March said. 'Meanwhile we'll take one or two precautions. Get ourselves properly organised. Jo-Jo, you and Sar'nt Lever go and make yourselves comfortable in Room 3 at the top of the stairs. There's an excellent view of the compound from there. Flight Sar'nt Smart, organise a watch roster at the landing window – that covers the front and side doors of the cinema. Henry, you take six NCOs up to the main compound. The guards up there'll be wondering what the score is. You can use the fifteen-hundredweight parked out in the street. OK?'

Bush nodded and stood up.

March said, 'Collect sandwiches and tea flasks from Ryder before you leave. Enough for yourselves and the guards. Everybody else to . . .' He broke off as the phone on the bar began to ring. 'So,' he said. 'Sooner than I thought.'

The orderly picked up the receiver and handed it to him.

'March.'

'Already? And here's me thinking it was still only October.' The voice was McCann's cocky, sneering, his accent magnified over the phone.

'Never mind the jokes, McCann,' March said evenly. 'I'm not in the mood.'

'Me neither, Wack. It's not exactly a load of laughs in here, y'know.'

'Did you ever think it would be, laddie?' March said and put the phone down. He pushed his tankard across the bar. 'Same again, Tommy, please.'

The orderly snapped the cap off a bottle and began to pour the beer carefully into the tankard. Everyone was silent, watching him, waiting for the phone to ring again, for March's gamble to come off. When it did, March let it ring three times before he picked it up. 'Well?'

'OK,' McCann said. 'This time you'd better listen.'

'I'm listening.'

'We've drawn up a list of demands and . . .'

'Yes,' March said. 'I thought you might have.'

'Look,' McCann said. 'Are you going to listen or not?' Behind his voice March could hear laughter, the clink of glasses. Which meant they had broken into the bar in the Sergeants Mess.

'Say your piece, McCann.'

228

'OK. First off, we want no more of those bloody Saturday morning bull inspections. Right? We want Saturdays off. Finish work Friday afternoon. Start again Monday morning. If there's a Pack Up we'll work weekends. Otherwise . . .'

'Good of you,' March said, not unsympathetically. It was, after all, the routine they had worked under Hammond. The routine most ME MUS were now working.

'Yeh, innit?' McCann said. 'We've got no quarrel with you, March. Or any of the other officers. Only with Gatley. We want him posted out a bit smartish.'

Amen to that, March thought. He said, 'Anything else?'

'We want your word that no further action will be taken over what's happened here today. Give us that and we'll hand Gatley over and go back to work this afternoon.'

'Just as though nothing had happened?'

'Right.'

'And you'd accept my word on that?'

McCann hesitated. 'Got no choice, have we?' he said then. It was what March had been waiting for. A plea for help. A hint that things were not going entirely his way in the cinema. 'One more thing while we're at it,' McCann said then. 'We want immediate leave. Seven days. Half the unit to go tomorrow morning. The other half when they come back.'

'I see,' March said. 'And that's it, is it?'

'Yeh. That's it.'

It could be worse, March thought. The demands were not altogether unreasonable. Phrased as requests submitted through the proper channels they would have deserved a sympathetic hearing from anyone but Gatley.

'We want your word, mind,' McCann said warningly.

Which March could not give. On the revised work schedules, perhaps. And on the leave. But not on the glossing over of the attempt on Roper's life. That had Court of Inquiry written all over it. With a Court Martial to follow. He said carefully, 'And if I refuse?'

'You can't,' McCann said, playing his trump card. 'Not while we hold the Preacher.'

March said sharply, 'If you mean Wing Commander Gatley, say so.'

'You know bloody well who I mean.'

'Then you'd be well-advised to treat him with the respect his rank deserves. If anything happens to him...'

'Now what could happen to him in here, surrounded by his happy, devoted lads?' McCann said. 'Miss Vince, now – or should I say Mrs Gatley – well that's another story. The way we see it, she's fair game.'

'All right, McCann,' March said. 'I've listened to you. Now you listen to me. I don't like demands and I'm not impressed by threats. Let's be quite clear about that. You're in over your head already. Don't make it worse for yourself.'

'And what's that supposed to mean?' McCann said, warily.

'It means it's time you stopped playing silly buggers and faced a few facts,' March said quietly. 'I can't make any promises, but there's still time to get this mess sorted out. Provided you ...'

'Wait a bit,' McCann said. 'Are you saying you agree to ...?'

'I'm not agreeing to anything, McCann. Not while you're in there. Get yourselves out into the compound and let's talk about it.'

'What about Gatley?' McCann's voice was less certain now, less arrogant. 'He's never going to let...'

'Let me speak to him. Put him on the line.'

'Can't do that.'

230

'Don't play games with me, McCann.'

'I'm not. Gatley's in the shower room. Him and Vince. I locked 'em in there myself.'

'You did what?' March said, shaken.

'It's for their own good,' McCann said. 'Safer see? They're not what you'd call popular with the lads.' Behind him a glass splintered on the floor.

March heard it, and the shout of laughter that followed it. He said quickly, 'All right, McCann. I get the picture. Now here's what I'll do. I'll meet you in the compound in five minutes. Just you and me. No guards. No rank. Hats off. Equal footing.'

'Just the two of us?'

'Just the two of us.'

'Man to man?'

'Right.'

McCann hesitated. 'You give me your word on that?'

'Yes,' March said. 'I give you my word.'

'I dunno,' McCann said.

'We've got to talk, McCann. Get this thing thrashed out. You owe it to your mates in there.'

'Yeh,' McCann said. 'OK. I'll think about it. Ask the lads. Then I'll ring you back.'

'No, wait,' March said. But McCann had hung up.

March put the phone down slowly. 'Damn,' he said. 'I nearly had him. I bloody nearly had him.'

'And did he ring back?' Hobey said.

'No,' Scobart said. 'At least, not for three hours.'

Bush had rung through from the main compound at 13.00 to say everything was quiet and under control. The watchers at the windows had nothing to report. Fisher was still on guard outside the Signals office. Ryder and Street produced a lunch of sorts – sandwiches, tea, biscuits and jam. Afterwards, March had sent two groups of officers and sergeants, four men in each group, to walk round the town, do a bit of shopping, put on a show of normality for the wogs. And the rest of them had waited. And waited.

'That'd be – when?' Hobey said. 'Around 15.00?'

Scobart nodded. 'After that.' After Smart had tricked Fisher and they had managed to get the Mayday signal off to Group.

6

'He's taking his time, sir,' Scobart said.
March looked at his watch. 14.55. 'Yes.' Damned fool, he thought. What the hell's going on in there, for God's sake?
'You could try ringing him.'
'No, Mr Scobart.' A dozen times in the last hour March had been tempted to do that. And resisted the temptation. 'It's got to come from him or it won't work.' The will behind the words, the motive behind the action.
'You still think he'll ring?'
'I don't know,' March said. 'I hope he will.'
'Yes, sir.' Scobart's voice was doubtful. 'It'll be dark in three hours. Could be dicey then. They'll have drunk the bar dry.'
'And fallen asleep.'
'Not all of them, sir.'
'No.' March suppressed a mental picture of McCann fighting drunk.
'I think we should make a contingency plan, sir,' Scobart said. 'If they come out after dark looking for trouble we're going to be pushed.'
'Reinforcements?'
'I think so. To contain them if necessary. And to mount a couple of street patrols in the town. The wogs already know there's something up. We could find ourselves later tonight with a mob riot on our hands.'

'So, we get Group in on it?'

'I don't think we've any choice, sir. Not now. There's a detachment of the Regiment they could send.'

'Hard men,' March said heavily. 'Once they get up here it's going to be bullets not words.'

'I realise that, sir. But what's the alternative?'

'There is none,' March said, suddenly brisk, his mind made up. 'So, how do we get through to Group?'

They stood in the narrow passage between the cinema and the Mess: Scobart, Smart and Fenner. Fenner was the Signals sergeant; an ex-WOP/AG from Auckland, New Zealand, who had been on holiday with his aunt in Westerham when the war started, had taken a refund on his return ticket and gone into bombers. Two tours in the upper turret of a Wimpy and grounded with chronic sinusitis. A wiry, resilient man, straight-faced, sad-eyed, with a mordant sense of humour.

The passage was deep in shadow and they looked down over the wicket gate into the hot glare of sunlight baking the compound. Fisher was sitting on the edge of the veranda with his rifle across his thighs, a haze of flies hovering over his head.

'Bored out of his skull, poor bastard,' Smart said. 'This'll be a doddle.'

'Box o' birds,' Fenner said.

Smart grinned, glad to be out of the Mess, keyed-up for action. 'Bloody colonial. Why the hell don't you learn to speak English?'

'And sound like you?' Fenner said.

'OK,' Scobart said. 'Run me through the drill one more time, Kiwi.'

'Easier if I went myself,' Fenner said.

'You might have to,' Scobart said, 'if Jack balls it up. But just in case he gets it right for once, give me the gen on that set.'

Fenner briefed him on the console layout and Group's

234

frequency. 'She's all shut down, remember,' he said finally. 'So don't forget the bloody main switch.'

'Got it,' Scobart said. 'OK, Jack. When you're ready.'

Smart grinned, patted the heavy adjustable spanner in the thigh pocket of his overalls and walked down to the wicket gate. He opened it casually and went into the compound. The C.O.'s pick-up was parked at the end of the line of trucks on his right. He walked round the bonnet, waved casually to Fisher, opened the cab door and got in behind the wheel.

Fisher stood up quickly, his rifle at the ready, uncertain what to do. He heard the whirr of the starter motor, the sudden snarl as the engine caught. Smart let the revs build up a little and held it on fast tickover. He took a piece of rag out of the side pocket and wiped over the windscreen carefully, taking his time, making a production of it. Then he let in the clutch and eased the pick-up out of the line, driving it slowly in a wide curve across the compound towards the MT office. He parked at an angle at the end of the veranda, the nose of the pick-up facing the main gates. As he climbed out of the cab, Fisher walked towards him down the veranda. Smart went into the office, leaving the door open. Fisher followed him in and stood just inside the door, watching him suspiciously.

'What's the big idea, Flight?'

Smart opened the booking-out book and picked up a pencil. 'Just booking out.'

'Oh, ah?' Fisher said. 'Why?'

Smart looked up, saw Fisher was correctly positioned with his back to the compound. 'You haven't heard, then?' he said.

'Heard what? I've been stuck out here on me todd three bleeding hours haven't I? Haven't heard a sodding thing.'

Smart grinned. Fed up, brassed-off and far from home,

235

he thought. 'The C.O. wants his gharry round at the Mess,' he said. 'Going up to the main compound for a quick shufti.' Over Fisher's shoulder he caught a glimpse of Scobart crossing from the wicket gate to slip in behind the wing of the block.

Fisher said, 'Gatley? You mean they've let the bastard out?' He settled the butt of his rifle on the floor and leaned on it; a thickset, untidy man, his face greasy with sweat, his finger nails bitten and ragged. What Fenner would call a no-hoper, with more jankers time in than most men had had pay-parades. Thanks very largely to Gatley.

'Let him out?' Smart said. 'Why not? It's all over, mate. Kaput. Collos.'

Scobart was round the back of the block now, outside the window of the Signals office, prising the edge of the fly-screening away from the wooden frame with his jack-knife.

'No bugger's told me,' Fisher said bitterly. 'Bloody hell. How long since they . . .'

'Ten minutes.'

'Yeh? So where are they?'

'Confined to billets till Gatley decides what action he's going to take.'

'Well, bloody roll on,' Fisher said. 'So what's going to happen now?'

Scobart pulled the last corner of the screen free and climbed in over the window sill. He pulled up a chair to the RT console, threw the main switch and began to adjust the tuning dials.

'Good question,' Smart said. He finished making the entry in the book and stood up. 'I reckon you'll all be on jankers for the rest of your bloody lives, mate.'

'That bastard McCann,' Fisher said. 'Always was too big for his boots.'

'Yeh. His idea, was it?'

'"Hold the C.O. hostage," he says. "We can ask for

236

anything we like then. Any damned thing.'" Fisher shook his head sullenly.

Smart grinned. 'Serves you right, you shouldn't have joined, should you?'

'Here,' Fisher said. 'Does this mean they've found out who clobbered Roper?'

'Why?' Smart said. 'You sweating or something?'

Scobart was sending now, in clear, the table microphone close to his lips, his voice low and urgent, chopping out the consonants. The way Fenner had briefed him. The way Fenner himself had spoken on so many nights, ten thousand feet above the North Sea, coming home from the flak and the fighters with the bomb bay empty and the fuel running out.

'Wasn't me, Flight,' Fisher said.

'You're laughing then, aren't you?' Smart said. He walked round Fisher and out on to the veranda. Fisher tagged along behind him.

'What d'you reckon I should do, then, Flight?'

Smart turned and held out his hand. 'Gimme that rifle for starters, then go and wait in the billet like a good boy.' His hand closed round the rifle barrel, took it gently out of Fisher's grip.

The bullet came in at a steep angle under the end of the veranda roof, struck the concrete inches from Smart's right boot and ricocheted away. Smart dropped down on to the sand, whipped open the cab door of the pick-up, crouched behind it and settled the rifle on the window ledge, sighting along the barrel at the man on the cinema roof. He was kneeling behind the parapet, only his head and shoulders visible. And the Lee-Enfield's muzzle swinging now towards the pick-up. Smart saw his face small in the sights. Mainston. Young, scared, trigger-happy Mainston. He tracked right, aiming deliberately wide of the target and squeezed the trigger. He saw the puff of dust as the bullet smacked into the roof, saw Mainston duck behind the parapet,

237

twisted round and ran to the back of the pick-up. He squeezed off another shot from there to keep Mainston's head down, went up the veranda steps in one long bound, snatched the adjustable wrench from his pocket, rammed it in behind the hasp of the padlock on the Signals office door and prised it off. He kicked the door open and dived inside as a bullet thwacked into the doorpost.

Scobart was hunched over the microphone, his back to the door. Smart squirmed round on his stomach and lay with elbows crooked, squinting up along the rifle barrel. He could just see the top of the parapet below the edge of the veranda roof and pumped off a couple of shots into the brickwork.

Mainston returned the fire, working the bolt of the rifle very fast. But he was unsighted by the veranda roof, aiming at the small oblong of light which was the lower half of the Signals office doorway, the bullets flying wild.

But even a wild bullet can be dangerous. His third shot whined low over Smart's head, passed close to Scobart's left thigh, went in under the steel desk of the console and buried itself in the main junction box screwed to the wall. It drilled a neat hole in the metal casing and exploded in the nest of cables inside. There was a brilliant, crackling shower of sparks as the main shorted out. The set went dead.

Smart fired the last shot in the clip, chipping the edge of the parapet, spraying Mainston with slivers of concrete. He pulled himself up into a crouch on the office floor. 'Through the window. Now.'

Scobart went out head-first, rolled on the sand and came up with his back to the wire. Smart tossed the rifle to him and vaulted out over the console. The two men ducked instinctively as another bullet glanced off the door frame and smashed into the console, destroying the tuning dial.

238

'Main gate,' Scobart said, breathing hard.

They ran down behind the block, turned right past the windows of the Armoury and MT office and stopped just short of the corner. Thirty yards in front of them the Guard Tent stood deserted. Beyond it were the open gates and the safety of the alley.

'Together?' Smart said. 'Or one at a time?' He was soaked in sweat, his face set in a grin of concentration.

'Together. He won't be expecting us on this side.'

'I hope to Christ you're right, mate,' Smart said. 'OK. Ready?'

'Ready.'

'Go.'

They lunged out, bent forward from the waist, fists clenched, arms pumping, boots pounding on the sand. Faster than Scobart, Smart was slightly in the lead when the bullet hit the sand beside him. He swerved left automatically, momentarily blocking Scobart's path. His left heel came up and struck Scobart's knee-cap hard. The SWO stumbled, tripped and went down heavily.

Just beyond the gate, Smart stopped and looked back. Scobart was up on one knee, winded by the awkward fall, gasping for breath, his head down on his chest, the rifle still clutched in his hand. He shook his head, mouth open wide, the air rasping in his throat; got up in a half-crouch and began to run unsteadily. In the last second before he reached the shelter of the alley, Mainston's bullet took him through the right instep, slicing down almost vertically from the parapet. He staggered and fell forward. Smart caught him, pulled him through the gate, twisted under his chest, got Scobart's arm round his shoulders and began to half-carry, half-drag him up the alley.

Scobart was not in pain yet, the nerves in his foot anaesthetised by shock. The sole of his right boot was

239

half ripped off and flapped untidily as the two men hobbled up the alley and into the side street, along the length of the cinema and round into Sharia Pasha, Scobart's foot leaving a thin trail of blood.

Fenner was waiting outside the Mess. He ran towards them and took Scobart's other arm and they got him up the steps and into the entrance hall.

March had been watching the compound from the bedroom window. He came down the stairs two at a time. 'Did you get through?'

Scobart nodded, grey-faced now, his eyes beginning to unfocus as the first thrust of pain skewered up his leg.

'Bloody good show,' March said. 'What's the damage?'

'Bullet through the foot,' Smart said.

'OK, Flight. Get him into the Mess. We'll have Frant take a look at it.'

'And that's when McCann rang back?' Hobey said.

Scobart nodded. He looked at his watch. 02.40. Eleven hours ago he had been sitting in this chair, sweating and shaking as Frant cut away the remains of his boot, slid off his sock and began to clean up the wound.

'Straight through,' Frant had said. 'You're lucky, SWO.'

Scobart had managed a twisted sort of grin, half-smile, half-grimace of pain. 'Always was,' he said. But he had not felt lucky; had felt rather that the luck was running out – for Gatley, for McCann, for the whole unit. In the pit of his stomach he had that cold, end-of-the-line-God-help-us feeling. A sort of dank, sodden slough of despair through which the phone bell cut sharply.

'Sod you, Fisher,' McCann said. 'You've really dropped us in it now.'

240

Fisher gulped flat beer out of a mug, wiped his hand across his mouth, belched and said, 'He said it was all over. Smart. He said you'd packed it in. Let Gatley go.'

'And you believed him?'

'Well, I . . . Yeh, sort of.' Fisher looked round at the men sitting on the benches at the trestle tables in the foyer, the empty beer bottles clustered in front of them. They had got through all the decent stuff – the Stella from the Sergeants Mess. Now they were on the thin, onion-flavoured rubbish reserved for the ORs. 'Well, what was I supposed to do, for Christ's sake? I'd been out there bloody hours and . . .'

'You were supposed to guard the Signals office, Wack,' McCann said. 'That's what I told you to do.'

'Oh, ah,' Fisher said bitterly. 'You're good at that, aren't you, McCann? Lashing out orders right, left and centre like you was top brass down in Cairo. Sitting in here swilling beer while some poor sod's out doing your dirty work. Just about your bloody mark, that is.'

McCann scowled. 'Somebody's got to do the thinking. It's bloody obvious you can't.'

'And you can, I suppose?' Fisher glared round the table. 'There's enough of you bastards in here doing damn-all. Why didn't you send somebody out to spell me if you're such a bloody genius?'

'I should've,' McCann said. 'Then we wouldn't have had Mainston doing his Buffalo Bill act.'

'Mainston did OK,' Fisher said. 'Clobbered the RT, didn't he?'

There was a growl of assent from the listening men.

'Yeh, too late,' McCann said quickly. 'And shot up Scobart into the bargain. That's a big help, that is. How the hell am I supposed to negotiate with March now, for Christ's sake?'

'Ah, what's the use?' That was Wooten at the end of the table. Big, solid, sullen. 'Gatley, March – they're all

241

the same. All officers, like. You can't trust the buggers.'

And again that growl of assent, ominous as the rattle
of pebbles in an undertow.

It's going bad on us, McCann thought, watching
them covertly. All we've done is argue among ourselves
ever since March made his offer. I should've taken him
up on it there and then. We'd have been in the clear
now. I've got to get a grip or the whole option's going
to fold. He stood up. 'OK. If that's the way they want
to play it, that's how it's going to be.'

Fisher said, 'What you going to do, then?'

'Go upstairs and phone March. Tell him what he can
do with his bloody offers.'

March picked up the phone in the suddenly silent Mess,
aware of the watching eyes, the taut faces. 'Yes,
McCann?' he said calmly.

'You bastard,' McCann said, his voice corrosive with
anger. 'You gave me your word.'

'And got no reply. You promised to ring back,
remember? When you didn't...'

'I'm ringing now, aren't I?' McCann said.

March heard the edge of anxiety under his anger,
knew McCann was worried. And therefore dangerous.
'I'm listening,' he said.

'The deal's off, Wack.'

'You're not prepared to meet me as I suggested?'

'And get my arse shot off? Do me a favour.'

'So far the shooting's been all on one side,' March said
evenly, 'your side.'

'Now who's threatening?' McCann jeered.

'I am. Only it's not a threat, McCann. It's a promise.
You had your chance and you passed it up. Now we play
it my way,' March said. And he thought: My God, I'm
beginning to sound like Gatley. Hard-nosed, regimental. By the book. Only there was no chapter in the book

242

headed mutiny, procedures for dealing with. Or if there were, he hadn't read it. 'It's 16.00 now. You have exactly one hour to change your minds, open the doors and come out of there with Wing Commander Gatley unharmed.'

'And if we don't?'

'You'll have the Regiment to reckon with.'

'Stuff the Regiment,' McCann said and rang off.

March put the phone down and turned to face the Mess. Scobart twisted awkwardly in the chair. 'No good, sir?'

March shook his head. 'They'll sit tight, I'm afraid.'

'So long as that's all they do,' Scobart said. 'They might decide to widen their perimeter. Occupy the compound.' He sucked in his breath sharply as Frant finished bandaging his foot.

'Bullying you a bit, is it?' Frant said.

'Just a twinge.'

Frant took a syringe from his kit and filled it. 'This'll help.' He injected the pain-killer into Scobart's calf. 'I think we'll get you up to bed, Mr Scobart.'

'The hell you will,' Scobart said tightly. 'Sorry, sir, but I'm staying put.'

March said, 'Sar'nt Lever, I want a new padlock on the main gates and I want the compound staked out – not too obviously. Take as many NCOs as you need. OK?'

'Sir.' Lever said, poker-faced, careful not to show his approval. He looked round the Mess, nodding to one man here, another there.

As they were going out, March said, 'No shooting unless you have to. And then aim off-target. The operative word is discouragement. Got it?' He turned to Scobart. 'I suppose Group picked up that signal?'

'I didn't get an acknowledgement, sir. There wasn't time. I was still sending when . . .'

243

'They'd be monitoring,' Prince said. 'Very keen types up at Group.'

'I hope you're right, Jo-Jo,' March said. 'The set's u/s, is it?'

Scobart nodded. 'Main junction box shorted right out.'

'Which means half the wiring'll be melted,' Fenner said.

'You can't fix it?'

'Sorry, sir. That's a job for Sloan, I'm afraid,' Fenner said. And Sloan, the electrical fitter, was in the cinema with the rest of them.

March shrugged. 'That's it, then. We're out of touch.' Like a ship separated from the convoy, its radio out, its crew mutinous.

'Unless . . .' Fenner said.

'Yes?'

'There's a few bits and pieces up in the main compound, sir. RT sets dismantled from pranged kites. I might be able to bodge something, wire up a battery bank and . . .' Fenner shook his head. 'It's a long shot, of course.'

'But worth a try,' March said. 'Smart'll run you up there in the pick-up. OK, Jack?'

'Sir,' Smart said.

'Just drop him off and come straight back.'

'Will do.'

Hobey said, 'We picked it up. Around 17.00. It was faint but we got it. Just.' He remembered the scene in Watson's office with Hanwell and Curtis and the Group Captain; the receiver on the squawk box and Jane's cool voice relaying the signal. Eleven hours ago. It seemed much longer. For Scobart, helpless in the chair, worried, in pain, it must have been an eternity.

'He's a wizard type, Kiwi Fenner,' Scobart said. He opened his cigarette packet and saw it was empty.

244

Hobey tossed his across to him. The SWO took one and lobbed the packet back. When they had both lit up, Scobart said, 'That was when it started to get a bit hairy.'

There were long shadows across the compound now, the air flat and stale, all the life baked out of it. From the cinema the sound of ragged singing drifted intermittently, muted, lonely. The two sergeants in the Guard Tent heard it. And the one covering the wicket gate from beneath the last three-tonner in the line. And the others stationed strategically around the office block. Prone on the roof of the Armoury, Lever brushed the flies off his face and took a fresh grip on his Mauser.

In the Mess they were drinking coffee. The two 'show-the-flag' groups who had been out in the town were back, reporting that everything was quiet in Marazag. A bit too quiet, perhaps.

'And David?' March asked Frant.

The MO shrugged. 'Comfortable.' A reassuring medical word belied by his intention to stay overnight. 'I'll know more tomorrow morning,' he said.

Won't we all? March thought. He sucked moodily at his pipe, chafed by the lack of action, dreading what action might yet be forced on him. His mind back-tracked over the events of the day, turning them over without hope like someone searching through a litter of pebbles for a lost ring. Damn McCann. If he had agreed to the meeting it would have all been settled now. If the others in the cinema had let him negotiate. If he hadn't walked off that idiotic parade in the first place. If Gatley hadn't panicked and ... March shook his head irritably. In the end it always came back to Gatley.

The phone interrupted his thoughts and he grabbed the receiver, hoping against hope McCann had seen sense. But the voice in his ear was not McCann's. It was Henry Bush.

'Yes, Henry?'

'How are things with you?'

'Quiet.'

'They're still . . .?'

'Yes. Everything all right up there?'

'So far.' Bush hesitated. 'But we're collecting an audience.'

'Wogs?'

'Citizens of Marazag,' Bush said in his polite voice.

Where there are carcases, March thought bitterly, the eagles will gather. Eagles, hell. Vultures, more like. He said, 'How many?'

'Rather a lot, I'm afraid.' Bush sounded apologetic. And worried.

'Where are they?'

'Just this side of the mosque at present. Beginning to drift this way a bit.'

'Probably just evening prayers, Henry,' March said, not believing it.

'Doesn't sound like Evensong to me,' Bush said. 'Listen.' He held the phone out of the Guard Room window.

March heard it, faint, menacing; a low, rumbling mutter spawning a burst of high-pitched chanting.

'See what I mean?' Bush said.

'Yes. When you say a lot, are you talking about . . .?'

'A hundred and fifty. That's a conservative estimate. There are more of 'em coming all the time now.'

'OK, Henry. Keep everything screwed down tight and stand by to let us in.' March put the phone down. 'There's something starting to build up outside the main compound.' It was what he had expected. And feared. In Marazag, as elsewhere, bad news travelled fast. 'Flight Sar'nt Smart.'

'Sir.'

'I want drivers for the trucks. All of them. Go in through the main gates. Sar'nt Lever's squad'll give you

cover if you need it. Ask him to stand by to issue arms.
We'll be out there in five minutes. I want it quick. No
hitches.'
Smart grinned. 'Sir.' He began to call out names.
Prince said, elaborately casual, 'If you're asking for
volunteers, Bobby . . .'
March shook his head. 'I'm not. We're all going.'
'All of us?'
'Except Mr Scobart and the Doc. And Sar'nt Ryder.'
'Going to leave the place a bit empty, isn't it?' Prince
said gently. 'When McCann and his merry men hear
those trucks rolling out . . .' He shrugged. 'When the
cat's away . . .'
'Don't panic, Jo-Jo.' March's smile was hard. 'I'm
about to take care of that.'
'I'm so glad,' Prince said.
March crossed to the phone and dialled the Sergeants
Mess. McCann answered.
'March here, McCann.'
'You've changed your mind,' McCann said. 'And just
in time, as the midwife said, brushing away the
confetti.'
'Shut up and listen,' March said curtly. 'I'm asking for
volunteers.'
'You what?'
'There's a mob gathering outside the main com-
pound. We're going up there now to sort 'em out. We
could use help.'
'Get stuffed.'
'Get a grip, McCann. Use your head for once. This is
your chance to start putting the record straight. Any
man who volunteers to go up there with us starts with
a clean sheet so far as I'm concerned.'
'Yeh?' McCann said. 'Maybe. But it's not up to you,
is it, Wack? It's up to Gatley. And I don't see him . . .'
'Look,' March said. 'Pass the word round in there. Tell
'em what the situation is. If they call off this nonsense

247

and come out now, I'll take care of the C.O.' He waited a moment and then said, 'Well?'

'Good try, Wack,' McCann said. 'Divide and conquer, eh? Not on your nelly, mate.'

'For God's sake,' March said. 'You've been over long enough. You know what one of these mobs can do once they get started.'

'Yeh. Well, if there is a mob – and I've only got your word for that – I reckon that's your problem.'

'I see. And that's your final answer, is it?'

'You wouldn't bloody chuckle.'

'Right. While you've been talking to me, Sar'nt Lever has been busy.'

'Doing what?'

'Wiring grenades to the cinema doors. All of them.'

'What the hell ...?' McCann spluttered, caught off-balance. 'You can't do that.'

'It's done, McCann. Anybody who tries to open those doors will lose a hand – if he's lucky.'

'Bloody hellfire. You must be ...'

'It's gone bad on you, McCann. You think you're safe in there. All snugged down with your hostages. Bolted and barred. In a fortress. Well, think again. It's not a fortress, it's a trap.'

'I don't believe you,' McCann said, a note of desperation in his voice. 'I don't bloody well believe you'd do...'

'That's up to you. If you think I'm bluffing, try opening the doors. I don't recommend it. But you can try.'

'Not me,' McCann said. 'Gatley, maybe. Or Vince.'

'Certainly,' March said, keeping his voice casual though his mouth was suddenly dry. 'If you want to face a murder charge on top of everything else.'

'Bull,' McCann said with an attempt at his old jauntiness.

'Is it?' March said and hung up.

248

'He was bluffing, of course,' Hobey said. 'About the grenades?'

Scobart nodded.

'Bit dicey, wasn't it?' Pulling out *en masse* with no insurance except a small seed of doubt sown in the mind of a man struggling to retain his uncertain authority over his fellows.

'It was all dicey, sir,' Scobart said, remembering.

They had left him the rifle and a revolver for Ryder, gone out and shut the hotel door, climbed into the trucks and driven away. Frant had gone back up to stay with Roper. Ryder to stand on the staircase by the landing window. The Mess suddenly empty and silent, the sound of the trucks fading as they accelerated away up Sharia Pasha. And the long, long time of waiting...

Through the long afternoon the noisome, cockroach-infested little shower room seemed to contract, the smooth grey walls leaning inwards, the ceiling pressing down on their heads. As the hours dragged by Vince had to steel himself increasingly against the contagion of Gatley's fear communicated in the touch of his body as they stood face to face on the iron grating; and in the sour smell of his sweat. A fear which grew from affronted indignation ('I'll make them pay dearly for this') through whining petulance ('They've never given me a chance') to a nerve-twitching panic which flared into something close to hysteria when Mainston and Smart began shooting in the compound outside. The impact of the bullets thudding into the brickwork was magnified in that vertical concrete shaft. Gatley began to shake uncontrollably, face contorted, teeth chattering, eyes glazed and staring. Vince put out a hand to steady him but Gatley twisted violently away and threw himself against the door, hammering with his fists, shouting hoarsely to be let out.

Vince hit him; hauled him away from the door and whipped the back of his hand across Gatley's face, jerking his head round sharply. Gatley staggered, knees buckling. Vince caught him as he crumpled and lowered him down on to the grating. Gatley slumped, sobbing and snuffling, tasting blood on his tongue.

'It's all right.' Vince bent over him, stroking the thin,

sweatsoaked hair. 'All right now.' He kept his voice low and calm, trying to inject reassurance into Gatley's mind.

Gatley gripped his hand blindly. 'Got to get out,' he mouthed. 'Got to get free.'

Vince nodded, watching that crumpled, working face. Beyond the door, out in the foyer, McCann was shouting. Feet pounded heavily up the stairs to the Sergeants Mess. Vince felt the walls of the shower room squeeze in on him. He looked up. The tiny, opaque window mocked him. Too high to reach, too small to squirm through. He looked down at Gatley sobbing on the grating.

The grating. And below it the drain. The door was locked, the window useless. But the grating...

He pulled Gatley off it, bundling him into the corner. It was like manhandling a warm corpse. Gatley huddled down against the wall, knees drawn up, arms wrapped protectively round himself, head sunk on his chest – the classic foetal position of a man who had passed through anger and fear into the limbo of total withdrawal. Vince set his feet firmly on the concrete surround, bent and gripped the grating and tugged. The grating lifted, heavy, slippery on the underside with congealed soap grease. He got it up on its end and propped it against the wall. There was a pool of scummy, stagnant water in the bottom of the drain. Vince stepped down into it, stooped and peered along the pipe.

When they had built the shower room and kitchen on opposite sides of the foyer, back in the early days when the unit had first moved up to Marazag, they had put in a common drain, running it under the floor of the foyer and out to a soakaway excavated under the compound. It had been a makeshift job and they had used what materials they could scrounge off the dump in the main compound – lengths of old lead piping, bags of reject cement and some sections of concrete culvert three feet in diameter. Absurdly oversize for the purpose, but all that was available.

Vince took off his watch and put it in the breast pocket of his shirt, rolled up his sleeves and knelt in the drain. An incredibly foul smell rose from the disturbed water. Under his knees the curved base of the drain was slippery with grease. He took a deep breath and ducked down, on hands and knees now, the water reaching up to his elbows. He began to crawl carefully along the drain. Great drifts of cockroaches clustered on the curved sides above the water level and were brushed off on to his back and into his hair as he inched his way forward in the evil-smelling darkness. Where the concrete pipes joined, the ridges were thickly coated with viscous, grey-white scum, inches thick, lard-smooth, lard-slippery. He negotiated the first of these successfully, grimacing with disgust as his hands sank into the gooey mess. But at the second the pipe had settled a little and his palms slid over the ridge away from him and he went down flat on his stomach, his face under the water. He jerked his head up, spitting the filthy liquid out of his mouth, retching over its foulness, gathered himself together and pressed forward. He shook the water out of his eyes and saw that the darkness ahead was less solid now, beginning to grey. Two minutes later he was below the grating let into the kitchen floor under the sink. The waste-pipe from the sink protruded down through the grating from which long threads of grease hung like seaweed under a jetty. The grating itself was smaller than the one in the shower room but still big enough to squeeze through. He straightened his back cautiously until the top of his head was up against the iron grille, setting his teeth against the horror of the strands of grease brushing against his face. He steadied himself on his knees and put up both hands and lifted the grating a couple of

252

inches. The kitchen floor came into view, looking vast from that angle. Vast and polished and deserted.

He turned awkwardly, slithering on the curved, slippery surface of the pipe, and began to crawl back. He emerged into the shower room, a nightmare figure rising up out of the drain. His hair was thickly coated with grey soap scum which streaked his face and hung in slimy strands from his shoulders. His fingers were clogged with it. As he rose to his feet, great lumps of it dropped off the knees of his trousers. The appalling stench filled the little room.

Gatley stared at him in horror, cowering back against the wall, making little pushing motions with his hands. Vince reached up and turned on the shower, letting the lukewarm water sluice down over him. He rubbed his hands vigorously, shuddering with disgust, and tilted his head back to let the clean water wash over his face. The soapy slime clung to him tenaciously but at least he was able to scrape the worst of it off with his fingers. He turned off the shower, slicked back his hair and grinned at Gatley. 'OK,' he said. 'After you, Mon Général.'

It took him nearly ten minutes to persuade Gatley to go down through the drain with him. Ten minutes of pleading and bullying, of threats and promises. Filleted of courage, his will to act atrophied by his claustrophobia, Gatley crouched on the lip of the open drain, wringing his hands, muttering to himself, cocooned in terror, his mind a blob of soft plastic.

'Damn you, then,' Vince said finally. 'Stay if you want to. I'm getting out of here. Now.' He knelt down in the drain, his face level with Gatley's. 'Are you coming or not?'

A boot thudded on the outside of the door. Gatley jerked convulsively. 'Hey, Preacher.' The voice beyond the door was coarse, jeering, ugly drunk. 'Better get praying, mate. We just shot bloody Scobart.' The boot thudded again. 'Your turn next, you bastard. You and your fancy boy.'

Vince said quietly, 'Well?'

Gatley licked his lips, his face white and drawn. He held out his hands like a child. 'Help me,' he whispered, 'for God's sake, help me.'

Vince got him down into the drain, floundering and slipping in the foul water. He reached up and pulled the grating back into place over their heads. He had wanted Gatley in front of him but he refused, kneeling with his hands braced against the curved sides of the culvert, whimpering to himself, his eyes glassy.

The crawl through to the kitchen took longer this time. Twice Gatley slipped and went under. Vince heard him gasping and vomiting behind him in the darkness but was powerless to help him. There was no room to turn in that grease-clogged, foetid tunnel. If Gatley drowned, he drowned.

But somehow the C.O. kept going, slathered in grease, the water squelching in his boots, penetrating his sodden clothes, the spidery touch of cockroach legs brushing against his face. When they got under the kitchen grating, Vince made him kneel upright. Gatley was moaning and muttering, splashing his hands in the filthy water, trying vainly to wash off the grease that coated his fingers and clogged under his nails.

'Shut up, damn you,' Vince hissed. He prised up the grating and peered out over the lip.

The man came in from the foyer. Vince saw him huge and distorted, enormous boots, long khaki-clad legs, trunk and head foreshortened. He ducked down and clamped his hand over Gatley's mouth. The toes of the boots appeared on the edge of the grating. A tap was turned on over the sink. Water came gushing out of the waste-pipe, cascading over their heads, cold enough to take away their breath. It sounded unnaturally loud; a deep, rushing roar echoing down the length of the drain.

254

A roar that, oddly, increased, as the tap was turned off and the flow of water stopped.

Vince recognised it then; knew it was not the sound of running water magnified by the drain but the full-throated throbbing of big V8 engines out in the compound as the trucks were started and run up.

The man standing at the sink recognised it, too. He turned and ran back into the foyer. Vince released Gatley and saw his mouth open in a silent scream. He was struggling to stand up, his eyes staring down the drain towards the soakaway. Vince followed his gaze and saw the rat. It was reared up out of the water, its front legs on the curved side of the culvert, its nose twitching inquisitively. A long-backed, black rat which looked as big as a small dog in that confined space. Vince reached up and gripped the grating with both hands, drew up his knees and lashed out with his right foot. The toe of his boot took the rat under its jaw, snapped its head up and back and broke its neck. It went over in a back somersault and disappeared into the darkness where the drain dipped out under the wall into the soakaway.

The noise of the trucks was very loud now, booming up along the concrete culvert. Vince felt the grating vibrating under his fingers. He set his feet in the water and thrust upwards, trying to tilt the iron grille to one side. The sink waste-pipe jammed in the grating and he wrenched at it fiercely, the muscles in his back and shoulders creaking. He was shaking with cold, saturated with greasy water, his hair plastered to his head, his fingers numb and slippery on the coated iron bars. Slowly the pipe began to give, bending up under the pressure, acting as a hook now, holding the grating half open at an angle. Vince squirmed his head and shoulders up through the opening and hauled himself out on to the kitchen floor. There was a heavy wooden meat-chopping table against the far wall near the door into the foyer. He dragged it out and rammed it against the door, turned and went back to the sink. Down on one knee, he reached into the drain, gripped Gatley by the front of his tunic and heaved him up savagely.

Soaked and filthy, they crouched together by the sink, water running out of their clothes to form a spreading puddle. In the foyer the men were shouting, their voices cutting through the roar of the truck engines. Angry voices, drunken, with an edge of panic in them. The trucks were pulling out now, gears grating, engines revving. At any moment the men in the foyer might be thrusting at the door to come through the kitchen and out into the passage. The table would not hold them more than a few seconds.

Vince grabbed the grating and forced it down, the waste-pipe straightening enough to let it drop. He pulled Gatley to his feet and pushed him towards the outer door. 'Get that open, man. Quickly.' There was a small pile of empty flour sacks, neatly folded, on the work-top by the sink. He snatched one up and shook it open, whipped up the lid of the big food chest, grabbed bread, a hunk of cheese, an opened tin of butter and dropped them into the sack.

Gatley was fumbling with the door key, shaking and sobbing. Vince shouldered him impatiently aside, his head throbbing to the roar of the trucks, his ears straining to catch the first thud of fists on the foyer door. He turned the key and inched the door ajar. The passage outside was empty. He pulled the door wide open, pushed Gatley through it, slipped the key out, shut the door and locked it on the outside.

He gripped Gatley's arm and hustled him down to the wicket gate. All the trucks had gone. Only the pick-up was there, parked in its usual place just inside the gate. He checked the compound quickly, his eyes flicking from the locked main gates to the empty Guard Tent to the silent HQ block. It was deserted, a dispersing haze of dust the only evidence of recent occupation.

'They've gone,' Gatley said. Out in the open, the nightmare of that dark, cockroach infested drain behind him, he was beginning to recover. He looked dreadful. Smeared with filthy, clinging grease, soaked to the skin, his boots oozing water; a bedraggled scarecrow, half-drowned, stinking. But he had stopped shaking. The air was warm on his face, the compound suddenly vast and spacious after the prison of the shower room. His eyes were focused again, his voice firmer with just a touch of his normal pompous precision. 'Very well,' he said, gathering his dignity round him like a tattered cloak. 'No point in standing here. We'll go round to the Mess and . . .'

'No,' Vince said, clipped, hard, his fingers locked on Gatley's upper arm like the jaws of a trap.

Gatley stiffened. 'What d'you mean, no?'

'What I say,' Vince snapped. The plan which had formed vaguely in his mind during those long hours in the shower room was sharp and clear now, every move, every detail. He was astonished by its clarity, its inevitability. Astonished and in a curiously cold way, excited.

Gatley's chin came up in the old, familiar, arrogant way, his mouth hard and thin. It was as if the knife-edge in Vince's voice had severed the last cords of his claustrophobia and set him free. 'Let me remind you, Corporal,' he said tartly, 'I'm still in command here.'

'You? In command?' Vince's lip curled. 'You couldn't command a rowing boat on a park lake. In command of what, for Christ's sake? The men you're supposed to lead have mutinied, God help 'em. Your officers and NCOs have baled out and left you. It's the end of the line for you. You've had it. From here on, I'm giving the orders.'

Gatley shrank back against the pick-up, water dripping down his face out of his hair, his eyes bewildered. 'I'm warning you, Corporal,' he said unsteadily. 'You've had a difficult experience. I realise that. I'm prepared to make allowances. But I'm warning you...'

'Wrap up,' Vince said. He thrust the bag of food into Gatley's hands, spun him round and began to force-march him across the sand.

The sun was well down now behind the blocks of flats, the compound in shadow. Gatley stumbled in his wet boots and Vince held him in that pitiless grip, dragged him up the steps on to the veranda and into the Orderly Room. He thrust him towards the bed. 'Those blankets. Get them.'

Caught off-balance, Gatley lurched across the floor and fell on the bed. Vince opened the filing cabinet and took out a small bunch of keys. 'Come on, man. Move yourself,' he snapped.

Gatley gathered up the blankets in an untidy bundle and got to his feet, shoulders hunched, head down, face very pale. 'For God's sake, Alec,' he said. 'Don't make it worse for yourself than...'

Vince reached out and grabbed the back of his tunic by the collar. 'Outside,' he said.

He took him down the veranda to the Armoury, selected a key and slid it into the lock.

Gatley's eyes widened. 'What are you doing with a key to the Armoury?'

'Opening the bloody door,' Vince said. He shoved Gatley inside, closed the door behind them and switched on the light. He tossed the bunch of keys on to Lever's workbench and began to unbutton his shirt. 'OK. Strip off.'

'Strip?' Gatley stood by the bench, the blankets and the bag of food clutched against his chest.

Vince looked at him with contempt. 'You heard.' He pulled his shirt over his head and dropped it on the floor.

258

He put his left foot up on the wooden form beside the workbench and began to unlace his boot.

Gatley watched him, dazed. This was a Vince he had never seen before; the neat, polite clerk transformed into – what? A soldier? An enemy? A killer? His mind shied away from the word, refusing to accept it. As Vince stood on one foot to pull off his boot, Gatley lunged forward, threw the blankets at him and made for the door. It was done clumsily, without conviction; the half-hearted action of a frightened man. Vince ducked and pivoted on his right foot. The fingers of his left hand, extended and rigid, dug deeply into Gatley's side just below the rib cage. Gatley jack-knifed in agony, caught in mid-stride. His forehead slammed against the door. He went down heavily, out cold.

When he came to he was lying naked on a blanket on the floor, cramped and chilled, his wet skin goose-pimpled. Vince stood over him dressed in a spare pair of Lever's bleached overalls, an old webbing belt buckled round his waist. In the harsh light of the unshaded bulb suspended from the ceiling his face looked thinner, older, the strength of the bones under the skin apparent now, the line of the jaw hard and unforgiving. The face of a stranger. He stared down at Gatley, taking in the pallid nakedness – the thin arms and legs, the rounded paunch fish-belly white, the cold-shrunken genitals – observing them impassively, without pity, without concern.

Squinting up at him, Gatley was suddenly afraid. A fear subtly different from the claustrophobia he had felt in the shower room and the drain. More searching, more unnerving, coming in from outside himself. And mingled with the fear, part of it yet separate from it, a terrible sense of foreknowledge, a kind of heart-stopping premonition. In a rare moment of honest self-appraisal, his mind as naked as his body, Gatley knew himself to be what he was, what he had always been under the

259

proud uniform, the cultivated, by-the-book authority –
a weak man of no consequence come unprepared to a
violent life or death crisis. He licked his lips, his mouth
dry, his gut aching from the stab of Vince's fingers, the
bruise on his forehead swollen and throbbing. 'Alec, for
God's sake,' he whispered. 'What are you going to do to
me?' But the question was already answered in his
mind.

Vince dropped a blanket on him. 'Dry yourself on
that,' he said, his voice as flat and disinterested as an
Ansafone. And he stood silent and unmoving while
Gatley scrambled unsteadily to his feet and began to rub
himself dry. He was trembling with cold and shock, his
eyes glazed, his face burning with humiliation – an
excessively modest inhibited person ashamed to be seen
naked by another man. Drying his stomach and down
between his legs, the blanket bulky and slippery, he was
acutely conscious of those cold eyes watching. What
had happened to change Vince from a trusted servant,
always polite, always willing, into this bleak-faced
stranger? His mind struggled wearily with this riddle,
failed to solve it and closed in upon itself, refusing to
contemplate what might lie ahead. He draped the
blanket over his shoulders, wrapped it round his waist
like a plaid and stood bare-footed, a grotesque, pathetic
figure with a dirt-streaked face and filthy, black-nailed
hands. Vince unhooked a rifle sling off the wall and
tossed it to him. Gatley pulled it tight round his waist
to hold the blanket in place.

'Sit down,' Vince said.

Gatley sat on the form, staring miserably at the floor,
stripped of all dignity, defeated.

Vince said, 'Now you know how it feels.'

'How what feels?' Gatley said. But he knew what
Vince meant. Knew with a jolting sickness in his
stomach, a glowing point of terrified understanding in
his closed, shrunken mind. He looked up at the corporal

260

and saw it written in his face; remembered how it had been between them that night when he had walked unexpectedly into the Orderly Room.

Fourth October, eleven days before JACK KNIFE. A Sunday. At 22.00 hours Vince closed his book and put it up on the shelf above his bed in the Orderly Room. He slid his feet into his boots, not bothering to tie the laces, and went out on to the veranda.

There was one arc lamp burning over the main gates, dappling the line of parked trucks with a pattern of shadows. The rest of the compound was in darkness. Above the roof of the cinema the sky was brilliant with stars. A fine, clear night, peaceful, serene.

In the blackness by the wicket gate the sentry was smoking. The tip of his cigarette glowed and faded. In the cinema some of the men were singing. Vince visualised the scene in there – the men lying on their beds reading comics, writing letters on pads of ruled paper, playing pontoon for matches; the air thick with smoke and the smell of beer and sweat; the monotonous, mind-eroding arguments ('It is, y'know. It isn't, y'know. It is, y'know. It bloody isn't, y'know') which always threatened to erupt into violence but seldom did; the songs that began as sentimental ballads and deteriorated into obscenities sung to Victorian hymn tunes – and he breathed in deeply, tasting the cool night air, his body warm and relaxed, showered, clean, free from sweat.

This was the best part of the day. Five minutes on the dark veranda before turning in to sleep in the quiet privacy of his Orderly Room. In the Guard Tent they would be brewing up on the primus. He thought about getting his mug and going over to join them and decided against it, tired of the jokes about being married to his job – and perhaps to Gatley. He yawned, rubbed his hand over his face and went back inside.

Five minutes later he was in bed, naked and comfortably cool between the sheets, a blanket folded neatly at the foot of the bed, handily placed for the early hours when the pre-dawn chill set in. The main light was out; just the small lamp on his locker beside the telephone, hooked in to the outside line for the night in case of emergencies. He looked round his little kingdom, pleased as always with its neatness, and was just about to switch off the light when the door opened and a girl came in.

She was in her twenties and beginning to run to fat, her face broad and pockmarked, the nose slightly hooked in the Arab fashion, the mouth wide, thickly-lipsticked. Her hair was black and wiry, frizzed out round her head and she was wearing a pink dress cut very low with narrow shoulder straps, the skirt short to display her heavy thighs. The dress fitted closely, clinging to her hips and breasts, outlining her nipples. Her legs and arms were bare, her feet thrust into high-heeled, open-toed sandals. She half-turned to close the door, the dress sliding over her hips so that Vince knew she was naked beneath it. He had never seen her before but he recognised her for what she was; a hostess-dancer from one of the out of bounds cabarets in Sharia Nasr.

She smiled down at him, showing small, uneven teeth yellow with nicotine. 'Allo, Tommee,' she said. 'Thees is the Emma Tee office?'

'La,' Vince said. 'No. This is the Orderly Room.'

The girl frowned. 'Where is Jack Essmart?'

'Not here.'

'He say to come.' She giggled. '"You come and I come," he say.'

Vince nodded. That sounded like Smart. 'Well, I'm sorry. He's not here.'

The girl shrugged. 'Maleesh. You are here.' She sat down on the edge of the bed. 'And you I like.' There was

262

dark hair in her armpits and she smelled of cheap scent and sweat.

Vince sat up, pulling the sheet round him. 'Look, you can't stay here.'

'No?' Her eyes were puzzled; dark eyes, experienced, the whites muddy. 'You do not like me?'

'It's not that,' Vince said embarrassed. 'Only...'

'Onlee?' She had the throaty voice of an Arab. A Cairo accent with just a hint of French. 'How did you manage to get in here?' Vince said.

She shrugged. 'The little gate. I give the man cigarettes. Every time, cigarettes.'

'You mean you've been before?'

'Aywah.' She reached out and touched his face. 'You Ingleez. Always many questions.' She giggled. 'Not Jack. He likes to – what you say – get cracking.' Her fingers traced the line of his jaw, moved down to the hollow of his throat; warm fingers, light, teasing, as experienced as her eyes.

Vince pressed back against the wall. Close to, her face was coarse under the make-up. There were beads of sweat on her upper lip. Her breath smelled of garlic. He was both appalled and fascinated, acutely aware of her body – the naked thighs below her rucked-up skirt, the smiling mouth, the full, heavy breasts. 'Please,' he said in a choked voice. 'You must go. I...'

She leaned over him, her hand moving to his chest and down over the sheet, her fingers probing gently through its thin folds, expertly finding the junction of his thighs. 'Wallahi.' She opened her eyes wide. 'It is a man, then.' She sat up and slipped the straps off her shoulders to expose her breasts in a frank, unselfconscious invitation. She pulled her shoulders back proudly, watching his face, her mouth open a little, the tip of her tongue moistening her lips. 'I am called Rose,' she said. 'What is your name?'

Vince stared at her breasts. 'Alec,' he said, his voice thick in his throat.

'Al-lick.' She cupped her breasts in both hands, lifting them, offering them to him. 'You like them, Al-lick? You like my..?'

'Evening, Vince. Everything all ...?' Gatley's voice froze.

Vince looked past the girl and saw him standing just inside the door, his eyes frosty, two red spots of anger burning in his cheeks.

'What is the meaning of this?' Gatley said, outraged.

The girl swung round, still holding her breasts. 'Allo, Tommee. You want Rose? OK. Him first, then you.' She giggled, her eyes sly.

Vince said, 'I'm sorry, sir. It's ...'

Gatley stared at the girl. 'Get out,' he snapped. 'Cover yourself up and get out.'

'It's not what you think, sir,' Vince said. 'I can...'

'Be quiet, Corporal.' Gatley's voice was like a fist in Vince's face.

The girl pouted. 'I give you good time. Good jig-a-jig. Cheap.'

Gatley stepped forward and slapped her face. Hard. 'You filthy slut. Get out. D'you hear me? Imshi. Yalla.'

The girl recoiled from the slap, springing to her feet, her face contorted, lips drawn back, eyes blazing. 'Ya ign kelp. You bloody bastard son of a ...' The words exploded out of her mouth, a long, guttural burst of Arabic and English. Every sexual insult, every foul name, every curse in the gutter vocabulary of the souk. Naked to the waist, hands on hips, her head up, her heavy breasts quivering, she scourged Gatley with words, her voice rising shrilly. He retreated, backing against the trestle table, overwhelmed by her fury – a man who had dislodged a pebble in a dam wall and

264

released a torrent. He was, as always, in full uniform, freshly-showered, groomed, polished, his hat brushed, the badges of rank in his epaulets newly-laundered. Yet he appeared insignificant, a nonentity. As did Vince, huddled naked under the sheet. They were both muted and pale, like ghosts. Only the cabaret girl in her sleazy semi-nudity was real; full-bodied, full-blooded, magnificently alive. A woman scorned whose blazing temper gave her a kind of presence.

Her tirade screeched to its climax. She spat on the floor at Gatley's feet, hauled up her dress, made an obscene gesture at him and banged out through the door.

In the silence that followed they heard her footsteps go down the veranda, the sound ceasing abruptly as she stepped on to the sand.

Gatley said, 'It is usual to stand up in the presence of an officer, Corporal.' And watched with compressed lips as Vince wrapped the sheet awkwardly round his waist and stood by the bed.

Embarrassed, feeling ridiculous, Vince said, 'I – I'm sorry, sir. It wasn't...'

'By God,' Gatley said thickly. 'So you should be. Rutting in here like an animal with that whore off the streets.' All his pent up anger, all his smarting resentment of the girl was in his voice, chopping up the words, spitting them out at Vince.

'It wasn't like that, sir. She just came in and...'

'I trusted you, Vince. I took you into my confidence.'

'Sir. Please let me explain. I was...'

'I thought you were different,' Gatley said. 'A cut above the others. I thought you had principles, values. A certain standard.' And he meant it; was genuinely shocked, disappointed. He had a high regard for Vince, thought of him privately as a son; was, in his own curious, inhibited way, proud of him.

265

'It was a mistake, sir,' Vince said.

'At least we're agreed on that.'

For God's sake, Vince thought, I haven't done anything. 'She was looking for someone else and...'

'I know what she was looking for,' Gatley said coldly. 'It was obvious enough when I came in here.'

'Sir,' Vince said hopelessly. He searched Gatley's face for the smallest sign of understanding. That was all it needed to put the whole unfortunate episode into perspective, cut it down to size, shrug it off. A little understanding. A willingness to listen, to make allowances.

Gatley met his eyes grimly.

Conscious of the absurd figure he presented, standing there swathed in the sheet, Vince felt the stir of anger, a sense of betrayal. He would have been astonished to know his feelings exactly matched Gatley's.

They stared at each other across an invisible barrier, two lonely men needing each other, unable to communicate.

'You will write a full report,' Gatley said then. 'To be on my desk first thing tomorrow morning. Is that clear?'

'Sir.' Vince hesitated. 'Is that really necessary, sir?'

'No. I could charge you now,' Gatley said. 'I have all the evidence I need. But in view of your past record I wish to give you every possible opportunity to...'

'Evidence?' Vince said. 'What evidence? And where are your witnesses to this charge you're ....?'

'That's enough, Vince,' Gatley said sharply.

'I've done nothing,' Vince said. 'And you know it.'

'I come in here to talk to you,' Gatley said, 'and find you in bed with a whore. That's good enough for me, Vince.'

'And if I walk out of that door with you now,' Vince said hotly. 'Just like this, wrapped in a sheet? Stand with you on the veranda and let the guard see us together?'

266

He looked at his watch. 'You've been in here – what? Twenty minutes? Longer? If the guard puts that in his report – will that be evidence enough for you?' He drew himself up, clutching the sheet. 'It isn't the first time you've come in here late at night. There's talk enough about that already.'

Gatley's face paled. 'If you're suggesting...'

Vince shook his head. 'Not me. The others.'

'I see.' Gatley bit his lip. 'Very well, Vince.' He walked to the door and turned. His face was set and hard but his eyes were hurt. 'Don't think you've heard the last of this, Corporal, because I assure you you haven't.'

Vince looked at him bleakly, seeing him as if for the first time. Not angry now, ashamed, disgusted. Not for himself, for Gatley. 'Good night, sir,' he said.

And now, Gatley thought, sitting huddled in a blanket on the wooden form with the weapons of war racked around him and Vince tall and forbidding like an avenging angel in those bleached overalls, now the wheel has come full circle. He looked at Vince's face. Was this how the corporal had planned it? They had lived five days in an armed truce. On the surface nothing had changed between them. Commanding Officer and Orderly Room clerk, they had carried out their duties, followed the routine, gone by the book, politely, coolly going through the motions. But underneath ... underneath Vince had been waiting, biding his time, making his plan.

'What are you going to do to me?' Gatley said again. That same hopeless question. And the answer becoming more obvious, more inevitable with every passing minute.

PART THREE

16 OCTOBER 1944

1. 03.30 – 05.00 HOURS

'So you reckon he'll make it?' March said.

'Roper?' Frant shrugged. 'Put it this way: he's got a sixty per cent chance now. He's reasonably comfortable and he's not deteriorating. There's always the chance of infection, of course. A dose of pneumonia in the next forty-eight hours – even a mild dose – and he's in trouble. But so far he's clean.'

'That's good,' March said. 'Bloody good.'

'Well,' Frant said with professional caution, 'it's not bad.'

'Thanks to you,' Hanwell said.

'And Jane,' Frant said. 'Mostly Jane. Just seeing her's put new life in him.' He grinned. 'Nothing like a spot of LTC.'

Loving tender care, Hanwell thought. There's not a lot of it about. Not in 87 MU.

'How is Jane?' March said, leaning his solid bulk comfortably against the bar, his pipe in his mouth, his shirt soiled and stiff with dried sweat.

'Bushed,' Frant said. 'She was out on her feet when

271

she got here.' He had left her curled up in a chair beside Roper's bed, fast asleep. Even the return of the trucks from the main compound had not disturbed her.

'Not the only one,' Hanwell said looking round the crowded Mess. They were all in there, packed together, officers, NCOs and ORs, drinking hot coffee in a blue haze of cigarette smoke, talking and laughing in quick, excited bursts, the over-casual, uptight conversation of men who had passed clean through the fatigue barrier and were way out beyond it, living on their nerves. He felt his own eyelids heavy in the warmth of the room, the dull ache of knotted muscles between his shoulder-blades. One more push, he thought, and we're home and dry. But it would be a dicey one; a game of bluff. Please God it wouldn't be a bloody one.

He hit the bar counter with the flat of his hand to catch their attention, saw their heads turn towards him expectantly as the buzz of conversation died. 'OK,' he said. 'Let's have a sit-rep shall we?' He looked round the room. 'Flight Sar'nt Smart?'

'Sir.' Jack Smart eased himself off the window-ledge and stood with his thumbs tucked into his silver-buckled belt.

'What've you done with your Dinky toys?' Hanwell said.

Smart grinned. This was a man he understood, responded to. 'North and south road blocks on Sharia Pasha in position, sir. A couple of three-tonners at each end. All ours. We've relieved your crew at the south end. Except Jackson. He opted to stay put.'

Hanwell nodded. Jackson would.

'The rest of the transport's round three sides of the cinema,' Smart said. 'The alley down to the main gates is completely blocked off. I've got a line of trucks right round from there to the jeep outside here.'

'Good show. Sar'nt Scott?'

'Sir.' Scott was standing just inside the door, clean

272

and workmanlike, his sten gun slung over his shoulder. 'We've got the compound staked out. Wicket gate, main gates, six men on the cinema roof.'

'Compound lights?'

'Fully operational, sir.'

'Anything moving in there?'

'No, sir. I've got thirty of our lads covering the trucks and the front of the cinema,' Scott said.

Hanwell heard the eagerness in the Scots voice. His sergeant had played a waiting game so far and he was impatient for action. 'What about the bod in the Armoury?'

'All quiet, sir.'

'Still in there, is he?'

'Aye,' Scott said grimly. 'He's still in there.'

'Stanna schweir.' That was Lever, his white overalls streaked with dirt, his face questioning. 'What's this about the Armoury?'

'Ah,' Hanwell said. 'You don't know, of course. There's somebody holed up in there.'

'The hell there is,' Lever said truculently. 'Doing what?'

'Colonel-bloody-Custer act,' Miller said bitterly. He was propped up in a chair with his arm strapped across his chest, the bruises on his face livid against the grey tiredness. 'He's OK if you keep your distance. It's people who want to shake hands with him he doesn't go a bundle on.'

'But who the hell is he?' Lever said. 'I left that place locked up tighter than a duck's arse this afternoon.'

The 87 MU personnel in the Mess looked at each other. A murmur of speculation ran round the room.

'OK,' Hanwell said, not too sharply but sharply enough to get hold of them again. 'We'll find out in due course.'

'All will be revealed, my children.' And that was Prince's languid, mocking drawl. He lounged against

273

the wall contriving a certain elegance in spite of the sweat stains and streaks of dirt on his uniform.

'Roger,' Hanwell said, a shade more sharply. He wasn't used to Prince. 'Meanwhile, Wing Commander Gatley's in that cinema and we've got to get him out. In one piece.'

'May one ask why?' Prince's voice was insolent now.

Hanwell cut through the laughter. 'You know damned well why. If anything happens to him this whole bloody unit's for the high jump.'

Prince shrugged. 'Might be worth it, at that.'

'All right, Jo-Jo,' March said. 'That's enough.' He turned to Hanwell. 'We're in your hands, Wing Commander.'

'It takes one to get one apparently,' Prince said, but quietly. He looked coolly across the room at Hanwell and said loudly, 'At your service, sir.'

Hanwell nodded. 'Thank you.' He glanced down at Scobart slumped in the chair by the bar, his foot on the low table. He and Hobey were beginning to look like ghosts as tiredness and pain sapped their strength. The return of the troops from the main compound had revived them temporarily but they had a brittle, fragile look about them as if, beneath the surface, they were dried out and eroded. 'No contact with the cinema since we left, Mr Scobart?' Hanwell said.

Scobart shook his head. 'The line's u/s anyway.'

'That's it then,' March said. 'We'll have to go in and get him out.'

Hanwell checked his watch. 03.50. Coming up to the bad time, the pre-dawn-chill-life-at-its-lowest-ebb time. But for the job in hand, the right time. He said, 'We're not going in to them. They're coming out to us.' He saw the disbelief in their faces and grinned. 'Psychological warfare, gentlemen. They think they're

274

safe so long as they stay in there with Gatley. It's down to us to show them they're wrong.'

'And how do we do that?' Henry Bush said quietly. Safe, dependable Bush, dogged, unimaginative, guaranteed to obey orders.

'We spread a little alarm and despondency,' Hanwell said. 'Put on a bit of a show.' He smiled. 'Like Joshua.'

Prince's eyebrows lifted. 'Joshua?'

'Of course,' Hobey said. 'By God, yes. The battle of Jericho.'

'Thank you, Hobo,' Hanwell said. 'I'm glad somebody knows his Old Testament.'

'For the benefit of those who don't – and I fancy I speak for the majority – could you perhaps enlighten us a little?' Prince said.

Hanwell grinned. 'Hobo?'

'It's a classic,' Hobey said. 'The people of Jericho sat tight inside the walls. Safe in their fortified city. Until Joshua persuaded them they were in a trap.'

'And the walls came tumbling down?' Prince drawled.

Hobey shook his head. 'They didn't tumble. They were pushed flat. Outwards. By the panic-stricken mob inside fighting to get out.'

Bush said slowly, 'And that's what we're going to...?'

Hanwell nodded. 'Roger.'

'I return to my previous question,' Bush said. 'How?'

How indeed? March thought. It was the idea he had tried to sell McCann over the phone. But he hadn't bought it then. And now the phone was dead – ripped out, probably, by McCann himself in a fit of temper. Or by the others in there with him, afraid he would sell them down the river.

Hanwell took up his briefing stance, back propped comfortably against the bar, arms folded across his chest. 'It's really very simple,' he said.

'The buggers are every-bloody-where,' Wooten said. 'On the roof. In the street. You name it, mate, they're there. There's a line of trucks from here to breakfast out there and...'

'Out there,' McCann said acidly. 'Not in here.'

They were sitting round one of the tables in the foyer; McCann, Wooten, Mainston and five others. A council of war while the rest of the men slept.

McCann looked at their faces – eyes red-rimmed, cheeks drawn and hollow under the stubble – and saw the tiredness there. Tiredness and boredom and something else. Something he had watched building up since the trucks had pulled out. Uncertainty, the beginnings of doubt. 'So long as we sit tight we'll be OK,' he said. 'We've got the Preacher, damn it. They're not going to come busting in here. Not while we've got Gatley.' He glared round the table, willing them to believe him. He had said it so often, hammering into their skulls, sweating to convince them, to convince himself. And at first it had been easy enough. Before the trucks left. Before the beer ran out. Before the Regiment came swanning up the street. But now...

'Y'know what I reckon?' Mainston said.

McCann looked at him bleakly. 'What?'

'I reckon they're just going to ignore us. Leave us here to...'

'No,' McCann said sharply. It was what he was afraid of. A stalemate with the ball in his court.

'Why not? It's bloody obvious, isn't it?' Mainston said. 'We can't stay in here for ever. We've got to go out sometime. All they need to do is sit tight and wait.'

The men round the table nodded glumly.

'Not while we've got Gatley,' McCann said. 'The bastards might write us off. But they can't afford to write him off, can they? They've got to come to terms with us. Negotiate.'

276

'Yeh?' Mainston said sceptically. He shifted restlessly on the hard wooden bench, the rifle propped against the table beside him.

You're twitched, mate, McCann thought watching him. 'Yeh,' he said vehemently, desperately. And he thought: They're twitched, too, aren't they? March and Scobart and all the bloody poncey officers. Up the bloody wall by now, wondering if Gatley's OK. 'Don't panic,' he said. 'All we've got to do is stick it out and call their bluff.'

'Right, lads,' Scott said, standing on the steps of the cinema at the end of the line of trucks. 'On my whistle. Pass the word.' He waited, his eyes fixed on the luminous second hand of his watch, his sten gun reversed and clubbed in his right hand, the whistle on its lanyard in his left. Thirty seconds. Fifteen. Five, four, three, two, one. 04.15. The time Hanwell had chosen.

He blew the whistle, swung the sten back underarm, rammed its steel butt forward hard against the shuttered doors, drew it back, counted two, swung it forward again.

THUD-pause-two-pause-THUD ... All down Sharia Pasha, the side street, the alley at the back, they hammered the cinema walls with gun butts, jack handles, heavy steel wrenches; the men from MONOP-OLY seeded with 87 MU's NCOs, swinging in unison, taking their time from Scott. THUD-pause-two-pause-THUD. Fifty blows. A hundred. A hundred and fifty. And Scott checking his watch and the whistle shrilling again. And silence. A five minute break and off again. THUD-pause-two-pause-THUD...

'Bloody hell.' In the foyer, Wooten's voice was harsh with panic. 'They're coming in through the bloody walls.'

Inside the cinema the concentrated, rhythmic ham-

277

moring, magnified in the great hollow space under the high ceiling, hit the sleeping men with an almost physical force. They sat up in their beds, rubbing their eyes, dazed and shocked, dry-mouthed from sleep, reaching clumsily for their boots.

In the foyer, McCann said, 'Don't panic. It's a trick, that's all. They're only trying to . . .'

'They're planting charges,' Mainston said. 'Gouging chunks out of the walls to ram bloody dynamite in and . . .'

'Don't talk so bloody wet,' McCann said tightly.

'He's right, though.' Wooten's eyes were round and anxious. 'Them Regiment bods – they're trained in demolition. Genned up on explosives. It's all part of . . .'

'Bull,' McCann snapped. 'Get a grip, for Christ's sake. Can't you see? That's what they want you to think.'

The men were crowding into the doorway from the stalls now, tousled, half-dressed, their faces puffy with sleep.

'What the hell's going on, McCann?'

'What you gonna do now, then?'

'Come on, mate. Get your bloody finger out. This place'll fall on top of us in a . . .'

Angry, frightened, their voices came at McCann like jagged shards of glass as the steady thudding splintered their morale. He jumped up on to the table and spread his arms wide, his mouth twisting contemptuously. 'Wrap up,' he shouted. 'Stupid buggers. What the hell's the matter with you? Like a bunch of bloody WAAFs in a bloody knocking-shop. A bit of noise, for Christ's sake. Anybody'd think they were . . .'

The thudding stopped abruptly.

'There, y'see?' McCann said. 'What did I tell you? It's just a trick.' He turned to face the shuttered doors. 'Knock, knock,' he jeered, hands on hips, legs straddled,

278

head thrown back. 'Who's there?' He waited a moment or two and then swung round. 'OK. Panic over.'

The men stared up at him, uncertain, sheepish. He spotted one of the cooks in his white tunic. 'Come on, Wack,' he said. 'Let's have some grub, eh? Chai up, lads. Big eats.' He stood grinning down at them, sweating with relief.

They grinned back shamefacedly. The cook pushed his way into the foyer and made for the kitchen. As if on cue, the thudding started again.

'How long did it take him?' March said.

'Him?' Hanwell said, standing beside him at the wicket gate, his face sharply etched in the harsh glare of the arc lamps.

'Joshua.'

Hanwell grinned. 'Best part of a week.'

'We haven't got that long,' March said.

At the far end of the cinema wall the blunt nose of a three-tonner protruded into the compound through the open gates. There were men stationed in the Guard Tent; crouched down on the sand by the end wall of the MT office; at the open door of the Signals office into which they had infiltrated through the back window.

'We won't need it,' Hanwell said. He looked at his watch. 04.35. Scott was stepping up the hammering now, increasing the tempo, shortening the intervals to two minutes. THUD-pause-THUD-pause-THUD. Even out here in the open the noise was intense, a giant time-bomb ticking. Inside it would be mind-breaking. 'Two more rounds on the big drum,' Hanwell said. 'Then we bring in the full orchestra.'

In the Armoury Vince was nearing the end of his preparations. The two ammunition boxes stood one on top of the other in the middle of the floor, carefully positioned under the main beam of the roof. On the

279

workbench behind them everything was laid out neatly, as if for inspection – the first field dressing unrolled on the sheet of oiled silk, the leather laces out of Gatley's boots, two rifle slings – one opened out, the other looped through its brass buckle. He ticked them off against the list in his mind, picked up a large screwdriver, walked across to a wooden case of grenades and began to lever off the lid. The wood splintered and he jerked it upwards, the nails shining in the light, ripped away the oiled paper and took out a grenade, hefting it in his hand like a cricketer preparing to bowl. He went back to the bench and set the grenade carefully beside the rifle slings, his movements deft, methodical, his face set.

Huddled on the form against the wall, Gatley clutched the blanket round him, his eyes glazed, unfocused, the lids drooping with tiredness. He was back in his cocoon now, withdrawn, shut away, suspended in a grey vacuum. The thudding on the cinema walls reached him only faintly through a grey mist of fatigue and fear, merged with the beat of his heart and went unremarked.

But inside the cinema it was inescapable; a manic, pounding pulse shared by two hundred men. The whole building vibrated, throbbing with sound. They stood in little groups between the beds, up on the stage, in the foyer, on the stairs leading up to the Sergeants Mess. The tired, smoke-wreathed air smelled of sweat and fear. They stared at each other like men trapped in a submarine being attacked by depth-charges, mesmerised by the noise, gripped by its rhythm, their nerve-endings frayed, their minds squeezed flat.

McCann saw the centre shutter over the glass doors bulge slightly, the wood cracking under the steel butt of Scott's sten gun. 'OK,' he shouted. 'This is it, lads.'
Mainston stood with his rifle in his hands, tight-

280

mouthed, his eyes screwed up against the pounding beat. 'What're you gonna do?'

'Get Gatley,' McCann bawled. He crossed the foyer, went into the narrow passage and slid the key into the lock on the shower room door. Mainston stood beside him, rifle levelled at his hip. McCann turned the key and whipped the door open wide.

'Sir,' Bell said, raising his voice above the thudding which was pulsing heavily down the passage between the cinema and the Mess.

'Yes?' Hanwell said.

Bell held out his hand with a key in it. 'That side door, sir. It's locked on the outside.'

Hanwell said, 'That's the kitchen, isn't it?'

March nodded, puzzled.

Hanwell stared out across the compound at the shuttered windows of the Armoury. 'So that's how he got out,' he said. 'Whoever he is.' He turned back to Bell. 'OK. Unlock it. But don't open it till I give the word.' He looked at the line of men in the passage. 'A couple of the lads to cover it.'

'Sir.'

As Bell went back towards the door the thudding stopped.

Hanwell grinned fiercely at March. 'Ten seconds,' he said. 'Then we let 'em have it.'

'Empty?' Wooten said. 'How the hell can it be empty?'

'Because there's nobody in it, you clot,' McCann snapped.

'You mean they've gone?' Wooten said. 'Gatley and Vince?'

'What a brain,' McCann said bitingly. 'Of course they've bloody gone.'

'Where?'

'How the hell do I know, for Christ's sake?' McCann said.

'But there's no way out of there,' Wooten said. 'They can't just bloody disappear, damn it.'

'Well, they have, Wack,' McCann said bitterly, the noise pounding in his head, his brain struggling to cope with this new situation. Without Gatley they were finished. Up the creek. No ace in the hole. He scowled at Wooten's heavy face. 'Well, don't just stand there chewing the bloody cud, man,' he said. 'Start looking for the buggers. They've got to be in here somewhere.'

'How?' Wooten said. 'How can they be in here?'

'Well, they've got to be, haven't they?' McCann said. 'There's nowhere else they bloody can be.' The last three words came out unnaturally loud in the sudden silence as the thudding stopped. McCann shook his head irritably. The pattern stamped on his tired brain now, the silences as demoralising as the noise. He needed the quiet to get his thoughts sorted out. But was unable to make use of it because his mind was screwed up tight, waiting for the thudding to start again. Through the open doorway into the stalls he could see the men sitting on their beds, their hands clamped over their ears; knew they were still hearing the noise even in the silence.

It's over, he thought. God help us, it's all over. He slumped on to one of the benches, elbows on the table, his head propped in his hands. God, he thought, what a mess. What a bloody, stinking, useless...

And then it came. A booming, blaring, unbelievable torrent of sound.

In every truck the driver clamped the flat of his hand on the horn button and held it down. The harsh, metallic blast was reinforced by renewed hammering, frenetic now, deliberately irregular, and by the bellowing shouts of the men in the street.

282

The effect was indescribable, apocalyptic. A shock wave of crude sound which burst into the cinema like a sonic bomb. The men inside sprang to their feet, stood rooted for a second or two, staring wildly at each other. And then broke. Those on the stage jumped down to join the stampede for the foyer. Beds were overturned, lockers sent flying. The floor was instantly littered with clothing, bedding, torn magazines, broken glass. Men went down, their feet tangled in blankets, and were trampled brutally as the mob swept up the sloping floor to the doorway of the foyer, kicking, punching, screaming, fighting to get out, to get away from the terror of the noise which yammered and howled around them.

McCann stood with his back to the kitchen door, his arms raised, his face contorted. 'The guns,' he yelled. 'They're waiting for us with guns. You'll all be . . .' But his voice was drowned in the uproar. He was hurled aside, thrown against the wall like a rag doll. The men charged into the kitchen, thrust tables and benches away to get at the wooden shutters guarding the big glass doors, jammed the staircase which led up to the Sergeants Mess and the windows overlooking the street. Guns, bayonets, grenades – anything was better than the braying, hammering, yowling hell which boiled and seethed over them and into them and through them.

Out in the passage Bell looked down towards the wicket gate. Hanwell and March were silhouetted there against the white glare of the compound arc lamps. He saw Hanwell's arm go up and drop sharply, whipped open the kitchen door and stepped back against the wall. The mob burst out into the passage, turned both ways and saw the sten guns levelled at them.

On the far side of Sharia Pasha, right opposite the cinema, Curtis stood in the doorway of a shop, six men with stens spaced out in a shallow arc in front of him. There was a sudden flood of light from the cinema as the foyer shutters were torn down. Through the big glass doors Curtis saw the press of bodies, the kicking feet, the threshing arms, the faces distorted with terror like masks in a Greek tragedy. And then the doors exploded outwards, glass showering down the steps into the street.

The terrible noise stopped as abruptly as it had begun. The screams of the struggling men petered out. The torrent of bodies hurtling through the kitchen door into the passage, tumbling down the front steps into the street, froze and was still. It was as if a waterfall had suddenly turned to ice in mid-flow. As shocked by the silence as they had been by the noise, the men waited, some standing, some lying where they had fallen.

Curtis shouted crisply, 'Sar'nt Scott.'

'Sir.' Scott stood in the mouth of the passage, phlegmatic, unruffled.

'I'll have these men fallen in. Three ranks facing the cinema.'

'Sir.' Scott had his sten gun cocked and levelled. He looked at the dazed faces of the men and knew he would not have to use the gun. He signalled to the trucks. Two of them started up and swung out and round, their headlights flooding the street with a bright, yellow-white glare. 'Let's be having you then. Come on, come on. Shake it up a bit.' Scott shouted, his voice brisk, authoritative. The familiar words brought the men up out of the passage and down the steps of the cinema. They moved listlessly, like zombies, still in shock, their overalls torn, some without boots, and began to form three ranks in the street.

When the last of them came out of the kitchen door, Bell went in with three men. They found McCann huddled on the floor by the big calor gas stove, bruised and bloodied, his overalls split across the shoulders. Bell prodded him with the muzzle of his sten. 'On your feet, mate,' he said. 'The party's over.'

284

Hanwell and March walked up the passage and joined Curtis who had crossed the street to stand by the jeep outside the Mess. The men stared at them blankly, chivvied into line by Scott and his squad, covered by rifles and stens, hang-dog, washed-up, finished.

Bell came out through the front doors of the cinema holding McCann by the right shoulder. 'That's the lot, sir.'

Curtis nodded. 'Who's this?'

'McCann,' March said, half-angry, half-sad. All the jauntiness was gone now, all the bounce, all the pert, grinning self-confidence. McCann's face was wrinkled and grey, his body slack. He stood on the steps, his right hand thrust inside his overalls, bent forward a little, his hair hanging over his eyes.

My God, March thought. Is this the man who's been holding us all to ransom for more than twelve hours?

'All right, McCann,' Curtis said. 'Fall in with the others.' He spoke firmly, his voice neutral, impersonal. A routine order in a routine tone. Which was the way Hanwell had briefed him. After the howling nightmare in the crowded cinema, a straightforward parade. Three ranks. Pick up your dressing. Properly at ease. The first, vital step back on the road to normality.

But McCann did not respond. He stood unmoving, head down, shoulders bowed.

'You heard the officer,' Bell said and gave him a push.

McCann moved then. He came down the steps in a crouching run. His hand slid out of the front of his overalls with a kitchen meat knife in it. A thin bladed, honed-down knife, sharp edged, pointed, protruding out of his fist like a steel extension of his arm. He tossed his hair back and his eyes were bright and blank, focused in a manic stare. He moved very fast, jinking in behind Curtis, making for Hanwell, his right arm rigid, the knife describing a tight, flickering arc.

285

In that moment he became the knife. It was his identity, his whole being. All the bitterness of defeat, all the sweat of those long, nerve-testing hours in the cinema, all the arguments, the boredom, the growing sense of futility – all this was focused now in that murderous point at the end of his arm. His right shoulder lifted a fraction, he gathered himself, his aching muscles forgotten, his tiredness washed away. And lunged for Hanwell's stomach.

Scott's sten barrel smashed down on his wrist, crunching the bones, striking so hard that McCann tipped forward, off-balance, carried by his momentum. The knife flew harmlessly out of his hand and he went over and down in a half-somersault, screaming in agony as his hand hit the street and the broken wrist bones were forced out through the skin.

The three officers stood like rocks, forcing themselves not to look down at him, their eyes searching the faces of the men paraded in front of them, watching for the first sign of reaction. There was none. The ranks stood silent, detached. As if McCann did not exist. As if the attack had never been made.

Curtis felt the sweat break out warm under his shirt, acutely aware of the sten gunners covering the parade, of the dilemma that would have presented itself had the ranks threatened to break. He waited a moment longer and then turned smartly, saluted Hanwell and said in a clear, steady voice, 'Parade ready, sir.'

Hanwell acknowledged the salute. 'Thank you, Mr Curtis.' He stepped coolly round McCann, now mercifully unconscious, crumpled on the sand. 'Sar'nt Scott.' His voice was meticulously polite.

'Sir.'

'Two men to carry McCann into the Mess. Put him in the hall. My compliments to the MO and ask him please to have a look at him.'

'Sir.'

286

Hanwell nodded and said quietly, 'And thank you, Sar'nt.'

March watched him turn to face the parade. Watched him with admiration and relief, visualising how Gatley would have handled such a situation, grateful for Hanwell's calm, casual authority.

'Right,' Hanwell said. 'Now pay attention. The quicker we get this sorted out and you chaps back in your beds the better I'll be pleased. It's been one helluva long day. For all of us.' He paused, his eyes watchful below the peak of his badgeless, operational hat. 'My name is Hanwell. I am temporarily in command of this unit. That means I expect my orders to be obeyed. Instantly. Without question.' He had their full attention now. The faces in front of him were drawn and tired but no longer disinterested. The shock was wearing off, the men discovering a kind of normality. 'You don't need me to spell out the situation. It's not good. I'm here to put it right. With your help or without it. The choice is for you to make. There are no excuses for your behaviour. But I am prepared to accept there may be explanations. Whether the Court of Inquiry will accept them is another matter. The facts are inescapable. But they can be presented in a sympathetic fashion. I am prepared to do that, so far as I am able. If you co-operate. I'm not saying I can make it easy for you. But I can make it damned hard. It's up to you. All of you. Are you with me?' He saw heads nodding. 'Right. First question. Where is Wing Commander Gatley?'

The men looked at each other, puzzled. Someone in the rear rank called out, 'In the shower room, sir. With Corporal Vince.'

Hanwell turned his head. 'Mr Curtis. My compliments to the Wing Commander and ask him please to join us here.'

'Sir.' Curtis turned towards the cinema steps.

In the centre front rank Mainston took one pace

forward, came to attention. 'Sir. Permission to speak, sir.'

Curtis waited.

'Name?' Hanwell said.

'Mainston, sir.'

'Yes, Mainston?'

'He's not there, sir. The C.O. Vince neither. They've both gone.'

Hanwell heard the murmur of surprise run through the ranks. So it was news to most of them, too. 'Gone where, Mainston?' he said. And felt the answer click into his mind.

Mainston shook his head. 'I dunno, sir.'

'Very well. Thank you, Mainston.'

'Sir.' Mainston stepped back into line.

Standing just behind Hanwell, March said quietly, 'The Armoury?'

Hanwell nodded. 'Has to be.'

'Why there, for God's sake?'

'A bolt-hole?' Hanwell said. 'Somewhere safe from the men?'

'No way,' March said. 'If that's what Gatley wanted he'd have made for the Mess.'

'Yes,' Hanwell said. 'That's what I thought.'

'Oh, my God,' March murmured. 'And I was hoping it was all over.'

2

'Anything from the Armoury?' Hanwell said. He was propped against the bonnet of the jeep outside the Mess, hands in his trouser pockets, hat tilted back slightly, his face creased with tiredness.

Scott shook his head. 'All quiet.'

Too damned quiet, Hanwell thought. And then: This is where we came in.

It was cold in the street, the air dry and crisp. Black dark, still, the light streaming out through the shattered doors of the cinema a pale gold wash, fragile as a false dawn. There was a rich smell of frying bacon, the sound of voices, of furniture being moved. Inside the foyer they were clearing up, getting ready for an early breakfast.

Hanwell's mouth watered. Damn Gatley and his bloody corporal, he thought. If they'd stayed put in that shower room we'd be home and dry now. 'OK,' he said. 'Tell your chaps we're working on it.'

'Will do, sir.'

'Meanwhile they're to keep their heads well down. No heroics.'

'Sir.' Scott went off down the passage to the wicket gate, his sten slung on his shoulder, his step as firm and springy as if he had just had a good night's sleep.

Hanwell walked up into the entrance hall of the Mess. Frant was there waiting for him. Hanwell nodded

289

and thought: Please God, no more panics. He said, 'How's Roper?'

'Better than he's any right to be.' Frant smiled. Briefed by Hanwell he had done his best to shield Roper from the impact of raw sound which had broken the siege of the cinema; wadded cotton wool into the Adjutant's ears, swathed his head in a thick towel, packed extra pillows round him. 'He's probably the only man here who hasn't got a headache.'

'And Jane?'

'She's coping.' She had put cotton wool in her ears too and sat by the bed holding her husband's hand as the room began to shake to the rhythmic hammering. 'What's the gen now?'

Hanwell shrugged. 'Nearly there. Just a couple of loose ends.' Called Vince and Gatley. It sounded like a music-hall turn; the comic and the straight feed man. An unexpected, unwelcome addition tacked on to the end of the bill.

Without McCann the so-called mutiny had collapsed. The men on parade in the street had been eager to co-operate, get back to normal. Talking to them with Curtis and March beside him, he had sensed this. Had chosen his words carefully, balancing the events of the night against the prospect of a new beginning, setting the whole incident in perspective, not playing it down but not magnifying it either. He had finished with simple, direct instructions. Something positive for them to do. Breakfast. A day off for all ranks. The cinema to be cleaned up, broken furniture repaired, the smashed glass of the main doors replaced with timber. 'And tomorrow,' he had said, and paused, holding their attention. 'Well, tomorrow's another day. Time enough to worry about that when it comes.'

March had listened with approval and a twinge of regret. Approval for the sensible, down-to-earth approach. Authority seasoned with understanding, compassion. Regret that this was something Gatley had never been able to do.

Frant said, 'They're still in the Armoury, then?'

'For the moment.' Hanwell gave him a sketchy grin. 'We'll get 'em out, Doc. Hopefully without filling your surgery.'

'Amen to that,' Frant said.

'What about McCann?'

'McCann is hurting. His arm's a mess. He's also very sorry for himself.'

'He's been that before,' Hanwell said. 'He'll survive.'

In the Mess they were waiting for him. Prince, Lever, Smart, March – all the key men, the genned-up types. And Scobart and Hobey, still propped up in their chairs, still refusing to be put to bed until the last piece of the puzzle had been dropped neatly into place. Hanwell pulled up a chair and sat down with them. 'Right, gentlemen,' he said. 'What can you tell me about this laddie Vince?' He raised an eyebrow. 'I take it he's the one with his finger on the trigger over there?'

'Well, it's definitely not Gatley,' Prince drawled. 'He's more the chaplain type. Strictly non-combatant.'

Hanwell nodded. He was beginning to get the measure of Prince; had heard from March the sort of show the languid Flight Lieutenant had put up in the main compound before the Regiment arrived. 'Behind that pretty-boy face,' March had said, 'there's a tiger. Very polished, highly dangerous.'

'Oh, it's Vince all right,' Scobart said.

Hanwell looked at him. 'And you're not surprised, are you, Mr Scobart?'

'Not really. No,' Scobart said. Not since that Sunday night just over a week ago. Something had happened then. Something decisive. A turning point. A watershed. Nothing had been said afterwards, no action

291

taken by Gatley. But something had gone sour between them. Vince had continued to work efficiently, politely; neat and methodical as always. But Scobart had sensed a change in him; a kind of sullen, brooding resentment. A disenchantment.

'He's not been himself,' Lever said. 'Not for a couple of weeks now.' Lever who sat in his Armoury and kept himself to himself, watching through the fly-screened window, seeing everything, saying nothing.

'He's bloody twitched, poor little bastard,' Smart said, as foul-mouthed in sympathy as in anger.

God, Hanwell thought, that's all we need. A nice, quiet, well-behaved airman who's gone round the twist and locked himself in the Armoury with a pompous idiot who thinks bull equals efficiency. 'How twitched?' he said and saw the three NCOs exchange uneasy glances. 'Twitched enough to shoot the Adjutant?'

'We've no proof of that,' Scobart said quickly.

'Hell, no,' Smart said. 'Vince's not the type. I know it's bloody hard to credit but he really likes Gatley. Admires him, anyway.'

Lever shook his head. 'Not now, he doesn't.'

'I see,' Hanwell said, keeping his voice neutral.

Scobart said, 'Even in the RAF, sir, a man's innocent till he's proved guilty.'

Hanwell's face was hard under the tiredness. 'But you think he did it?'

Scobart hesitated. 'I don't know. It's out of character, but ...'

'But he's twitched,' Hanwell said.

'Yes.'

Hanwell turned to Hobey. 'Hobo, you've got more of the background than I have. What d'you think?'

'It's a possibility we have to reckon with,' Hobey said carefully.

Hanwell nodded. 'I agree.'

292

'In which case,' Prince said, 'we don't have a lot of time, do we?'

'Meaning?' Hanwell said sharply.

Prince shrugged, spreading his hands. 'If it is Vince – and I'm inclined to that opinion myself – then he's out to get Gatley. He tried yesterday morning. Execution by firing squad at dawn, sort of thing.'

Hanwell said impatiently, 'If that's what he wants he's already had ample time to do it over there in the Armoury. Might already have done it, in fact.'

'I don't think so,' Prince said. 'What we've got here is an imaginative sensitive man who's got the twitch. So he's not thinking too straight. My guess is he doesn't just want to kill Gatley now. He wants to kill him publicly, in front of witnesses.' He smiled apologetically. 'Justice being seen to be done.' He looked at his watch. 'A dawn execution gives us just twenty minutes to stop him.'

'But that's madness,' March said. March who lived in a logical, machine-tooled world in which gear-teeth meshed sweetly and shafts always spun true.

'Yes, Bobby love,' Prince said gently. 'That's exactly what it is.'

The coil of thin cord Lever used to make up pull-throughs for the Lee-Enfields was hanging from a hook on the wall behind the work bench. Vince took it down and ran it through his fingers, feeling the strength of its greased thinness. He crossed to the door, inserted the key in the lock and threaded the cord through it, knotting it neatly. He ran the cord back over the hook and down to the bench, looped it over the vice and turned to face Gatley.

Gatley stared at him dumbly, his skin crawling under the blanket, his teeth digging into his lower lip. It seemed to him that he had been huddled on that wooden form for a week, his bare feet numb with cold, fear a dull, persistent ache behind his eyes. He had watched Vince's meticulous, almost clinical preparations with mounting terror, his mind shying away from the evidence of his eyes, wanting to know, afraid to know. His mouth was dry, his stomach muscles cramped and knotted, the bruise on his forehead dark and angry. He knew what was happening concerned him, every movement Vince made wrapped itself round him, binding him to the grim-faced, silent figure in the white overalls. And yet he felt curiously detached; a spectator at his own execution. For that was what it was. He knew that. How and when were questions he dared not ask himself. But what—that he knew. And felt the knowledge bloom in his mind like a cold, poisonous mushroom.

'Stand up and turn round,' Vince said, his voice matter of fact, without warmth or feeling.

Gatley got to his feet, clutching the blanket round his shoulders. Vince turned him, pulled down the blanket so that it hung from the rifle sling tied round Gatley's waist. 'Hands behind your back,' Vince said. He picked up Gatley's boot laces off the workbench, knotted them together and used them to bind the C.O.'s hands in the small of his back. He turned him again then, saw his face close to, smelled the fear on his breath. He pushed him down on the form.

'What . . .?' Gatley said, his voice a croak.

'Shut up.' Vince turned his back, opened the front of his overalls and picked up the first field dressing he had laid out on the bench. Above his head, slung over the centre beam, the two rifle slings hung down.

Lying flat on his stomach on the veranda, Lever pressed his ear against the Armoury door. He had wedged the outer fly-screen open inch by inch, careful not to make a noise. The wooden surface of the heavy inner door was warm against his ear. There was a faint line of light

294

under it but no sound came through. He waited a few more seconds and then back-crawled under the shuttered window, got to his feet and walked quietly past the MT office and down on to the sand.

Hanwell was waiting there with Scott and six of his men.

Lever shook his head. 'Nothing doing.'

So what the hell did you expect, Hanwell asked himself. The sound of singing?

The men looked at him expectantly.

'Do we go in and get 'em, sir?' Scott said.

It was the problem Miller had faced earlier. Lob a grenade down the veranda, blow in the door, rush the Armoury with stens? What Armoury? According to Lever the place was stuffed solid with explosives. 'Not yet,' Hanwell said. 'If we have to, we have to. But not yet.' And he felt the grip of his watch-strap on his left wrist, was aware of the time ticking away. 'OK, Sar'nt,' he said. 'We'll have the compound lights off.'

Scott sent one of the men to the Guard Tent. The lights died as he threw the switch. They blinked in the sudden darkness, the after-image of the arc lamps glowing on their retinas. Hanwell looked up and saw the sky growing pale in the east, the blocks of flats standing out blackly now, their outlines clearer every second.

Hanwell said, 'I'm going to take a look. Cover me. No shooting unless he shoots first. And then to wound only. Clear?'

'Sir.' Scott began to deploy his men, fanning them out in a curved line to cover the Armoury door.

Hanwell walked across the sand and up on to the veranda outside the Orderly Room. He stood by one of the roof supports, staring down towards the Armoury. The thin line of light under the door was bright in the darkness under the veranda roof. He looked out and saw the men in position, stens levelled. Above and behind them the roof of the cinema was turning grey-pink in the first tentative rays of the sun. He looked back at the Armoury, saw the door beginning to open, the light expanding, growing, widening. He held his hands out from his sides, palms turned forward, well away from the holstered revolver on his belt. The door was fully open now. He took a slow pace forward. A second. A third. And stopped.

The scene framed in the doorway hit him like a fist in the gut. Vince was standing, feet planted firmly apart, on the two ammunition boxes. He had a rifle in his hands, the muzzle pointing directly, unwaveringly at Hanwell's chest. On his shoulders Gatley was sitting, the blanket ruffled like a huge collar round the back of Vince's neck, hands tied behind his back, bare legs hanging down, the feet tucked back under Vince's arms. Hanwell's eyes travelled upwards, saw Gatley's head tilted slightly to one side, the looped rifle sling round his neck under his chin, the brass buckle under his left ear, the second sling running up to the beam above.

'Hullo, Vince,' Hanwell said, every ounce of training commandeered to keep his voice calm. 'It is Corporal Vince, isn't it?' He took another step forward, sliding his foot on the veranda, careful to keep his hands in view.

'Stand still.' Vince's voice was strained, pitched too high, flawed. 'Scobart. I want Scobart.'

'Mr Scobart's wounded in the foot,' Hanwell said. 'He can't ..'

'Get him. Scobart. Get Scobart. Now,' Vince said, the words like buckshot, hard, abrupt. In the crazed logic of his plan it was important to have Scobart there. He would understand.

'Look, old chap,' Hanwell said. 'It's just not on. He can't walk. I'm sorry but ...'

'Carry him,' Vince said. 'Drag him by the hair if you have to. I don't give a damn. Just get him here.'

296

Without turning his head, standing very still, his eyes fixed on Vince's face, Hanwell called, 'Sar'nt Scott.'

'Sir.' Imperturbable, correct.

'Bring Mr Scobart, will you? Get Jackson to give him a hand. Jackson's a good strong lad.'

'Jackson? Yes, sir,' Scott called, to show he had got the message.

Hanwell smiled apologetically at Vince. 'It'll take him a good five minutes to hobble ...'

'I'll wait. Five minutes. No more.' It might have been Gatley speaking. The same abrupt, precise, almost disdainful authority.

Hanwell said casually, 'There are rather a lot of us out here, y'know. We don't have to take your orders. We could have you out of there in ten seconds flat, no sweat.' But it was an empty threat and Vince knew it.

'Use your eyes, man,' he said. 'If I go down, Gatley hangs himself.'

By God, he means it, Hanwell thought watching that white, set face, those over-bright eyes, the hands clenched on the rifle. He really means it, the poor mad bastard. 'But you'll talk to Scobart?' he said.

'I owe him that,' Vince said, his voice subtly different, tinged with a certain sadness. If he had seen his father in Gatley – the same unswerving allegiance to a code of behaviour, the same obsessive rigidity of purpose – Scobart had been the elder brother he had never had. No brother, no sisters. No mother he could remember. Only his father to bring him up, graft into him his own unbending moral virtues; neatness, punctuality, deference to one's seniors, cleanliness of body and mind, probity, obedience. A senior clerk with no further ambitions. A man who knew his place and accepted it. Took a pride in accepting it. Who had privately thought there was too much of the boy's mother in Alec and had been at pains to subdue, if not eradicate, it. There had been no teenage rebellion, no

297

dramatic break-out into manhood. All that had been supressed, packed down hard inside, left to ferment. Until now.

He stood on the ammunition boxes, making his demands, hugging his secret. The secret that was his ultimate strength, his passport to freedom. He tightened his right hand round the rifle stock, felt the gentle pull of the length of thin cord looped round his little finger leading down to the secret strapped to his stomach under the overalls, held in position by the first field dressing.

'You married, son?' Hanwell said, looking for a way into his mind.

'No.' No wife, no girl friend. Nobody. His father had seen to that, injecting his own shyness with women into the boy, sublimating his natural urges. Study not sweethearting. Duty not dalliance.

'How long've you been over?' Hanwell said.

'Long enough.' Vince twisted his wrist, checked the time on his watch. 'Two minutes now.'

Hanwell turned his head. Jackson was coming through the wicket gate, his rifle in his hand. And someone else. Not big enough for Scobart, quick-moving, slight. It was light in the compound now, the grey-white walls of the flats golden in the morning sun. As she stepped out on to the sand he saw it was Jane Roper.

'Is he there?' Vince said sharply.

'Just coming.' Hanwell looked at him. 'OK if I give him a leg up?'

Vince nodded. 'No tricks.'

Hanwell stepped down off the veranda and hurried across the compound.

'He wanted to come,' Jane said breathlessly. 'Scobart. He's on his feet – on one foot anyway – but he'll never make it.'

Hanwell nodded. 'OK. Jackson.'

298

'Sir.'

'Round the back. In through the Signals office window. The door's open. Stay in there until I give you the wire. Then it's one step out and one quick shot. Smack through the centre of the Armoury doorway. Twelve feet high.'

Jackson nodded. 'What's the target, sir?'

Hanwell grinned, his face hard. 'A rifle sling,' he said, 'connecting Gatley's neck to the roof beam.'

'Oh God,' Jane said. 'Oh dear God.'

'It's got to be spot on,' Hanwell said. 'A snapshot. OK?'

Jackson nodded. 'Twelve feet high, centre doorway. Got it, sir.'

'Roger. I'll try to distract his attention.'

'Vince?' Jane said.

'Vince. He's got Gatley on his shoulders.'

'Bloody hell,' Jackson said. 'Begging your pardon, Miss.'

'When I put my hand on the veranda roof support,' Hanwell said. 'OK?

'Sir.' Jackson turned and ran in a wide curve across the compound, round the end of the MT office, up the side of the block to the back. He stopped under the back window of the Signals office, put his rifle inside carefully, hoisted himself up over the sill and stood listening.

' . . . said, no tricks.' That would be Vince.

'It's not a trick, old chap.' Hanwell's voice, calm, easy. 'He's doing his best to get here.'

The scene in the Armoury under the naked bulb was even more bizarre than he had remembered; a still from a horror film. Tilted grotesquely by the pull of the rifle slings, Gatley's face was a mask of fear, the eyes sunken and staring, the mouth twisted open. The face of a man already dead. Between his thighs swaddled in the blanket, Vince's head protruded, pushed forward slightly by the weight on his shoulders in a ghastly parody of birth. Hanwell saw the corporal's legs trembling a little. The man was dog tired, kept upright only by his crazed will, liable at any moment to buckle at the knees and go down.

'Good man, Scobart,' Hanwell said. 'He sends his best wishes, by the way. Says for you to hang on till he can get himself over here.' He wasn't watching Vince's face now. He was watching the muzzle of the rifle, looking for the slightest waver, the merest suggestion of a droop. But the rifle remained steady, trained unerringly on his heart. It's not going to work, he thought. He's too far round the twist for words to reach him.

The open door of the Signals office was two feet in front of him. He saw Jackson take up his position just inside, the rifle held ready, his face composed, alert.

Scott came into the edge of his vision, cat-walking silently along the veranda to his right, his sten gun in his hands. He stopped short, just past the shuttered Armoury windows, and froze.

Hanwell heard the footsteps then, quick and light on the veranda behind him. He felt the hairs rise along his spine, the sweat break cold between his shoulders. He turned his head slowly, slowly. Jane walked round the corner by Scobart's office and came down towards him. 'For God's sake,' he breathed.

She was smiling. Her face was very white, her eyes enormous. But her chin was up and she was smiling. 'Hullo, Alec Vince,' she said gently, clearly. And in a whisper to Hanwell, 'It's all right.' She stood by his left shoulder. 'Alec, you're not to worry about David. He's going to be OK.'

Vince looked at her blankly, shocked by her cool assurance, the poised femininity of her figure, the caress in her voice. But the rifle did not waver.

'David Roper,' she said. 'He's my husband. He says he

300

realises it was all a mistake. That you didn't intend to...'

Vince saw her lips moving, heard the sound of her voice. But the words failed to enter his mind. Just by being there she disoriented him, all the crazily logical steps in his plan crumbling under her smile. He felt Gatley's weight driving him down into the ammunition boxes. The secret passport to life under his overalls pressed hard against his stomach, a mostrous steel erection which both shamed and excited him. Jane's face blurred as tears formed in his eyes, became Rose's face, wavered and changed and came back into focus. But distant, remote. A face in another world; a sane, real world from which he had withdrawn, to which he could never return.

Flawed by a sudden, hairline crack of doubt, his concentration wavered.

Hanwell saw the muzzle of the rifle levelled at his chest dip and drift off target. He scooped Jane in behind him with his left arm and put his right hand on the roof support.

Jackson came out of the Signals office as if on a coiled spring, his rifle hugged into his shoulder, his cheek pressed against the stock, his finger taking first pressure on the trigger. Out and round he came in one swift, smooth movement, his finger squeezing all the way home, the bullet flying true.

Eight inches above Gatley's head the rifle sling parted, the kick of the bullet jerking the metal buckle under his ear. He slumped heavily, his stomach butting the back of Vince's neck. Vince's knees bent, his shoulders bowed, his bare toes clawed for a grip on the edge of the ammunition box. He brought the rifle up sharply in an automatic reflex action as he tried desperately to keep his balance. The cord looped round his little finger pulled tight, jerking the arming pin out of the grenade strapped to his stomach. He jack-knifed

301

over the rifle knowing he had now only seconds to live.

Gatley was catapulted forward, his hands still lashed behind his back. He landed on his feet, bent double. The folds of the blanket wrapped themselves round his legs. He staggered two paces towards the door and fell awkwardly, kicking and sliding, helpless as a fish in a net.

Scott saw Gatley's head and shoulders lurch out through the doorway. He stooped quickly and grabbed his arm. Vince was on his knees on the Armoury floor, off-balance, bowed over the rifle. Scott saw his head come up, saw the strained, contorted face, the mouth wide open sucking in air, the bright, mad eyes. His fingers closed over Gatley's upper arm and he hauled him savagely to one side as Vince got the rifle up at last, the muzzle lifting, searching.

Jackson's second shot, aimed at Vince's face, coincided with the explosion of the grenade. When the dust cleared there was nothing left of him but torn flesh and shattered bone and a welter of blood.

'It's over,' Hanwell said quietly. 'All over.' He was crouched behind the roof support with Jane held tightly in his arms, pressed against him, trembling, weeping, her tears wet on his shirt, her hair brushing his face. 'All done,' he said. 'All finished.'

He lifted her to her feet, turning her away from the Armoury; from Gatley crumpled in his blanket outside the shuttered window, from what was left of Vince shredded under the naked lamp bulb, his passport stamped in blood, his freedom secured.

He looked at his watch and up at the sky above the compound. The Daks would be over the beach-head now, JACK KNIFE's life support system secured. He hoped it had all been worth it. 'Sar'nt Scott.'

'Sir.' Scott had cut Gatley's hands free and came down

302

the veranda, sliding his knife back into his bayonet frog.

'My compliments to Mr Curtis. Ask him to raise Group on the jeep radio.'

'Sir. What message?'

'COLLECT £200,' Hanwell said.

Objective achieved. It was, in its cryptic way, not a bad epitaph for Vince. Whatever the verdict of the Court of Inquiry, Gatley was finished at Marazag.

STUART JACKMAN

Born in Manchester, England, in 1922, Stuart Jackman served with the RAF during World War II in India and the Middle East, and since then has traveled widely on both sides of the Iron Curtain and has lived and worked in South Africa and New Zealand. He is the author of several novels, including *The Davidson Affair,* which has been published in five languages and adapted for television by the CBC. He has also written numerous radio plays and is an experienced boadcaster. Married, with three sons and a daughter, he now lives in Surrey, England.